She slammed th... moment the front door and they could hear her footsteps outside as she ran along the square until they vanished into the distant rumble of the traffic in Holland Park Avenue, and then there was a sudden burst of chatter from Lee and from Sophie and Penny who had been sitting enthralled and open mouthed. Barbara was weeping noisily in a mixture of anticlimax and relief and Lally was comforting her, and even Robin was talking to Sam as Poppy and Lee and Jeremy sat with their heads together chattering busily.

David got up quietly and under cover of the chatter, went out of the room and upstairs to Bertie. He liked the same telly programme and anyway he needed time to dry his eyes. The boy could still make him weep, even after thirteen years, he thought. Only tonight it was a different sort of weeping. The right sort.

SIXTIES

The Poppy Chronicles VI

....

Claire Rayner

ORION

An Orion paperback
First published in Great Britain by
George Weidenfeld & Nicolson Ltd in 1992
This paperback edition published in 1994
by Orion Books Ltd,
Orion House, 5 Upper St Martin's Lane,
London WC2H 9EA

A CIP catalogue record for this book is available from
the British Library.

ISBN: 1 85797 412 3

Printed in England by Clays Ltd, St Ives plc

For Patty Coombs,
my dear funny friend,
with love

The Poppy Chronicles Family Trees

The Amberley Family

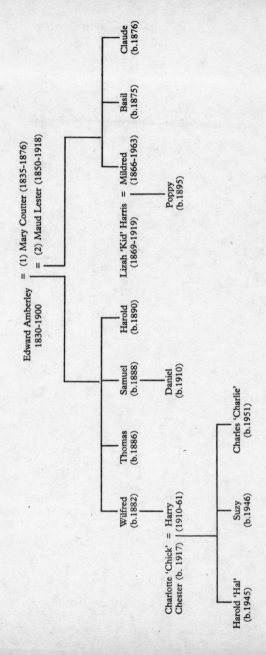

The Harris Family

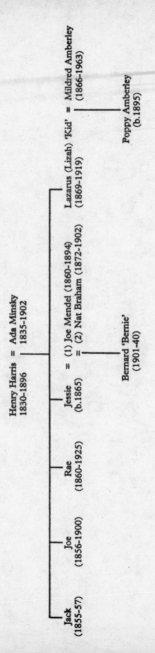

Henry Harris = Ada Minsky
1830-1896   1835-1902

Jack (1855-57)

Joe (1856-1900)

Rae (1860-1925)

Jessie (b.1865) = (1) Joe Mendel (1860-1894)
                  (2) Nat Braham (1872-1902)

Bernard 'Bernie' (1901-40)

Lazarus (Lizah) 'Kid' = Mildred Amberley
(1869-1919)   (1866-1963)

Poppy Amberley (b.1895)

The Bradman Family

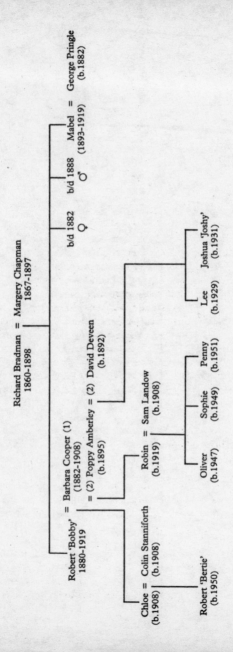

BOOK SIX

1

The dust motes hovering in the wash of sunshine that was spreading itself over the big empty room swirled and danced as somewhere below a door was slammed and a loud voice called hoarsely; and Poppy fixed her eyes on a larger than average fragment and tried to concentrate on its movement. It moved a lot, caught in the draughts from the tall windows which rattled busily in the sharp winds that were whipping Leinster Terrace into a froth of scraps of rubbish and last year's dead leaves; waltzing along the empty walls past the faint oblong marks where once Mildred's pictures had hung and across the marble fireplace with its frosting of cold ashes to end up bouncing along the naked floorboards until it lost itself among its myriad companions in the film of dust that lay there; and Poppy sighed and stopped trying to concentrate on anything at all, just letting her thoughts go where they would.

The upturned wooden box on which she sat was hard beneath her and she knew she'd snagged her stockings on it, but that didn't matter. Nothing mattered really. There was just here and now, sitting alone on this cold March morning in a world where Mildred no longer was.

Stop being so mawkish, she told herself then, her eyes still fixed on the patch of floor into which her dust mote had vanished; it's absurd to feel so bereft. Mildred had had a long life, an incredibly long life. To die at the age of ninety-seven had been a considerable achievement. Hadn't it?

Not really, she thought then. Not really. Poor Mamma had actually died five years ago, after she had that stroke. She may have lingered on, but it had been a twilight existence, unaware, unreachable, silent. She hadn't responded to anyone, not even to

1

her beloved Josh who had visited her as often as ever, and certainly not to Poppy who had also come with religious regularity to sit at her mother's bedside. To grieve now after five such empty years was absurd, and at my age too; and Poppy managed to smile wryly as the word slid into her mind. Orphaned. I'm an orphan, at sixty-eight. How sad to be orphaned at only sixty-eight.

She got to her feet as again the voice shouted hoarsely downstairs. They were trying to get her to come down, the removal men, she knew that. They'd taken the last of the bits and pieces that had cluttered the big echoing rooms and now it was time to move on; but they could wait a little longer. They'd have to. So much of her life had been tied up in this great house, and to be hurried out of it at this last moment wasn't to be borne. So she set her mouth into a stubborn line and began to prowl about the room, trying to see it as it had been in the old days when Mildred had sat in her high-backed chair beside the fire and watched her only daughter make her way across the old red Turkey carpet to sit beside her on her dutiful evening visits –

But she couldn't. It was as though the familiar furniture had never been here, as though the Turkey carpet with the pattern she had known so well had been torn beyond repair and memory. All she could see as she stared through the tall windows and at the high ceilings were rows of shadowy beds and lockers. Or would they, the new owners, put up flimsy partition walls and make these beautifully proportioned spaces into nasty mean little enclosures to give the overseas students for whom the old house was destined 'rooms' of their own? She shuddered at the thought and found herself almost running out of what had been Mildred's drawing-room, pulling the door closed behind her with never a backward glance to stand trembling a little in the echoing hallway outside.

Really, this was totally ridiculous, she told herself firmly. It has to stop. It's just reaction to the last few weeks, the funeral and the dickering with those hateful estate agents and lawyers and dealing with the new owners and all the rest of it. And the anxiety about how the children might react to the provisions in Mildred's will. Mama had obviously given very careful thought to her dispositions and had shared out her large estate with scrupulous care, and everyone had seemed to accept the apparent inequalities with – and she smiled as the word came into her mind – with equanimity. Josh had been the only one to demur, but then he would, of course. He had by far the lion's share and he was the least greedy of people. But Robin hadn't minded a bit and neither had Lee; Josh was much blessed in his sisters if not in his worldly success and his inheritance would be of great value to him, a value enhanced by his sisters' generous reaction to it.

As for Poppy herself, she had been glad that Mildred had bypassed her so completely. It was much easier to have the money go directly to the children, since Poppy herself was so very well off. The business was thriving and even though she no longer owned it virtually outright but was answerable to a Board, still Poppy's rewards were more than adequate for her needs. Mine and David's, she whispered to herself then as slowly she made her way down the broad staircase. Mine and David's. We need little enough at our ages. David, gone seventy. It doesn't bear thinking about.

As she reached the midpoint of the staircase she had a sudden memory so sharp that she could almost see her there below her. Not Mamma, but Jessie. Dear Auntie Jessie, struggling to climb the stairs on her twisted painful legs, pretending it didn't hurt, damned if she was going to let one of Hitler's bloody bombs do her down and spoil her fun at Mildred's New Year's Eve party, and again Poppy smiled, this time widely and with a sort of gratitude. It didn't seem possible that Jessie was still with them, and not at all as Mildred had been, living in a silent half-world where she knew nothing. Jessie sat in her flat at Marble Arch with Lally and Barbara fussing around her like anxious hens with a strangely elderly chick, and meddled in all their lives. Almost blind now, but as sharp in mind and tongue as she had ever been, and she was a year older than Mildred. I'll go and see her today, Poppy promised herself, her spirits lifting. This very day. Then I'll feel better. And she hurried down the last steps and across the hall and out of the front door, much to the relief of the removal men who had been lounging against the side of their van with their racing papers and their battered enamel tea mugs, waiting for her.

'Right, lady!' the senior of them said briskly and shoved his paper into his pocket. 'All right to lock up, is it? Keys go to Number Seventy-seven Queensway, Mr Aziz – '

'Yes – yes, thank you,' Poppy said and reached into her bag for the half-crowns she had prepared for their tips. 'And tell the Repository that the receipt for the furniture and the documentation is to be sent to this address, at Norland Square – '

3

'Right, lady,' the man said and tucked the card too into his pocket. 'Though I 'as to say, lady, there's not going to be no percentage in paying expensive prices to a Repository to 'ang on to stuff like this. This 'eavy Victorian gear – no call for it, you see. I'll gladly take it off your 'ands and charge you nothin' to get rid of it – '

'No thank you,' Poppy said frostily, knowing perfectly well that Victorian furniture was in fact becoming popular again (and therefore valuable) among some of the smarter young people who wanted to cut a dash that was clearly different from the sort of Scandinavian inspired design that was everywhere these days. 'I prefer to keep it.'

'Suit yourself, lady,' the man said good-humouredly and swung himself up into the cab. 'We'll be on our way then. Good morning to you!'

And the engine coughed into life and sent the van lumbering away down the terrace towards the Bayswater Road, carrying the last remnants of Mildred Amberley's ninety years of living in this house with it, and leaving her daughter to stand in the blustery street with her hair blowing in the capricious breeze and her eyes watering with cold – or so she told herself with some ferocity as she watched it go.

'Yes, I've finished,' Poppy said and smoothed her gloves on her knee. 'You got the chiffonier safely?'

'Mmm. It looks lovely in the upstairs hall,' Robin said. 'Helga polished it half to death and it looks like satin. I've arranged dried flowers on it. Very *House and Garden* it looks. Grandmamma would have approved, I think. Are you all right? You look a bit – '

'A bit what?' Poppy said as lightly as she could. 'Elderly? Past it? Feeble?'

'No,' Robin said equably, refusing to rise to the bait. 'Just bothered. You should have let me come and help this morning. You know I wanted to.'

'Yes, I know,' Poppy sighed and lifted her chin and managed a smile. 'I'm sorry, darling. It's just that – I had to do it alone. There were things to sort out – anyway, it's done now. And I'm sorry if I sounded crabby. It's just that I feel so – '

Robin reached forward and touched her mother's hand. 'I know. Me too. When someone dies, however old they were and

4

however ready to die, it makes you think of when it'll be your own turn – concentrates the mind wonderfully, death.'

Poppy grimaced. 'Doesn't it just? No more of that now. Not another word. Let's order, shall we? Have you checked the specials?'

'Would I dare do that before you got here?' Robin said and laughed. 'Jerome'd pay no attention even if I tried, anyway.'

'Of course he would,' Poppy said, but her tone was a little absent as she looked round the restaurant with the sharp gaze that her employees had long ago learned to respect. Everything seemed to be all right at first glance: the tables with their pale-blue and green cloths and the bamboo-handled cutlery set just so; the waiters in the neat uniform of blue waistcoat over dark-green trousers and pale-blue shirts to match the overall decor, moving quietly and skilfully between the crowded tables, but she noticed smears on a water jug on the next table and a diner eating fish with a meat fork, and tucked the observations away to be delivered to Jerome, the head waiter of 'Bertie's', later on.

'Mrs Poppy!' Jerome was there beside her, deftly twitching napkins, pouring water, snapping his fingers at his juniors to scurry with ice and lemon and the bread basket. 'I haven't seen you since – well, my deepest sympathies, and the same goes for all of us.'

'Thank you, Jerome,' Poppy said as briskly as she could, and smiled brightly at him. 'My mother was very old, of course – '

'Yes, indeed, but all the same – '

'Well, yes,' Poppy surged on. 'Now, about the specials? What have you for my daughter today? She looks hungry to me – '

'Oh, Ma, really!' Robin said and smoothed her hands over her hips. 'I'm on a diet, you know that – '

'As if you needed it, Mrs Robin!' Jerome said and smiled at her as approvingly as his sharp little features would allow. 'But you needn't worry. I've got some really lovely fillet steak and you can have that grilled with a nice salad – '

'Perfect,' Robin said. 'Ma – you need a bit more than that. You're looking peaky.'

'Nonsense!' Poppy said. 'I'm fine. I just want an omelette, Jerome. No, don't argue with me. *Fines herbes* and a little baveuse. You know how I like it. And no wine, thanks – too early in the day for me – Robin? No? I didn't think so. Just water – '

Jerome fussed away at last and Robin laughed. 'Poor Ma. Maybe you should eat in other people's restaurants instead of your own. Then you wouldn't be twittered over so much.'

'Other people's restaurants? How could I? I have to keep an eye on them all – '

'I doubt you *have* to. They run themselves these days.'

'There's no better muck than on the farmer's boots,' Poppy said with a brave try at a bucolic accent. 'Now tell me, how is everyone?'

Robin was at once distracted and launched herself into an account of her children's doings. Both the girls, Sophie, a leggy and bright-eyed fourteen and Penny, at a year younger, already displaying a formidable brain, were doing well at their expensive girls' public day school, and Robin chatted happily about their achievements in class and out of it – Sophie, it appeared, was a notable netballer – and Poppy watched her as much as listened to her, enjoying her animation. She looks marvellous, she thought, staring appraisingly at her daughter. It's not just because I'm her mother, she really does look wonderful. She's – Poppy did a quick computation – forty-six, for heaven's sake! It doesn't seem possible; and she had a sudden intense visual memory of the small Robin, puzzled and wide eyed, staring up at her big half-sister Chloe, and her brows tightened. Poppy didn't think often about Chloe, but when she did it was always with pain. Not just because Chloe had been so much trouble to her stepmother, but because of the way she had behaved over her son, Bertie. And Poppy let her eyes roam around the restaurant again as she thought about Chloe and Bertie, for this, the most recent of the acquisitions of the 'Food by Poppy' group of companies, had been named for him, and sighed softly. Poor Chloe, to have missed so much. Poor Bertie, to have been so rejected.

'And the boys?' she said then as Robin paused for breath. 'How are the boys?'

'Bertie's fine, of course,' Robin said and leaned back as the waiter set her steak before her, thus avoiding Poppy's direct gaze. 'But you saw him last week – '

'And I'll see him tomorrow,' Poppy said, still looking at her with her brows raised. 'It was Oliver I was thinking about.'

'Fine, fine,' Robin said quickly. Too quickly, for Poppy pounced.

'What's he been up to now?'

'Ma, really!'

'Don't Ma really me! I know perfectly well when you're trying to hide something. So, what is it this time?'

'Oh, damn!' Robin said and put down her knife and fork, her steak untasted. 'I do so hate it when Oliver gets into some sort of scrape. Any boy of sixteen gets into trouble sometimes – but you always make such a drama out of it.'

'I do not!' Poppy said. 'Though I can't deny it upsets me, when it seems to me so avoidable. If he was at a proper school, where they taught the children some manners and respect – '

'Ma, let's not go into all that again,' Robin said and her voice was sharp. 'We chose Lord Peter's because it was the best sort of school for Oliver. He doesn't do well when he's pushed and nagged – both Sam and I agreed on that. He needs the more relaxed and open atmosphere he gets there – better than one of those awful Dotheboys Hall sorts of place where they beat them and – '

'There's a world of difference between Dotheboys Hall and the sort of school where the children call the teachers by their first names and choose whether or not they'll bother to go to classes, and well you know it,' Poppy said tartly. 'I'm not surprised Oliver gets into so many pickles, when he's never been taught to behave any better. Keep him at home and send him to a day school. Surely that'd be better for him – '

'Ma, I won't discuss it. We've gone over this time and again. I prefer Lord Peter's, Oliver's happy there, and there's an end of it. I knew we'd have a fight if Oliver was mentioned, damn it – ' And she seized the knife and fork and cut a piece of steak and began to chew with great ferocity.

There was a little silence as Poppy played with her omelette and then she said, 'I'm sorry, Robin. You're right, of course. I've no business sticking my nose in. I try not to – it's just that today – '

Robin's knife and fork clattered onto her plate and she reached forward to take her mother's hands in hers. 'Oh, I'm sorry too! I don't mean to rise to – well, we'll never agree on this. And I can't deny that I do worry dreadfully over Oliver. He can be such a darling and such a villain too – I despair sometimes – ' She managed a small laugh then as she returned to her steak. 'Sam says it's a judgement on him. It's his fault for being a psychiatrist.'

Poppy smiled a little crookedly. 'I know. I've heard him on the subject. But it's nothing to do with him, or with you. People are what they're born to be, and our Oliver was born to be a rogue. Enormous charm and wit, but a rogue all the same.' And she shook her head, remembering suddenly – what a tiresome day this was becoming with all the memories dredged up by the morning's activities! – remembering Bernie, Aunt Jessie's son, who had also been a charmer and good looking and thoroughly villainous. But then she shook herself mentally; Oliver was no more than a young tearaway who took the bit between his teeth from time to time. There was nothing of his long-dead cousin's real amorality in him. He was just in need of a little sensible firm guidance –

Determinedly she pulled her mind away from Oliver and began to chatter of Chick and her children, for the whole family had visited her last weekend. 'Suzy's turning out to be so pretty,' she said. 'I used to worry about her when she was six or seven for she was so much plainer than Sophie and they were so close I thought it'd make problems for her – but now she's – '

'I know,' Robin said, warmly grateful for the change of subject. 'She's sweet too. Like darling old Chick – '

'I thought she seemed well?' Poppy looked at her daughter questioningly. 'Is there anyone else on the scene for her? Is that why she seemed to be so – '

Robin shook her head, regretfully. 'No, not Chick. She'll never marry again. As far as she's concerned Harry was the only man in her life and that still goes even though he's dead.' She sighed then. 'I try to make her go out and about more, to meet people, but she won't. She says she's happy as she is – and the Clinic does do awfully well.'

'It's good for Sam to have her,' Poppy said, and looked sharply at her daughter. 'No regrets you didn't take it on?'

'None at all,' Robin said and her voice was a little sharp. 'When Sam wanted a Matron for the place Penny was only ten – how could it have been right to leave her as much as I'd have had to? And in the event it worked out right because if I'd taken it on, the job wouldn't have been there for Chick when Harry died, and you have to admit it saved her life one way and another.'

'I suppose so. But still it seems a pity you can't find something to do – ' Poppy looked at her quizzically and laughed. 'There I go! I'm off again. I'm sorry. I don't mean to meddle, darling, truly I don't. It's just that – well, work means so much to me, that I can't imagine a life without a job. But if you're happy – '

'I'm fine,' Robin said. 'I dare say I'll find something to do eventually that'll suit me. Right now, I just enjoy freedom. It's fun – I can shop and spend time with friends and – '

'Yes,' Poppy said and left it at that. But Robin could feel the doubt hanging in the air between them and ducked her head to concentrate on eating her salad. This was another subject not to be discussed with her mother. At least, not today.

'I can't stay for coffee,' Poppy said eventually. 'I'm sorry, darling, but there's a Board meeting at four.'

'Can't you miss it?' Robin said. 'I thought it'd be fun to go and look at the new French designs they're showing at Harrods – '

'Miss it? Heavens, no! I'm the Managing Director as well as a member of the Board – I have to be there – '

'If you were Chairman you could take the afternoon off,' Robin said. 'I still think you should have been.'

Poppy shook her head as she began to collect her bag and gloves. She'd eaten only half of her omelette and hoped Robin wouldn't notice because she tended to fuss over such things. 'I've got quite enough to do with running things at the sharp end of the stick. We're thinking of taking on three more hotels, you know. In Bournemouth and Brighton and Torquay. They should do very nicely – but it all takes a lot of supervision, what with the London end and the factory, as well as the restaurants – I couldn't deal with the Chairmanship too; Richard's doing perfectly well.'

'Oh, I'm sure he is, but it makes me a little irritable, I have to say, to see you working so hard when Gillian does so little and gets just as much out of the business as you do.'

'We were partners at the start, so we still are,' Poppy said firmly and got to her feet. 'And Richard's working in her place. What's a husband for, after all?' And she laughed. 'Darling, I must go. I'll deal with the bill on the way out – no, I insist we pay it. It ruins the bookkeeping if people just waltz in and eat for nothing. I don't allow anyone else to do it, so we won't. But I'll deal with it. Forgive me if I fly, I'll only just make it as it is – and darling, don't worry about Oliver. I'm sure whatever it is'll be sorted out eventually. It usually is, after all.'

She bent and kissed her daughter's cheek and made for the door with Jerome, materializing out of nowhere, fussing her on her way, and Robin sat and watched her go and bit her lip, thinking about Oliver.

It would be maddening to have to admit her mother was right and they'd sent him to the wrong school, but she was beginning to wonder. And she thought for a while and then took herself off to Jerome's office to claim the privilege of using the phone. Talking to Oliver would help, and today was a half day. With a bit of luck someone would be able to find him and fetch him to the phone, and she made her way across the restaurant, her spirits lifting absurdly at the prospect of hearing her son's voice.

2

Oliver wasn't there. 'Out somewhere, Lord knows where,' a young voice said blithely – 'Try at tea-time. He always gets in for meals,' and slammed down the phone, leaving her holding the earpiece as it buzzed insolently, and she could have stamped her foot in irritation.

'So what now?' she asked herself as she cradled the phone. To go to the French fashion show alone wouldn't be much fun; it had been too much to hope her mother would take the afternoon off to go with her, and Robin stood and stared unseeingly at the wall, trying to feel as her mother must, busy and useful and content; and couldn't.

She's right, dammit, she thought as she pulled on her gloves and checked her face in the fly-blown mirror on the wall behind Jerome's cluttered desk. I need something to do. And she thought of Chick, serenely busy about the small clinic that Sam had started five years ago for those of his private patients who couldn't face the prospect of being admitted to an NHS psychiatric hospital ('And who can blame them?' Sam would ask savagely. 'Seeing the sort of dumps they call hospitals – ') and almost envied her. And then felt guilty, for that was tantamount to wishing Sam as dead as Harry was, and she didn't mean that at all.

'Are you sure?' an inner voice murmured nastily in her ear as she walked out of 'Bertie's' amid Jerome's fulsome farewells and made her way along the crowded pavements of Beauchamp Place to pick up a taxi in the Brompton Road. Would it make all that much difference? For all you see him and all the attention he pays you when you do, he might as well be – well, somewhere else at any rate.

'No!' she said aloud, to the surprise of an elderly passerby. And

11

then bit her lip in embarrassment as she hurried on. Of course she didn't mean that. She loved Sam, of course she did, but it was all so *dull* at home, so everyday, so tedious, and she stopped to stare at one of the shop windows, though she would have been hard put to it to say just what she was looking at. What had happened to her? Life had been so busy and such fun when the children were small. There'd been so much to do and so little time to do it in. But now the girls were absorbed in their own lives at school, and spent all their time at home either head down in homework or talking to friends on the phone or making appalling rows with their record players, and Oliver was away at his boarding school and Sam was always at the clinic or his consulting rooms, and Helga ran the house superbly, so they'd hardly notice, any of them, that she wasn't there, if she chose to go. But where would I go? she asked herself piteously and had a vision of the way they'd be if she did suddenly pack her bags and walk out, or even died herself; the way they'd all look a bit sad for a day or two, but soon settle back into their old ways, with Helga cooking for them and cleaning for them – and I thought I was lucky to get such a good mother's help! she thought with some indignation – and forget all about her –

This is perfectly ridiculous, she told herself then, and turned into the Brompton Road with her head high and her step springing. She would go to the fashion show after all, why not? She was perfectly well able to spend an afternoon on her own, for heaven's sake! Didn't she usually, after all? As for the situation at home, well, it was as much her fault as Sam's, no doubt. All those years of her being child besotted must have made him feel less at home in his own home than he'd choose; now she had to make things better for him. Just the way it said in the women's magazines.

Harrods was its usual comforting self, warm and scented and quite remote from any sense of the real world. Here was all money and smartness and elegance and nothing at all vulgar, like women's magazine problems, and she slipped into its cosiness with a sense of relief. She bought a lipstick she didn't need on her way through the perfumery department and then took herself to the Food Hall to browse among exotic teas and calorie-bursting biscuits and managed to come out without buying more than a jar of ridiculously expensive mustard, and went up to the fashion floor for the show feeling a little better. Life after all was treating her well. She had a home and husband and children and now some money of her own; Mildred's death had seen to that. And she thought with a faint frisson of pleasure of the twenty-five thousand pounds that now lay in her private account and considered the possibility of buying more than just a lipstick, a ridiculously expensive dress perhaps –

She settled to watch the skinny mannequins make their sinuous way across the catwalk, all with the same look of ineffable boredom on their perfectly painted faces, ready to enjoy herself. She'd consider buying one, seeing what they had that would be right for her, and she caught a glimpse of herself in a mirror and was well pleased. I don't look my age, she thought. I may be nearer fifty than forty, but I don't look too bad at all. Good hair and teeth and not that much larger than I was before the children.

She was disappointed. The clothes all looked so predictable, she thought; neat pinstripe suits from Dior with rather silly little truncated leg o'mutton sleeves, and skimpy shirt dresses that looked well enough on the impossibly thin models but which would look, Robin knew, absurd on her, and vividly checked suits with droopy revers and collars that made her feel depressed rather than elevated, and did nothing at all to cheer her; and she found herself imagining the sort of things she'd like to wear rather than this obvious chic; things that were ridiculous and loud and that would make her laugh.

She got up to go before the end of the show and the inevitable wedding dress. She wasn't in the mood for this sort of thing after all, no matter how hard she tried, and she made her way out of the store and came out at the side, and without thinking much about where she was going, cut along Basil Street to Sloane Street, and on an impulse jumped on a bus that was going up to the King's Road. Ma's offices were there, and maybe the Board meeting would be over, and they could talk a little more. She'd been less than kind to Ma over lunch; she'd feel better if she made sure they were really comfortable together before she made the trek home to Hampstead.

But she didn't get there. She left the bus at Peter Jones, remembering she needed some school socks for Sophie, and on her way back out of the store into the bustle of King's Road, literally bumped into someone who was rushing in.

'Oh, you idiot!' the other wailed and bent to rub her ankle. 'I mean, I'm madly sorry – it was my fault – I mean, I'm the idiot, not you – Good grief! Robin!'

'Susan?' Robin said after a moment. 'Susan Monk? What on earth are you doing here? Oh, what a silly thing to say! Same as me I imagine – shopping – '

'Not shopping – buying. Or, sort of. And not right this minute – I've got to pick up some of my eye cream first – it works wonders, darling, actually gets rid of those awful bulges. Or if it doesn't I'd rather not know – do come with me – I'm dying for a gossip with someone sensible – '

Robin hesitated for a moment and then agreed. Ma, after all, might still be closeted with her Board, and Susan, who had once lived quite near her when the children were young, had always been great fun.

'How's Edward?' she asked as Susan riffled through her enormous and clearly over-loaded bag for money to buy her magic cream – which Robin couldn't help but notice was criminally expensive – and Susan made a grimace.

'Gone, darling. Long since. Ran off with someone from the office – what could I do? Still – ' She brightened and looked up at Robin, who was red with embarrassment. 'Oh, don't look so mortified, darling! It was the best thing he ever did for me! I've had the most marvellous time, with all sorts of wicked men – you've no idea what fun it is to be footloose. You ought to try it sometime.'

'Footloose?' Robin said. 'Me? Hardly.'

'Oh, darling, I know! Your Sam was always too perfect for words. I'm just saying for me, stuck with boring old Edward all those years and no lovely fat babies like yours to take the heat off, well, leaving me was the best thing he could possibly have done, I do promise you. I'm not as flighty now as I was, though. I've met this marvellous chap in the diplomatic, would you believe? Not very high up or anything, but still, Foreign Office and all that! Such fun – we go to the most glorious parties, I adore them. Now, do come on, sweetie. I have to get some ideas for the wretched shop. I'll be so glad when I can get it off my hands – '

'Shop?' Robin was bewildered as she followed the other woman's twinkling high heels out of the store and into the street again. 'What shop?'

'Oh dear, so much to explain!' Susan pushed her hair (which was exceedingly curly and excessively blonde in a way that Robin found highly unlikely, remembering the rather duller Susan she had known all those years ago) back from her forehead and beamed. 'It was my mother's, you see, and she died and then I ran it and then Edward ran off with his office manageress, the dreariest creature but obviously what he wanted because I'm told they've had two children already – ' There was a sudden glint of pain behind the brightness and Robin felt a pang of sympathy, but Susan ran on before she had a chance to say anything. ' – So I decided to manage it myself, but it's all so much work! I try to find interesting things to put in it, but it's madly difficult. People want the best of stuff for the lowest of money where we are – I'm just off Regent Street, you see, but not where the people with money shop, like Liberty and Dickens and Jones – heavens no! I'm in Foubert's Place. It's a little turning off by Liberty's, and the people who come to me are office girls and so forth, very badly off, and wanting lots of fun stuff, but no money to spend on it. Which means I can't really get them all I'd like. Still, I come here to look – they have some amazing shops here, darling, did you know? Do come and see – '

She was still talking busily as Robin, a little stunned, followed her, and she took her at great speed down one side of the King's Road and then up the other, darting in and out of the little shops they passed, picking over the clothes on the rails with pursed lips and giving a fast running commentary – much of it highly critical –as Robin stood beside her and tried to take it all in.

And had an amazingly enjoyable time. It was absorbing in a way she wouldn't have thought possible. They found a shop where the walls were splashed with whitewash and covered in cheap and cheerful posters and there was no real furniture at all apart from hanging rails and a curtained corner where people could try on the clothes. It was run by a couple of extremely cheerful young men in very tight black trousers and polo-necked sweaters who whooped and hooted at their customers, insulting them in every possible way, which the customers clearly adored, as they pulled themselves into gaudy skirts and tight skinny little tops and climbed into high boots made of shiny patent leather or absurd sandals which were little more than the soles and strings, and floppy hats which looked endearingly old-fashioned over

15

round young faces, and altogether had a wonderful time. Robin found herself caught up in it all, and by the time they'd reached the fourth shop was as eager in her pawing of the stock as Susan was.

'Are you going to buy?' Robin asked as they pushed their way through the crowds in a shop that seemed to sell only glittery tops and berets dripping in sequins, and Susan roared with laughter and patted the notebook in which she had been scribbling all the time.

'Darling, of course not! These are retailers like me. I just come for ideas and there's plenty of them here, see for yourself! I note the names of the manufacturer if there is one – there usually isn't –and I draw the designs – see?'

Robin looked at the little notebook and indeed Susan had covered the pages with rapid but accurate scrawls of several of the garments they'd looked at.

'What use is that?' she asked and Susan crowed with laughter again and hurried her on the way to the next shop, which was filled with rails holding only trousers of all colours but mostly in a rough blue cloth, like overalls.

'What use? Why, so that I can copy them. I've got some outworkers who make up to my spec, you see – ' Robin looked puzzled and Susan amplified. 'My specification! I just look at what people are going in for here and then I go and try to get the same sort of stuff for my little place. Of course it's easier for them round here. There are so many shops like this that lots of people come to the area and that encourages others and so it goes on. Never mind. There's some interesting people looking at the shops near me, I'm told, so here's hoping we start to do well. It's time we did.' She made a face. 'I can't pretend I make a fortune. I wish I did.'

'Still, if it's what you live on. On your own – ' Robin ventured and Susan looked at her sharply.

'Yes, I can live on it, just about. Why darling? Thinking of cutting loose, are you?'

Robin crimsoned. 'Of course not! It's just that, well, it just sounds so much fun.'

'It's bloody hard work, sweetie. But yes, it can be fun. I wouldn't be thinking of budging if it weren't for Clive.'

'Clive?'

'My diplomatic sweetheart. There's a chance he's going to get a foreign posting, he says – ' She dimpled suddenly, and looked positively girlish. 'If he does he says we'll have to get married because abroad they'll never tolerate people who live in sin. It has to be legal. So I'll have to be legal! It'll be such a joy – at my age too!'

Robin computed and Susan glanced at her and laughed.

'You're quite right, sweetie. As far as Clive's concerned I'm a very well-kept forty, even though you know and I know I'm the same age as you, near enough. But what the heart doesn't know and all that – and he's thirty-seven after all! Oh, I'm exhausted! Come back to the shop and see my little place? It's been such fun meeting you again, do let's have more time for a lovely gossip. Tell me about the children – '

They took a cab to the shop and Robin talked all the way of the children and Susan nodded and listened and showed no hint of the pain she had seemed to feel before when children were mentioned, and Robin relaxed and talked even more. By the time their taxi had fought its way through the traffic to Oxford Circus and made its tortuous turn into little Foubert's Place, which was tucked away, as Susan had described it, in a knot of little streets behind Liberty's, she felt as though she and Susan had never been apart. It was a very comfortable way to feel, for since Chick's assumption of the job of Matron at Sam's private clinic, she'd lacked the close woman friend she most needed. It wasn't that Chick didn't care any more; it was simply that she hadn't the time she'd been used to have for Robin.

Which was probably why Robin found herself confiding even more in Susan as they shared a cup of tea at the back of her tiny shop. It was cluttered with as many rails and shelves as the King's Road shops had been, but the main difference was the lack of customers. Where the King's Road had been heaving with people these little streets were almost empty, for the shoppers who thronged Regent Street never turned their heads to peer down dim Foubert's Place. The young assistant who had been in charge in Susan's absence reported only one sale, of a skirt which had put the princely sum of twenty-seven shillings and sixpence in the till, a full afternoon's takings, and had gone home gratefully when Susan sent her, and left them to relax together.

Susan kicked off her shoes and Robin needed little encourage-

17

ment to do the same and they sat there and gossiped as the afternoon grew darker and the lights outside glinted into life, and Robin talked and Susan, with what seemed uncharacteristic silence, listened.

'So you see, it's me. It's not Sam or the house or the children. It's me – ' Robin ended. 'I want to – oh, I don't know. I want to *do* something. Not just sit about and be – well, nothing. I want to be busy and useful and – '

'You'd better take this then,' Susan said and bent her head to peer into her cup. 'I read the tea leaves this morning and they said something would come my way and I think it's you. Some more?'

Robin was staring at her. 'Take what?' she said.

'This.' Susan made a comprehensive gesture and then got to her feet and poured another cup from the battered old tin teapot behind the curtain that led to what she laughingly called her office. 'The shop. I told you – Clive says we'll have to get married if he gets a posting and – '

'If he gets a posting – ' Robin said, trying to avoid thinking about what Susan might be suggesting. 'You said *if* – '

'Darling, poor bugger won't know what's hit him! He only had to mention it, you see. If he's ready to get married if he gets a foreign posting then, by golly, he can get married if he doesn't. The shop'll have to go either way, you see. And who in their right mind would buy a place like this? It needs someone with a bit of imagination and willing to take a chance.' She gazed limpidly at Robin. 'So, why not you? It won't matter too much if you don't make a lot of money, and you can afford it – '

'Are you mad?' Robin gaped at her. 'How do you mean, I can afford it – '

'You said your grandmother had died and left you some cash, didn't you? You didn't say how much, mind you – ' She set her head to one side like an inquisitive bird. 'But I don't want too much here. Just for the lease, you know. It's for seven years. And then there's a bit for goodwill, I suppose, and stock and so forth – the rent's not bad – you could have the whole caboodle for – oh, trousseau money! Say five thousand pounds – ' And she set her head even more to one side and smiled beatifically.

Robin stared again and then began to laugh. 'Susan, you really are quite mad! What do I know about shops, for heaven's sake?

I've never even worked in a shop; I wouldn't have the first idea what to do.'

'Oh, it's not difficult.' Susan waved one hand airily. 'All you need is a bit of an eye for fashion and you've got that – I mean, you said some very sensible things there in those King's Road places –and a bit of charm to sell the things. That's all. Oh, and a bit of book-keeping, but I dare say that'll come easy to you. Your mother's in a business of some sort, isn't she?'

'Susan, how much money have you lost here?' Robin said, keeping her face as expressionless as she could, and Susan smiled blissfully again.

'Oh, masses, but that's because I'm so stupid, darling! I mean, I never did it right. I took out what I need to live on, you see, and always wore clothes from stock, so you see it couldn't have worked with me. I was always more interested in my private life than this shop. It could have been a gold mine, Clive said so,' she ended, as though that clinched it for good and all.

Robin got to her feet and pushed on her shoes. 'Susan, love, it's been good to see you again, really great. And I've had a lovely afternoon with you – but do please forgive me if I run now. I've got to get home to the girls – they're late in tonight because of some school club or other, but it's getting on now and I'll have to hurry for the tube. I hope you sort it all out with your Clive and I do hope you get someone to take your shop.'

She looked round at the little crowded space and her lips quirked. It looked very lonely and unloved, with its drooping rails and its rather lack-lustre lighting. 'And if you'll take my advice you won't tell anyone else how bad it is to trade here and you won't admit you lost so much money. Then maybe you'll do better – '

'I'd go down to four and a half thousand,' Susan said hopefully. 'No? Oh well – be sure to let me know if you change your mind – '

Robin laughed. 'I will,' she said. 'But don't hold your breath. And forgive me if I run. I must get back in time to phone Oliver at school – I've missed his tea-time but he'll be there for supper. I'll just make it. Do keep in touch, Susan.' She kissed her and made for the door. 'I'll really want to know how you get on!' and she went, hurrying away from the dull little street into the bright cheerfulness of Regent's Street.

She'd filled in the afternoon nicely and now it was time to get back to real life; especially to phoning Oliver. And she thought about what she'd have to say to him all the way home.

3

'Did she give you hell?' Jamie asked sympathetically and Oliver raised a supercilious eyebrow, as he dropped the phone back into its cradle.

'Good God, no! Ma's a pushover – flaps a good deal but there's no harm in her.'

'Then why's she phoning so often? Tried at lunch time, didn't she? I mean, whoever it was who rang for you sounded motherish!'

'I told you, she flaps a lot. The original wet hen, that's my Ma. Listen, are you on for tonight?'

The other made a face. He was sitting with his legs hanging over the side of one of the battered armchairs that littered the Fifth Form common room, eating an apple. 'I'm a bit pushed,' he said with his mouth full. 'Three weeks behind with chemistry prep. Not sure I can – '

'Drip!' Oliver said scathingly. 'What's chemistry got to do with your love life, for God's sake?'

'I thought it was mostly a matter of chemistry,' someone murmured from the other side of the room. 'Or physics, perhaps? Light the blue touch paper and retire.'

'It's all right for you, Landow.' The apple eater threw the core in the general direction of the waste basket and missed. 'You don't give a damn, but me, I've got A levels to worry about. If I don't get into Uni, life won't be worth living at home.'

'Mine won't be any better,' Oliver said. 'So why should you worry if I don't? Anyway, I'm not going to waste time begging you, James Major, take it from me. There's plenty more'll be glad of the chance. These are three very remarkable wenches, take it from me.'

'Surely that's what they'll have to do?' the boy at the other side of the room said. 'From all you say – '

21

Oliver smirked. 'Oh, they do, they do. And don't they love it. Jamie, where are you going?'

Jamie was on his feet and making for the door. 'I told you, I've got three weeks of chemistry notes to do, and if I don't do 'em tonight, Joe Crimmond says he won't let me do the exam. So he's got me by the short and curlies.'

'Some freedom school this turned out to be,' Oliver said with disgust. 'You can call 'em by their bloody first names, the beaks, but when it comes to any real control over our lives they're the buggers with the whips in their hands. And my father thinks I have it easy! I should cocoa!'

'Looks like you've got your three wenches to yourself, doesn't it?' The other boy got to his feet too. 'A bit like your pub – did you ever get any customers?'

Oliver laughed. 'Who cares? There were four of us had a great party – '

'On your booze, I'm sure you did. But you said people were going to pay for their own drinks and that'd make money for you.'

'Sod the money!' Oliver said blithely. 'We had fun and that always comes first. Listen, it'll be fun with these three too. They're all goers, from all accounts and – '

'Whose accounts?'

Oliver laughed again. 'Do me a favour, Danny. That'd be giving away all my stock in trade! Just take it from me they're good news. Have I ever lied to you? One of 'em works here in the kitchen – got the reddest hair you ever saw and *the* most incredible shape.' And his hands described the shape in the air and he set his head to one side and looked beguilingly at the other.

Danny looked back at him and wavered. There was something very exciting about Oliver Landow. It wasn't just that he was good looking in a rather obvious curly-haired and dark-eyed way; it was the couldn't-care-less air that he carried with him all the time, the sense of danger mixed with a wicked childlike glee that made him almost irresistible. But Danny too had a great deal hanging on his A·levels and he shook his head firmly to make resistance easier.

'Not on your sweet nelly,' he said and headed for the door. 'Me, I've got the magical world of mathematics hanging over the old bonce. Try me after the mocks and we'll see then. Tonight, like I said, you get all three to yourself, including the redheaded pneumatic one. See you – '

Oliver, left behind in the shabby room, swore loudly and then, after a little thought, made for the phone again, digging in his pocket for the necessary pennies. If it was a choice between losing the fun and losing face there was little he could do; his hand was forced: and he waited till the ringing stopped and a breathless voice said, 'Hello? Yes? *Who* is it?' and then tucked his chin into his chest and said in a husky tone, 'Jacky? Hello sweetie – '

'Who's that?' The little voice clacked in tinny suspicion. 'Olly? What's the matter with you?'

'Got a lousy cold, haven't I?' Oliver said, huskier than ever. 'They're going to put me in the bloody sickroom for the night. I'll never get away. And anyway, don't want to give you my bugs, do I?'

'Oh, poor Olly!' The voice softened and lost its suspicion. 'You be careful now. You don't want to get really ill – you wrap up warm.'

'I'd rather wrap you up warm.' His voice was so husky now it was a lascivious whisper and the distant voice giggled.

'Ooh, you are a one!'

'Promise we'll make another time,' Oliver croaked. 'The other fellas are mad with disappointment – and frustration! Tell your mates, yes? Next week maybe? I'll be fine by then – '

And the mocks'll be over and those stupid sods'll join in. 'Say yes. It'll give me something to look forward to while I'm locked up in the sickroom.'

'We – ell,' said the little voice coquettishly, and mentally Oliver sighed. There'd have to be five minutes or more of coaxing and flirting now, or he'd lose the three of them altogether, and especially this one. And he really fancied her a lot. The red hair was quite something, let alone the figure. 'We – ell – maybe – '

When he hung up the phone again almost ten minutes later he'd worked the oracle and had made a firm date with the three girls for the following week, but that didn't solve the problem of tonight. He'd been really keyed up for this escapade. Setting up smoking groups in the cellars and drinking dens in the woods was small beer compared with getting three willing girls lined up for a party in the swimming-pool enclosure. He'd planned it all so beautifully, making sure he had a copy of the pool-house key and there were cushions on the long loungers that were stored in the cupboard at the back of the pool, and it had never occurred to him that the stupid bastards would refuse to join in. Mock A levels, for God's sake – as if they mattered compared with the chance of getting a bit of real life with girls like Jacky and her friends!

He wandered over to the window and stared down into the garden, skulking wet and grey in the March twilight, and the feeling settled over him like a cloak coming down from the ceiling, that all too familiar sick black bored sensation that said, 'Nothing good will ever happen again. Life isn't worth the bother. Everything's flat and dead and dreary.' And he kicked the wall beneath the window in an attempt to dislodge the feeling, but it sat there on his shoulders, gloating at him like some heartless animal. Again he kicked the wall, so hard this time he hurt his foot, and swore. He'd have to think of something to do or go out of his mind. This was one hell of a way to feel on a Friday night with the whole weekend ahead. He could have wept with the frustration of it all.

Somewhere behind him a door opened and slammed and then opened again and he could hear a radio blaring down the fifth-form corridor; the new record everyone was so mad about but which he personally loathed. 'Won't you please please me,' the Liverpool voices burbled as the thumping background made the walls seem to vibrate – it was a very loud radio – and he shook his head in scorn. The things these kids went in for! He could imagine his Uncle Josh's face if he were here. Uncle Josh who was a successful composer as well as a great trumpeter and had the greatest jazz record collection anyone could ever have and who played his own trumpet like an angel –

And then his head seemed to burst with light. That, of course, was the answer to the weekend and its miseries. The black cloak lifted from his shoulders, trembled and vanished. He dug into his pockets and counted the cash he found there and then ran over to the door and peered out. No one was in sight and the door down the corridor had been closed to deaden the thump of the music, and he withdrew his head into the room and made for the battered old briefcase Danny had left there when he'd gone, taking only his maths books under his arm. If he knew Danny, there'd be a stash of some sort there.

There was; and he scribbled a note on a piece of paper he tore from one of Danny's exercise books: 'I.O.U. two pounds, borrowed in your absence, to be returned as soon as I've got the necessary.' and signed it with a flourish with his new signature, the one with the extra tail on the final 'r' of his first name which embraced his surname with a sort of scroll. He thought it looked rather fetching and then snorted with laughter as he imagined Danny Plaistow's face when he found it in the front pocket of his briefcase. He'd be livid. Well, serve him right. He shouldn't be such a boring old swot, and leave his things lying around.

Getting out of school wasn't difficult. It never was because it was school policy to treat the boys as people who were more likely to behave well with less supervision rather than with more, and as individuals responsible for themselves; considerably to Oliver's scorn and that of many of his cronies. That was why there were telephones in all the form common rooms and why people who wanted to go home for the weekend had only to sign themselves out in the porter's book and no questions asked.

Stupid gits, thought Oliver and signed, waiting till the porter was not there before he did it. They'd had a couple of brushes lately, Jeffcoate and he. Oliver consistently broke the only real rules the school had, which were that there was to be no smoking and no alcohol on the premises, and Jeffcoate had caught him three times in the last fortnight. It had cost a fair bit to buy him off and he'd want more than ever if he saw Oliver tonight, considering he hadn't paid him all he'd promised after their last run in. Better just to slope off quietly while he and most of the masters were at supper. No time for collecting any gear from his dorm, and anyway, why bother? He'd be able to borrow some of Josh's. Josh wore interesting clothes, much better than the boring blazers and battered flannels in which Oliver had to spend his time.

It was a much more cheerful boy who swung himself on the Green Line bus and paid the fare from Danny's two pounds that would take him to Marble Arch in just a couple of hours; a weekend with Josh! That was more like it. As long, of course, as Josh didn't rat on him and tell his parents what he was up to. But he'd have to gamble on that, and worry about it if it happened. That was the way Oliver usually operated and he saw no reason to change now. He was whistling softly between his teeth as the bus drew away into the darkness and left the school behind.

'No thanks. No, really,' Josh said and pushed the door a little closer. 'I'll call you if there is anything, Mrs Chesterfield, I do promise. Good night!' And at last she stepped back and took her worried face away and he was able to close the door properly and go padding back to the armchair out of which she'd summoned him with her urgent rapping.

Of course he'd have to go out now. She'd made him lie when he refused her offer of a 'nice home-cooked supper, Mr Deveen, just what a man wants on a chilly night. You don't eat enough to keep body and soul together, you don't – ' And when he'd said that no, really, no, he couldn't, he was invited out to eat tonight, but it was very kind of her, the look on her face compounded of equal measures of doubt and inquisitiveness had made his heart sink.

At first he'd thought her the perfect landlady, when he and Adrian had taken her top two floors to be their home. She'd cleaned and laundered for them, and sometimes cooked, and never showed the slightest interest in their private lives, nor made any comments about meeting nice young ladies, the way every other member of his family did – well, almost every other member. She'd just accepted that Nice Mr Deveen and his Nice Friend, Mr Kingsman, were co-tenants and were nice quiet tidy gentlemen, and that had been that.

Nice quiet tidy gentlemen, thought Josh, throwing himself back into his armchair and looking round the room. Oh dear! What would Adrian say if he could come back now? 'Josh, you're like a bug, you know that? A nasty messy old bedbug. This place looks like it was hit by a bomb – ' And he'd go about quietly tidying up and cleaning the little kitchen and the even smaller bathroom and then he'd cook them something or other and they'd settle to a quiet evening, Adrian writing as always and Josh absorbed in his music, and they wouldn't say a word to each other for hours on end.

'Oh God,' Josh said aloud and switched on the radio to drown out the thoughts. 'Oh, God!'

And then turned off the radio, because it was playing another of those awful Liverpool songs that he so disliked. Not the melodies; they were good enough, but the driving mindless beat that had no real soul in it, that was as far from his view of what music was as this room was from the way it had been when Adrian was alive.

'No!' he said, aloud again and switched on the radio again and found another station. This was going to be a bad evening, no question. It'd be just as well if he did go out. If he sat here he'd drive himself mad with retrospection, all the regrets and miseries that Adrian would have jeered at; and he got to his feet and stretched. A bath first. That'd ease things a little maybe. A hot bath and a shave and clean clothes.

He slouched off to the bathroom and turned on the tap and began to whistle, trying to find a way through the tangle of notes he'd fallen into with the new score. It was devilishly difficult, and he didn't know why; he didn't usually make such heavy weather over a new commission. Maybe he was tired? A holiday, perhaps? Even abroad somewhere in the sun? He could afford it now, with darling old Grandma's bequest.

He stood there in his bathroom in the steam, naked except for one sock, the other held in his hand, and let the tears fill his eyes as he thought of Mildred. Imagining the world without her was horrendous. Those long hours he had spent at her bedside when she had lain there not talking, barely even seeming to breathe, had been so important a time for him, something precious. A time to stop and think, to talk to her inside his head and hear her wise answers. When Adrian had been killed the first thing he'd done after he left the morgue where they'd made him go to identify his body had been to Leinster Terrace to sit and hold Mildred's dry little bony hand and talk to her and cry with her. She might have seemed unconscious to everyone else, but to him she had been responsive, warm, her old sharp-tongued self.

And now she, like Adrian, was gone, and who was there to talk to or share the pain with? No one at all. And he thought confusedly of his mother and his sister and wept even more, for they loved him as he loved them, but it was different with them. He couldn't talk to them, not ever. He never had, even when Adrian had been here – even though Adrian had said they should, both of them, talk to Poppy and David – but anyway, that was out of the question now. There was just himself, alone, and somehow he'd have to manage.

27

He pulled off his other sock and got into the bath and sank gratefully into its caressing heat and closed his eyes. Just ten minutes of this would work magic –

He woke with such a start when the rapping came that he sat up suddenly and sent a great wash of water cascading out of the bath and all over the floor, and he cursed and shivered, all at the same time, for the water had gone cold as he'd slept; and he climbed out of the bath, suddenly aware of the darkness, and groped for a towel and wrapped himself in it and then turned on the light to stand blinking in its unaccustomed brightness for a moment to regain his composure.

There was another rapping at the door and he went out, barefoot across the lino, leaving damp footprints, and opened the door to the hallway and could have sworn as he saw Mrs Chesterfield's anxious wrinkled pippin of a face peering back at him.

'Oh, Mr Deveen, I was that worried when you didn't answer! I told the young man you was in, you see, seeing as how I hadn't seen you go out, but then you didn't answer and you *didn't* answer, and I thought, well, I thought, maybe I got it wrong and you went out quietly and me never noticed, though I have to say I don't miss much sitting there in my front room as I do all the time and then I thought, well, maybe I better knock again and – '

'Hello, Uncle Josh!' Oliver peered out from behind Mrs Chesterfield's comfortable bulk and looked uncharacteristically uneasy as he gazed at Josh's damp hair and the towel beneath his wet chest and shoulders. 'Maybe I should have phoned first but I thought, well, I just thought it'd be nice to drop in – '

'Drop in?' Josh said and blinked. 'I thought you were at school.'

'Oh, I am!' The boy slipped past Mrs Chesterfield and ducked under Josh's arm as he held his door. 'I just thought – let's go up to Town and see good old Josh! I was getting absolutely stifled there, you know how it is. I ache for some music – real music, not this awful new stuff – '

He looked appealingly at Josh, who gazed back at him and shook his head a little ruefully and managed a grin.

'You're a villain, Oliver. Your mother will – well, we'll talk about it. Thank you, Mrs Chesterfield, that'll be fine now. What?

no, not a thing – we really will be going out to eat – ' And he closed the door on her disappointed face.

'Out to eat? Fab!'

'Who invited you?'

Oliver grinned cheekily. 'You did. You said *we* – didn't you? Where shall it be? Make it Chinese. Oh, do please make it Chinese! I love that – '

'Don't we all know it,' Josh said and went padding back to the bathroom. 'Sit down and shut up. There's a magazine there, and there's the radio, or you can play a record. I'll get dressed.'

He got dressed to the strains of Fats Waller – which was the record he knew Oliver would play, for whatever other faults the boy might have, his taste in jazz was faultless – and felt his spirits rise a little. The boy could be a nuisance, heaven knew, but he was a distraction. And there was a friend playing tonight at One Hundred Oxford Street – Oliver would like that. Of course, he'd have to call his sister Robin and tell her the boy wasn't at school but that shouldn't cause any problems; and he was actually whistling in time to the 'Jitterbug Waltz' as he came out of the bedroom, knotting his tie.

'Have you called Robin?' he asked as he checked the knot in the mirror over his fireplace, and Oliver grinned.

'Oh, Josh, don't be a bore, please! You know what Ma is! Treats me like a three-year-old, dammit. All I want is a decent night out with some adult company – the people at school are really such infants – and no drama. Can't I just spend a couple of days with you and then go quietly back with no one any the wiser? Be a sport, Josh, please!'

Josh looked at him consideringly.

'What have you been up to?'

Oliver looked back with equal thoughtfulness. His mind was clicking its gears at a great rate. Tell a lie and risk being caught out? Or try the honesty tack? He opted for the latter and produced the most disarming grin he could.

'Been smoking in the cellar. Got caught by the Stalag Luft Oberführer, Jeffcoate. He sneaked on me to the Head because I didn't have enough cash to buy him off. Ma was told and she's a bit – well, you know.'

Josh shook his head. 'Oliver, for heaven's sake, what's the matter with you? You're at a school where they let you get away

29

with blue bloody murder, only two rules, and you delight in breaking both of 'em. What's so special about smoking, for God's sake?'

Oliver thought for a moment and then smiled brilliantly. 'It's a rule,' he said simply and this time Josh couldn't stop himself laughing.

'Yes, well I can understand that – oh, damn you. You make it very difficult for me. Look, let's put it this way. I won't tell Ma tonight that you're here, okay? But come tomorrow she'll have to know –'

'Oh, Josh!' wailed Oliver.

' – because tomorrow it's Lee's birthday and she's having a party and we're all going to be there. I'll take you with me, and you can say you're there to surprise her for her birthday, and then Robin won't get quite so mad. And at least she'll not have been kept in the dark about your comings and goings, which could upset her a lot. Is it a deal?'

'It's a deal!' Oliver said exultantly. 'On one condition.'

'You've got a nerve making conditions!'

'Can't help it,' Oliver said. 'I've got no cash, kind Uncle, dear Uncle, need some to buy Lee a present – '

'Damn your avaricious soul, it's a deal,' Josh said. 'But not a penny more than you really need – '

'Not a penny more. Not after you've bought me all the egg rolls I can eat! Can we go to Ley On's? I just love Ley On's – and then maybe a jazz session somewhere. How about it, Josh? Let's paint the town, as they say in all the best films – '

'Do they indeed,' Josh said dryly. 'All right. Let's paint the town. But it's going to be a very pale pink, take it from me. I'm not made of money – '

'No,' Oliver agreed and leapt to his feet. 'Of course not. But you've got more'n I have what with Grandma's and all – don't look like that! Of course I know about it. Everyone does. I don't care! Why should I? I say, before we go, dear old Josh, may I borrow that green shirt of yours and the matching silk scarf and the duffle coat with the tartan lining? I mean, you don't want to look as though you're out with just a kid, do you? I have to dress the part!'

'No,' Josh said and was suddenly less amused than he had been. 'No I don't, do I? Yes, you can have them. And I can improve on those godawful flannels too. Come on then. Let's get on with it.'

4

Lee's house was heaving with people when Josh and Oliver arrived, walking up from St Martin's Lane and ducking through the little arch that brought them into the Court. 'London's oldest street,' Josh said, looking at its narrow cobbled length and the tiny bow windows of the small houses that lined it. 'Trust Lee to come and live somewhere like this, and to fill her house up with the sort of things she does.'

'I like it,' Oliver said. 'The new stuff's miles better than all that awful old-fashioned muck like there is at home – I can't think why Ma and Pa don't have the sort of furniture Lee does. It'd be much more interesting – '

He stopped chattering then as they reached the door with the large brass knocker and bell pull and the polished brass plate which read 'Foxlee Agency' in discreet letters, seeming for the first time since he'd arrived last night in Josh's flat to be a boy of sixteen. All Friday evening and the daytime of Saturday he'd been his usual brash and bouncing self. Now he seemed subdued and Josh glanced at him and was amused. Do the boy no harm to worry about what his parents might say, no harm at all. His trouble was he had to worry too rarely.

'Josh darling!' Lee carolled from the top of the stairs inside as the door was opened to their ring by a man in a servant's white coat. 'Such heaven to see you!' And she hurled herself down the stairs to hug her brother and then to look in amazed delight over his shoulder at Oliver.

'Dear Oliver – what are you doing here? Why aren't you at school?'

'I wanted to come and say happy birthday, Auntie Lee,' Oliver said and held out to her the bowl of hyacinths, a blue bowl

32

wrapped in cellophane and adorned with a blue ribbon, that he'd been carrying, and she took them and hugged him and then kissed him and hugged him again, and set the flowers on the low glass table beside the front door and unwrapped them so that the scent could drift up to fill the rooms above.

'Come on, my darlings!' she cried. 'Come and get a drink. You're among the first, which is lovely. At least there's still room to breathe – ' And she led them into the drawing-room above, which stretched the width and depth of the building, which was not a large one. Oliver had thought the first time he'd seen his aunt's home, just after she had married, that it was a perfect miniature. The single office on the ground floor where she and her husband worked at a big double desk with a battery of phones on it, and a secretary tucked away in the corner, and here above the drawing-room and the tiny kitchen-cum-dining-room, and right up in the eaves the bedroom with its gables and oddly arranged ceiling and the minuscule bathroom, seemed to him the epitome of sophisticated living.

'Perfect for a newly married pair!' Jeremy Fox had said and laughed when Oliver had agreed. 'Since we choose to live and work in each other's pockets, what more space do we want?'

Oliver followed Lee and Josh upstairs with alacrity and threw himself happily into one of the huge bean bags in the corner which were so much a feature of the room and took the glass of lemonade Jeremy gave him ('No, don't look at me like an injured gazelle! Your parents'll be here soon and I don't want to be accused of debauching their only son! Anyway, booze isn't good for you. I should know – I have far too much of it.') and the dish of peanuts he was able to filch from another nearby glass table and looked around him approvingly. How could they abandon him to life in a grotty old school like Lord Peter's, when there was this sort of life to be lived in the real world? The extraordinary paintings on the otherwise blank white walls, all strident greens and aching blues and screaming reds; the boldly black and white striped swags of curtains that slashed the far wall; the spindly legged furniture in the palest of wood but mostly in glass, all of it enchanted him and he settled to make the best of his surroundings and of the party that he could before his parents and retribution arrived.

Josh was already in a cluster of people beside the fireplace, which was little more than a hole in the wall surmounted by a vast copper hood that went right up to the ceiling, and Oliver looked at the sharply defined bones in his face as the firelight flickered on it and thought – at least that's one relation I don't have to be ashamed of. And Auntie Lee's all right, living here and being a theatrical agent and knowing all these madly famous people – for several of the other guests who were now arriving thick and fast had extremely familiar faces – but why did Ma and Pa have to be so awful? If anyone at school ever found out Pa wasn't just a doctor like I said but a specialist in loonies I'd never live it down. And as for Sophie and Penny – he grimaced and finished his lemonade and got to his feet to go prowling for more.

Across the room Lee watched him and shook her head. 'Something tells me that Robin doesn't know he's here,' she murmured to Jeremy. 'She'll go spare – perhaps I ought to – '

'Do nothing at all,' Jeremy said with considerable force. 'Don't meddle, there's a love. I know you and your family are as close as bedbugs in a soldier's blanket, but you don't have to get involved in what's private to them – '

'Bedbugs!' Lee was immediately diverted. 'You wretch! How dare you call my relations bugs?'

But she wasn't at all offended in truth and Jeremy knew it perfectly well. They'd been friends long before they became lovers and then married; Jeremy had been her agent when he'd worked for the huge company which had agreed graciously to take on the aspiring actress that had been the younger Lee back in the middle nineteen fifties, and they'd always got on well, even after he'd told her with what might have seemed brutal candour that she was at best an indifferent actress, but that her understanding of the business of theatre and her grasp of such matters as contracts, union arrangements and cash returns on investment was second to none. They'd started the agency together on the basis of that judgement, a lot of hope and not much money, three years before, and now were sitting happily on a small but very select heap of exceedingly hard-working and successful actors and a few directors and cameramen too. They'd married as much for practical business reasons as any other, since they'd been lovers for most of the three years anyway (not that Lee ever mentioned the fact to her family, Poppy especially, fearing she'd be appalled) and happily they were as contented as they'd ever been before.

To Lee, looking around her very fashionable drawing-room with its sprinkling of gossip-column faces and important business contacts, with more coming up the stairs all the time, it was clear that her lines had fallen in pleasant places. She had the perfect husband, an enthralling business, and a delightful family; even the scapegrace Oliver had gone to the trouble to take a day off from his school life to visit her on her birthday and had brought her a gift, and she softened as she looked at him sitting hugging his knees on her biggest bean bag, and staring around bright eyed at his fellow-guests like a large bird waiting to see where the crumbs would fall thickest. He'll do very well, Lee thought, when he's as old as he likes to think he is already. Very well indeed – as long as he doesn't get himself into big trouble first. I'm glad he's just my nephew and not my child.

And she looked thoughtfully at Jeremy and wondered what his reaction might be if she did in fact change her mind and say she thought it might be nice to produce a potential junior partner for the firm. After all, this was her thirty-sixth birthday; time was not on her side as far as babies were concerned. But then she saw Robin and Sam appear at the top of the stairs and at once forgot her musings.

'Darling!' she hugged Robin warmly and took her bow-bedecked parcel with delight but made no effort to open it. 'Listen, I can't tell you how thrilled I was when he arrived – it was the sweetest thing any child could have done. It only goes to show how much good upbringing sticks!'

Robin stared at her, puzzled. 'What on earth – ?'

Lee rattled on, certain now that she was on the right track to getting Oliver's unexpected presence accepted by his parents, and behind her, Oliver, who had also seen his parents arrive and was skulking rather low on his beans in consequence, could have hugged her in gratitude. Good old Lee – exactly the right fertilizer to make Robin blossom forth in pretty flowers.

'I was amazed when I saw him but then I thought – of course it's just the sort of thing he would do for the family – now where is he? He arrived with Josh – Oh!' Lee said with a nice air of surprise, as Oliver unwound himself from his low seat and stood straight. 'There you are, Oliver!'

'Oliver!' Robin gasped and without hesitation threw her arms round him and hugged him, and over her shoulder Oliver caught his aunt's eye and winked hugely, conveying all the gratitude he could; and then noticed his father's quizzical face as he interpreted the wink and blushed redly.

But Robin seemed not to notice his colour change as she held him away from her to look at him and then hugged him again.

'You didn't say you were going to do this!' she said then, putting on her scolding face. 'When we spoke on the phone yesterday!'

'I wanted it to be a surprise,' Oliver said. 'I thought I'll pop up to town and to make sure you don't accidentally let Auntie Lee know I'm here, I'll go to Josh and so I did and – '

'Robin,' Josh said behind her and Robin turned and smiled and kissed him. 'Did the young wretch tell you what he's been up to?'

Robin looked fondly at Oliver. 'No, he didn't have to, Lee did. Coming up specially to surprise her – so nice!'

Oliver, who for one ghastly moment had thought that his uncle was after all going to tell tales on him, smiled back with great fervour as Josh said no more, and basked in his mother's delight in his company. She made him mad, often, but she was a good soul, his mum, and God help anyone who ever said otherwise.

'Oliver, my boy, come and get your glass filled with me,' his father said and Oliver glanced at him and felt his ebullient spirits falter. Surely Pa wasn't going to cut up rough?

Obediently he went, leaving the sisters talking in great animation with their mother, who had just arrived, both explaining to her in point and counterpoint how splendid her grandson was to visit his aunt as a birthday surprise for her, and accepted the lemonade his father gave him.

'Well, now, young man,' Sam said, looking at him with a very straight face. 'Let's have the truth of it, shall we?'

Oliver thought fast. Tell his father one of his more elegant stories about why he'd taken off for the weekend? No benefit in that. The wretch could always see through tales. Doing a job like his made it very difficult for any son to live a life of his own, he thought, aggrieved, and then sighed. Why waste time?

'I was bored,' he said. 'I was in trouble for smoking and the other fellers were all heads down in their revision instead of being ready to spend a fun evening with me.' He thought it prudent to leave out mention of the girls in the hope that that possibility might not occur to his omniscient father. ' – And well, it seemed a good idea to come and see old Josh. He's always such good value – and then when Josh was mad at me and said I had to tell you I was here and – well, he said it was Auntie Lee's birthday and I thought – ' He shrugged and let the words tail away.

His father sipped his drink gravely and looked at him, thinking; it was difficult, as it always had been, to assess the things Oliver said. From his earliest childhood he'd had a trick of looking at you with huge candour beneath those ridiculously thick lashes, a wide dark-eyed gaze that was ever hard to resist. He'd learned by painful trial and error that his son was as happy lying as speaking the truth and didn't always know the difference between his fantasies and reality; now the same problem presented itself. Was this sudden jaunt from his boarding-school to London no more that a whim based on boredom? Or had there been more to it than Oliver had said?

He was tired. It had been a harder than average day, with one of his more manic patients taking it into her head to abscond from the Clinic, leaving Chick in a state of considerable alarm, and by the time she'd been found, as she clearly had intended herself to be, in a local tea-shop and coaxed back, he'd been late to pick up Robin for the party. She'd been frosty because he'd had to go to the Clinic on a Saturday anyway – she regarded it as the one day she ought to be able to count on her husband's company – and his lateness had been the crowning insult. She had sat beside him in the car in stony silence, refusing to respond to his overtures of peace in the least, and now, here was Oliver and –

No, he couldn't cope with a further row with Robin over her undoubtedly favourite child. She adored Sophie and Penny, of course she did, but her first-born and only son was clearly the one who owned her heart and soul above all others, and to probe more deeply into his present behaviour and the situation at school would be fuel to the flames. Their life was dry enough and more than ready to catch fire. To tinder a conflagration from sparks thrown off by a fight with Oliver would be stupid. And very exhausting.

So Sam sighed softly and nodded with some resignation and Oliver perked up happily and dodged away to join the group of people talking to – or rather listening to – the self-indulgent chatter of a particularly pretty young actress who was currently all the rage because of her appearance in a TV show in which she had scant lines to speak but even scantier costumes to wear so no one minded, least of all herself. There are all sorts of storms brewing for the future with Olly, he thought. But that's the least of it. Why has it all gone so sour? Was it my fault, always, as Robin said the last time we managed to talk about it without getting so angry we lost our tempers? How could it be? I wasn't building the practice and the Clinic just for my own career satisfaction. It was for Robin and the children so that they'd always have enough. He could still remember the poverty of his own childhood in the black years that had led up to the Great Depression, and the struggle he'd had to make any sort of meeting between ends during the Depression itself, when he'd been a medical student and then a young house physician subsisting on what he could filch to eat from the ward kitchens. He wanted no such penny-pinching for his fiercely loved family. So how could Robin not see that there were good reasons for his absorption in his work?

And anyway, what else could he have done? He looked at her now and felt the familiar ache deep in his belly. He wanted her as much as he ever had, as much as he had the first time he'd seen her in her neat student nurse's uniform at the old London Hospital during the Blitz; a desire that had grown over the years and became more clamorous. Watching her now, chattering with one of her sister's more handsome clients, he felt again the old jealousy that had filled him then, when he'd seen Robin – talking so eagerly and somehow so intimately – with that dour Scottish orderly they'd had, and with whom she'd – oh, well, what was the use of thinking about it now? The years had done it to them, driving this heavy wedge between them. The years when she'd been so absorbed in the babies and then the children as they grew ever more vociferous and demanding, and had seemed to have less and less need for him. No wonder he'd become so wrapped up in the practice. What else did he have, after all? She excluded him from so much to do with the children; for the best of reasons, he knew, wanting to protect him from the exhaustion of small feet thundering over him and loud shrill little voices demanding attention from him at the end of a harsh and difficult day. Though there had been times when he'd have found it refreshing rather than wearing and –

He shook himself slightly. It was absurd to think this way. What he'd have to do was find a way to make Robin listen to him, away from the usual surroundings of home where it was always so easy to escape into the girls' demands, or the phone rang and was insistent on an answer or a tradesman called. He'd plan a small holiday; that was the thing to do. Plan a holiday, and take his Robin away and reforge the old love affair that had fallen into tired grey embers over the years. That the heart was still there glowing he was quite certain. It was just a matter of fanning the flames –

With which unusually fanciful idea for so pragmatic a man, he switched off his ponderings and paid attention to the person for whom the party was being given, his sister-in-law, Lee. She was standing on a small coffee table very precariously and banging a spoon on a glass.

'Darlings – all of you! Listen. I want to make a speech. No, I insist. It's my birthday and I will if I want to. I won't be stopped. I want to say thank you all for being here. I want to say please go on just as you are, because I love you all the way you are. I want time to stand still as it is at this moment. I can't say anything else or I'll cry. On account of I get sentimental sometimes – '

'Does she ever,' Jeremy said sotto voce so that everyone could hear and there was an ironic cheer.

'So I'll be practical instead. Now, you have to have food at a party, but in this tiny house of ours I certainly couldn't cook for fifty of you. Even if I was a good cook which I'm not – '

'That's a myth,' Jeremy said loudly. 'She pretends she can't do it so that I have to take her out to dinner a lot.'

'Clever!' called someone from the back of the room. 'I'll have to use the same technique!' And there was considerable laughter.

'Anyway, you won't go hungry!' Lee cried, flushed with excitement and happiness. 'Any minute now – ' Somewhere below the doorbell rang again and she clapped. 'How's that for right on cue? I was going to say, any moment now there will be arriving newspaper parcels of fish and chips! Lots of salt and vinegar, the real McCoy. So tuck in, and enjoy it – and afterwards there's an ice-cream wagon down in the court and you can all go down and get yourself the cornets of your choice. How's that for sophisticated fun?'

There were loud cheers of approval and the party broke into

chattering groups all extolling Lee's brilliant trendiness in doing something so stunningly original for a party, and the scent of freshly fried food drifted in to mix itself with the heaviness of the hyacinths from downstairs which were very heady indeed. The party got louder and more boisterous and everyone seemed to be having a lot of fun. Especially Oliver, now flushed and flirting quite outrageously with the little actress from the TV show.

But the family members, clustered together on one side of the room – Robin and her mother, and David and Sam – seemed less happy. Robin was watching Oliver with a slightly troubled crease between her brows and Poppy was clearly miles away and thinking of something quite other than where she was. Sam too was abstracted, though David, standing beside him with his now completely white head set on one side and his rather pouched and saggy old face set in a more than lugubrious expression, seemed not to notice. He too was occupied with his own thoughts, and suddenly gave them speech.

'It's time she got on with it,' he said abruptly, and Sam, pulled out of his introspection, was startled.

'What?'

David reddened. 'I'm sorry. Thinking aloud.'

Sam followed his gaze and saw him looking at Lee and nodded. He and David had become close friends over the years as well as father- and son-in-law, and he knew how David felt about grandchildren. He adored all he had, and ached for more.

'Yes, I know. But if she isn't ready for children, she isn't. She can't be bullied into it.'

'Who's bullying?' David raised his eyebrows. 'Would I bully?'

Sam chuckled. 'In your own way you put on a good deal of pressure – oh, hello, Josh! Leaving already?'

Josh had come up to them and bent to hug his father and David lifted his face unselfconsciously and kissed his son's cheek.

'I'm leaving your son to your own tender care now,' he said to Sam. 'Keep an eye on him.'

Sam looked at him sharply and then lifted his chin in acknowledgement. 'I will.'

'Where are you going in such a rush, Josh? Got a date to work, have you?' David said.

Josh shook his head. 'Thought I'd drop in on Auntie Jessie. Haven't seen her for a week or two – 'Night Dad. Sam – '

And he was gone.

There was a little silence between the two men as they watched Josh make his way down the stairs and then David sighed and said, as much to himself as to Sam, 'Now, if I really was a bully about having grandchildren, wouldn't I bully him?'

'No,' Sam said. 'You've got more sense.'

David looked at him and made a small grimace. 'Yes, I have. I wish my Poppy, bless her, had as much.'

'Don't we all wish our wives had the same sort of sense we have?' Sam said and though he spoke the words lightly, there was a note of bitterness in his voice. David looked at him sharply and sighed.

'I'll tell you what, Sam,' he said and took him by the elbow. 'Me and you, to hell with the fish and chips. It's a nice drink we need. And I know where Jeremy keeps his Scotch –'

'Ah,' said Sam approvingly. 'Now you're talking. Let's go and find it then.'

And they did.

5

The television set murmuring softly in the corner of the room was the only sound when Josh put his head round the drawing-room door, and Lally looked up and set a finger to her lips, and he nodded and came in quietly to stand for a moment in the dimness, waiting for his eyes to accustom themselves.

In front of the fire, which was burning low now and glowing dully in the grate, Jessie sat in her big armchair with her feet up on a low stool and her head on one side, and he looked down at her in the faint blue flicker sent by the TV set and slowly picked out the lines of her face. She's beautiful now she's old, Josh thought; in her younger years she had been stout, with a couple of chins and plump cheeks to blur the shape of the bones, but now all that had fallen away and her skin, soft and crumpled like dead flower petals, was stretched tightly over the skull beneath. Even the body had shrunk; the strength that had been so much a part of her was quite gone and he looked at her old hands, bent now and dry skinned, resting on the rug over her knees, and sighed. Ninety-eight. An amazing age. She'd outlived so many of them, and looked fair to outlive them all the way she was going.

She'll never die. She's forgotten how, if she ever knew, Josh told himself, standing there as the room's bulky furniture at last loomed into his view. She'll go on sitting there long after we've all vanished —

She seemed to become aware of his regard in her sleep, and stirred and turned her head and opened her eyes to look up at him, and at once the image of frailty seemed to vanish. Her eyes seemed not to have changed at all; they were as dark and as sharp as they had ever been and there was the same look of hopeful excitement in their depths that had been part of her for as long as he could

42

remember, and he bent and kissed her; and she lifted her chin with exhilaration.

'Josh,' she said in her cracked old voice and raised her hands to him and he took them in his and kissed her again and she nodded with satisfaction, for she knew she had made the right identification. The truth was that despite her bright gaze her vision was sadly depleted. She couldn't read as much as she had done once, unless the print was very large, and could only recognize people when they were close by but her mind was as sharp as it had ever been and so, oddly, was her hearing. She spent her time listening to her beloved radio and sometimes watching TV. 'Although,' as she had once confided in Josh, 'it really is such stupid stuff. But the girls like it, so what can I do? You got to put up with things sometimes – '

He looked down at Lally, sitting in her usual place on the little tuffet at Jessie's feet and grinned at the memory. To call Lally and Barbara 'girls' was to stretch credulity thin, for they were both around fifty and looked every minute of it. Lally was now wrapped in a large and shabby greenish plaid dressing-gown, her hair tied up in curlers and her feet thrust into large fleecy slippers that Josh strongly suspected she had bought in a men's shop, and her face was shiny with the attentions of soap and cold cream. Her eyes were fixed on the TV screen and its gyrating little figures and Josh patted her on the shoulder in greeting which she returned by touching his hand, though she never moved her gaze, and Josh went and took the chair on Jessie's other side.

They sat in silence for a while, he with his hand on Jessie's, both deep in their own thoughts, and there was a tranquillity that made Josh at last unknit his shoulders and relax. It had been a difficult weekend with Oliver. Not because the boy had been particularly difficult; he hadn't, taking enormous pleasure in his Chinese supper and his visit to the jazz club, but because being with him meant that Josh had to put on a show of some sort of jollity. He couldn't bury himself as he usually did in his loneliness and grief for Adrian. Now he could and he felt better for it.

And then he realized that he wasn't thinking about Adrian at all, or at least not in a miserable way. He was just sitting here with Aunt Jessie's old hands beneath his, relaxing and feeling pleasantly drowsy as agreeable memories drifted through his mind. It wasn't at all a bad way to be.

The peace was broken as Barbara came in through the door backwards, bearing a large tray, and at the same moment the show that Lally was watching ended, and she got heavily to her feet and switched off the set and turned on the low table lights as Barbara set her tray down on the big table and said with loud cheerfulness, 'Nightcap time!'

Jessie struggled to sit forward, and Josh helped her, pushing the spare pillow that lay ready beside the chair down her back with expert ease; he'd done it for her many times before and she sat upright now, bright eyed and birdlike, looking greedily towards the sound of clinking tea cups and the scent of toasted teacakes.

'What I'd really like is a piece of cheesecake,' she announced in her reedy voice and Barbara tutted loudly.

'At this time of night? You know it'll upset you.'

'So what? I fancy a bissel cheesecake.'

'I haven't got any,' Lally said. 'Tomorrow I'll get some for you. You can have some in the morning.'

'Now,' Jessie said implacably. 'You've got some. You always have. Who's the one who pays for it around here, hey? You tell me that. A bissel cheesecake. You can keep your toasted bits of rubbish.'

Barbara sighed and looked at Lally who shook her head gloomily. Barbara too was in dressing-gown but no curlers; she had a plait of grey hair down her back and looked like an elderly and decidedly bulky schoolgirl, for she was round and rosy now she was middle aged, and clearly a contented person.

'You might as well get it,' Lally growled. 'We'll have ructions if you don't.' And she looked at Josh. 'Can't you persuade her? She'll only wake up in the small hours with a pain – '

'I do that anyway,' Jessie said. 'And if I'm not entitled to wake people up at my time of life, it's a poor thing. Josh, you have cheesecake, too.'

'Too rich for me, Auntie Jessie,' he said. 'It'd keep me awake.'

'Such stuff,' Jessie said and chuckled. 'So, give me my tea and my cake and go away, you two. Me and my boy here, we want to talk private, hey Josh?'

'Not really – ' Josh began and then grinned. 'Yes, of course. If you want to,' and winked at the two women who looked glumly back at him and obeyed. Lally poured the tea and set a cup on the small over-table beside Jessie's chair and then pulled it round so that it was in front of her, and Barbara came bustling back from the kitchen with a minuscule portion of cheesecake and then, still saying nothing, the two of them equipped Josh with tea and a piece of cake and went out together.

'Good night,' Josh called and Lally looked back over her shoulder and lifted her brows expressively at him and said, 'We'll be in the kitchen. Get her to bed after you've gone – '

'Thank you, Lally. And Barbara,' Josh said in a quiet voice as Jessie, oblivious, began shakily but efficiently to demolish her cheesecake. 'I don't know where we'd be without you.'

'Neither do we,' Lally said tartly and then they were gone and he heard them thump along the corridor to the kitchen and smiled. Their watchful love for the old lady was a legend in the family and all of them were used to the jealousy it engendered; they were really only happy, Lally and Barbara, when they had their beloved Jessie to themselves, allowing only one other person to intrude into the charmed circle with a welcome; Bertie, who had been Barbara's nursling in his precarious infancy. The rest of them were only grudgingly allowed in, and as David said, 'Frankly, we should all be damned grateful. What we'd do without them to care for her I can't imagine – '

Looking now at Auntie Jessie, Josh had to agree. That she had lived so long was an amazing tribute to their excellent care, after all she had suffered. The injuries she had received in the Blitz had left her with permanent pain and her legs were still encased in the irons on which she'd been dependent for over twenty years; yet she seemed not to care at all. And then she moved one leg slightly and he saw the faint shadow of pain that passed over her face and revised his opinion. It was sheer effort of will that kept her going, clearly. Will was something she'd always had in overflowing quantity.

'So, how's my Josh?' she said as she pushed her empty plate away from her and tried to lean back. He went to help her, taking out the pillow that held her upright for eating so that she could relax again. 'Still in the dumps?'

'Who said I was in the dumps?' he said lightly and took her plate and empty cup away. 'I'm fine – '

She managed a faint snort. 'This is your old Jessie you're talking to. Not some flighty – me, I can smell it when people're in the dumps. You were.'

45

She closed her eyes and he waited, wondering if she had drifted into sleep as she so often did, but after a moment she opened them again and struggled to focus on his face. 'Come closer,' she ordered. 'So I can see you.'

He obeyed, sitting well within her line of vision and she drew a deep breath and nodded contentedly.

'That's better,' she said and then she did drift into sleep for a few minutes as he sat and watched her, and again let his own shoulders relax.

'I tell you what it is,' she said, suddenly opening her eyes as though their conversation hadn't lapsed. 'I can't talk to you properly when you're in the dumps.'

'I'm sorry,' he said. 'I didn't mean to – someone close to me died.'

'I know,' she said and again closed her eyes. 'It happens. It's a funny thing, it happens and you stop feeling it. You care, but it doesn't hurt so much no more – '

'Really?' he said with some bitterness and she turned her head to look at him.

'Really.'

There was a long silence and then she said. 'I want you should do something for me.'

'Anything, Auntie Jessie.'

'It's Poppy. I'm worried about Poppy – '

'Ma?' His voice sharpened. 'What's the matter with her?'

'Business,' Jessie said drowsily. 'I don't know what it is, but it's something. She's bothered. She comes to talk to me. I ask her about the business and why shouldn't I? Ain't I interested still? But she don't answer and and I worry – you should find out for me, Josh. You're her son. A woman needs a son to look out for her – ' Her eyes snapped open again, for they had closed as though they had a will of their own. 'My son, he didn't look out for me. A woman needs a son to look out for her.'

'Yes, Auntie Jessie,' he said soothingly, and put his hand over hers and gently stroked it and again her eyes closed and she drifted into sleep and he thought – bless her, she's wandering a little. She has no son. Never did, to my knowledge.

He waited and the embers in the fireplace settled with a soft rustle and still she slept on, and he let go of her hand and tiptoed to the door. It was Barbara and Lally's turn now. He'd go home and try to get some sleep himself. He rather thought he would tonight. Visiting Auntie Jessie had helped a lot. Not as much as it had helped to visit his beloved grandmother, but a little. He had good cause to be grateful to her.

Later, as he fell asleep, he remembered and was puzzled. Why should Jessie say his mother needed her son to look out for her? She had David and Gillian to help her with the business, and Gillian's husband Richard. What on earth could the old lady have meant? He turned over then and let sleep come back. Nothing probably. Just a very old lady's confusion, mixing up past and present, remembering sons she never had, seeing problems that weren't there.

He slept.

David was lying in his favourite position, huddled on his side with a book propped up against a pillow. No matter what time they went to bed he read for an hour or so, claiming it was impossible to sleep unless he did, and Poppy had become used to falling asleep in the faint glow of his bedside lamp, hearing the rustle of the pages as he turned them and feeling his back and bottom warm against her. It was the most comforting moment of the day and she needed it as much as – more than – she needed food and drink.

Tonight, though, she couldn't sleep and after a while she prodded him.

'David.'

'Hmm?' He clearly wasn't listening.

'I'm wondering – do you think I'm right about the hotels?'

'Oh, sure, love,' David said but he still wasn't listening and she prodded him harder.

'Put the book down for a while, David. I do want to talk to you. I've got another meeting with him in the morning and I'm just – I need to practise my ideas a bit – '

'It's awfully late,' David turned his head and looked at her over his glasses, his forefinger marking his place on the page he had so reluctantly left. 'Can't it wait till tomorrow?'

'I told you – I've got a meeting with him first thing.'

He sighed and turned towards her, closing the book but keeping his finger still between the pages. 'Tell me about it. What is it?'

47

'I told Richard I thought we were going too fast. The hotels, you remember? Three of them, all over the South. Making sure they're run right'll mean I'll have to spend a hell of a lot of time driving between them. It bothers me.'

'Then don't do it.'

She was irritated by the calmness of his voice and turned over onto her back sharply. 'It's not as easy as that! I'm managing director. If we have major new assets, then I have to be fully aware of what's going on in them – and that'll mean with hotels in Brighton and Bournemouth and Torquay – '

'You're being absurd, Poppy,' David said firmly. 'I don't want to labour a point, but dammit, woman, you're close on seventy! Most people at your age will have retired and – '

'Two years is a long time,' she said acidly. 'When I'm nearer my next birthday you can talk about being nearly seventy. Not yet – '

'If you were fifty-eight instead of sixty-eight I'd say it was too much. It's so silly! Running around the roads from one place to another is a young person's job. You can use someone else to be your legs, for pity's sake, surely! You get someone on your staff to go to the hotels, you stay in London doing whatever it is you insist only you can do in London – though I reckon you could get a deputy for a lot of that too – and take life a bit easier. I'm longing for a holiday.' He sounded a little plaintive. 'But what the hell chance do we have of getting away into some real sunshine while you're so obsessive about the damned business?'

'It's not a damned business,' she snapped. 'It's my – '

He put a hand out and covered her mouth. 'No, not that again. I'm sorry I said it. I just get so – well, anyway, let's not start that stupid row again. You asked me what you should do about Richard wanting to enlarge the business so fast and adding on all these hotels. I've told you. Get yourself a young deputy to do the legwork for you. It's what good editors do! They get poor crummy writers like me to do the donkey work and then they sit at their desks like lords and ladies telling you where you went wrong and making you change things. That's what I *call* being in charge, for God's sake! You do the same! Get yourself a deputy –'

'Who?' she said, and clasped her hands behind her head to lie staring at the ceiling. 'It has to be someone I can trust – '

David lay thinking for a while and then his lips curved. 'Why not talk to Robin?' he said. 'She's got more time on her hands these days. She might be just the person you need to see you right. She's got the car, drives a lot – I bet she'll just love the idea of running around and having a look at your hotels.'

Poppy stared at him with her brows furrowed and then slowly smiled.

'You old – do you know I think you could be right? I could trust Robin – '

'Are you sure?' he asked dryly.

She very properly ignored him. 'And it'd give her something extra to do. I told her she needed a job. She wasn't keen, but I bet I could persuade her. She's been a bit bored lately, and she could earn a little extra for herself and that's no bad thing, especially when you love shopping as much as Robin does! I can have her put on the staff establishment without any problems – Richard would have no say in it. She'd be my personal assistant – '

'May I read again now?' David said hopefully and opened his book.

She laughed. 'Oh, go read yourself stupid, stupid. Mmm. I like that idea. I'll sleep on it – ' And she burrowed down into his back again as once more he turned into his favourite position and began to read. 'If I can sleep for worrying, that is.'

She slept.

'Ma was on at me again about getting a job of some kind,' Robin said suddenly as Sam began to brush his teeth, timing it so that he couldn't speak until she had said all she wanted to. 'I told her I was happy as I am, of course, because I don't want to get like her, all obsessed with the job. But it did make me think a bit – '

Sam spat, rinsed and spat again and towelled his mouth vigorously. 'What are you trying to tell me, Robin?' he asked.

She shook her head, grimacing a little. 'Nothing. Just what Ma said when we met for lunch. I thought she was looking rather well tonight, though she's a bit tired. But I must say you'd never think she was almost seventy, would you? It must be the job that keeps her on her toes so well.'

'Dear Robin,' Sam said and sat down heavily on his side of the bed, as he reached for his watch and began to wind it. 'Don't let's go round in circles, hmm? I've got a rough day tomorrow, we're late now and – '

'It's Sunday tomorrow!'

'I know. I can't help it. I've got to go to the Clinic and see Mrs Meredith – she was in a hell of a state today – and I've got some notes to sort out for Monday's conference. After next week it'll be a lot easier, but right now – so do tell me what it is you have to say, and then we'll get some sleep, hmm?'

You're doing this all wrong, a voice shouted inside his head. You're treating her like a child, you bloody fool! So what if you're tired? Do use your common sense –

But it was too late. 'It doesn't matter,' she said. 'I was just chattering, really. Good night, Sam.'

And she turned her back and rolled herself up into the sort of ball she did when she was angry with him and he sat there on his side of the bed and looked down at her huddled shape and sighed. Tomorrow he'd pull out all the stops and get home early and talk to her properly. No use trying now – she was angry and he was exhausted and desperately in need of sleep. Tomorrow, after I've had a good night, he promised himself as he pulled the covers over him and punched his pillows to submission. When I feel rested.

But he didn't sleep.

6

Poppy parked in her special corner, tucking the car behind the row of vans that bore the familiar sweeping 'Food by Poppy' logo, and sat in it for a while after switching off the ignition, watching the bustle around her as the prepared foods were brought from the factory section at the back of the yard and loaded into the vans. She watched the trays with their neatly fitted white cotton covers being slipped into place along the special runnels with which each van's interior was fitted and thought – there go the chicken pies and cheesecakes for the Golders Green shop and the apple cakes and the salmon croquettes for Crouch End. She'd actually taken that order herself, small as it was, since she'd happened to be in the factory manager's office when the call had come through, and lofty though her status was in the company she was not above dealing with basic jobs like order taking. I'd do the washing up too if it had to be done, she thought and felt a surprising pang of yearning for the good old days when all this had been just a small lock-up office with only herself and Gillian sweating over the orders and making each job pay for itself. It had been fun in those days. What was it now?

She looked as dispassionately as she could at the bustle around her and the way the seven adjoining properties that 'Food by Poppy' had swallowed up had been connected by the elegantly painted timber fascia that bore her logo, just as the vans did. She ought to be proud and happy to see all that her efforts had led to. Instead she felt melancholy and homesick for – what she didn't know, and she shook her head sharply at her own foolishness and got out of the car and made her way across the yard to the stairs that led to her first-floor office and the big boardroom that lay between it and the row of offices in which the rest of the senior staff were ensconced.

Her secretary Marilyn, a dour woman of some forty years and a forbidding expression, was waiting for her as usual with the day's letters ready opened and annotated and yesterday's neatly typed and stacked waiting for her signature. There was a scent of coffee from the pot that Marilyn always had perking in the corner and two 'Food by Poppy' honey biscuits on the small porcelain plate beside the matching beaker, and she sighed as she settled down to the first half-hour of the day's work.

This was the best time when she dealt with the odds and ends, made sure her desk was clear and braced herself for whatever was to come. At ten o'clock, when she'd finished it all and was fortified by Marilyn's carefully made coffee (she never allowed anyone else to brew it, since no one but she, she told everyone, could possibly make it the way Mrs Poppy insisted on having it – though Poppy herself had never said a word on the subject) she felt ready for anything. Even Richard Melhuish.

She began to go through the hotel files that Marilyn, ready as ever just in advance of what she wanted, had put in front of her. This matter had to be settled today. Either Richard would see it her way and allow the option to lapse, since they had a deal that permitted them to withdraw from the contract with no financial penalty within three months of taking over, if they so chose, or she would be forced to accept this extension of the empire and her own responsibility. She had argued as eloquently as she could with Richard and she was almost ready to admit defeat. He had most of the Board on his side, since he had painted for them such a dizzying picture of the value to the company of enlargement of their hotel arm, and her own doubts and warnings had, she knew, come across as very dreary and fuddy duddy. The world according to Richard was poised on the edge of a commercial explosion. There was money about, lots of it, and he wanted 'Food by Poppy' to make its fair share of it. More, even. No wonder the Board preferred to be dazzled by his vision than her own much more cautious view.

There was a buzz from her intercom and Marilyn's voice, frosty with disapproval, clacked at her, 'Mrs Melhuish to see you, Mrs Poppy.' She didn't say it but Poppy could hear her thoughts as though she were shouting them – 'and her with no appointment and you the Managing Director! Partner she may be, and Mrs Melhuish she may be, but what right has she got to come marching in here without so much as a by your leave?'

Poppy got to her feet and hurried over to the door that led to Marilyn's outer office to welcome Gillian with open arms. She always had to do that to overcome Marilyn's all too clearly displayed hostility. Gillian, who had been standing peering at the framed award certificates that decorated the walls, hadn't noticed, of course. She never did. Even if Marilyn had been downright rude to her she would probably just have smiled in a vaguely amiable way and nodded cheerfully.

'My dear Gillian, do come in! More coffee, Marilyn, please. You're looking well! Is that new?'

Gillian turned and beamed at her rather shortsightedly. She'd needed glasses for years now but was much too vain to wear them; which might account for the rather odd effect her clothes always had. They were expensive, undoubtedly, but somehow they never looked quite right. Today she was in a cream mink jacket that clearly cost a small fortune, worn over a suit of brown suede, an outfit that was totally ruined in effect by the clumsy black brogue shoes she was wearing over stockings in a muddy beige that shrieked at the rich tones of the suede. She had a costly Hermes silk square in vivid crimson and blue tied over her head and was carrying a white plastic airline bag with BOAC emblazoned on it.

'Hello, Poppy. Thought I'd drop in,' she said vaguely and beamed again. 'Are you well?'

'Couldn't be better.' Poppy made herself sound as hearty as she could. 'Do come in and sit down. How's Caroline?'

Gillian made a face. 'Oh, just the same. All over the place. You know what she's like, but when I get really mad at her, I remember how you used to have such problems with your stepdaughter and it cheers me up no end. Caro's not as bad as *she* was – awful, wasn't she?'

Poppy blinked. Even from Gillian this was a bit direct, and for once some awareness of her reaction seemed to get through Gillian's usually impenetrable skin.

'Oh, I'm sorry, Poppy, but I mean – you used to get so upset. I remember how it was when your Bertie was born and how she tried to take him away from you after you'd saved him from being thrown into a Home for Incurables and – well, all I mean is that Caroline's a bit noisy and thoughtless but she hasn't done anything like that – '

53

Poppy relaxed and was glad that Marilyn arrived with the extra coffee cup and a face like thunder, and waited till she'd gone again, shutting the door behind her with almost insulting delicacy, before she answered.

'I suppose you're right. Girls can be difficult, though – '

'Your Robin wasn't, was she? I remember, she was marvellous, with her babies and all. I wish I'd had one of my own.' She looked wistful suddenly. 'It'd be nice to have grandchildren.'

'Well, you will have,' Poppy said, trying to be bracing. 'Caroline'll settle down in time, I'm sure, and have lots of babies and then you can have the time of your life. And you're right – grandchildren are fun.'

'She'll have to put a move on,' Gillian said a little sourly. 'She's thirty next birthday.'

Poppy laughed. 'That's a great age! Biscuit?'

'No thanks. Well, it is as far as having children's concerned. I should know. I left it too late – '

Poppy was uncomfortable. Richard might be her colleague now and a senior member of the Board but knowing too much about his private life didn't seem right somehow.

' – by the time Richard and I got married I was thirty-three and there you are – no children of my own.'

'It's wasn't because of your age, though, Gillian,' Poppy said gently and Gillian looked at her with a moment of misery.

'It sort of was,' she said. 'If I'd have married younger I'd have had a younger husband probably and he would have wanted children like I did, only with Richard being so much older than me – '

Her voice dwindled away and there was an awkward silence and Gillian said with a great air of cheerfulness, 'Not that it's all bad. I mean, I've got him all to myself really. Caro's still in our house of course, but she's out and about so much it's like she isn't there at all. Comes in late, goes out early, off to the country or wherever most weekends and I don't see much of her.'

'Then why complain?' Poppy asked and Gillian shook her head.

'It's Richard. He gets so bothered about her being out so much. Then I have to soothe him – ' She sighed. 'It's not always so easy.'

There was another little silence as they both slid into their private thoughts and then Gillian roused herself and smiled brightly at Poppy.

'Anyway, that isn't what I wanted to talk about. Listen, Poppy. I was thinking. Let's get away for a holiday.'

'What?' Poppy gaped at her. 'What *are* you talking about?'

'I was thinking. It'd be fun, just the two of us, go away somewhere to sort of do women's things, you know, shop all day and all that – ' She was chattering now, not meeting Poppy's direct gaze and Poppy frowned sharply.

'Where on earth did you get such an extraordinary notion? I can't think of anything that'd bore me more, frankly, than to spend a holiday shopping. And why should we go on a holiday together? I mean, no insult, Gillian, but it's not as though we had all that much in common. We're not bosom friends exactly, are we?'

'I love shopping all day,' Gillian said, still not meeting her eye. 'I thought you might too – '

'You should know me better than that after all these years. Come on, why? There has to be a reason for such a daft notion.'

Gillian looked a little sulky. 'I don't see what you're making such a fuss about. Richard said it'd be fun for you and I thought so too.'

'Oh,' Poppy said, and bent her head to study her hands on her lap. 'I see. Richard thought. Hmm. And when did you both plan this holiday would start?'

'Oh, right away!' Gillian said, eagerly, and now she did look directly at Poppy. 'Richard – I checked and we could take a plane, you know and go to New York and stay at the Plaza and it wouldn't be too expensive and – '

'And when would we come back?' Poppy said with a dangerous note in her voice that Gillian seemed not to notice at all.

'Mmm – Oh – I don't know. Richard said two weeks'd be about right.'

Poppy got to her feet and went over to her desk to flick her calendar.

'I see,' she said. 'Two weeks. That'd bring us back at around the beginning of April.'

'Something like that.' Gillian was beginning to get a little uneasy.

'After the option on the three new hotels was past its due date.'

'I don't know about that.' Gillian looked up at her with her brows a little creased. 'What hotels?'

Poppy tightened her jaw. 'The hotels in Brighton and Bournemouth and Torquay that we talked about at the last three Board meetings, for God's sake!' she said.

'Oh, that,' Gillian shook her head. 'I didn't pay much attention to that.'

'I don't know why you bother to come to meetings of the Board at all!' Poppy kept her temper under control with a strong effort. 'You sit there and say nothing and just – '

'I'm a partner!' Gillian said indignantly. 'I've every right to be there! I've been with you ever since we started and – '

'Gillian, I know the history! You don't have to remind me. I insisted you be on the Board *because* you'd been with me from the start! I wanted you to help run things. But you say and do less and less. Only what Richard tells you to do – '

'He's my husband,' Gillian said. 'Of course I agree with him! It's what wives do. Don't you agree with David?'

'Not all the time. And I'm not trying to run a business with him. If we did, we'd probably disagree quite a lot. A hell of a lot in fact. Look, Gillian, you've got a responsibility to the Board and to me as well as to Richard, you know, and it's high time you realized that. Don't you see what your precious husband's trying to do? He wants to get me out of the way until the option lapses so that he can get his own way over those three hotels. I think we're growing too fast and I want us to consolidate a bit, and then reconsider stretching ourselves a bit next year. So I'd like to let the hotels option go. But your Richard wants to do it his way, helter skelter, and he doesn't seem to mind what tricks he pulls to win! I don't object to your sticking with him if that's really what you want to do, but I do object to being treated like a daft woman who'll drop everything including important business decisions for the chance to shop in New York! I've a bit more meat on my bones than that, let me assure you.'

Gillian was staring at her with her face crumpled. 'I really don't understand all this. All I did was what Richard said – I thought a holiday'd be nice too. I didn't know anything about this hotel business, really I didn't. I leave it all to Richard. He understands things much better than I do.'

Poppy came and stood in front of her desk, leaning forward so that she could look directly into Gillian's face.

'Listen, Gillian. You know more than you think you do. You were my partner, for heaven's sake, when Richard was just a waiter – and not too good a one at that.'

Gillian flared into anger. 'You've always been against him! You thought he wasn't good enough to come into the business, even though he was good enough to work for you! Well, I wanted him to have a better job and I don't see – '

'He got a better job,' Poppy said, and straightened her back wearily. 'I let him become the manager of the wholesale foods department, didn't I?'

'And you said he was very good.'

'He was. He is. He's ten times better a business man than ever he was a waiter.'

'I told you that when I first went out with him, and you weren't sure about him. He's just had back luck – his business going under when his first wife ran off and all that, and him left with a youngster to look after on his own and no money coming in – he took the best job he could. Of course he wasn't a good waiter. He was a much cleverer person than that!'

Poppy sighed. 'Gillian, we've been together too long to fight over Richard, for heaven's sake. And I do value him. He's got a great business head and he makes a very good Chairman, though I sometimes think I should have – well, that's water under the bridge. He does what he does very well, I just wish he wouldn't try so hard to push us faster than we ought to go and above all I wish he wouldn't be so – so manipulative. He seems to want to get his own way just for the hell of it rather than because he genuinely believes it's the best way for the company. Trying to get me to go off on some sort of silly jaunt so that he can go ahead on his own is typical – and I'm going to tell him so.'

'Oh, please don't.' Gillian was alarmed. 'He'll be furious with me, because I've probably got it all wrong. You know what I'm like – please, don't start a fight, Poppy. I couldn't bear it – '

She began to cry, twisting her face into an ugly rictus and letting the tears wash down her cheeks without making any attempt to mop them up, and Poppy looked at her in exasperation.

'Oh, Gillian, do stop being so silly! Of course we have to talk about this! He has to understand that I'm in control of my business, Chairman of the Board though he may be. I hold the majority of the shares and – '

'Richard says – ' Gillian swallowed and sniffed and tried again, for her voice had soared to the ceiling with its load of tears. 'Richard says it's all so wrong to have the controlling shares in other people's hands, even if they are your family. I mean, I'm supposed to be a partner and – '

'Look, Gillian, let me explain again. I did tell you all this when we started to grow. You'd worked hard and I wanted to be fair. I kept sixty-six per cent and you had the rest. Then when we had to expand and needed more cash, we put ourselves on the open market and we each sold some of our own shares, remember?'

Gillian nodded. 'That was when Richard bought some. He was ever so pleased.'

Poppy nodded a little grimly. 'Indeed he was. And I ended up with thirty per cent just as you did, and he bought ten per cent – do you remember that too?'

'I never was any good at mathematics.' Gillian sounded piteous.

'Then concentrate. You really have to understand properly. I own a third still. You chose to give your proxy to Richard after he bought up ten per cent on the Stock Exchange – '

Gillian brightened. 'Richard told me that. It means we have more shares than you.'

'No it doesn't!' Poppy almost shouted it. 'How often do I have to get across to all of you that you do not have a controlling interest? I do! My family own thirty per cent and I hold their proxies. So that gives me the controlling interest, doesn't it? I hold sixty per cent and you and Richard between you forty per cent. Do you understand that? It's *my* business – and if I don't choose to allow Richard to push the Board the way he wants to go, I have the deciding power. So, you go back and tell your Richard that, with my compliments. Because if you don't, I damned well will – '

'Oh, I'll try.' Gillian sounded plaintive now. 'I'll do my best. He'll be livid with me of course, because of not getting it right with you. But I did my best.'

She stopped at the door. 'Look, we're still all right, aren't we?'

'All right?'

'Me and Richard and you. I couldn't bear it if we were enemies or anything.'

Poppy sighed. 'Of course we're all right! This is business, quite separate from being friends. You've been my friend for years and you always will be.' And she went across the room and hugged Gillian who sniffed loudly and at last wiped her face with her handkerchief.

'That's all right then,' she said and went, apparently not noticing that Poppy had made no mention of any friendly feeling towards Richard. But that was Gillian all over. She'd always been vague about such matters as words and ideas. She'd been a marvellous working partner, a genius at cooking and table laying and the running of a complex banquet and above all the clearing up, but beyond that she lacked any sense at all. She was putty in the hands of her much adored and often, Poppy suspected, equally greatly feared husband. Poppy sometimes wondered if he'd been astute enough back in those days when he'd been an impecunious ex-business man grateful for odd evenings of work as a waiter, to foresee the way the business would go, and had married Gillian in a cynical plan to get himself into so rich a gravy boat. Certainly he had wormed his way into the business with great success. In those early days he'd been as charming as he'd been hard-working and clever and Poppy had been charmed by and grateful for his efforts. The business had certainly grown with his assistance. But now the veneer of charm sometimes wore thin and she could see the steely ambition and hunger beneath it, as she could now. And it made her shiver a little.

She went back to her desk and picked up her papers with a sigh. The meeting was to be at three this afternoon. She had a good deal of work to do on those documents before then. Because one thing was sure. Richard Melhuish was not going to get his own way this time. The real fighting had to begin now.

7

Robin's line had been engaged the first twice she'd tried to call her, and that had irritated her; by the time she got through she was edgy and allowed herself to snap somewhat.

'Robin? It's me. I've been trying to get you for ages.'

'Well, I was on the phone!' Robin said, nettled by the implied criticism. 'I do have other people to talk to sometimes, you know, Ma.'

'Oh, I know. I'm sorry. Look, something rather urgent's come up. Can you get up to town to see me? I've got a Board meeting at three and I must talk to you before that.'

'Come up to town? No, I can't possibly – it's Helga's afternoon off.'

'Oh, damn it all to hell and back,' Poppy said. 'I'd never get to you and back here in time.'

'Ma, what is this?' Robin was alarmed. It was very unlike Poppy to lose her temper, even as mildly as she just had. She might be crisp to the point of sharpness with other people, but never with her own family, and least of all her daughter.

'I'll have to do this on the phone. And I hate doing that. It's not that I think anyone can overhear – '

'It's unlikely in this day and age, darling.' Robin was amused now. 'It's been a long time since manual exchanges and people listening in.'

'Crossed lines can happen! No, it's not because of that. It's just that it's easier to talk face to face. Oh, well, if I have to I have to – '

'Have to what?'

'Sit down, Robin. Or are you already?'

Robin giggled. 'Are you sitting comfortably? Then I'll begin.'

'Robin, this is serious. I'm not playing baby games with you,'

Poppy sounded thoroughly rattled and Robin shook her head at the phone in surprise.

'Ma, I was only joking – you did sound a bit like "Listen With Mother". Anyway, yes, I'm sitting down. Now, what is it you want to talk about? If it's Oliver and school – '

'No, of course not. This is my business, not yours.'

'Oh? Then you agree Oliver's school is none of your affair? That's quite an admission. Can I have it in writing?'

'Robin, stop being so – listen, I have to talk to you about the business. About "Food by Poppy".'

Robin stopped being amused. 'Is something wrong?'

'I'm making damned sure it won't be. Look, we were talking the other day about you getting some sort of a job.'

'We weren't,' Robin said. 'You were.'

'Well, yes, I was. I said then – and I said it because I was thinking of you – that I thought you needed some sort of a job.'

'And I said – '

'Well, now I'm saying it because I'm thinking of me too.'

There was a little silence and then Robin said in an oddly flat little voice, 'You'd better explain.'

Poppy took a deep breath and did. About the three hotels they'd taken on a three-month option to test the business and their own readiness to deal with them and how Richard Melhuish was trying to force her hand into taking them.

'It's a hair's-breadth thing, Robin,' Poppy said. 'It's possible we can absorb them – and if we can there's no doubt they'll improve our equity hugely. If we let them go we could be depriving ourselves of considerable benefit. The thing is I'm worried about the management side and that's my department. I'm afraid that I simply won't be able to cope with it. Not driving off to three different chunks of the South Coast every week, to oversee and so forth. But I could do it with help. I need a personal assistant I can really trust and who'll report to me and only me and won't be suborned by Richard.'

'Ma, if he's that bad, why on earth don't you get rid of him? I mean, you're the boss and – '

'It's not so easy. Over the years he's become closer and closer to – well, he owns a minor but sizeable piece, through Gillian who lets him do what the hell he likes and – it's not that easy. I have a meeting at three and I have to decide whether to fight off this attempt of his to hold on to the hotels or to demand that he let the option lapse without completing. And I need your help.'

Robin was guarded. 'If you're going to say to me what I think you are – '

'Darling, you could do it for me. Now the girls are at school more than they're at home and you've got Helga who's the best au pair you've ever had – could you? If I thought I had you to be my arms and legs on this project then I think I could make it work. You could be a part of the business yourself and – '

'Ma, you've tried this before. I don't really want to be part of it. I applaud all you've done building it up and so forth, but I don't want to be part of it. I really can't.'

'But – '

'Ma, I've got plans of my own. Look, why not ask Dad? He'd do anything you want and – '

'He's older than I am,' Poppy said almost savagely. 'I wouldn't ask him to do what I can't do myself. Anyway,' she hesitated. 'It's not his style. He's a writer, dammit. No business man.'

'You think I am?' Robin brightened.

'I'm damned sure you could learn,' Poppy said. 'You're bright and quick and although you trained for something quite different, I get the impression it was the sort of training that makes you able to turn your hand to almost anything. You could develop a business head.'

'I'm delighted to hear you say so.' Robin took a deep breath. 'Because I'm going to need it. A business head, I mean.'

Now it was Poppy's turn to be silenced. 'Why?' she said at length.

'That was why I was on the phone, Ma. Do you remember a girl – well, woman – who used to live near us? When the children were small – Susan Monk. A rather scatty thing with a lot of curly hair and – well, anyway, I ran into her again the other day. In Harrods. The day we had lunch, actually. I – it was a bit because of what you said that afternoon actually.'

'What was?' Poppy was getting irritable again as she glanced over her shoulder at the clock. Almost half past two. 'You're not making sense.'

Robin took a deep breath. 'I've bought a shop,' she said and sat there holding the phone so tightly that her knuckles were white.

'You've done what?'

'A shop. Fashion shop. Bought it. Or promised to. Foubert's Place, sort of behind Liberty's and Dickens, well, quite near Dickens – in Regent Street. Very small, and it's a bargain. I got her down to three and a half thousand for a six-year lease which really is a snip, she said, and – '

'Three and a half thousand? Where did you – oh.' Poppy stopped. 'Stupid of me. Mamma's money.'

'She left it to me, didn't she?' Robin said defensively. 'It's mine to do with as I choose.'

'Well, yes, of course it is, though I doubt she thought you'd choose – a fashion shop, Robin? What do you know about fashion?'

'I don't exactly walk around looking like a rag doll,' Robin said tartly.

'There's more to any business than just liking the products.' Poppy said, crisp again. 'You need a grasp of bookkeeping, of cash control, of – '

'What did you know when you started? As I recall, you were a nurse too, weren't you? We used to laugh about that, how we'd both started in the same career, but you'd gone off sideways to be a woman in a business. Well, now, I'm going to follow in my mother's footsteps. I'd have expected cheers from you, not drears. Or is it just that I'm not available to do your job for you? Is that why you sound so down on me?'

Poppy took the phone away from her ear and sat with her eyes closed for a moment. And then put it back and said, 'I'm sorry. You're quite right. It's – well, put it down to surprise. Tell me more. Only quickly, darling – I have to go into the meeting soon and I want to get my head together before I do.'

'I'll give you the details later. You go to your meeting – just let me say I saw the place and she wanted to sell it and she rang me again this morning. I didn't think I wanted to but she was very persuasive and I remembered what you'd said and I thought – why not? So I agreed it on the phone. I have to go round to her solicitors to discuss the contract – '

'See a lawyer of your own first,' Poppy cried. 'Sign nothing till you've seen your own advisor! There'll have to be searches made of the leases and all sorts of things – '

Robin laughed. 'I know, Ma! I've already talked to Mike

Shelton about it. I'm in safe hands with him – he's the best solicitor there is. He's meeting me at the other solicitor's to sort it all out. I'm not that green, you know.'

'No. I'm sure you're not. Good luck, darling – '

'Thanks, Ma. And good luck with your Board meeting. I'll call you tonight. Then we can both report progress with each other.'

'Yes,' Poppy said. 'Yes, we'll do that – ' and then said quickly, 'Robin?' But she was too late. Robin had hung up and only a soft burring filled her ear.

I wonder if she's talked about this to Sam? she asked herself as she cradled the phone. I hope so. And I wonder how he'll feel about it?

Richard was sitting in his place at the head of the Board table when she went in, his head down over his own pile of papers, and she stood for a moment looking at him before he was aware she was there.

That he was an attractive and interesting man to look at was undoubted; she couldn't blame Gillian for being so besotted with him, even though he was so many years her senior. His head was high domed and the fringe of grey hair that ran round the bald pate looked dignified rather than slightly ridiculous as it did on so many bald men. He was bulky with heavy shoulders and upper arms and looked large and imposing until he stood up and then he seemed to dwindle into neat little feet and legs, so that he looked a little like a buffalo, especially as he had a tendency to stand with his head poked forwards on his short neck. His eyes were a bright and apparently cheerful grey and quite disarming. He never showed any sign of what he was thinking, looking always benign, a gift that Poppy envied him since she herself had a tendency to show every fleeting thought on her face. It was no accident he played poker as a way of relaxing, Poppy had told him once and he had laughed his usual merry laugh and agreed with her and she couldn't tell whether he was gratified or angered by her comment.

He looked up then, seeming to become aware of her scrutiny, and got to his feet at once.

'Poppy, my dear! I'm so glad you're early! We can sort out this business of you and Gillian and the holiday you're so suspicious about before the others come in.'

'Can we?' she said grimly and came and sat down on his left in her usual place, putting down her files of paper with a little thump. 'There's nothing to sort out, I thought. I'm not going anywhere.'

'Of course you're not! I was a clumsy oaf.' He smiled his wide warm smile and she was hard put to it not to smile back. That was the trouble with Richard; he was so very beguiling a man. Don't trust him, she warned herself inside her head. Don't trust him.

'I'll come clean.' He was sitting down again now she'd taken her chair. 'I was trying it on. I was heart-set on these hotels. They're a good price in good sites and I reckon they're money waiting to be dug out of the ground. But they do have to be properly run and if you feel you're not ready yet to take them on, then fair enough.'

'Suppose I told you I never will be? That I think it's stretching ourselves way beyond our reach if we try to leave London? We've got one London hotel, the three restaurants, the factory. Do we have to have more?'

'Businesses have to grow, Poppy.'

'Do they? I never quite saw why. I think it's possible to destroy a business by letting it get too big and sprawly. Like rose bushes. Keep it small and well in control, inside defined limits, and you can really care for it in every detail because you can reach every branch. Let it grow long and leggy and out of your hands, and it stops producing so many flowers – and those it does produce are poor – '

'A pretty analogy, but I don't think it stands up,' Richard said. 'It's stagnation to stay the same size.'

'I haven't stagnated ever,' Poppy said quietly. 'I grew this company from – '

'I know, a tiny room in the first building and a couple of functions a week, you and Gillian with a few part-timers. And now it's one of the biggest and best catering firms in London. But it could be the biggest in the country! Why not? That's why I wanted the South Coast hotels.'

'Wanted?' She was swift to pounce and he laughed.

'It's a joy working with you. You don't miss anything. Yes, past tense. I know better than to try to drag an unwilling Board along with me. I need a really enthusiastic team with everyone pulling the same way. These three places are bargains, yes, but they won't be the last and it's better to wait and consolidate than to split the Board by pushing ahead now.'

She took a deep breath, trying to hide her relief. It hadn't seemed possible that she'd win this easily, without a lot of deal making. But it looked as though she had.

'That is really my point of view. I want to take time, that's all. I want to find a good young person I can train up to be my deputy, to hand over to. Someone who really cares, who'll put his or her heart into the business the way we have, and then, once they're trained –then you can grow. They'll be younger and more energetic than we are. After all, Richard,' and she smiled a little wickedly, 'You're only eight years younger than I am. You can't go on for ever either.'

'I know, I know. No need to rub it in! And you're right. You need to expand the staff before you can expand the business. Invest in people before you invest in bricks and mortar, hmm? It's not the commonest business way but it makes sense to me – '

'And me. So we have an agreement?'

'That we'll let the options lapse on the three South Coast hotels. Yes. I'll put it to the Board and we'll see what they say. I have no doubt that – ' He stopped and smiled.

'That they'll see it your way,' Poppy said a little bitterly. 'They usually do. They'd have said yes to the hotels if you'd really made up your mind to it. That's why I'm glad that you've seen it my way.'

He lifted his brows and laughed. 'Our way, Poppy, surely?'

She had to laugh too. 'I suppose so. Yes, our way. Well, I'm relieved, I won't deny it. I thought I'd have a heavier battle with you than this. I thought you were dead set on those hotels.'

'I know when I'm licked. And I know that I value friendship and amity a great deal more than getting my own way in the business.'

She looked at him a touch suspiciously, and he laughed aloud. 'My, but you look doubtful! You do me an injustice, you know. Why should you look like that?'

'Frankly, you surprise me,' she said. 'I had you sorted in my mind as very, very ambitious – '

'So I am.'

' – too ambitious to give in quite so gracefully when you fail to get what you want.'

He shrugged and then looked up as the rest of the Board began to drift in. 'You'll see. It's possible to be ambitious and civilized as well. There are more than a dozen ways to skin a cat, you know. And then a few more. Hello, Gilmore. Good to see you. How's the wife?'

She watched him as he went through his usual emollient routine, settling the Board members, including the rather boring old buffers who had only become included because they added status to the company's letter heading and encouraged confidence in the City, and couldn't deny he was a remarkable operator. The meeting went smoothly as it always did and they all agreed in a slightly bemused way that the options on the three South Coast hotels should be allowed to lapse, and that they would consider further expansion in the future, and left happily filled with Marilyn's tea and biscuits and mantled in Richard Melhuish's blessing.

When they were alone again she lifted her brows at him. 'Mellifluous Melhuish!' she said. 'So honey tongued!'

'Why not be nice to people? You get on faster than if you're nasty, I find. It's friendship that oils the wheels of business. A propos of which, it's time you dined with us.'

'Oh!' She was a little startled. She knew that Gillian hated entertaining. Good as she was at catering for other people, in her own home she felt inept and awkward, and it showed. But Richard seemed not to worry about Gillian.

'Yes, a dinner party would be delightful. Tell you what, my Caro's home at present. Promised she'd spend a few more weekends under the domestic roof instead of going gadding around the smart set. Help me entertain her, Poppy, do. Bring your David and that nice son of yours, Josh. Not married or engaged or anything yet? Good. My daughter's mad about music and I'm sure they'd get on very well. I'll fix dates with Gillian and my secretary'll see to it that Marilyn has all the details and sorts it out with your diary. Don't forget now.' And he was gone, leaving her standing staring at the empty boardroom with a line between her brows.

So that was his tack. She could see it clearly now and she had to admit it had a certain charm. If they could persuade the younger members of the families to pair up, it could be perfect for the business. There'd be far fewer squabbles over who had the lion's share of the company if both had children who were going to inherit the bulk of it together. And if one of them chose to work in the business, so much the better. That Richard would like his daughter to work with him was obvious; he'd suggested it, she knew, many times. She had flatly refused, according to Gillian (somewhat to Poppy's relief; she'd thought it a bad idea) but if she were married to the majority shareholder's son, that might change things a good deal.

Josh, she thought, as she walked slowly to the door. Lonely, unhappy Josh. Is he ready to settle down? It would be such a comfort to her if he did. She'd worried a lot about him when Adrian had been alive, not sure just what their relationship had been, and had been sad for Josh when Adrian had been killed. But he seemed over it now, though still a little remote. Maybe it was just loneliness, and a girl like Caro could lift him out of it? After all, he was much older now. To develop an intense close relationship with a friend when a boy is young is natural enough. But now at thirty-two, Josh was well past that stage. A man, no longer a boy. It could well be that he needed someone who could lift him from his gloom, which by now could be as much a habit as anything else. It had been almost a year ago that Adrian had been killed, after all.

Her spirits began to lift as she took herself back to her office to end the day at last. They would go to Richard's dinner party and Josh would join in to please her, she was sure he would. And after that – Let's see what happens. It could be very tidy if things worked out the right way.

8

'Are you saying you'd have sacked Chick?' Robin said, and lifted her chin in an aggressive little gesture that made Sam frown sharply. This conversation wasn't working out at all as he'd planned it.

'No.' He tried to sound patient. 'Of course not. There's enough for both of you to do and –'

'I see.' She sounded dangerously close to anger. 'A job that was just right for Chick when it suited you can be split to keep me out of mischief and under your eye, again when it suits you. What about the people involved? Are we wax dolls to be shaped and pushed around the way you fancy with nothing to say for ourselves?'

'Robin, why are you being so obstructive?' He looked at his watch. 'Oh, hell, we shouldn't have started talking about this this morning. There isn't enough time. All I'm trying to say is that if you want to take a job why not work with me rather than in some tatty little shop in a –'

'That really does it!' she said and got to her feet. 'You haven't even seen it and you start to be insulting –'

'You said that yourself! You told me it was in a back street, and needs a lot doing to it and there wasn't a great deal of trade there and –'

'That doesn't give you the right to call it tatty!' she blazed at him. 'It needs some work, of course it does, but I can do it. Why be so – so damned condescending about it? I want something for myself, dammit. I've been working for other people all my life – nursing and then Auntie Jessie and then Ma and Pa and then you and the children and I need something that's mine –'

He stared at her with her face blank, but she could see the look in his eyes and she chose not to recognize it. So what if she'd hurt his feelings? What about her?

'Was it that bad?' he said quietly.

'Of course not!' She began to clear the breakfast dishes, slamming them down on the draining board noisily. Helga, displaying rare tact, had vanished as soon as the girls had left for school, and somewhere upstairs the vacuum was whining, so they could argue safely, and Robin made the most of her opportunity, letting her voice rise luxuriously, whipping herself up into a richer anger with every word. 'That's just like you, trying to make me feel guilty when there's nothing to feel guilty about. I'm bored, for God's sake. I've been bored for ages. The children aren't really children any more – they've got enough to keep them busy, and you're up to your elbows in your practice and I want something of my own. To work with you in the way you want would be just like staying home. I'd be there to do what you said when you said it. That isn't what I want. Now this chance has come up and I'm taking it. I sign the contract today and there's an end of it. I'd have asked you to come and see for yourself, if you hadn't been so nasty about it, but now I shan't. I'll just go ahead and do it and you can come and look when you can spare the time. Which probably won't be till the year dot anyway. I can manage perfectly well for myself.'

'I'm sure you can.' He was on his feet too now. 'I'm sorry if I upset you, Robin. I meant no harm. I never do. But you were determined to be angry, so – '

'If you don't stop analysing every word I say I'll really lose my temper!' Robin snapped. 'I'm sick of the way you – '

'There's no point in talking any further on this.' Sam was a little white around the mouth now. 'You seem determined to have an argument and I'm not going to. I hate arguments, you know that perfectly well. I'm not analysing you, I never do and – well, as I say, there's no point in discussing it further and anyway there's no time. I'll see you tonight – '

'If I'm home in time,' Robin said not looking at him, as she kept her head down over a cup she was washing with unnecessary vigour. 'I've got a lot to do and the girls are having supper with Chick so I've got even more time to call my own. Which I'm going to use in my own way – '

'Yes,' he said. 'Yes, Robin.' And went, and the back door

closed behind him with a little click and she watched covertly as he went past the kitchen window on his way to the garage and his car. And for one moment wanted to run after him and hug him and say she hadn't meant to be so hateful –

But of course she didn't. She left the kitchen as it was, in its post-breakfast muddle, and ran upstairs to dress properly and give Helga her last instructions for the day. She could make Sam's supper, do one of those concoctions of sauerkraut and sausages she was so good at and which he rather liked, and then she herself could leave and hurry up to Foubert's Place and get on with the fun of her own day, in her own life. 'It's my turn – ' she whispered to herself ' – my turn to have fun.'

Fun. She stood and stared at herself in her dressing-table mirror and could have wept. That was why she had been so hateful to Sam. She'd made the wrong decision as well as a complete and utter fool of herself, that was the thing of it. She knew it all the way through to her middle, and as the childish phrase which had been invented long ago by the very young Oliver came into her mind tears of self-pity collected in her eyes, and threatened to spill over.

It wasn't going to be fun at all. She'd been carried along by Susan's ridiculous optimism and the sheer absurdity of the whole idea. If her solicitor had been a little more forbidding she might have been halted in her headlong rush but he'd been as she imagined solicitors always were, calm and non-committal and polite, and had offered no opinion. So she'd stifled the small niggle of doubt that had started to pierce her certainty and gone ahead, and now they were to sign the contracts today and there was no way she could get out of it –

'I'll have to,' she said aloud to her mirrored image, and set to work on her make-up. 'When I get there I'll tell them I've changed my mind. I'll have to pay Mr Shelton's fees, of course, and Susan'll be furious and make a lot of noise, but it's the only way. I must have been mad to even think of it.'

But by the time she got to town, after struggling through the morning crush on the tube, she'd calmed down. She wouldn't make a scene when she got there. She'd read the contract and ask more penetrating questions about the way the business was run, and then show them her doubts. That'd be the businesslike way to do it; she might lose some of her money, but at least she wouldn't lose quite so much face.

71

Regent Street looked bright and inviting in the Spring sunshine. The women were in the first of the thinner lighter-coloured clothes that would appear everywhere in another few weeks and she looked at passersby with a sharp new eye, assessing their tastes and their style, and thought that people would look so much better if they only tried. It takes so little to wake clothes up, to make them more than mere coverings to keep out the weather. I could show that girl the way to improve that suit no end, and that woman there needs someone to tell her she'd be much better off in brighter colours and –

She shook her head at her own weakness as she hurried past Dickins and Jones with their coolly elegant windows and Liberty's with its usual swathes of fabric cramming its displays and turned into Foubert's Place with a firm step. She'd made up her mind to it. This contract was not going to be signed and there was an end of it. It had been a madcap idea and thank heaven she'd seen sense in good time.

Her lawyer, a neat man in a well-cut suit and a handsome camel overcoat was standing at the far side of the street staring up at the property next door to Susan's shop. His lips were pursed in a soundless whistle and he looked pleased with himself.

'Good morning, Mrs Landow!' he said cheerfully. 'All set, are we?'

'Well, I'm not sure,' she began. 'There are details I have to check – '

'Oh, don't fret over that,' he said. 'I've made it watertight, I do assure you. You've really got a very nice proposition here, you know. Very nice.'

She gaped at him. Where was the non-committal blankness she'd become used to in him? He caught her eye and looked embarrassed for a moment. 'I have to say I thought at first you'd be hard put to it to make a go of this, but that was before I'd made further enquiries.'

'Oh?' She was alert and followed his gaze to the building at which he was still looking. 'And what do you think now?'

'Well, I hope I'm right, but if not, then at least I'll suffer the consequences with you!' he said and grinned. 'I've taken the building next door.'

'You've – ' She opened her eyes wide and stared at him. 'What on earth for?'

'Investment,' he said and smiled widely. 'Even lawyers take chances sometimes, you know.'

'Well, I suppose so, but – ' She shook her head, still confused. 'What do you want the building for?'

'If you can run a shop here then other people can too. I might as well be the landlord and join in the benefit.'

'But what makes you so sure that – I mean, I've been worrying dreadfully! Thought I must be mad to be taking such a chance – '

'Well, that's healthy. You'd have more to worry about if you weren't full of doubt. You need to be worried to make anything work. Like exams – no use expecting to pass unless you're scared silly at the thought of failing.'

'But I still don't understand,' she said. 'What have you found out that made you do such a thing as buy a building here?'

'Carnaby Street,' he said. 'Round the corner. Come and see. We've got time.' And he took her elbow and led her further along narrow Foubert's Place towards the tangle of streets at the back. 'Come and see.'

It looked to her like any other dull little side street in London; mean shops and clusters of tired-looking people. But then her eyes brightened as she caught sight of a small group at the far end of the street. Three young men brightly dressed in corduroys and vivid shirts with knotted scarves in the neck were leaning against a shop front, laughing and talking. They looked as exotic as parrots in a hen run and she stared at them with fascination.

'It's a bit early for the sort of people who made me change my mind,' Mr Shelton said in her ear. 'But I thought – ah – There we are – ' And he lifted his chin towards the three young men Robin had noticed. 'Now, look at them. In another couple of hours this street'll be full of chaps like that.'

'Who are they? And why are they here?'

'Actors mostly,' the lawyer said. 'A few of them are in other businesses, interior decorating and so forth, but mostly actors. They come here to buy their clothes.'

She looked at the vividly bright trousers on the man nearest to her and smiled faintly. They were a deep purple, rather like the aubergines she'd seen piled on stalls in French market places, and over them he wore a lilac-coloured shirt and an even darker purple jacket. His hair was rather longer than average, well over his ears, and he was standing in a relaxed but very self-aware pose that showed off his shape extremely well.

'I can see they'd have trouble finding things like that in most men's shops. I buy Sam's stuff and I've never seen anything like those trousers anywhere.'

'Precisely. These shops here cater to a special market. It mightn't be huge, but it's there – see? Here are some more.' He indicated with another jerk of his chin a further couple of men who were walking down towards the others. They were wearing matching yellow trousers and were even more vivid than the men they now joined with much laughter and chatter.

'I asked around,' Shelton said in her ear. 'It's a growing centre, this street, for this sort of unusual fashion. So I thought, maybe this is the time to invest when property's cheap. You are. So I will – you gave me the idea – '

She was alarmed. 'Don't blame me if you lose your money!'

'Good heavens no! Any more than I'll credit you if I make it.' He stood there in a patch of warm sunshine, his hands in his trouser pockets and his coat bunched over his back and smiled at her and she smiled back. There was something so very hopeful about him and for a glorious moment the feeling of excitement that had been part of the whole plan at the beginning came back into her. She felt it bubble inside her and the street around her stopped looking drab and dirty but seemed to glitter.

But then her common sense, boring and dull, lifted its head again. 'But these are men,' she said. 'Maybe there are shops for them here, but if there aren't any for women, how can I expect to do well?'

'You make it as interesting to actresses as these men's shops seem to be to actors,' he said. 'Where you get one of a species you're likely to get the other. I learned that in biology class at school.'

Robin looked over her shoulder. 'I doubt these chaps'll have many actresses with them,' she said dryly.

'Don't jump to conclusions. These young men may not look as though they're interested in women as women, but they'll be interested in them as fashionable creatures. I know.' He nodded wisely. 'My wife goes to a dressmaker who's like these chaps – and she thinks the world of him. Makes her just the sort of things she needs. Thinks like a woman when it comes to fashion, she says.'

She stood for a while longer, looking back over her shoulder. More people had come to join the first group, and then there was a ragged cheer as another man came panting up the street. He was small and dark and looked rather dully dressed in comparison with the others. But there was a great air of style about him for all that and she watched as he unlocked the door of the shop where they were all waiting and then, as they all trooped inside, the street became dull and quiet again, and she turned in response to Michael Shelton's urging and began to walk back to Foubert's Place.

He looked at his watch. 'She'll be ready for us,' he said. 'And her chap – there's the inventory to deal with of course, and so on. We'll need all the time we have. I've another appointment at twelve thirty, so we'll have to get on with it. Are you sure you're going ahead, Mrs Landow? Now's the time to say yea or nay. Frankly, I wouldn't want to spend a couple of hours on an inventory with you and then have you backing down.'

She stood at the junction of the two streets, still looking back into Carnaby Street. There were a few more people now, coming in from the far end and they too seemed to her to have the raffish exciting stylish look of the people who had followed the dark little man into his shop and amongst them there was a girl who wore her hair long and who had a pair of tight red trousers on beneath a matching sweater. She looked vibrant and alive and Robin was suddenly very aware of her own sensible dark dress and matching shoes and gloves. *Surely* she could make a go of this idea? Surely it was meant to be, the way the whole thing had happened. Not an accident but fate had made her bump into Susan Monk that afternoon.

She turned and looked at the lawyer and managed a grin.

'All right,' she said. 'All right. The worst thing I can do is lose all my grandmother's money, I suppose, and she won't be here to complain. Let's get on with it – '

9

'The trouble with this house,' Poppy said softly in David's ear, 'is that it always makes me very aware of how shabby ours is.'

David looked at her with blank astonishment. 'Our house, shabby?' he said. 'It's perfect the way it is! You wouldn't want to live somewhere like *this*, would you?' And he looked around the big drawing-room with his face clearly showing his distaste.

'Hush,' she murmured and pinched his arm. 'They'll be in in a moment.' And she too looked round the room, trying to see it through David's eyes.

It was a porridge room. The carpets, the walls, the severe furniture, were all the same softly greyish-beige colour. The wallpaper had tasteful stripes of closely toning colour of the sort commonly called Regency although Poppy couldn't imagine that insipid satin ribbon had ever pleased the garish Prinny, and there were swathes of slightly darker oatmeal satin picking out the heavy curtains. There was an imitation coal fire, glowing red with a repeated flicker pattern that soon became repetitive to the watching eye, and a tall slender vase with a single daffodil carefully displayed in it. Poppy thought of her own drawing-room with its great open fire on which they burned logs that left a silken veil of grey ash in the hearth, and the blissfully comfortable sagging old red velvet armchairs and cushions against the warm faded flowered wallpaper and the blue faience bowls crammed full of flowers, and knew herself to be totally out of touch with modern taste. Her drawing-room had grown up over the long years of living in Norland Square (and she did a hasty computation and was amazed to realize that that had been well over forty) and this one had clearly been Designed. How could she possibly compete? The rest of the house she knew was much the same; the identical

76

oatmeal carpet was everywhere including, to David's particular disgust, the bathrooms, and there were a lot more bleached wood furnishings and low glass coffee tables carefully ornamented with single perfect pieces of sculpture. Here and there on the pale striped walls were good prints of well-known Old Masters, something which David again found mystifying, for he liked their walls at home, which were hugger-mugger with the pictures he couldn't resist buying every time he went to an exhibition or met an artist, which was extremely often. The dining-room, which they could see beyond the open glass doors that separated it from the room they were in, was already set with a great deal of glittering silver and crystal on a polished wooden table. (I still use tablecloths, Poppy thought, mournfully. Oh dear!) and the lighting was low, carefully planned and a touch dispiriting.

'Perhaps we should make a few changes at home,' she murmured then, but David shook his head firmly.

'Not if I can stop you,' he said. 'I like us the way we are, comfortable. This is straight out of a magazine, for heaven's sake! What could be drearier?'

The door swung open and Gillian came in, clearly agitated. 'Oh dear, I'm so sorry. I should have been ready for you, but when I'd done my hair Richard didn't like it – ' She looked around the room a little vaguely. 'I thought he'd be down here by now – '

'It's all right,' Poppy said soothingly. 'He gave us drinks and then went off to find Caro – '

'Oh dear!' Gillian looked doleful. 'Oh dear, yes, Caroline – '

'Is something wrong?' Poppy asked quickly and her heart sank. She'd gone to a lot of trouble to persuade Josh to come tonight, moving him by degrees from a terrified, 'Not on your Nelly! I wouldn't be caught dead spending an evening at a formal dinner party. I hate 'em!' to a grudging, 'Well, if it matters that much to you, I suppose I must.' If after all that Richard's daughter wasn't going to be here, all her efforts would be wasted and Josh would be justifiably furious.

She'd been as honest with him as she could, telling him that the point of the dinner party was to cement the Board's decision to do things her way, though she hadn't told him that she suspected that Richard Melhuish had designs on him as a son-in-law (let alone her own feelings on the possibility) but she had said the girl was to be here and he was needed to help entertain her in the midst of the old fuddy duddies who were the rest of the guests.

'It's the whole Board, almost, darling,' she'd told him. 'Imagine how dreary for a young girl. Do, please, help us out!'

And now it seemed there were problems; and she looked at Gillian with almost a scowl on her face.

'Oh, it's all right!' Gillian said quickly. 'It's just that the dress she put on – well, Richard was livid. It's a bit – well, extreme – you see, so he made her go up and change. I don't know how he persuaded her, because she was so angry. But – '

There was a little bustle outside in the hallway and then the door opened and Gilmore and his wife came in and Poppy schooled her face into a polite smile, as did Gillian. He was almost the most boring member of the Board – though there were several others who competed with him for the title – and talking to him, Poppy had told David privately, was like walking over a ploughed field in high-heeled shoes; steadily more difficult.

Now she moved forward with one hand out.

'Hello John! Good to see you!'

'Hello Gillian, Poppy,' Gilmore said and made an odd sound in his throat. 'What a drive! All that traffic – took us over a quarter of an hour longer on the North Circular than I'd planned. Why you live so far out I can't imagine. Ought to try town, you know – '

'Richard likes Stanmore,' Gillian murmured and hurried over to the drinks table at the far end of the room. 'What can I get you? Elizabeth?'

Gilmore's mousy little wife demonstrated a surprising taste for whisky and Gillian busied herself with ice and glasses as more people began to arrive. And then to Poppy's relief Richard came in, with his daughter close behind him.

Poppy hadn't seen her for some time, not since she was little more than a schoolgirl on her way to France, ostensibly to work as an au pair in an aristocratic French family, but in fact to have a fairly wild time of it, as she later discovered from Gillian. But that had been all of ten years ago, and the young woman who stood in the doorway now was a very different creature from the rather large and sulky girl Poppy remembered.

She was thinner of course, but then all girls were nowadays.

The buxom look that had been so familiar all through the nineteen fifties seemed to be giving way to a half-starved appearance and this girl was clearly nothing if not fashionable. She was wearing a dress in huge black and white squares, with a very short skirt and very high boots, one black and one white. Her hair, which was thick and dark, was cut in an almost brutal bob close to her neck at the back and set in strange geometrical shapes round her face, which was painted extremely vividly indeed about the eyes, which themselves were adorned with obviously artificial eyelashes. There was a little silence from the women as she came in and then a sudden burst of chatter and Poppy was amused. What on earth had she been wearing before that her father had objected to? This was outrageous enough an outfit for anyone, and particularly for a suburban dinner party.

She glanced at Richard then and knew that she had guessed wrong, and that the girl had won their argument. He was scowling and she had an air about her of a cat that has supped on cream, and Poppy smiled to herself. So there were people who stood up to Richard, just as she did herself! He didn't get things all his own way, even in his own home. And she saw him look at the other women in their neat and obvious cocktail frocks in stiff dark taffeta and then again at his daughter's ridiculous piebald boots and could have laughed aloud. Whatever Caro had been like in the past, clearly she had developed into a strong-minded young woman and Poppy found herself well inclined to like her for that.

The chatter went on as more people arrived until the party was complete, but for one; and Poppy looked round at the waiting eleven would-be diners and again her heart sank, but this time for herself rather than because of Josh. Surely he wasn't going to let her down? He had promised to be here on time, well before eight, and now it was – and she looked surreptitiously at her watch – just past the half hour. Gillian was looking restless as she thought about the people in the kitchen; even though they had been brought in from the staff of 'Food by Poppy' for the evening she still was anxious about it all. And here was Josh not yet arrived and –

She heard it then and relaxed; the sound of the front door being opened and the murmur of voices as the 'Food by Poppy' maid let someone in and she breathed again gratefully and glanced at Caro.

She was leaning against the fireplace, staring down into the false fire and her face was gloomy. She had a drink in her hand – and she

79

too, Poppy had noticed, seemed to like whisky – and was patently bored by her company. But she looked up as the door opened and Poppy saw her face change as Josh came in. And smiled contentedly as she too turned to the door to greet her son after he'd paid his respects to his host and hostess.

He had clearly made an effort, for he was wearing what Poppy knew was his newest sports jacket over some carefully pressed grey flannel trousers and also a tie in the neck of his slightly crumpled shirt. Usually he wore loosely knotted scarves and a battered comfortable old corduroy jacket that showed its age on every rubbed seam. The effect tonight of his efforts was rather endearing, Poppy thought, though she would have been happier to see him looking as the other men did, even David neat in a lounge suit in dark grey. But there it was, he was as formal as he could be, and she was too glad to see him there at all to mind that some of the men were obviously disapproving of his casual look. And then bit her lip in shame as she remembered how she'd mentally applauded Caro for dressing to please herself rather than her father; how could she be so hypocritical as to criticize her son in the same sort of way?

She linked her arm in Josh's as Gillian went hurrying out to the kitchen to tell them they could go ahead and serve dinner, and led him with apparent nonchalance but very definite intention towards Caro, who was still standing by the fireplace, introducing him to people as they went.

'Elizabeth, you've met my son, I think? Josh – yes of course, last year. And Mary, you, I know, haven't met – yes, my middle child, though hardly a child now of course! Yes, they do grow up quickly, don't they? – '

And then at last they were with Caro and she said cheerfully, 'Caro, I don't think you ever met Josh. I hardly met you myself all that time ago before you went to France! Anyway, here you both are – Josh, this is Caro Melhuish.'

Josh smiled in his usual rather vague and friendly way and Caro held out one hand.

'Heavens, but I'm glad to see you!' she said, and her voice was high and clear and easily heard by at least half the room. 'I thought tonight was going to be impossible.'

'Caro!' Poppy said warningly and she looked at her and laughed. But she dropped her voice a little.

'Well, you must admit I'm a bit out of my generation,' she said. 'It's such a comfort to see someone who isn't older than God – if you'll forgive me, Mrs Deveen. And I have to say Daddy was being impossibly boring about it all, and wanting me to put on sackcloth and ashes – you can't blame me for being miserable, or for being grateful to see someone fit to talk to.'

Poppy blinked. She'd thought herself used to young out-spokennesss, but this girl really went further than most; and she glanced at Josh to see his reaction.

He was frowning and looking at Caro in silence, but then he said a little stiffly, 'I find people interesting for all sorts of reasons. Youth or age is rarely one of them.'

'Whoops, put my foot in it!' Caro said and made a little face. 'I'm sorry, I didn't mean to be rude to you or yours. It's just that – well, do look around! Apart from your own parents, I ask you!'

He looked over his shoulder, just as Elizabeth, talking earnestly to Mary Cooper, said in an intense tone, 'And what regulo do you start to bake it?' and all three of them laughed.

'I told you!' Caro said triumphantly. 'A huger collection of stuffed shirts never never breathed. Promise me you'll sit next to me at dinner and make me laugh.'

Josh lifted his brows, still a little stiff. 'It depends on how Mrs Melhuish sits us,' he said and Caro set her head on one side and grinned.

'No problem there,' she said airily. 'Don't go away!' and she dodged under his arm and went wriggling through the group of older people just as Gillian came back from the kitchen to announce dinner was ready.

Caro murmured in her ear and Gillian looked harassed and then nodded, and Caro stepped back, looked across the room at Poppy and Josh and winked outrageously and almost in spite of himself Josh chuckled.

'You have to give her top marks for cheek,' he murmured as Gillian began to corral her guests for all the world like an eager but not very well co-ordinated sheepdog. 'She's not going to be bored if she can help it.'

'Then she won't be boring,' Poppy said. 'And looking after her won't be that difficult. Thanks so much, Josh, for agreeing to come. It'll help the evening along no end, for me as well as for Richard.'

'It's a pleasure,' he said and then smiled as Caro appeared at his side.

'As stepmothers go she could be worse,' she announced. 'She'd already put us together. Now we can gossip and be rude about everyone. Except your parents, of course.' And she smiled disarmingly up at Poppy who found herself smiling back, in spite of herself.

The dinner was good. Poppy couldn't stop from assessing the choice of menu and the quality of the food just as she always did at any event catered by 'Food by Poppy' and she had to agree that this time they'd excelled themselves. The first course of avocado pears served with peach halves containing a whipped cream cheese with horseradish was delicate and looked as good as it tasted and the lamb cutlets in herbed pastry that followed were a triumph. Once she was sure of that – although no credit could accrue to her any more than discredit would attach itself – she felt able to relax and pay some attention to the rest of the party. Gillian, she saw, was still as tense as a trampoline, watching Richard for signs of approval or otherwise, but he seemed happy enough, talking cheerfully and easily to Elizabeth Gilmore on one side, leaving his other neighbour, Poppy, free to watch the young ones.

Which she did with considerable pleasure. To start with, there was no doubt that Josh had been uncertain and rather aloof, but as Caro had chattered on all through the meal – eating little and smoking between each course, using a long ivory and ebony cigarette holder – he began to melt and by the time they reached the pudding, a truly delectable lemon souffle, he was laughing as much as she was. Poppy caught his eye at one point and he sketched a wink at her and as clearly as if he had said it, she heard his thoughts: that this dinner party which he'd dreaded and was only attending as a favour to her, his mother, was turning out to be quite good fun after all. And she relaxed and grinned across the table at David, who was sitting peaceably eating between two women who were chatting cookery over his head, and thought – it's all right. We'll be able to go home as soon as the coffee's served, and I'll have done my duty by Richard. Such a relief.

On the other side of the table Caro giggled. 'Your mum looks a lot less glum than she did,' she observed.

'Ma? Glum? What an odd word to use for her.' Josh frowned again and she laughed.

'Oh, don't be so prickly! I only meant she isn't as bored as she was. I like your mother. She's the sort of woman I want to be one of these days. You know, successful in her own right.'

He looked at her and relaxed. 'I like her too. She's good fun. Most of the time.'

'Oh, when isn't she?'

He laughed. 'When she tries to get me to wear serious clothes instead of things I like. When she gets into a sweat about the state of my flat.'

'I wouldn't complain,' she said and there was a sudden note of bitterness in her voice. 'I bet she isn't as bad as my father.'

Josh glanced at Richard. 'What's so bad about him?'

She grimaced. 'A fusspot.'

'Father's privilege, perhaps.'

'Always on about what I'm wearing – not just sometimes, but all the time. Hates this outfit – I ask you! It's the latest thing from a new chap in Paris. I adore it – '

'It's striking,' Josh said after a moment and she laughed, throwing her head back in delight.

'Wow! There's a slap in the face. Great. It means it's really something. If it weren't you wouldn't have noticed what I had on, as long as it was something to keep me decent. Well, just you wait till next year or so. Never mind striking. He'll be the biggest thing to hit fashion this century. You see if he isn't. Courrèges, his name is.'

'I'm not terribly interested in fashion,' he said. 'Sorry.'

'Oh, don't be boring. It's madly exciting.'

'Not for me.' He was amused now, and she pouted at him.

'All right. What is exciting for you?'

'Music.'

'What sort?'

'Any sort?'

'The Beatles.'

It was his turn to grimace. 'Not really. I prefer something a little more – let's just say they're not as interesting as they might be, considering how popular they are.'

'You're beginning to sound as stuffy as the rest of them here.'

'Can't help that. I prefer more complicated music. Jazz – '

'You said you liked all sorts.'

'Except the wrong kind.'

'I tell you what,' she said and took a sharp little breath. 'I'll bet I can make you change your mind.'

'Why on earth should you make such a silly bet? I wouldn't change just because – '

'Ah! Don't confuse me with anything new. I know what I like – or is it I like what I know?' She looked at him with eyes glittering with mischief and he had to laugh.

'Touché! Perhaps, a little. But allow me an excuse. Life's too busy, too short, to waste on rubbish – '

'Let me show you that it isn't rubbish.'

'How?'

'A concert. I've got tickets for a Beatles concert.'

'Then maybe you ought to sell them. I hear they're as valuable as gold dust.' He couldn't help the little sneer in his voice, and she pounced.

'That's what you dislike about the Beatles, isn't it? Not the music, but the fuss over them!'

'Not at all. Why should I mind the fuss?'

'Because,' she said with sudden shrewdness, 'you've studied music for as long as you can remember, and worked hard and struggled and struggled and no one's paid any attention to you, and they've just popped up from nowhere with no training at all and stolen the world.'

'Nonsense!' he said. 'I never heard such – ' And then stopped.

'I knew I'd like you,' she said with satisfaction. 'You're sensible. You stop and think. So, is the concert on?'

'It depends on when and where – '

'Next Saturday. As for where – leave that to me – ' She was masterful suddenly. 'It's my bet and I want to do it my way. Just come here to pick me up – let me see – eleven next Saturday – '

'Eleven? Ye Gods, a midnight concert?'

'Stupid! No, eleven in the morning, it's a bit of a journey – '

'Now, look here. I don't want to – '

'You made a deal,' she said and fixed him with a glittering gaze. 'Are you welching on it?'

He burst into laughter and across the table Poppy looked at him again and smiled contentedly. 'You really are the pushiest girl I've ever met,' he said.

'Poor you! So limited an acquaintance. All right then. It's all

set. You'll pick me up next Saturday at eleven. Glory be –
something to really look forward to. Bless you for that.'

He looked at her curiously. 'You can't be that bored, surely – '

'Oh, I'm not bored – not with most things. It's living here that's
driving me potty. I want a place of my own and Daddy goes mad
whenever I talk about it. I'll get it in the end of course – I always
do. But in the meantime it's no end of a bore.'

'What do you do with yourself all day?'

She opened her eyes wide at him. 'Oh, I've got a job! Did you
think I was just a lily of the field? Of course I work.'

'Let me guess. You're – a model?'

She opened her eyes even wider and clapped her hands
together. 'You're a wizard. How did you know that?'

'Not very difficult. Obsessed with clothes and pop music – '

She made a moue. 'I think you're being rude. Don't care. You'll
find out after Saturday. Anyway, it's not just modelling I do. There
isn't enough work, frankly.' She looked at him disarmingly. 'So I
work in an ad agency as a receptionist. It's quite a laugh really. People
coming in and out all the time. You see the world and his wife.'

'Then why not take them to the Beatles concert?' He looked
rather quizzical.

'Because they want to go, silly! It'll be much more interesting
with you. Anyway, you've agreed. No wriggling out.'

'I'm not wriggling,' he said gravely. 'I know when I'm beaten.
But don't expect me to enjoy it.'

'I expect nothing,' she said joyously. 'Just a fun day. And we'll
have it.'

'If you say so,' he said and then got to his feet as the rest of the
diners did, and followed her into the drawing-room for coffee.

He took a cup to his mother and she peered up at him and said as
casually as she could, 'Hope you found dinner fun?'

He laughed and shook his head at her. 'You win in spades,' he
said. 'Wretched girl's making me go to a Beatles concert, would
you believe? Sugar?'

'No thanks,' she said and contentedly watched him go back to
the coffee tray to continue fetching and carrying cups for his
hostess. Whatever he was wearing he was an asset to the party and
from the way Gillian was looking at him so gratefully, she thought
so too. And who knew? Maybe the concert outing would lead to
better things.

85

And across the room she saw Richard looking at his daughter and Josh thoughtfully as well and was struck by the oddness of the fact that for once, both she and he actually seemed to want the same thing. It made an interesting change, to say the least.

10

Robin couldn't remember the last time she'd been so filthy. There was a muddy tidemark straggling up both her arms, her knees were blackened inside her laddered stockings and her face was streaked with dirt. Furthermore, she strongly suspected that she smelled as hot as she felt. Not at all an appetizing person, she told herself blissfully. Not even a little bit.

But she'd finished and she stood at the back of her little shop with her hands set over her aching back and surveyed it. The walls were hung with a gathered blue and white striped coarse mattress ticking, and had four full length mirrors set against them at intervals, and looked marvellous. The ticking had been her own idea and at first she thought she'd made a terrible mistake, buying so much of it, and had cursed the difficulties of threading each strip onto stretch cords so that they could be fixed just beneath ceiling level and at the skirting board. But it had worked and that was all that mattered. The floor was gleaming now, paying sizeable dividends for the effort she had put into the scrubbing that had occupied the last hour. What she thought to be a nondescript brownish surface had turned out to be a rich crimson linoleum that showed up well against the blue and white striped walls. The whole effect was lively and fresh and exciting.

She stretched and groaned softly and took herself to the tiny space at the back that was the only private accommodation they had. The minuscule sink in the corner beside the shelf where the gas ring stood offered only a cold water supply. Perhaps sometime she'd see about putting in a gas geyser, but that was for the future. Right now she had to wash and change into her street clothes, and drive herself home. It was past eleven and Sam would be worrying.

Won't think about Sam, she told herself, lathering her arms in the cold water. Won't. And spent the next ten minutes as she scrubbed herself as industriously as she'd done the floor doing just that. He'd been amazingly polite and nice about the shop since that morning when they'd both been so angry with each other. Well, she'd been angry with him; he, in his usual exasperating way, had refused to get angry back. Now he was being even more exasperating with the general goodness of his behaviour. He asked after progress every day, offered her supper on a tray because she'd missed the family's evening meal, ran her bath for her and generally made her feel wretched. If he'd shouted and nagged it would have been much easier, she thought, now towelling herself to a rosy glow on the dirty old roller towel on the back of the door that led out to the yard. Then I'd have had something to kick against. As it is, all I've got is a guilty conscience.

Well, blow that. I've got the shop now and it's lovely. Now the fun'll really begin.

Her heart actually began to beat harder and faster at the thought and she stood with both hands clasped over her middle and thought about it. The stock she'd inherited from Susan with the lease and the keys was to be sold at give-away prices, as a bait to get people into the shop. Then they'd see the new stuff she was to buy tomorrow and it would be that which would make them realize that the brand new shop 'Glad Rags', which would unveil itself to the public next week, wasn't at all like the dreary 'Susan's Modes' which had stood on the site previously. But first she had to find that new stock, and that was what was so frightening. She had a list of places she intended to visit, collected from labels she had inspected in the King's Road shops and discussions with those of her friends who wore the sort of things she liked. But it would all take money and it was that that caused the main fear that filled her.

'It'll take a couple of thousand to stock it the way you plan, Robin,' Susan had told her when Robin had explained her strategy. 'I mean, it's a great idea, but you'll have no credit yet, will you?'

'Credit?'

Susan was patient. 'You have to establish a customer relationship with the fashion houses. They let you have stock and you pay anything up to eight weeks later, by which time if you've bought well, you've sold some stuff and you've got the necessary to pay the fashion house's bills. Of course, if you can find a couple of referees to stand for you and guarantee your debts, you may be able to get credit right away – '

'Who can I ask to do that?' Robin was aghast. 'I've never been in debt in my life.'

'Don't look so scared. It's normal practice to go into debt when you run a shop. Try the bank. And maybe your solicitor chappie? Or Sam?'

'Never Sam,' Robin said firmly. 'I'm doing this on my own.'

'Like that, is it, sweetie?' Susan was sympathetic. 'Doesn't want the little woman to be independent? Bastards, men are. Some of 'em.' And she smiled fondly, obviously thinking of her diplomat.

'Not at all.' Robin tried to be dignified. 'I just want to do this all on my own.' She thought for a while. 'I won't ask for credit. I'll spend the money and ask for a discount as I won't be in debt and then when I do start selling and getting cash back at least I'll know it's my money – '

'That's the way to think!' Susan said admiringly. 'Not about not going into debt, I don't mean, because that doesn't matter, but because of asking for a discount if you pay cash. That makes sense.'

And tomorrow she had to go and convince these fashions manufacturers that she made sense. She hadn't the least idea what to buy, let alone how much, but she had to do it. It was, she knew, the hardest part of any business. Choosing what other people would be willing to buy from you. And if you couldn't you were stuck with a lot of expensive goods you'd pretty well have to give away in a sale, just like the stuff Susan had left behind –

She shivered and finished her clean-up by changing her stockings, and went home. A decent night's sleep and a proper supper before it, that was what she needed. Then when tomorrow came, she'd be fit for anything. Or so she tried to persuade herself all the way home on the tube. It wasn't easy.

'Darling, I can't tell you! He's such fun. Quite mad you know, but enormous fun.' Caro filed her left third finger-nail industriously, the phone tucked precariously between her chin and shoulder. 'I mean, told me he loathed the Beatles – I ask you! And then at the concert actually thought they were rather good. So he's not entirely – what? No, he has not. And that's half the charm. I loathe it when they're paddling around all over you the first time they take you out. He's a real poppet. Shakes hands when he sees me home, would you believe? I adore it – what? Oh, blast. Hang on!'

She flicked a switch and pushed a plug into place and said sweetly, 'Freeman, Fussell and Garrard!' in the most fluting tones, 'Mr Fussell is away on a photo session. Mr Garrard is taking his calls – shall I – thank you! Hold on, please, – putting you through.' She pulled on more cords and plugs. 'Mr Garrard, I have a call for Mr Fussell, thank you – '

She made the connection and went back to her conversation. 'As I was saying, he really is awfully nice. I'm bringing him to Jeffrey's party. What? Well, suppose it does? It won't do Jeff any harm at all to see there's more than one man who likes me. No, I'm not. I don't play tricks like that. I really like this fella. Hmm? Oh, Josh. Yes I know. Rather old-fashioned all round, but there it is. His people and mine are in business together. Yes, that's right. "Food by Poppy". What? Oh, money – no, it's not come up, but I suppose – well, Dad gives me enough, so frankly I couldn't care less – well, if we ever get round to talking then I'll think about it, but I'm not in a hurry to marry anyone, so don't go getting ideas. Listen, such fun! Old Fussell says he can use me for a soap powder ad he has to do next week. Isn't that fab? Well, it's better than last time. That was lavatory powder, but you have to take what you can get in this business. Oh blast, the board's waking up. I'll have to go – see you tomorrow night at Jeff's, then? Then you can see Josh for yourself. And listen – hands off!' And she chuckled and turned back to her board with a sigh.

'Freeman, Fussell and Garrard! No, I'm sorry, Mr Fussell is away on a photo session today – '

'Well, there's a treat,' Barbara cried and opened her arms wide. 'I didn't expect you today!'

Bertie hugged her back as hard as she hugged him and said in a muffled voice, because his head was buried in her bosom, 'Gramma said I could. I'm supposed to be with her this afternoon but she has an extra thing to do at her office or something, and GranDave has to go to see his publisher. So here I am.' He disentangled himself and smiled at Barbara. 'So I thought I might as well come over here as be on my own at home. Is that all right?'

'What a question!' Barbara took his coat from him, helping him out of it as though he were a child, and goodnaturedly he let her, for all he was thirteen and well past any need for such services. But it pleased her to do it and he knew it. 'Come into the kitchen now. Your Auntie Jessie's having a nap – '

'She's always napping,' Bertie said and followed her down the hall towards the kitchen door, his slight limp giving him a rather rolling gait.

'So would you if you were nearly a hundred,' Barbara said, with the pride she always displayed when Auntie Jessie's age was mentioned. Both she and Lally took it as a personal credit that the old lady was still alive and tolerably well, and Bertie grinned at her back. Funny old Barbara, he thought, and then as he went into the kitchen, grinned at Lally too.

'Hello, Lally, Have you got some tea for a starving person? With gingerbread?'

'What a boy,' Lally said delightedly. 'Always gingerbread! You'd think it was the only thing there was in the world worth eating.'

'Yours is. All sticky and soggy. I love it.'

'It's supposed to be light and easy,' Lally said. 'But it always comes out that way – ' She put a large slice on a plate and pushed it across the scrubbed kitchen table and he scrambled into a chair and began to eat it greedily as Barbara fetched more from the fridge.

They sat and watched him, two bulky middle-aged women sitting on either side of the table with their elbows on it and their eyes fixed benevolently on the boy between them. He was worth looking at; a great deal of thick hair that he liked to wear fairly long, and which neither his grandmother nor his aunt, who shared his care, objected to, and a pale face, in which his eyes, large, dark-blue and absurdly lashed, shone brightly. He was small for his age, but lively, and apart from the lagging movement of one leg which gave him his limping gait, showed no evidence of the handicap with which he'd been born. To Barbara, remembering

91

how scrawny and sick he'd been as a baby when she had taken on his care and before he had had the operation that closed the lesion in his back and gave him virtually complete mobility, it was a miracle to see him. Every time he came to visit – and it was often, for he was a devoted and grateful child – she marvelled at the beauty of him and preened a little at her own success in rearing him.

'If it hadn't been for me, he'd ha' died, two or three times,' she would say to Lally as they waved goodbye to him from the flat window after his visits. 'Saved his little life, I did.' And Lally, knowing how important it was to Barbara to remember that fact, never complained at its repetition, but patted her beloved friend's shoulder and went back to the kitchen to work on Auntie Jessie's next meal.

Now, Bertie finished his cake, wiped his mouth with the back of his hand, looked at the plate and contemplated another slice and decided regretfully he had no room at present.

'So,' Barbara said with satisfaction, and settled even more comfortably in her chair. 'What news?'

Once or twice Lally had demurred, told her she shouldn't encourage the boy to chatter so about the families and their private lives, but she had stopped complaining after a while, not least because she had come to find it all as fascinating as Barbara did. Bertie would talk and they would ask apparently artless questions and he would talk more and more and all of it was enthralling. To Barbara and Lally it was better hearing even than the doings of their much loved Ena Sharples and Minnie Caldwell and Elsie Tanner and her naughtiness on their favourite TV show.

'Well, Auntie Robin's got a shop,' he announced, and Lally's eyes rounded with disbelief.

'No! What sort of shop?'

'Fashion. It's in the West End. She says we can all go and see it one day – not yet because it isn't quite ready. She's getting stuff ordered and all that. She's ever so excited.'

'I'll bet she is,' Barbara said. 'But what about your uncle?'

Bertie looked troubled. 'I don't know. He listens all the time when she talks about it, but he doesn't seem – I don't know. He's not excited like Auntie Robin is.' He stopped to think then. 'Mind you, Uncle Sam never does get excited, does he?'

'I don't know,' Lally said. 'I don't live with him.'

'Well, I only do sometimes.' He laughed then. 'My friend Ronnie, he gets really jealous of me. He says it's much more fun to have two houses that are yours than just one. I suppose he's right –'

'Don't you think so?' Barbara said, anxious suddenly. Any threat to her Bertie's happiness was a personal affront to her.

'Probably,' Bertie said and looked at the cake. 'Maybe I can manage another piece. Not too big – '

He got it and talked through the mouthfuls, muffled and happy. 'Like I told Ronnie, it's funny to have two of most things. Except important ones, like bikes. But two bedrooms and everything – '

He wiped his mouth again and said with a fine artless air, 'He says it'd be a great way to get out and about. I'd just have to say to Auntie Robin I was in Norland Square and tell Gramma I was at Auntie Robin's, wouldn't I?'

'Oh, yes?' Lally said. 'And where would you be, I'd like to know?'

'Here,' Bertie said and giggled. 'Because I've got three places really, haven't I?'

'Indeed you have,' Barbara said warmly. 'And never you forget it, my lamb.' She leaned over and kissed him soundly which he, good-natured as ever, accepted with a reasonable grace.

'So,' Lally said, her nose back on the scent. 'They're a bit miserable in Hampstead, are they?'

He shook his head. 'I wouldn't say miserable. Auntie Robin gets fed up, I think. Sophie and Penny and me are at school all the time and Uncle Sam's at the practice and now even Auntie Chick's not around to be with, what with looking after the Clinic. So she gets bored. She won't any more, though. Not now that she's got a shop. I wish it was a different sort of shop.'

'What sort? Sweeties, I suppose.'

'Not at all,' Bertie said with great dignity. 'I'm not a baby, you know! No, I'd like it to be a bicycle shop. Then I could get all the bits and make my bike into a ten-gear one and go everywhere, with a bag and a tent on the pannier and all. Ronnie and me, we're planning a holiday like that, just on our bikes going round France.'

Barbara opened her eyes wide. 'France? Heaven help us, you'll get into terrible trouble there. They'll rob you and everything!'

'No they won't,' Bertie said with sublime certainty. 'I talk French now, you know. I'm ever so good at it. They'd think I was French and not English and be very nice to us.'

'Hmm,' Lally said. 'Let's hear you.'

Bertie pursed his lips and thought and then said, 'S'il vous plâit, Lally, est-il possible pour moi – er – er – manger un morceau de gâteau?'

'There,' Barbara said proudly. 'What do you think of that, then Lally? What did you say, Bertie?'

Lally cut the cake and pushed it towards him. 'Greedy little tyke. Asking for another piece of cake. You won't be able to get out of the door at this rate.'

Bertie gave a little cackle of laughter. 'Je suis un grand cochon,' he announced. 'A big pig, Barbie!'

'Don't they give you enough to eat at home?' Barbara asked anxiously again, looking at his thin frame.

'I never stop eating,' he said with pride. 'Everyone says I've got the biggest appetite of anyone they know. It's nice being greedy, and not getting fat like poor old Ronnie. When we're grown up I'll have all the girlfriends and he won't have any.' And he cackled again.

'Girlfriends? Such a thing to talk of at your age!' Barbara said. 'You're much too young.'

'I said when I was grown up.' Bertie stretched and drank some more milk. 'I wouldn't want to be as grown as Uncle Josh though before I do. He's more than thirty and he's only just got a girlfriend for the first time.'

The two women exchanged glances. 'Josh, a girlfriend? Who would that be?' Lally asked casually.

'Oh, someone from Gramma's office.' Bertie got to his feet as the sound of a bell came down the hallway. 'Is that Auntie Jessie awake? Can I go and see her?'

Lally was already on her feet and bustling to the stove to put the kettle on again. 'I'll be there in five minutes with her tea, tell her,' she said over her shoulder, as Barbara equally busily made for the toaster. 'Don't get her over-excited, now – '

He went along the hall whistling softly between his teeth, for he greatly admired his Aunt Jessie, not just because her great age was a source of much boastful talk to his friends, as because her salty wit was the kind he most enjoyed. And the two women busied themselves for a moment or two; and then Barbara said uneasily, 'Do you believe it?'

'What?'

'About Josh?'

'Not for me to say,' Lally said, her head down over the kettle. 'Nor you, come to that.'

'All the same,' Barbara was staring down at the toaster, her brows creased. 'It does bother me. He's so – I worry about him. He's so good really and ever since last year when that Adrian died, well, I can't say I haven't been worried. But maybe I got it all wrong? Mind you, if I did, you did too. You said he was – '

'Never mind what I said,' Lally said. 'And if you've any sense, Barbara, frankly you won't say any more on the subject either. It's one thing to make guesses and so forth between ourselves but another to start getting involved.'

'Who said I was getting involved?' Barbara was indignant.

'Well, I know you. You take people under your wing. Bertie's all right, because he was your baby, but Josh, he never was – '

'I've known him long enough,' Barbara said. 'He feels like one of my own. Anyway, I like him and I want to help him. I mean if people like us don't help each other then who will?'

Lally took the toast from her and arranged it on the tray and hoisted it on to her hip. 'Barbara, not another word,' she said sternly. 'We're here to look after Mrs Jessie and there's as far as it goes. If Josh wants to be helped he'll come to us soon enough, I have no doubt – but keep your tongue where it belongs, between your teeth, till then. It's the best advice you could have.'

'I suppose so,' Barbara said and followed her out into the hall. 'I wish though that – well, never mind. Let's give Mrs Jessie her tea.'

11

'I say!' Chick stopped at the top of Foubert's Place and stared in amazement. 'You have pushed the boat out!'

'Haven't I just?' Robin said gleefully. 'But I think I'm entitled. After all – six months! Do come and look – ' And she hustled her along the street so fast that Chick almost had to break into a run.

Overhead, in the late afternoon September sunshine, the rows of balloons Robin had strung from one side to the other bobbed cheerfully like so many lollipops, red and yellow, blue and green, and streamers of glittering aluminium foil floated in amongst them. The shop itself had its entire window surrounded by more aluminium frosting interspersed with fairy lights, and Robin stopped her outside and said breathlessly, 'Wait here. Watch what it's like – ' and darted inside.

After a few moments the fairy lights blinked on and began a pattern of flicking off and on that made them seem to be circling the window and Chick laughed at the absurdity of it as Robin came hurtling out of the shop again.

'It's ridiculous – ' she cried. 'It looks more like a toy shop than a grown-up dress one – and what have you done inside?' And she went closer to peer into the window itself.

Robin had created a sort of party scene there with clothes pinned and pulled by threads in different directions so that the dresses themselves seemed to be alive, covering invisible bodies. The lack of mannequins, far from making the display meagre, added to the fun as the dresses and trousers and shirts seemed to become personalities in their own right and pranced and pirouetted round each other, and Chick shook her head in admiration.

'Who'd have thought you could do anything like that?' she

said. 'It's so – it's so – well, it certainly isn't anything you learned in hospital! I've never seen a window display like it.'

'I know,' Robin said happily. 'One of the girls from Liberty's came in and she showed me how to do the bits with the threads and pins, but the actual idea of doing them like a party was mine. I'm amazed myself. Oh, and I'm going to have music too – just a sec,' and she put her head round the shop door and shouted, 'Beckie! Put the player on!' and after another moment or two the sound of the latest Beatles record began to blare over their heads, filling the street with sound. People walking past the end of Foubert's Place along Regent Street stopped to look in some surprise, and after a moment or two, some of them began to turn into the street towards them, curiosity written all over their faces.

'See,' Robin said, even more excited, if that were possible. 'It works. Come on in – have a look round while I sort out the last details – I'm so glad you could come, Chick! It's cheered me up no end. I thought I'd never get you here.' And she hugged her warmly and beamed.

'I'm sorry,' Chick said, as she followed her inside the shop. 'It's just been so difficult fitting in everything, what with the Clinic and the children. Hal and Suzy aren't a problem of course, at their age, but Charlie is still rather young to be on his own as often as he has to be.'

'I told you, let him come round to us when you're busy. There's always someone there.'

Chick sighed. 'If it were only that easy! The truth of it is Charlie just doesn't get on with your lot and there's nothing we can do to change that. If only our kids were as contented in each other's company as we are – but if they're not, they're not – ' And she thought of Oliver, and Hal and Suzy's loathing of him and his behaviour loudly expressed to her, and prudently said no more.

Inside the shop she stopped to stare round. 'It's lovely!' she said after a moment, turning from side to side to take it all in. 'Really lovely.' The striped walls were also glittering with a fringe of foil that had been pinned up round the edge of the ceiling against the striped ticking, and the mirrors had been framed with winking lights like the window outside, but it was the clothes that startled Chick most. She moved from rail to rail, picking up hangers and trying them against herself, and then exchanging them for others with increasing consternation.

Robin had gone to the back of the shop and was talking with her young assistant, Beckie, a girl of incredible thinness who was wearing very tight blue canvas trousers adorned with brass rivets that Chick thought were the sort her own son Hal had been yearning to get, and who had long black hair that hung half-way to her waist and which she kept parting in front with her hands so that she could see where she was going. Chick thought that she looked rather ill, until she was close enough to realize that the girl's very white face was achieved entirely with make-up rather than anaemia.

Beckie wandered off to talk to a couple of young girls who looked much like herself and who had come into the shop, and Chick looked at Robin again and looked at the outfits the two were wearing, and said carefully, 'They're – well, a bit odd, aren't they?'

Robin grinned. 'Aren't they just? I love 'em, don't you?'

Chick looked dubiously at the very short dress in emerald-green crêpe with purple trim on neck and shoulders that just covered the taller of the two, and shook her head. 'I can't say I'd actually wear one myself,' she said cautiously.

'Oh, darling, of course you wouldn't! They're not for you. They're for people like Beckie. Seventeen and tuned in to every new thing there is. They adore way-out clothes, these kids and –'

'Way what?'

'Way out. It's the thing they say these days. You have to keep up with the way teenagers talk in this business if you want to get anywhere.' Robin preened a little. 'I'm getting rather good at it, according to Sophie.'

'Yes,' Chick said and looked at her thoughtfully. She was wearing a pair of black and white checked trousers with a scarlet shirt and matching red boots, and her hair had been cut into a square bob that was so hard to the sides of her face that it looked rather like a close-fitting helmet. Her face had been made up with considerable skill and though Chick privately thought it looked a little ridiculous, with its heavy mascara and elongated lashes and very pale lipstick, she had to admit that her friend looked ten years younger than she used to.

'I'll have to get things ready, Chick – ' Robin said and peered through the dress rails at Beckie and her two customers, one of whom was climbing out of her dress in order to try on a pair of the same sort of trousers that Beckie was wearing and seeming quite happy to be in her bra and pants in the middle of the open shop. 'I hope they hurry up – I don't want to turn customers away, but I did hope we could have this celebration just for ourselves – you know, friends and family, and so forth.'

'I'll help you,' Chick offered and followed Robin out to the back area and through the door into the yard outside.

'I had this put up to give me extra space,' Robin said, as she unlocked the door of a small cabin which seemed to Chick to have been built of plywood. 'I dare say there'd be trouble from the council if they knew, but it's fully portable and if I have to get rid of it, I will. It's helped me a lot, though.'

Inside was a bigger space than appeared possible from the look of the building and it was filled with rails, like the shop, but also with a couple of long tables on which trays of food and glasses and wine bottles had been set.

'If you could uncover all the sandwiches and peanuts and so forth,' Robin said. 'I'll take the glasses through and then together we'll haul the tables in. Then there's just the wine to open – '

The next half hour was busy as the two customers were seen on their way with their purchases and the shop was officially shut (though lots of passing people peered in through the windows and tried the door before going away disappointed) and the three of them organized the party. The rails of clothes in the shop were pushed back and covered with sheets of transparent plastic, and the tables in front of the shed at the back were brightly covered in paper cloths and adorned with food, drink and pots of paper flowers, while the record player blared out its eternity of current pop songs until Chick's head began to ache. But Robin was clearly delighted with herself and all she was doing and bustled around among her preparations like a child at her own birthday party. Chick who had spent the day at Sam's Clinic, dealing with a few refractory patients and all the irritations that running any twenty-bedded psychiatric unit is likely to create, felt jaded and, as she watched Robin, positively dowdy.

They had been friends ever since their late teens when they'd been student nurses during the war; and there was Robin, bouncing with excitement and looking as young as her own daughter, while Chick, widowed, lined and heavy, still grieving for the loss of her husband, looked more like Robin's mother than her contemporary. And then, as Poppy arrived to the warmest possible welcome from Robin she thought a little sourly, 'I could be Poppy's mother too, dammit. Even she looks younger and better than I do.'

Or so she thought until she got a closer look at Poppy and saw the weary lines around her mouth and the violet shadows in her temples and changed her mind. Poppy was showing every minute of her twenty or so years' seniority, and on an impulse Chick took her arm and said softly, 'Everything all right, Poppy?'

'Hmm?' Poppy looked up at her and smiled affectionately, 'Oh, fine my dear, fine. Although I'm a bit busy at present and a touch worried – I can't pretend I'm not.'

'Over this place?' Chick looked over her shoulder at the hubbub beyond as several more people arrived in a cluster, all of them making a considerable noise as they looked about and squealed delightedly at each other and at Robin. 'It seems to be doing all right, though, doesn't it? And Robin's never looked better.'

'Oh, she's having a wonderful time,' Poppy agreed. 'Wonderful. But she's working all the hours God sends, and then there's Sam – '

He too had arrived and was standing unnoticed by the door as Robin busied herself with the earlier arrivals, none of whom Chick knew at all.

'Who are they?' she wondered aloud and Poppy shook her head. 'I've no idea. Customers perhaps? Though the way they're carrying on – no, I think they must be people in the fashion trade. Suppliers maybe. They seem to be all over Robin anyway,' as two of the noisiest of the women almost carried Robin away to the back of the shop to look at something on one of the back rails they wanted to discuss with her, and she went, hardly noticing Sam was hovering there behind them. 'I'm going to talk to Sam,' Poppy said and she went, leaving Chick where she was to observe what was happening around her.

Sam, she thought, looking at him covertly over the heads of the crowd, Sam; and her heart sank. He looked dreadful, pale and tired, but more than that. Defeated, somehow, and she could have wept suddenly, for him and for herself. It seemed to her the golden years had been so short, those happy years when the children had been young and Harry had been alive, and the two families had been so close and happy. Sam had been her greatest friend after Robin and she had thought the world of him; when he'd offered her a job after Harry died she'd been first scared and then grateful. And now?

She looked at Sam again and this time he caught her eye and smiled at her over Poppy's shoulder as she chattered up at him and Chick felt her belly swoop again. This was ridiculous; Sam had been good to her, as any friend would be. There was no more to it than that. To feel as she did when she saw him now, this extraordinarily queasy mixture of excitement and fear and hope was – well, ridiculous, and as the word came to her mind again she found herself repeating it over and over again under her breath. Ridiculous. Ri-dic-u-lous –

She made a convulsive little movement as she saw Josh at the door and hurried over to him and greeted him effusively, paying no attention at all to the conversation Poppy was having with Sam, though she ached to know what it was she was saying to him so earnestly. Warning him to persuade Robin to give up her silly little shop so that she could spend more time with him? No, she wouldn't do that. She wanted Robin to have a job; Robin herself had told Chick many times of the way her mother had positively nagged her about having some sort of interest of her own. Maybe she was just suggesting ways he could heal the obvious breach that was opening between them? 'No,' she murmured aloud. This all had to stop; it was none of her business how Robin and Sam got on, and she was being perfectly ridiculous to think otherwise. Ri-dic-u-lous –

'Chick,' Josh said warmly. 'Lovely to see you. It's been ages.'

'Too long,' Chick agreed. 'I've been working rather hard. Can I fetch you a drink? Over there – '

'We'll go and get one together,' Josh said and followed her through the press of people to the tables at the end where Beckie was dispensing wine with a lavish hand. 'This is all very smart, isn't it?'

'Mm.' Chick was noncommittal. 'Is this the first time you've seen it?'

'Oh, no,' said Josh. 'I come down this way quite often. I buy my own gear around here – no, don't look like that! I have to work quite hard to get this relaxed look.'

Chick laughed. 'Relaxed? Well you could call it that. From where I stand, dear boy, you're as shabby as last year's haystack. You were tidier when you were ten and I can't say worse than that.'

'Exactly.' Josh beamed. 'It's the madly casual look. Young, easy-going, just the ticket these trendy days. I look like me, and not like everyone else.'

'That's for sure,' Chick said and looked round again. 'All these people beavering away to make themselves look like fashion plates. So silly – oh!' She jumped as a brilliant light flashed across the room. 'What was that?'

'Robin's getting very smart!' Josh said admiringly. 'The place's only been open six months and there she is getting all the fashion magazine photographers out. She'll do even better after this evening.'

Chick looked at him curiously. 'Then she really is doing well?'

He laughed at her expression. 'Are you kidding? She's one of the names these days, keeps being talked about in the pop magazines. She's doing fine.'

'Why?' Chick reddened. 'Sorry, I didn't mean to sound so blunt, but honestly – this tiny shop and the things she sells – so weird, some of them.'

'Precisely. It's what the journalists adore. Anyone can go to boring old Harrods or Selfridges or wherever and find the same boring old stuff there – what journalists want is to find a "simply divine little place, darling, tucked away in sweet little Foubert's Place, madly chic, such way-out things – " '

Chick nodded. 'Robin said that. Way out. Way out of what?'

'Common sense! Or you could say beyond the usual. Different, I suppose. Trendy. It's the only thing to be in the fashion trade. Either that or dreadfully boring, so that you go on selling liberty bodices to people who've worn them since they were three and intend to go on wearing them till they're ninety-three.'

'You sound very knowledgeable about fashion,' Chick said and laughed. 'You're just making all this up to reassure me – '

He shook his head. 'No, I'm serious. She *is* doing well, because all of a sudden all people care about is fashion. World's gone mad, if you ask me. There used to be clothes you wore to keep warm and look all right and clothes you wore for best, and whatever it was you had, you wanted them to last. All those years of rationing concentrated the mind wonderfully. But now, what with all the new factories and the extra money everyone seems to have, well – it's all fashion, fashion, fashion. Robin's timed it just right. She's older than the usual run of new clothes queens, but none the worse for that. Most of this stuff here she gets made to her own ideas, you know. She found some people who sew and so forth – those girls there – see?' And he pointed with his chin at the noisy group of girls in the corner who were still monopolizing Robin. 'And they make the stuff up cheaply and she sells it fairly expensively. She's really doing very well indeed.'

'I'm delighted to know it,' Chick said and finished her drink. 'I know Sam was worried and I thought Poppy was too, so I just – ' She shrugged.

'My family do nothing better than they do worrying,' Josh said lightly. 'I know you're one of us, Chick, but please, love, do hold on to your common sense. That was always the most delightful thing about you, your-feet-on-the-ground attitude. I'd miss it like hell if you lost it.'

She reached up and kissed him lightly. 'Thanks, Josh. And I'd miss your all-round niceness. So stay as sweet as you are.'

She blushed then, and picked up her glass. 'I'll get another of these. You too?'

'No thanks. I have to go on to a party. Better keep my head at this early stage of the evening.' He grinned and looked over her shoulder at the door. 'And unless I mistake me, there's the lady's who's making me go.'

'Making you?' Chick was a little startled. 'The one thing about you, Josh, was always that no one could make you do anything you didn't want to. Who is this miracle worker?' She turned to look and was startled. 'Oh,' she said and no more.

'Well, I'm a peaceful soul and that one nags so much,' he said easily. 'And I like to please Ma. Her father's the Chairman of the Board of "Food by Poppy" and she asked me to keep the girl happy. So I take her around here and there. And she, dammit, then insists on taking me around.' He laughed as he caught Chick's considering eye. 'No need to look like that, Chick. I'm a confirmed bachelor as well you know and there's an end of it. This girl's just a friend. A very good one because she's so scatty and silly she makes me laugh and that's not to be sneezed at, if you'll forgive the bad imagery. But more than that? Forget it.'

And he smiled at her a little crookedly and made his way through the crowd towards the door where the dark girl in a bright scarlet jacket over the shortest of skirts and the whitest of stockinged legs stood looking coolly about her, and Chick shook her head and wondered, just for a moment, if she'd been wrong in her assessment of Josh, and decided, as she watched him bend his head to kiss the girl lightly on the cheek, that she had not. He was as he said, no more than a friend. You could always tell if there was more to a relationship than that, by the way a man behaved with people – well, women. And Josh was the way he always had been, remote and cool, friendly and cheerful, but remote. And then she moved her head and saw Sam leaning against the wall with an empty glass in his hand, his eyes fixed on his wife, and again her belly tightened a little and she hurried across the room as fast as she could, considering the number of people who were in the way, to find Robin and tell her that it had been a wonderful evening, thanks, she was thrilled to have been part of her six months' birthday party but now it was time to go home. She'd had quite enough to cope with for one day.

12

Sam saw Chick go and felt a moment of compunction. He hadn't bothered to go and speak to her and he should have done. She worked hard at his Clinic and deserved better of him. Of course they talked there, but it was always on a professional level, never a personal one, and he shouldn't have ignored her now, not considering all the years of friendship that lay behind them. But it was no use; he couldn't think of anything other than Robin and the dreadful row they'd had this morning; until they'd sorted it all out, he couldn't really spare any thought or energy for anyone else.

Even talking to the children this afternoon when they'd come in from school had been extraordinarily effortful, and Bertie had been sulky and Penny whining and Sophie irascible in consequence. He'd known it was his fault they'd started to squabble with each other and gone off to their respective rooms in a huff, but he'd made no attempt to go and make things up with them, though normally he would have done. All that had mattered had been getting out of the house and off to Robin's shop to make things right between them.

Now he stood with an empty glass in his hand, his head a little muzzy from the noise and the cigarette smoke that was making the air blue, watching her sombrely over the heads of the crowd. She was having a marvellous time; there was no doubt about that. There was also no doubt about the fact that she was making a considerable success of her shop; and that was the hardest thing to cope with.

It wasn't that he'd wished her endeavour ill; when she'd first told him of what she intended to do with her grandmother's legacy he'd actually been quite pleased for her. It would give her an agreeable hobby, he'd thought, something to occupy her mind when she wasn't busy with the children or the house or him. That it would take over her life to the extent it had simply hadn't occurred to him, and he didn't like the way it had done so, and that was the truth of it. That was why they'd had so major an argument this morning; and why he felt so wretched now.

He tried to nurse his anger, to remind himself that he was entitled to be annoyed. After all, surely he and the family came before this shop? He'd certainly felt that this morning. That was why he'd spoken as he had. But he hadn't meant to offend her quite so much –

He looked back over the morning to see where it had all started, trying to identify the point at which he'd gone off at a tangent and said the wrong thing. Once he could do that he'd be able to find the right thing to say now to put matters right. It was a technique that worked with his schizophrenic patients when they got angry with him in therapy – which sometimes happened. Why shouldn't the same technique work in his dealings with his wife?

She'd been abstracted as she sat at the table in her dressing-gown, a pretty enough one, short and a little fluffy in pale blue, and she'd looked charming in it; so charming that he'd felt a frisson of desire for her which, he had to admit, didn't happen as often these days as it once had. And he'd been a little embarrassed by the reaction at such a time and in such a setting, and that had made him a touch gruff. That had been the point at which the train had rocked on the rails, he told himself now. *That* had been when he found the wrong thing to say.

'Oh. Not getting dressed this morning?'

'What? Oh, I'm dressing after breakfast. A new outfit and I don't want to risk getting a mark on it – do you mind?'

She looked up at him, her head on one side, and he'd thought –for all the world as though she were a patient – she's being hostile, angry. I wonder why? And he reacted as he would to a patient, answering the question with one of his own. And she had realized that.

'Is there any reason why I should mind?'

'I know of none. Perhaps you do.' She had bristled at once. It was almost as though he could see the back of her neck rising.

'Not at all. It was just that it's not what you usually do and – ' He was floundering and he knew it.

'This morning isn't a usual morning,' she'd said and looked at him sharply. 'Is it?'

'I don't know. Is it?' Again the psychiatrist's reaction to a patient's question. And this time she really had lost her temper.

'Damn you, Sam! Don't sit there talking at me as though I was one of your bloody half-wits! I'm not! I'm your wife and I have important things to deal with today. It's the six months' anniversary party of the shop and it matters a great deal to me. And all you do is sit there and – '

He'd forgotten. That was the unforgivable thing. The most important event in her life at present and he'd forgotten. Yet instead of admitting he was wrong and apologizing, all he could do was fly to the defence of his patients.

'My patients are not half-wits. You display a colossal ignorance in speaking so, Robin, and I'm surprised at you.'

'Oh, are you? Surprised at me? It's amazing that I don't surprise you all the time, seeing how little you care about what I'm doing and why I'm doing it. You'd forgotten about today, hadn't you? You don't give a damn about me. I've told you and told you, and – well, to hell with you. If you want to go on pretending my business is just a silly little game I can enjoy myself with as long as I'm always home in time to organize your dinner, and always get up in time to look perfect over breakfast coffee, that's up to you. As far as I'm concerned my business comes way in front of your bloody coffee! There! What do you say to that?'

'There's nothing to say,' he'd said stuffily. 'You seem determined to have an argument, so where's the point in my saying anything?'

That had been a mistake too. Telling her she was picking a fight had been his way of preventing any sensible talk about their real differences. He knew that; and he should have had more sense than to say so stupid a thing.

But he'd said it, and she had tightened her lips and looked at him with eyes as hard as pebbles and then had turned and gone upstairs. He'd followed her after a while, hoping to mend the rift, but it was too late. She was in the bathroom with the door locked –which was something she never usually did – and would only call back with false brightness when he knocked on the door.

'Busy, I'm afraid.'

'Robin, I want to talk to you – '

'No time now – Got too much to do. Some other time!' And she'd turned the shower on so that she couldn't hear him any more and, defeated, he'd gone downstairs, paying no attention to Helga as he passed her on the stairs, where she was polishing the woodwork, glad the children had already left for school. Bad enough Helga had heard it all; no need for them to be embroiled too.

So it had been a hateful day and it still was, for she'd seen him come into the shop and ignored him thereafter. Now he stood and watched her laughing and chattering as though she hadn't a care in the world and could have wept with the loneliness of it.

Poppy came back to him from the corner where she'd been taken by Lee, who had arrived late and full of a burning desire to talk to her mother, and patted his hand.

'You'd be better off with something in that glass,' she said.

'Drown my sorrows?' He looked down at her and managed a crooked smile. 'Not my style, I'm afraid.'

'Nonsense. No need to exaggerate. Offering you a drink is hardly a suggestion you should become an alcoholic. For heaven's sake, Sam, stop looking like doom! So she's too busy for you –can't you wait a bit? I'm sure if this were the Clinic and you were busy with your patients you wouldn't expect Robin to go into a sulk – '

'Poppy, I'm not sulking.' He almost snapped it and she sighed softly.

'Oh dear, I'm being a meddling mother-in-law. Not another word. I'm sorry.'

'Oh, it's all right.' He relented. 'You're not meddling. And I'm not sulking. We had a row this morning, and I want to make it up, but I don't think Robin does.'

Poppy looked over her shoulder at Robin. 'Oh, don't jump to conclusions. She's just a little above herself, that's all. She'll be fine later.'

'I hope so,' he said gloomily. 'It's very tiring, being this way.'

'I'll get that drink,' Poppy said, and went away with his glass, and took as long as she could over it; it would be diplomatic, she decided, to give him time to get over the embarrassment of admitting to his wife's mother that they were arguing. Or, perhaps, she amended, to give myself the time. She had a horror of seeming to interfere in her children's lives, and she had rather badgered Sam, she couldn't deny.

The crowd was at its thickest now, and the sound was an uproar of laughter and shouted conversation and her head was aching and she saw David in the middle of the room talking with Lee and Jeremy and thought with a sudden aching longing of home and sofa and fireside. 'A little eggy something on a tray,' she murmured and smiled at the thought. That was what David always asked for with great pathos when he was tired, and as though he had heard the thought, he looked up, caught her eye and made his way to her side through the crowd.

'Ready for home?'

'You're psychic. I'd love to. But it wouldn't be fair. Robin needs us and – '

He lifted his brows at that. 'Robin needs us like the sea needs you to spit in it, honey. Look at this place!'

'Well, yes, I know that. Lots of people here. But we're family and – '

'And Lee and Jeremy are here and so is Josh and she's got Sam, of course. Come on. I'm taking you home. You're absolutely bushed –'

She wavered. 'It would be nice.'

'A little eggy something on a tray?' he said and they both laughed and slid away between the people to the door, not needing to discuss whether or not they should say goodnight to Robin. Poppy would phone her in the morning, they both knew that; and how could they not? After all these years together they thought through each other's heads, she and her David.

It was half past nine and about half of the guests had gone, which wasn't too bad, seeing the invitations had said clearly that the party was from five thirty to eight thirty, and Robin, looking round at the remainder of them, was deeply satisfied. It had worked. They'd all come, the journalists and photographers as well as the suppliers and her own little group of makers-up; after this, the publicity would jack her right up into the Big League.

'You'll be needing a factory of your own,' someone had murmured in her ear and her spirits had lifted like a bubble at the thought. It would be marvellous to have her own label. 'Clothes by Robin', perhaps to match Ma's enterprise. The women in this family are the best, she thought, with a great burst of exhilaration; absolutely the best. There's Lee with her agency and now me –

And then she saw Sam, still standing where he'd been all evening, near the entrance to the shop against the wall, and her cheerfulness melted and ran out through the soles of her feet into the floor beneath. He looked drawn and tired and she had to be firm with herself to avoid rushing over to hug him and tell him she was sorry about this morning, really sorry –

I won't, she thought then. It wasn't my fault. He was so sneering and so – and I won't think about it. I won't. And deliberately she turned away to find someone else to talk to; and then saw Beckie waving at her from the back of the shop, by the little office door.

'It's the phone,' she called. 'Just heard it. Says it's important – ' And she waved the hand-piece in the air, and Robin went over to take it from her, and at once Beckie shot back to join the noisiest group of people who were still hanging round the tables where the drinks were.

'Hello?' She had to shout it, for even though the crowd had diminished there was still a good deal of noise.

'Ma, at last!' He sounded fretful the way he had been used to when he was much younger and she stiffened at the sound of his voice. 'I've been ringing and ringing. Helga said you were there but you just didn't answer – '

'Oliver? What's the matter? Are you ill?'

'No, of course I'm not ill. But – well – there is something – '

'What have you done now?' Her anxiety sharpened her voice and he began to shout back, clearly aggrieved.

'Why do you jump to the conclusion that it's always me that's done something? It doesn't have to be. Anyway, it takes two – '

'What takes two?'

'Well, I can't explain properly now. But I'm going to come home. You hear me? I'm coming home.'

'Oh, Oliver, for God's sake, what's happened? And what takes two? Who else is involved? What's *happening*?'

'Has the Head reached you?'

'The Head? Now, look, if you don't tell me what's going on there, I'll – '

'I'll tell you as soon as I get there. Where will you be?'

'How will you get here? I mean – '

'I've arranged to borrow a car,' Oliver said and she could hear the defensive note in his voice. 'And don't tell me I can't because I have. I'm not hanging around for trains, and I've got the use of this car and it's one I can leave at his house in Chiswick – it's Bentley's, Joey Bentley's – and I'll come wherever you are. Will you be home by the time I get there? It's getting on for ten and I'll be there by midnight I imagine – '

'Oliver, you are to tell me at once what's happening,' Robin cried. 'Because if you don't – '

'Oh, all right!' He shouted it so loudly she winced and had to pull the phone back from her ear. 'All right – I've been expelled. Happy now?'

'Ex – ' She took a deep breath and tried again. 'Expelled? What for?'

'That's the bit I'm not going to tell you on the phone. I'm leaving now. It'll take the best part of two hours to do it – I'll come home. You'll be there, will you?'

'Of course. Where else – ' But the phone went dead and then the dialling tone buzzed in her ear and she recradled it and stood there for a moment and then turned and almost ran out of the little office and across the shop to Sam.

'It's Oliver,' she said baldly. 'He's been expelled.'

Sam stood very still, staring down at her and then said very quietly, 'Get your coat. I'll take you home and we can talk about this. Can someone else lock up?'

She nodded miserably. 'Beckie.'

'I'll talk to her. No, not another word. Where's your coat?'

'In the office – '

'Right. Wait here.'

He came back a few minutes later with her coat over his arm, took her elbow and headed for the door. 'It's all right. Lee says she'll stay till the last guest has gone and help Beckie tidy up. Beckie says she'll open up in the morning. Come on – '

It was as though she were another person. The shop and the party, which had been the only things that mattered for the last few weeks, seemed to dwindle in her mind to nothing. All she could think of was Oliver's hard little voice on the phone and the way her fears were taking over her mind. Expelled – what for?

These days schools only expelled boys for really heinous crimes. Stealing, perhaps? Would there be some sort of public court case? Would her son be splashed over the papers, even the TV, as a criminal? Or had he been drinking again? Was he already an alcoholic? Had she let him down so badly, her only special boy, that he'd turned to drink to such an extent that he'd destroyed his life?

And now he was driving home – perhaps he'd been drinking today already? He'd speed on the road and get into a dreadful accident and – the fantasies rolled and spun themselves into horrible images in her head; Oliver trapped in a burning car; Oliver stretched on a mortuary table. Oliver's funeral, her own total collapse –

'I'll phone the Head as soon as we get home,' Sam said tersely, and held her arm warmly in one firm hand. 'We'll see what's going on. Don't panic.'

She said nothing, only nodding, and got into the car and sat there in silence all the way home to Hampstead, staring out at the street lamps and headlights from oncoming cars swooping and dipping in and out of her vision, cold and stiff with apprehension. Whatever it was, it was dreadful; she knew that as certainly as she knew the sun would rise tomorrow.

Sam left the car in the road outside, not even stopping to open the garage doors and put it away, and she was suddenly absurdly grateful for that. He understood how she was feeling and she was about to reach out and hug him and say as much when she stiffened with fear again. Surely his hurry wasn't aimed at comforting her, but was an indication of how alarmed he was himself? And she felt a great deal worse, if that were possible.

By the time she followed him into the hall, moving stiffly up the path, pushing on the front door, he was already sitting beside the table in the hall where the phone was, leafing through their personal phone book for the number, and as Helga appeared at the top of the stairs looking startled and not a little alarmed, he dialled and then sat there with his hand clutching the phone so tightly that his knuckles were white, and staring blindly at the wall.

'Mr Manningtree?' he said at length and took a deep breath. 'This is Dr Landow – Sam Landow. Has something – '

He sat for a long time listening and Robin stood beside the

still-open front door, not able to move to close it, staring at him, and Helga came down the stairs and went padding into the kitchen, where Robin could hear her putting on the kettle and rattling tea cups. Good old Helga, she managed to think somewhere in a corner of her mind that wasn't invaded with terror for Oliver; always practical.

'I suppose there's no doubt that Oliver is – that it is Oliver?' Sam said then and listened again.

'I see,' he said then and nodded. 'I see. Well, thank you, Mr Manningtree. No, I understand. And no blame attaches to you. I can quite see that. What? Oh, I dare say he'll be able to put me in touch himself. We, of course, will deal with the whole thing as – well, as decently as we can. It's difficult, of course – Yes. Well, as I say, thank you and – er – Mr Manningtree.' He stopped then and looked up at Robin and his face creased a little, losing its mask-like intensity. 'I'm truly sorry you've had such a difficult time with him. What? Oh, yes. Oliver has never lacked charm, whatever else might be less than – well, anyway, thank you. Good night.'

Slowly he hung up the phone and now Robin did move, a little stiffly, coming into the hall, and pushing the front door closed behind her.

'Sam?' She was hoarse, which seemed to her suddenly to be very odd. 'Sam, what is it?'

He turned on the stool and looked up at her, and then began, very slowly to smile. It was an odd smile, stretched and painful rather than mirthful, and he shook his head at her and said, 'You'd better sit down for this one, Robin. The thing is – '

He got up and took her elbow and half led, half pushed her to the telephone stool, and she gave at the knees and thumped down on it, staring up at him.

'The thing is, darling, he's made a girl who works in the school pregnant. And the Head feels he can't keep a pupil who's an expectant father. So he's coming home for good.'

13

They sat in different corners of the room, exhausted, pale and silent. Robin felt strangely dreamy, as though she weren't there at all; as if she were really somewhere else, outside in the dark road perhaps, and peering in through the window to look at everyone and guess how they were feeling. She certainly didn't know how she felt herself; there had been too much feeling altogether this evening. Now she was aware only of a deep fatigue, and it was almost comforting after all the emotion that had gone before.

Sam sat up suddenly then and got to his feet and at once the Robin who had been outside peering in through the window vanished and Robin in her armchair sat up sharply too as the sick miserable hopelessness flooded back into her.

'We'll get nowhere sitting here like this at this time of the morning,' Sam said harshly. 'It's gone two, and I have to work tomorrow. So has your mother. Go to bed. We'll sort the rest of it out another time. Tomorrow – '

'As long as you know I'm never going to a school again,' Oliver said, not moving from his place. 'Not ever. Nor to university or any place full of lousy teachers – ' He sounded sullen and miserable, but there was energy in him still and Robin felt the strength of it and that made her feel even more tired. I must be getting older faster than I thought, she told herself muzzily and rubbed her eyes, trying to concentrate on what Sam was saying.

'If you're adamant, you're adamant,' he said. 'I think it's a waste, a wicked waste, but if you're sure – '

'I'm sure,' Oliver said. 'I'm bloody sure.'

'Swearing doesn't prove you're an adult,' Sam said. 'Just that you're a rather childish person with a limited vocabulary.'

Oliver flushed patchily and flicked a glance at his mother. 'Sorry, Ma, but really – '

'Swearing's the least of my problems,' Robin said. 'It's what you're going to do with your life that matters to me.'

'Well, for pity's sake!' Now Oliver did move, getting to his feet in one tight little movement. 'I'm only just seventeen – hardly over the hill, you know. I could do all sorts of things, make my fortune a dozen ways – '

'Is that what you want? To make a fortune?' Sam said and his voice was full of distaste.

'Why not? I know you despise money, you think that being noble and compassionate and all that stuff is all that matters, but I see no harm in wanting to be rich and have fun and live a little.'

'You've done a fair bit of living already for someone your age,' Sam said dryly and Oliver flushed again, but this time it was with pride.

'I grew up a long time ago,' he said with a triumphant note. 'Stopped being a kid years back – you didn't notice.'

'Is it being grown up to get a girl pregnant and leave her in the lurch?' Sam said.

'It's as much her fault as it is mine!' Oliver cried. 'I keep telling you that! She wanted to do it as much as I did – went on and on about how we'd – well, she wanted to get married. I told her I couldn't, didn't have any prospects or anything like that, but she went on and on. Probably thought I'd *have* to marry her if she got pregnant, though I told her it wasn't on – '

'What are you going to do about her?' Robin said.

Oliver looked sullen again. 'I dunno. It was as much her fault as mine.' And now he looked every inch the sulky schoolboy he denied being. 'What can I do?'

'Do you love her?' Robin asked and he lifted his head and stared at her, aghast.

'Here, Ma, do me a favour! Just because we – well, yes, we did it, but that doesn't mean I – I *fancied* her, of course I did, but if you mean do I want to be with her all the time, no I don't. Ever since this happened she's done nothing but moan at me. It was her who shopped me to old Manningtree. Anyway, no. I don't love her.'

'That doesn't alter the fact that you've got a responsibility,' Sam said and Oliver shrugged.

'It's a long time till I have to worry about that. And by then I'll have a job and some money.'

'Oh?' Sam cocked his head at him and suddenly stifled a yawn. He looked grey with fatigue, and Robin for a moment could have slapped Oliver for having that effect on him. 'What sort of a job?'

'I'll think of something,' Oliver said with sublime confidence. 'There's a million jobs you can get. You'll see. Listen, let's go to bed, hey? You look awful.'

'I feel awful,' Sam said. 'And however hard you wriggle, you can't get out of the responsibility for *that*.'

'No,' Oliver said and flicked a glance at Robin. 'I'm sorry, honestly I am, that you're both upset. And I suppose it has been rotten for both of you. But I didn't mean it, and anyway, you never listened to what I wanted, just told me I had to do what you thought best, and – '

He stopped then as he saw the anger gathering again on Sam's face and said hurriedly, 'I'll sort out Tracey, you see if I don't. And the good thing is that at least I've persuaded you to let me get out of that lousy school. I'm just not right there.'

'You've won that much,' Sam said. 'I can't deny that.'

'And tomorrow – or in a day or two – I'll go and get myself a job – '

'And I'll see to that,' Robin said and started for the door, her legs dragging heavily as she went. 'God knows what you'd finish up doing if I left it to you. You can join the training scheme Ma's got at the Bittacy Hotel. There are worse careers – Sam?'

'I suppose so,' Sam said and he too made for the door. 'But this isn't the time to decide. Tomorrow. Go to bed, Oliver – '

'Absolutely!' Oliver said joyously and was gone in a matter of seconds.

They stood in the hall after he'd run up the stairs and listened to him whistling in his room as he undressed, and Sam shook his head.

'I don't think the Bittacy is a very good idea,' he said. 'He needs a tougher job, with better supervision. In a hotel he can get away with all sorts of things – '

'You make him sound like some sort of criminal!' Robin was on the defensive at once. 'He doesn't have to be watched all the time, for heaven's sake!'

'Doesn't he?' Sam asked quietly. 'I know he's not a criminal, but he can be criminally irresponsible, and that can be dangerous. I'd rather take him to the Clinic and make him work with us here for a while. It can be hard work and it could be an eye-opener for him.'

'No,' Robin said and started to climb the stairs. 'No. What sort of future would he have there? He's not going to medical school now, obviously, and that means in hospital work he'd never be more than an attendant, a glorified porter. At least in the hotel business there are possibilities for him. A career, even.'

Sam followed her into their bedroom, and said nothing but after they'd undressed and were in bed and about to switch off the light he said in a low voice, 'Robin, can we at least be friends again? I'm sorry about this morning.'

She lay down, turning her back to him, and stared at the dimness of the window, a dark square in a darker wall.

'Nothing to be sorry for,' she said after a long moment and then sighed deeply, a long shuddering breath that she hoped he hadn't noticed. 'Anyway, what does that matter now? We've got real problems to think about now.'

She didn't notice the way Sam winced. She just closed her eyes and fell into the deepest sleep she'd ever known.

'I don't know what I'd have done without the shop this past two weeks,' Robin said and Chick nodded in agreement.

'Work's the most therapeutic thing I know. I'd have gone completely out of my mind if Sam's Clinic hadn't come up.'

Robin glanced at her and then suddenly and somewhat to her surprise was embarrassed, and looked away. 'Are you still enjoying it?'

'Oh yes,' Chick said and went faintly red herself. 'Oh yes.'

'That's all right then.' Robin lapsed into silence, looking down into her coffee cup, and Chick sat and watched her and felt the guilt spread and burn into her.

It was hell sitting here listening to Robin pouring out all her misery about Oliver; not because she didn't commiserate with and even share some of her distress, but because she'd had to do the same for Sam. And he had asked her not to tell Robin they'd talked.

'She's got enough to worry about as it is,' he'd said. 'She might feel I was – oh, I don't know. Disloyal perhaps to discuss it with

117

you, even though you're family and so close. I didn't mean to drag you into it, but you're so easy to talk to – '

And now Robin had said much the same thing. She had turned up at Chick's back door this morning, on one of Chick's precious days off from the Clinic, to invite herself in for coffee, and had blurted it all out. Her fears for Oliver, her anger at Sam who was being so stupid about what the boy ought to do now and then had begged her not to tell Sam they'd talked, 'Because it'd only upset him to know I was worried so much,' she'd said. 'Keep it between us.'

I'm between a rock and a hard place, Chick thought wryly and wanted to laugh. It was all so silly; after all these years to be almost presiding over the split between her oldest friends at the same time as discovering she had a personal reason for perhaps being glad to see them split –

But I don't, she thought then. It's the last thing I'd want. I can't imagine Robin and Sam parting, however hard things are for them at the moment, and how much they're fighting over Oliver. Young wretch. If he were mine he wouldn't behave so –

She got to her feet and went over to the cooker to pick up the percolator, moving a little convulsively, needing to change the pattern of her thinking, fast.

'More coffee?'

'If I drink much more I'll twitch like a rabbit's nose,' Robin said and tried to smile. But it was a sharp little grimace with no humour in it. 'I'm sorry to put this burden on you, Chick. You've got enough problems of your own.'

'Haven't we all?' Chick tried to sound light. 'Anyway, what are friends for?'

'Not for making your life a misery.' Robin sat up and made a visible effort to cheer up. 'How are things anyway? I haven't asked, selfish object that I am. Are the kids well?'

'Couldn't be better. Hal's loving it at Bristol – ' She stopped then and made a face, screwing up her eyes. 'Oh, goddammit, I forgot. I'm sorry.'

'Don't apologize because your son's happy at University, for pity's sake! I couldn't bear that – I'm delighted to hear it. It's not easy the first term, they tell me. He's definitely reading English?'

'Mm. Got himself very involved with all sorts of things already, though, apart from the degree course, I mean. The music group, and the newspaper and debating, all sorts.'

'Good for him. I sometimes wish I'd been able to go to University – '

'I don't,' Chick said firmly. 'A hospital training was the best possible thing for me. I've no regret at all – and you're daft if you overvalue a degree. There's more to success than having letters after your name.'

'Stop trying to comfort me,' Robin said. 'It doesn't help – '

'But it's true! I'm not just being comforting. I think you've fallen into the trap of thinking you've got the right to plan your children's lives for them. You – and Sam – had ambitions to see Oliver at University and you're devastated because he just isn't academic. But he has other gifts and he'll do well in the hotel business, with all his charm, and he loves being with people. My Hal, who's a bit dour and loves to spend all his time with his nose in a book, was born to be an academic – so he's gone down that road. But it isn't a better road. Just a different one – '

'Oh, Chick, I do love you!' Robin said and jumped up and came round the kitchen table to hug her warmly and Chick hugged her back and just for a moment it was like the old days when they'd been girls together, sharing the complexities of nursing life at the London Hospital.

But only for a second. Robin sat down again and slid into a brown study, still staring into her coffee cup, and Chick looked at her with her lower lip caught between her teeth and thought.

'I've got an idea,' she said at length. 'Hear me out before you argue. I'll get Suzy to have a party. She'll ask the crowd of people she goes around with – they're a really good bunch. You'd like them. Then Oliver'll get some new friends to replace the people he knew at school and who mightn't have been good for him.'

Robin smiled a little wanly. 'Darling, you're sweet, but I'm not stupid. If anyone was in bad company it was the boys who got involved with our Oliver. He's always been the ringleader, according to Mr Manningtree. But it's a kind thought – '

'It's a practical one,' Chick said strongly. 'That's what matters. I'll fix it up with Suzy.'

'You said your lot don't really like ours – ' Robin said and Chick shook her head.

'Getting ratty with each other over details the way people do when they've known each other since infancy is one thing – actually disliking them and not caring is quite another, I promise you. Suzy and Charlie care a lot about your Oliver, even if he gets on their nerves sometimes. I can't speak for Hal,' she added honestly. 'He's such a dreamer I never know who he cares about, to tell you the truth. I think he cares about them but I can't even be sure of that.'

'He cares,' Robin said very definitely. 'You needn't doubt that. I've known him all his life, too, remember, and I know.'

'Well, yes, I suppose so.' Chick grinned. 'It was just a figure of speech, if you know what I mean. Anyway, I'll fix it up with Suzy.'

'It won't sort out the problem of this girl and her baby,' Robin burst out. 'It makes life easier for Oliver, sure, to have new friends, just as I've made it a lot easier for him by getting him a job in one of Ma's hotels. That's what Sam complains about. He says he's got to take responsibility for this girl and the child. His child – ' Her voice trailed away and she looked miserably at Chick. 'It's that that's driving me potty, Chick. How on earth can he be a father? He's the most childish person for his age I can think of. Your Hal and Suzy are – oh, streets ahead in common sense. He's got the charm and the looks and the style of an adult, I know that. I may be his mother but I'm neither blind nor stupid. But I know that he'll be hopeless taking on a wife and a child – '

'He doesn't have to marry her to be responsible,' Chick said. 'If he makes sure he hands over a set sum of the money he earns towards the baby's keep and visits a lot and – '

Robin shook her head. 'There's more to it than that, Chick. You know there is – '

They lapsed into silence and sat for a long time thinking their own thoughts and then, as a door somewhere in the house above them opened and the sound of radio music came out, Robin moved and looked at her watch.

'Ye Gods, look at the time – I must fly – they'll be wondering where I am. And I want to do the shop's books this afternoon anyway. Chick, thank you for letting me bend your ear, and – ' She hesitated. 'I don't have to say it again, do I? About not saying anything to – '

'No,' Chick said firmly. 'You don't. Go home. Stop driving yourself mad. It'll sort itself out somehow. These things usually do.'

★

Chick's phone rang the following morning at half past seven, as she was rushing around the kitchen sorting out the evening's supper plans with Mrs Chapman, her daily, and she cursed. She had to be at the Clinic by eight and the traffic these mornings was no joke. She almost didn't answer it, but the ringing was too insistent to ignore.

'Chick?' Robin sounded ecstatic, her voice lilting and bright, and Chick's brows rose. 'It's incredible – you were quite right!'

'I was?' Chick was cautious. 'What about?'

'You said these things sorted themselves out, didn't you? Well they have!'

'Darling, I'm a bit pushed for time – can we talk this evening?' Chick's heart had sunk. The last thing she wanted to do now was get into further discussions with Robin about her errant son. But Robin was oblivious.

'It's unbelievable. I'm so relieved. The girl phoned Oliver this morning at six o'clock! Sam wasn't best pleased – he thought it was some sort of Clinic emergency – but it was the girl, Tracey. Dear Chick, she's miscarried! Isn't it wonderful?'

Chick stared down at the phone in her hand and thought for a while. And then said it because she felt she had to.

'I find it hard to celebrate a death, even one as early in life as a miscarriage,' she said. 'Even if it does get Oliver out of a pickle.'

There was a sharp silence at the other end of the phone and then Robin said in a changed voice, 'Oh, I suppose – I hadn't thought about that. I mean, I was just so relieved for Oliver and he was – well, incandescent with delight.'

'I hope he didn't show that to Tracey,' Chick said and her voice was caustic. 'It may suit her too, of course – we can't know. But miscarrying is no fun. It happened to me once, remember. I do know what it feels like.'

'Yes,' Robin said and her thin disembodied voice had lost all its sparkle. 'I'd forgotten. Oh, Chick, I'm so sorry. You see how I've changed? I'd never have been so – well, like that, once – '

Well, I can understand it,' Chick said, her anger beginning to ooze away. 'It's been horrid for you all. At least now – well, there it is. Now it's up to you to make sure Oliver behaves better in future.'

'By God, he will,' Robin said strongly. 'You see if he doesn't!

I'll – I don't know what I'll do, but believe me, he'll change. He has to.'

'Yes,' Chick said. 'He has to. I must go, Robin – forgive me.'

'Of course,' Robin said and hung up the phone and Chick replaced her own and stood there staring at the blank wall above it for a long moment. She'd had her Harry to help her when she'd miscarried, Harry to hold her close as she wept her disappointment and her grief onto his chest, and what had this unknown girl in Sussex had? Just a jubilant boy at the end of the phone. She'd called him as soon as it happened, obviously, almost certainly needing comfort and love and concern, and what had she got?

For a moment Chick hated Oliver. Hated him as she'd never hated anyone before. It was a painful feeling.

14

The year turned mildly, with green in the parks instead of last year's prolonged snow banks, and Poppy's New Year's Eve party, to which as usual every member of the family came, should have been a cheerful one. After all, things were going well for the clan. It was true that they had lost Mildred, but she had been ailing as well as old and there was still Auntie Jessie who, as was usual for this event, was carefully bundled into rugs and carried tenderly to David's car by both Lally and Barbara, and fetched to the party to be among them all, albeit often falling asleep. And there were other good things too; Hal was doing well at University, and Suzy, who was working hard in her last year at school, looked all set to follow him, while Robin's Sophie and Penny were flying as high as kites at their school. Robin's shop was thriving, as was Sam's Clinic, and Lee's agency and 'Food by Poppy' had made record profits. 'We should all,' said David a little sententiously when he proposed the usual toast to the New Year, nineteen sixty-four, 'be as happy as kings.'

But there was an unease among them, and it was Josh who gave it voice.

'You're all sitting here looking like the world's come to an end instead of just the old year,' he said. 'I know it was a pretty cruddy year in some ways – people shooting American presidents and scandals in Parliament and millions stolen from trains and so forth – but we're all alive and well and you can't ask for more.'

'Can't you?' Oliver muttered sotto voce in the corner and was rewarded with a sharp glare from his father.

'It's tiredness, I think,' Poppy said, trying to be lively and not succeeding too well. 'You have to admit it's been a hectic year. For you too – '

123

'Oh, I've been busy enough,' Josh admitted. 'Two scores to write in one year – it's a lot.'

'I'll bet they'll be smashing when they're launched!' Caro said from her place on the sofa between Gillian and her father and beamed at Josh and he nodded his agreement. Richard was looking flushed and a touch glazed, and Poppy had already made a private mental note to see to it that his next drink was more diluted than he usually had it.

' 'Course it will! Smashing! Be great to have a famous musician in the family, won't it?'

David raised his brows at Poppy across the room, and Poppy shook her head imperceptibly at him. As though they'd spoken aloud, they'd conversed, and both knew it. David's glance had asked Poppy where Melhuish thought he got off making statements about his, David's, family when he wasn't even a member and had talked himself into attending this New Year's Eve party with his own small household, and Poppy had reassured him that the man meant no harm, he was a bit drunk and anyway it was the time of year to be kind to people, especially business partners, and the Melhuishes only had each other, a small family compared with the lucky Deveen lot –

'He's already famous,' Caro said and dimpled at Josh. 'Aren't you, my duck? Really well known by all the people who matter.'

'Oh, and who would they be?' her father asked owlishly as Caro laughed and rumpled his already untidy hair – what there was of it – with a rough hand.

'Oh, the trendy ones, the really fashionable people. At "La Poubelle" in Great Marlborough Street and at Humph's and all those super clubs in Soho – when we go there it's like he's holding court!'

Josh looked a little flummoxed and shook his head in some irritation. 'Shut up, Caro. You can exaggerate better than anyone I know. Or worse, rather – '

'Well, it's true, darling!' she protested and flashed a bright glance round the room. 'Honestly, it is!'

Someone put on a record and Lee and Jeremy began to dance and then Hal pulled his mother to her feet and made her join in, and soon several couples were milling around in the available space in the middle of Poppy's drawing-room and David watched for a while and then strolled round the edge of the room to stand beside Poppy and murmur in her ear, 'She's getting a bit proprietorial, isn't she?'

'Hmm? Who?' Poppy said.

'Miss Melhuish,' David said and there was a hint of distaste in his voice. 'I wish I really liked her. She's so – oh, I don't know. Makes me think of an egg after someone's blown out the insides, know what I mean?'

'Horrid! Don't be so unkind. She's a nice child. Not the world's brightest but sweet enough and she's been very good for Josh. Taken him out of himself. He used to sit at home all the time he wasn't working. Now, according to Gillian, they're out all over the place, night after night.'

'Hmm. I wonder whose idea that is?'

'Does it matter?'

'I suppose as long as he doesn't get himself embroiled in something he can't handle – '

'David, for heaven's sake! He's not a baby. Josh is very much his own man. He can look after himself.'

'In which case, why do you fuss over him so? It was you who persuaded him to see this girl in the first place,' David said a little triumphantly, looking at her over the top of his glasses, and Poppy reddened.

'David, you're being most unfair!'

'No, I'm not. You do and you did. Deny it if you can.'

'Oh, pooh!' she said and laughed up at him. 'Why do I take you seriously? You'd think after all this time I'd know when you were teasing. Do stop, darling – or better still, go and put on another record. That one's nearly finished and they'll want to go on dancing.'

He went, grinning at her cheerfully, but he hadn't been teasing entirely and both of them knew it. But he said no more. There seemed little point. But he did watch Josh as Caro dragged him to his feet and insisted he dance with her; Josh laughed and protested but she was adamant and he tried to follow her steps but with small success. Excellent musician though he was, he had never really learned to dance and was thoroughly awkward on the floor; but it didn't matter because they laughed a lot as did the other dancers who were accidentally kicked by them when they got in the way. But at least their antics lifted the mood and the party came to an end at around one thirty with everyone seeming happy enough with the prospect of the year to come.

The Melhuishes were the last to leave with Gillian, murmuring a little distractedly a mixture of apologies and explanations, leading Richard to their car and insisting on taking the car keys from him; and Josh, in his usual good-natured way, seeing how anxious she was, said, 'Not to worry, Gillian, I'll drive you home. I can get a taxi back to my place – come on.' And he bundled them into Richard's car – and he promptly fell asleep against his wife's shoulder – as Caro climbed into the front seat beside Josh.

'This is super!' she said below the sound of the engine as he put his foot down on the Bayswater Road heading west for Shepherd's Bush, where he would turn north to go towards Stanmore. 'Then we can go out afterwards – it's so *boring* to go to bed at two o'clock on New Year's Day. I fully intend to be up all night – '

'Do you indeed?' Josh said and settled down to enjoy the drive. He liked good cars, and Melhuish's Jaguar was a very good one. Maybe now he had a little money to call his own he'd buy one? It was an agreeable thought. 'I hope you enjoy yourself.'

'Oh, you will too,' she said severely, snuggling down into the fur collar of her white coat. 'You'll see.'

'Who said I'm going to agree to go out again with you?'

'Oh, you wouldn't be such a bore as to refuse, would you? Have a heart, Josh – it's New Year – you don't expect me to go to bed like a good little girl, do you? Daddy and Gillian won't mind – he's too smashed to notice and she's in too much of a flap to give a damn what I do anyway. So say yes. Or at least take me up to town so that I can have fun – '

'Oh, I see,' Josh said. 'And how are you supposed to get home again?'

'In the car, of course. You drive it like an angel – you know you'd love to go back to town and then drive it back. I can tell –'

And she was right. There was something very enjoyable about driving the big purring engine and he took a deep breath and inhaled the smell of leather upholstery and the faint scent of the cigars Richard had smoked in the past and capitulated. To start the New Year driving around in a top-rate Jaguar had a lot going for it.

He helped Gillian lead Richard upstairs and offerd to help undress him but she was firm about that. 'No need,' she said and closed the bedroom door in his face. 'I can manage – ' and didn't respond when Caro called, 'We're going out again and taking the car, Gillian – see you in the morning!'

'You see?' Caro said joyously to Josh and seized his arm. 'No one gives a damn what we do! So let's leg it back to town and see what's going on! I've got membership cards to a couple of the clubs – I'll sort 'em out in the car – Do come on!'

And Josh sighed and came on. It would be agreeable to drive that car and there was no harm in giving this silly child what she wanted. And Josh grinned inside his head at himself. If I get any more avuncular, he thought, white whiskers will sprout on my chin and children from miles around will gather at my ancient knees to be told stories –

The clubs of course were full and they were turned away from three before Caro struck gold in a rather dark little jazz cellar in Greek Street, not far down from Shaftesbury Avenue. It was called 'Hang About A Bit', a title that was spelled out in rather battered lights outside and the noise that was coming from it seemed to Josh to be tolerable. Someone down there blows a good clarinet, he thought, and followed Caro into the depths.

It was as smoky and dark as he'd expected but the music at close quarters was even better than he'd hoped and he sat there happily enough listening as Caro sat beside him chattering about the other people there and jigging in time to the music. She'd given up asking him to dance. He was very firm on that point, so she had to.

'Caro, my little duck, it's one thing to dance at my Mama's party, quite another to do it in public. I have three left feet and there's an end of it. Look about you, catch some likely chap's eye and dance with him. I'll rescue you if he gets objectionable.'

'Oh, it'd be all right if you danced. No one would watch,' Caro said and she pouted prettily, but it made no difference.

'Learn, girl,' he said equably, but there was steel in his voice. 'I said no, and when I say no, it's precisely what I mean, believe it or not.'

She took him at his word at last when a dark and rather thin boy in tight black trousers and a cropped Edwardian-style jacket, with his hair slicked back into a fashionable DA cut, came and jerked his head at them and then at the floor; Josh nodded amiably and she got up and began to dance.

Josh watched her for a while and saw she was blissfully happy;

the boy might not be much of a conversationalist – as far as Josh could see, he hadn't opened his mouth at all – but he danced well, moving his body sinuously and giving Caro plenty of opportunity to enjoy showing off in her own right, and Josh relaxed and turned his attention back to the band on the minute stand in the corner.

He could see more easily now, as his eyes had become accustomed to the dark, and he picked out the people who were playing. As well as the clarinettist there was a pianist, a drummer and a double bass, and the sound they were making was really excellent, and after a while Josh got to his feet and moved closer to them, feeling the itch to join in. He didn't have his trumpet with him, dammit, and no one would lend him one, even if he wanted to play a strange instrument, but the itch got stronger, and soon he was leaning against the wall, very close to the musicians, watching their every move.

The boy on the drums was tall and blond and had a thick sheet of hair drooping over his forehead and into his eyes, and every so often he flicked his head back and the hair fell into place on his scalp, but within seconds it had fallen down again and needed the flick once more. Josh watched, amused, almost mesmerized and suddenly realized that the drummer was aware of his scrutiny and was staring back at him.

Josh caught his eye, and the boy winked and lifted one eyebrow and after a moment Josh lifted his own and then almost shrank back against the wall. He shouldn't have done that. It wasn't right. Adrian might be dead but it wasn't right, and he turned abruptly and went back to the table in the corner where he'd been sitting and fixed his regard on Caro.

After a while the band ended their set and announced a break and disappeared and then the club's host appeared on the small stage and offered the customers records to fill the band's meal time and people shouted their choice – and Caro's voice was loud among them – and soon the inevitable Beatles record began and Josh leaned his head back against the wall and closed his eyes. Another ten minutes or so and he'd tell Caro it was time to go, and he'd take her home. It was past three thirty, after all. She couldn't really expect him to stay up all night.

'Hello,' a voice said above his head and his eyes snapped open. The drummer was standing there, his hands in his jeans pockets, and smiling down at him.

'Oh,' Josh said. 'Er – hello – '

'I saw you listening to us.' The boy slid into the chair alongside Josh and smiled even more widely. 'It's a pleasure to play when you can see someone listening who really understands. You like jazz, don't you?'

'I love it,' Josh said fervently and tried not to look at the boy. Adrian, he was thinking. Adrian.

'You can always tell.' The boy sounded very satisfied. 'Can I buy you a drink?'

'I have one,' Josh said and then looked over the dance floor to where Caro was happily leaping about to the best of the Beatles. 'We both have.'

'Both?'

'That girl there. She's with me.' He sounded a little desperate in his own ears, and tried to look relaxed and calm.

The boy laughed, and shook his head. 'Well, maybe she is, in a way. But not really, is she?'

'How do you mean, not really?'

'Oh, come on, love. I'm not as daft as I look! You're not dancing with her are you? Left it to old Gary there.'

'Gary – '

'Comes here most nights. Mad on dancing. Hates girls, but it's so hard to dance with fellas, isn't it? Unless the place is closed to the public and that's not often. I mean, Stan keeps open as long as there's a punter ready to spend so much as fourpence ha'penny on a lemonade. So Gary comes and finds a girl to dance with – these days it's so individual, isn't it? Dancing?' He cocked his head to the dance floor again. Josh looked and of course knew the boy was right. Gary was weaving in and out, his eyes half closed, his feet moving in an intricate series of steps, and Caro, equally self absorbed, was weaving her own pattern into his. They were dancing apart, ostensibly together but each locked in their own rhythm.

'So there you are. How about that drink then?'

'I don't think so,' Josh said and was furious with himself, because his voice was cracking and the drummer laughed softly.

'Oh, you will, I reckon – Stan! Send someone over with a – what's that you're drinking? Gin?'

Josh shook his head. 'Just tonic water, straight.'

'Wise man. Getting smashed does nothing for your love life,

does it? We'll both have tonics, Stan.' And he leaned back and rested his head against the wall, but turned sideways so that he could contemplate Josh's face more easily. 'My name's Gregory. You can call me Greg.'

'How do you do,' Josh said stiffly and Gregory chuckled.

'Oooh, we are stiff and starchy! Come on, love. Call me Greg! What's your name?'

Josh took a deep breath. What he ought to do was get up and go and get Caro and make her leave with him. He sat and thought about that, seeing himself doing it, pushing the table back, ignoring the boy, walking over to Caro, saying the words –

The drinks arrived and he reached for his without thinking and swallowed half of it.

'My name's Josh,' he said. 'Silly, isn't it?'

They went on talking after that, laughing a lot and Caro, still dancing dreamily in the middle of the room, looked at him once or twice and was pleased. She was dancing, Josh had someone to talk to so she could go on dancing. Lovely –

The records ended and Greg went back to the band, and the band back to the little stage and played till four thirty and by then even Caro was wilting. The place was still fairly full, but there were empty spaces at the tables now and the atmosphere was so thick with smoke that it had become darker than ever as the few reddish tinted lights were blanked out, and she yawned hugely.

'Ready for home?' Josh said and got to his feet and she nodded drowsily.

'I suppose so. It was fun though. He's a great dancer, that chap – but do you know what? He never said a single word to me – Isn't that funny?'

'Hilarious,' Josh said and helped her into her coat. She looked fragile and rather touching, with her rumpled hair and her smudged make-up, peering at him over her fur collar, and he pinched her cheek affectionately.

'Come on, baby face,' he said good-naturedly. 'Time I saw you home.'

They were half-way to the door when the music stopped for a rest, and there was a small buzz of talk, and Caro decided to stop at the ladies' before the drive home. He stood there waiting for her, and knew perfectly well what was going to happen. It was inevitable, something that was beyond his control now, and why not? He thought again of Adrian but it was all right this time. He wouldn't be upset, Josh was certain of it. Not now, not after so long.

The drummer was beside him then, and pushed a piece of card into his hand. 'That's the number. Do call me when you're coming here again,' he said. 'Or you can come over to see me. It doesn't make a lot of difference, does it?'

'No,' Josh said and looked at the card. 'No, not a lot.' And then as Caro came back and tucked her hand into his arm, he looked directly at Greg and smiled. 'Goodbye. Thank you for some great music.'

'Our pleasure,' Greg said. 'And have a great New Year, you hear me? It's fun isn't it, not knowing how 'sixty-four'll be? Who you'll meet, where you'll go, how you'll end up.'

'Yes,' Josh said. 'Funny. Good night. And a – er – Happy New Year to you too.'

And he took Caro home, and was glad she slept all the way.

15

'Listen, Poppy. I know he's your grandson and that has to have an effect on the way you think. But he isn't mine and as far as I'm concerned this is just another kid looking for a job. And I have to know, is he reliable? Is he the sort of young man we needn't be ashamed of turning out of our training scheme?'

'And you can listen to me, Richard.' Poppy's colour was a little high, but she was proud of the control she was keeping over her voice and her temper. What she would have liked to tell him as witheringly as she could was that 'Food by Poppy' was her business, her baby, a major operator in its field that wouldn't exist if it hadn't been for her efforts, and that being so, she had every right to employ anyone she chose, including her scapegrace grandson.

But she didn't say it; that wasn't the way to keep the business sailing steadily forward as it had done for the past ten years or more. Richard was an important part of it, so she had to be circumspect. But her anger sharpened her voice and Richard couldn't help but be aware of it.

'You listen to me. I'm not suggesting we take Oliver out of pity as a bolthole. I can assure you that if he shows the least sign of being anything but an asset to us, out he goes. I want him because I truly think this could be his metier, and therefore good for us. He mayn't be as academic as his parents want him to be, but he's energetic, good with people and has a lively intelligence. With the good training of the sort Corbett will give him at the Bittacy, he could turn out to be more than a credit to us –'

Richard sighed and got to his feet to come round his desk and stand at the window looking down into the yard where the day's vans were being loaded.

'Let him start here then, if you're so keen to have him. I'll be able to keep an eye on him and so will you and then if he shows he can take the sort of pressure there is here, we can move him on.'

'I thought of that, but it isn't the right way. Not for him. He'll be bored too soon. That's been half his problem at that wretched school he was at – boredom. No one ever expected enough of him. The boys called the teachers by their first names, for heaven's sake! That's why I want him at the Bittacy, well away from me. Corbett'll give him a hard time but he won't be bored – and he certainly won't call his elders and betters by their first names. Here it wouldn't be so clear cut – '

Richard's shoulders had tightened as the argument had gone on, but now he seemed to relax and turned to look at her, his face showing nothing but bonhomie and not a hint of the irritation she was sure was there. He's getting more and more difficult to deal with, a corner of her mind complained. Trying to bully her, wanting to get his own way all the time. She shouldn't have to fight him so hard on so minor a matter, dammit. She'd never objected when he'd wanted to bring friends of his own on to the Board; why should she have this sort of opposition when all she wanted to do was to put her grandson in at just about the lowest level of their business, as a mere clerk and learner? She'd have to do something definite about Richard soon, she feared. Not yet, not yet; there was too much else to deal with to think of the upheaval involved in trying to uproot a Chairman of the Board. But it would have to be considered –

'Well, let's not squabble over him,' Richard said and smiled winningly. 'It's only a clerkship, after all, I suppose. It's just that I take every detail of the business so seriously – '

'Don't you think I do?' Poppy said with what could have been a dangerous calm and he seemed to recognize it, and laughed a little too loudly, a little too eagerly.

'Of course you do, I know that. I suppose I was just fussing – no more. Oliver can join the Bittacy team, and welcome. And I'm sure he'll do well there. Do you want him to live in like some of the others? I imagine Corbett could find space.'

Poppy considered that. 'I'll talk to his parents, but no, I don't think so. It'd be too easy for him to whoop it up – not enough supervision of his private time. He's been living well away from

London all through his school years, and it could be tempting. Better to be where his parents can keep an eye on him.'

'Well, it's up to you,' Richard said. 'Though unless he gets extra cash from home – '

'Which he won't,' Poppy said swiftly.

' – he won't be able to afford to do much whooping up anyway.'

'Then that'll be another safeguard,' Poppy finished crisply. 'I'll see to it that his parents keep him on a tight financial rein. Believe me, this time next year you'll apologize to me for your doubts. He'll do well.' I hope, I hope, I hope, whispered her secret voice and she spoke more loudly to overwhelm it. 'He'll do very well indeed.'

'I'm sure,' Richard said and smiled again, and went back to his desk. 'Now, those accounts from the wholesale department – '

The Bittacy, decided Oliver, could be a lot worse. There were drawbacks, of course. It wasn't in the West End, where the real action was found, but in Chelsea which, though the area was improving as far as street life was concerned, still remained at heart a rather stuffy area, which meant that the guests were not exactly the most glamorous of people. Most of them were in fact dreary to an incredible degree; old women who'd lived there on half board for ages, keeping little kettles and teapots hidden in their bedside tables even though they weren't supposed to use bedrooms for any form of cooking; country people up for a few days' shopping and theatre going; occasional foreigners on a tour of the country, starting in London; but each of them were of value to him.

Half the fun of working at the Bittacy was putting one over on old Corbett, the manager who thought himself so clever and so sharp; but Oliver was sharper than he was and made good use of the fact. The little old ladies learned to send him to fetch the milk, sugar and biscuits they wanted and paid him handsome (to their minds) tips for his quietness on the matter and though the tips were in fact little more than average, to Oliver they came to constitute useful income, for there were enough little old ladies to provide a most useful sum between them.

The country people, he discovered, could be successfully

milked by the provision of theatre tickets for shows which, Oliver would assure them with wide-eyed honesty, were frightfully difficult to get hold of and for which they therefore gladly paid him extra, though how they felt when they reached the theatres and found several rows of seats empty, Oliver prudently didn't wait around to find out, always keeping well out of the way of the guests he had served until they checked out.

As for the foreigners – well, he soon found how to make himself useful to them. Some of them wanted to find exciting nightclubs and others wanted more direct personal services, and Oliver very quickly learned how to collect the information and the introductions they wanted. Altogether, he told himself contentedly, it wasn't a bad life, being an all-purpose assistant at the Bittacy. Wherever he was around the place, there was always an easy alibi he could trot out about having been somewhere else and busy there, and even Corbett, with his otherwise eagle eye, could be fooled by someone as clever as Oliver was. And Oliver knew himself to be very clever.

Until he almost came a cropper. He had perhaps been too successful. Certainly he had been lulled into carelessness.

He had settled in comfortably at home, telling his parents he was working on those evenings he chose to be somewhere else, and they never doubted him. There was no reason why they should: they knew that he would work different patterns of hours at the Bittacy; a hotel, after all, is a twenty-four-hour operation, and they had been told firmly by Poppy that Oliver would be expected to do his share of disagreeable jobs, including being night porter from time to time. Oliver had found, of course, that being night porter suited him very well indeed. There was rarely a great deal to do that constituted real work, but plenty of opportunity to earn extra by allowing into the hotel people whom old Corbett would have regarded with horror. Pretty and highly dubious girls who turned up to visit out-of-town men in their rooms were not at all what Mr Corbett would regard as persona grata, but Oliver found them very profitable indeed. So, he worked a large number of nights all through March and April, and then relaxed a little. He wanted to do a certain amount of night living on his own account. To have evenings off became desirable, so he arranged to have them. But he didn't tell his parents. They, out all day themselves, had no way of knowing whether he was in bed and asleep at home during the day as he assured them innocently he was, when in fact he was working. Then, come the evening, and his free time, he could change into the trendy clothes he had bought, and kept judiciously hidden at the Bittacy, and take himself off to some of his private and much more interesting times in Soho and the West End, without their questioning his absence. It all went, he told himself gleefully, as merrily as a marriage bell. Until the evening Chick tried to be kind to him.

She hadn't forgotten her promise to Robin to arrange for her own Suzy and Hal to take care of Oliver, to help him find new friends in London, but Hal flatly refused to oblige her and because of Suzy's own busy diary and – Chick couldn't deny – general unwillingness to get involved more with Oliver than she had to (Suzy had always found him an irritating person) it wasn't until early May that she could be persuaded to make an effort for Oliver.

'Oh, Mum, all right,' she said at length, exasperated and too weary to argue further. 'I'll go round and talk to him. But if he tries any of his nonsense, showing off the way he used to, don't expect me to do anything about introducing him to my friends. I'd be too embarrassed.'

'At least give him a chance,' Chick said, thinking of how anxious Sam always looked when she asked after Oliver's welfare. 'For your aunt and uncle if not for him.'

'I'm doing it for you, sweetie,' Suzy retorted and then hugged her. 'You get more mother-hennish every day that passes. Oliver isn't your responsibility – '

'But Robin and Sam are my friends as well as family,' Chick said. 'So que voulez vous?'

'Shouldn't that be "tu"?' Suzy said and grinned. 'Some linguist you are!'

'Don't change the subject! Are you going to talk to Oliver or do I have to – '

'I'll talk to him, I'll talk to him!' Suzy said. 'I can only manage this evening. I'm head over ears for the next week – so much revision and so forth – '

'Then go and see him this evening,' Chick said. 'Now – '

'I'll phone first,' Suzy said, to come back and tell her mother with some satisfaction that Oliver, Helga had said, was at work.

'Then go and see him there,' Chick said, implacable. 'If he's working at nights, he might have time to have a chat. Go to the hotel and have coffee or something. Show willing!'

And Suzy, less averse to visiting a hotel to drink coffee in the lounge and perhaps listen to some piano music, went. She took a tube to Sloane Square and then walked down towards the hotel in Sloane Street, enjoying the warmth of the spring air and the scent of lilacs from the pairs of tubs that stood flanking the doors of the small blocks of flats that lined the street and tried to think generally benevolent thoughts about the boy she was on her way to see. It couldn't have been easy for him, after all, she told herself, being at that awful school. To Suzy, who enjoyed home more than most girls of her age, the thought of boarding school was anathema, and she couldn't imagine anyone enjoying it. No wonder Oliver had gone off the rails, she told herself and wondered what form his rail-leaving had taken. No one had said, even her mother, usually talkative, clamping her lips shut and saying that she'd promised not to make Oliver the object of gossip. Oh, well, Suzy told herself as she arrived at the Bittacy, a neat and unpretentious place, I dare say he'll tell me. He's never been averse to showing off, that one.

There was a girl behind the desk in reception and she looked blankly at Suzy when she asked for Oliver.

'Oliver? Oh, he's on days,' she said. 'I took over from him about half an hour ago.'

Suzy looked blank. 'Oh! They said at his house he was working nights – '

The girl shook her head. 'Hasn't done this past fortnight. Got me lumbered with it, didn't he? He's good at that.'

Suzy smiled fleetingly, remembering times in childhood when Oliver had managed to get someone else blamed for one of his peccadilloes. 'Then you don't know where he is?'

'Could be anywhere,' the girl said, bored, and returned to her novel. 'I couldn't say, I'm sure.'

'I'll leave him a note, I think – ' Suzy said after a moment. 'Might I have some paper and a pen?'

The girl gave a martyred sigh and scrabbled among the papers on her desk and gave Suzy a sheet of scrap and a battered pencil and Suzy took them and after a moment moved away to the back of the lounge to write her note there. She certainly wouldn't want that miserable creature looking over her shoulder, she told herself. It's none of her business –

She sat staring at the staircase across the lounge hall, thinking, and was about to bend her head to start writing when she saw him. He came down the stairs two at a time, lithe and eager, and she stared at the tight blue jeans and the casually knotted scarf in the neck of his brightly coloured shirt and the gloss of his slicked-back hair and was so startled that she couldn't move for a moment.

He winked at the girl at the desk who gaped back at him and opened her mouth to speak, but he didn't wait, and was gone, out of the hotel and jumping down the steps outside even before Suzy had gathered her wits about her and jumped up to follow him.

By the time she got outside he was little more than a fading figure in the distance, barely seen in the half-light of the early summer night, and she watched him get even smaller and then, on an impulse, went in pursuit. She'd promised her mother she'd talk to him. Tonight was one of the few chances she was likely to get, and, anyway, her curiosity was piqued. He looked so unlike the way he had been used to look; in his parents' company which was when she usually saw him after all, at family affairs of one kind or another, he'd been – well, just Oliver. Now, he looked startling, also, she had to admit, he looked rather attractive. He didn't seem like a sullen schoolboy now, but an interesting young man, and she was as interested in interesting-looking young men as the next girl. So she walked at a rapid striding pace along Sloane Street after him.

He led her up across the Square and into the King's Road and her spirits began to lift. Busy as she was with her own life, her studies and her friends, she had heard of the excitements of the King's Road these days. All the new boutiques, the pubs and the cafés and the noise; above all the noise. Several of the cafés and restaurants were roaring with business, and had tables outside on the pavement, and their doors open, and all of them were playing very loud records, mostly, she thought, Beatles, but some even louder. The Rolling Stones, she decided and sniffed. In her set at school it was fashionable to despise such music and Suzy was nothing if not part of her set; but hearing it here spilling out into the swirling crowds in the street, as she hurried on keeping the vivid red of Oliver's shirt well in view, she had to admit it sounded exciting and dramatic and she began to walk even faster, spurred on by the heavy beat.

She caught up with him just as he was about to turn into the door of a pub, and she reached out and pulled on his sleeve, and he stopped and stared down at her.

'Oliver – ' she managed and then had to stop, because she was more breathless from her chase than she realized and he gaped at her in amazement.

'Suzy? It is Suzy Amberley, isn't it? Good God! What are you doing here?'

'Following you,' she said and managed to take a deep breath and blew it out and then grinned. 'I had to talk to you.'

'Er – ' He moved away from the open door and stood there in the light thrown out of the windows and looked at her a little warily. 'Is something wrong?'

'Wrong? I don't know. Is there?' She was beginning to enjoy this. He was clearly rattled by seeing her and that made a change for the lordly Oliver who had, in their childhood, made such a nuisance of himself so often.

'I mean, at home – '

'Oh! No. No need to worry. No one there knows you're not working when you told them you were – '

'Phew!' He blew a mock sigh of relief. 'Then that's all right. What the eye doesn't see and so forth – ' He frowned then. 'But what are you doing here?'

'Look, do we have to stand outside like this?' She peered across him to the pub where the door stood invitingly open. 'That looks like fun. And the music and all – '

'Er, no,' he said quickly and took her elbow. 'Not for you – I'll find somewhere for a – a cup of coffee if you like – ' And he tried to pull her away.

Suzy was incensed. He was treating her like a child and she knew it; yet in fact she was a year older than he was, and had passed her eighteenth birthday. Come September, all being well with her exams, she'd be at University. And here this pup was trying to prevent her from going into a pub. How dare he?

She shook his hand off and said crisply. 'To hell with coffee. I fancy a drink. I'm going in. You can do as you like – ' And she marched across the pavement and up the steps into the pub, and then stood for a moment, blinking in the brightness.

Truth to tell, Suzy didn't drink much. She and her friends occasionally had wine at home, and had been known to enjoy a little Martini or something of the sort at parties, but pubs were not their natural habitat. And certainly not pubs like this. She looked around and was aware of feeling intimidated; these people were very glamorous, very up to the minute, everything she wasn't. For a start everyone looked young. There didn't seem to be anyone over twenty-five in the place, jammed as it was. The boys were dressed in neat, smart yet casual clothes very like Oliver's, and the girls in tight skirts and with hair teased up into tall beehives which they wore over carefully painted faces were breathlessly fashionable. Suzy at once knew herself to be uniquely dowdy and painfully aware of her sensible skirt and blouse and shoes and her dull coat and above all her face, which was totally innocent of make-up, she could have wept.

He was at her elbow and said with some laughter, clearly aware of how she was feeling. 'Sure you wouldn't rather have coffee somewhere *naice*?' and that angered her and she snapped loudly, 'No!' and marched towards the bar.

'All right, all right, if you insist,' he said and came with her, and leaned over the bar and called cheerfully to the barman, 'Joe? Joe, over here!'

The barman looked up and grinned and nodded and Suzy thought – he comes here a lot; and watched as several other people looked up and waved at him and he called greetings back. That he was a regular and popular customer was undoubted.

He bought her a gin and tonic and a vodka for himself – which she found breathtakingly daring, but wouldn't have admitted for the world – and stood there looking down at her.

'Well, cheers and so forth!' and he lifted his glass. 'And what can I do for you? Why were you following me?'

'I'll tell you why,' she said bitterly. 'I wanted to help you. My ma made an arrangement with your ma that I'd try and arrange for you to meet some of my friends so that you wouldn't be lonely in London. Huh!' And she almost snorted her derision. 'Well, at least you've let me off the hook. I'll tell 'em you've no need for any sort of help, seem to have plenty of friends of your own and – '

He looked alarmed. 'No need to tell anyone anything,' he said firmly. 'My private life is my own.'

She peered up at him, a little glittery now from the gin in her drink. She wasn't used to the stuff, and had only asked for it out of bravado. 'So it would seem. But why shouldn't they know you've got friends? There's nothing wrong with that, is there?'

'Not in my opinion. But they – your aunt and uncle – they have different views. Bloody dull and stuffy views – '

'They're your parents, Oliver. You've no right to speak so of them – '

'If I haven't, who has? You really ought to grow up, ducky. The world doesn't rise and fall in the olds, you know. We're the people who count now, and it's all wrong they should be able to run our lives the way they do – or used to, in my case,' he said and swallowed the rest of his drink and gestured at the barman for a refill.

She stared at him curiously. 'What are you up to? You tell 'em at home that you're working at night and then you turn out to be hanging around pubs – and doing it a lot, going by the way people are talking to you – ' for several had greeted him while they'd been talking. 'Are you up to more trouble? I mean, is that why you were chucked out of school?'

He cocked his head at her. 'They didn't tell you why?'

She shook her head. 'I supposed it was drinking and smoking. You used to pinch stuff like that when you were twelve or so, I remember. I know more about you than most – you always do when you were kids together – '

'Mmm,' he said thoughtfully, and looked at her for a long moment and then said abruptly, 'Another drink?'

'I don't think I should,' Suzy said prudently, and put her glass on the bar. 'I've got a lot to do tomorrow. Revision all morning – I've got exams coming up – you know how it is – '

'Poor you,' he said absently, clearly thinking, and then smiled at her, devastatingly. 'I should have said thank you, Suzy.'

'What for – '

'For being so kind. I'm not lonely but I might have been. It was kind of you to care – '

'I did as I was asked,' she said brusquely, embarrassed. 'My ma said would I, so – '

'Well, yes, but you didn't have to agree. And you could have made life hell for me by rushing back and telling tales about what I was up to – And you didn't.'

'What *are* you up to? I still don't know – '

He made an odd sound, half laugh, half snort. 'Oh, damn all really. I just like to come here and to some of the clubs and so forth, where the fun is – I don't want to waste my best years being serious and learning about bloody hotels, for God's sake. Bad enough at school – at least I'm out of that. Now I want to get on with a bit of life of my own, without people breathing down my neck. Is that such a crime?'

'I suppose not,' she said doubtfully. The gin had really gone to her head now and she felt light and giggly. 'It is a bit boring, the way they fuss over you. Not that Ma's not an angel of course, because she is – but all the same – ' She looked over her shoulder at the girls surrounding her. 'It'd be fun to look more modern, wouldn't it?'

'A lot of fun.' His hand slid round her arm and held on, warmly. 'And you could, you know.'

'Oh, sure. What on?' Suzy scoffed. 'Buttons?'

He shook his head and laughed, a pleasant sound that she liked, even though the hubbub around them made it hard to hear. 'No buttons needed. I can help you. I'm earning now, doing quite nicely – '

'What, in Grandma's hotel?'

He slid over that. 'Oh, I have a couple of other interests. Thing is, I've a few bob to call my own. So I could help you get a few things of your own – '

She looked suspicious. 'Auntie Robin said she'd let me get some stuff at her shop. She's modern enough – I just don't think I'm the type really.'

'You could be. With me to help you.' Oliver said and smiled winningly. 'Stick with me, not a word at home to anyone about tonight and we'll have some fun. It can't be all exams, for heaven's sake, can it?'

'I suppose not,' she said with sudden longing. 'I suppose not.'

'Well then!' Oliver sounded triumphant, realizing that he'd saved his bacon by a hair's breadth. She wouldn't tell on him. Not now. He just had to keep her sweet – and it wouldn't be too difficult. She was quite a nice-looking girl really, and with a bit of

help from him could look great. 'Trust me. I'll look after you.
Just don't tell tales on me, that's all I ask.'

16

It should have been the best summer of her life. The shop was thriving, and not only because of the extra publicity she now had regularly and which had increased even more on the occasion of the shop's first anniversary, but also because of the weather.

It rained a good deal that summer and that meant that office workers in their lunch hours couldn't just wander the streets or stand outside the pubs in the sunshine giggling and drinking; they needed shelter and came into shops for it – and especially hers. And they spent money. So that was good.

Also Oliver seemed happy at last, and contented, and that was very good, though she had to work quite hard to stifle the diagreeable feelings that had been mobilized by Chick's reaction to the news of the end of the threat of fatherhood that had hung over him. That had been horrid, but it had all been some time ago now, and she thought of it less often, and experienced less guilt about the girl Tracey she had never met but felt she ought to have done. But if she had said any such thing to Oliver, she could have expected only anger and arguments, that she knew, so she said nothing.

But the really unpleasant part of the summer was the way she was with Sam. She knew now that the trouble was that they hadn't made up their big argument on the day of the shop's six month anniversary. They'd had their share of arguments over the years, of course they had, but they'd always kept to the old saw about not letting the sun set on their wrath. But that September argument had never had a chance of settlement, what with Oliver and then the way they'd sparred over him; so the unease and coolness between them had lingered on and on – and now was, it seemed, part of their lives for ever.

They saw each other at breakfast of course, but the girls and Bertie were always there then, and they talked so much and made such a general noise that it was possible for no one to notice that Sam and she never spoke directly to each other; and in the evenings her fatigue at the end of the day, married to her frequent need to deal with paperwork, meant there was no real opportunity for conversation, and anyway he often had meetings and extra work of his own to do at the Clinic. And so they went on living an ever more semi-detached lifestyle, and busy and happy though her shop made her, her awareness of that seemed to leave her very chilly somewhere deep inside.

All of which, she was to tell herself later, played a part in how the whole thing happened. But at the time she hadn't realized that, not even thought about it. It had all been too much to cope with, too immediate and exciting to think about logically at all —

The day had started gloomily, with rain pouring from a dead June sky, and the roads splashed and the gutters chattered round the scraps of garbage they carried as she went splashing through the puddles in Foubert's Place to open the shop about fifteen minutes later than she should have done. There'd been trouble at one of the underground stations on her route (she suspected gloomily that it had been an attempted suicide which hadn't helped her low mood at all) and she had had to sit steaming miserably with a great many other equally damp people for what seemed an eternity outside Oxford Circus tube station, waiting till the train could be allowed in. To find then, as she did, that Beckie was even later than she was didn't help her mood at all.

She unlocked and set about getting the shop ready for the day, while at the same time serving the customers who seemed to have been waiting for her to unlock, and it was past eleven before she could deal with the fact that Beckie still hadn't come in, and managed to find a moment to phone her.

'Oh, help,' Beckie squawked when at last she answered the phone. 'I s'pose I slept in. Late last night – see you tomorrow, hmm?' and hung up, to Robin's rage. And when she tried to call her back to insist she came in, the phone only buzzed an engaged tone. Beckie had left it off the hook and there wasn't a thing Robin could do about it.

She thought for a moment of sacking Beckie, but knew she wouldn't. The girl was unreliable and given to taking these extra days off, but she was so right for the shop, with her odd looks and sense of style, brought a lot of customers in from her wide circle of friends, and above all, good help was hard to find these days with more jobs around than workers. So Robin sighed and settled to coping on her own as best she could in a shop that, as the lunch-hour burst over her, filled itself to the brim with eager buyers.

At half past two, when at last the rush died down, she began to tidy up, for far too many of her customers just dropped clothes on the floor when they'd finished looking at them, and she emerged an hour later flushed, irritable and looking far from her usual tidy fashionable self. She thought for a moment of closing early, putting a sign on the window saying that Owing to Unforeseen Circumstances This Shop Is Closed till Tomorrow Morning, but pushed that away. That would be an amateurish way to go on. The sensible thing to do was to try to find some extra help; the shop could afford it now, for it was taking a lot of money and even at the low prices she charged and which were one of the major attractions, there was some slack she could take up, and she went to her little curtained-off office and started to draft an advertisement to send out to the agencies, to see who they could find for her.

She felt the shop door open as a rush of damp air came in and she wanted to curse, but put on her polite smile and went out, and was startled. There were three people standing there, and one of them she knew immediately: Sally Sampson, the star of the most popular current top soap opera on TV, and she looked at the girl more closely and was amused because she wasn't after all quite as dewy and girlish as she appeared on the screen. At least thirty-five if not more, she thought and then moved forward with her polite trained Can I Help You look, bright and not too obsequious, lively and alert but not pushy.

'Hi,' the dark woman standing alongside Sally Sampson said in an American accent. 'Would you be Robin?'

'I would and I am,' Robin said and the man barked an approving laugh.

'One of these days you'll learn to speak good English, Buffy,' he said. 'She got you fair and square.'

Robin was scarlet. 'Heavens, I didn't mean to be rude. It was just that I – '

146

'It doesn't matter,' the dark woman said graciously. 'Now, listen, we don't have a great deal of time. We have this new story-line for Sally here – you know who Sally is? – Yeah, of course you do. Who doesn't? Well, like I say, a new story-line. Secret now, don't tell a soul, but she's got to be a naughty girl in the plot – add a bit of spice. So we have to get her out of her uniform and into a few more interesting outfits. Which is where you come in. Everyone says you're hot stuff, so how much is it worth to you to get your gear seen on TV?'

Robin was cagey. 'Well, of course I'd be happy to help, but unless I got an actual advertisement saying who I am and where I am, it wouldn't really be worth it to me to give you clothes, would it?'

The man barked his mocking laughter again. 'Told you it wouldn't work! Not here in London. Forget it, Buffy. We don't do things that way – '

Robin was nettled. The woman seemed a cheerful enough soul and anyway, Robin didn't like other people speaking for her.

'I could let you have a discount though,' she said. 'Not much, mind you. I keep my prices as low as I can anyway. But I could manage something – and it could be a good chance to do a bit of what you might call below the line advertising. Would you let me have a signed photograph, a big one, of you wearing the clothes? For the window?' And she looked directly at Sally Sampson.

She had been staring moodily at the rails of clothes and now seemed to come to some sort of life. 'Mmm? All right with me if it's all right with them.'

'It's fine with me, but for the photo and all – well, we'd need more than just a discount,' Buffy said.

'I reckon – well, listen. Suppose – I'm not guaranteeing this, mind, but suppose I make a couple of new designs? I'm always trying out new ideas – suppose I try them for you, and if they work, fine, I'll go into production. I never expect to sell my samples – so you could have those for nothing – '

'Good on you, kid!' Buffy squealed and looked triumphantly at the man. 'Who said people in this country don't speak my language?'

'You're potty,' the man said and went to lean against the door. 'If they find out at the office you're throwing signed publicity photos about they'll have your guts for garters.'

'If they see my budget's in good health, they'll not notice anything else,' Buffy said. 'So, we're in business, Robin. Let's look at this gear you've got here, talk ideas and possibilities. Sally, you too. George, you can go play with yourself some place else. You'll be a bore here – '

'You bet I will,' he said and straightened up. 'Coffee and a wad, that's for me – whoops, sorry!' for the door behind him had opened, as someone tried to get in. 'I'll wait for you over the way,' he said over his shoulder and pushed past the newcomers and was gone.

'I'm on my own,' Robin said to Buffy. 'Do you mind if – '

'No way!' Buffy said. 'We were here first. Hey, you don't mind looking around while the boss here does business with me, do you?' she called and the people at the doorway looked up. Robin had tried to get past Buffy to talk to her new customers herself, but she was a large woman as well as a determined one and there was no way that Robin could, so she dodged round the other side of the clothes rail by which they'd been standing to say a little breathlessly to the newcomers, 'Do look around – if you want to try something on there's room at the back. Sorry, I'm here on my own today – Oh!' And she stood staring, her mouth half open with surprise.

She'd have known him anywhere; it wasn't just the height of him, at least six foot three, nor the bulk of him, for his body matched his height, but the whole look of him. When she'd last known him he'd usually been wearing the brown overall of the hospital orderly, but now he was spruce and very neat in a dark suit with a shirt of such blinding whiteness it almost made her blink. Yet still he was unmistakable. His hair, once rather curly and thick, seemed thinner now and was certainly combed closer to his skull and his face, once smooth and round, now had a number of ridges and clefts that made him look positively craggy. And then he smiled and the memory was complete; those endearingly uneven very white teeth.

'Hamish Todd,' she said. 'Of all people, Hamish Todd.'

He lifted his head in polite enquiry and she remembered that too, and was suddenly bitterly hurt. He looked a little puzzled and worried, but there was a wary look in his eyes that might have been a hint of recognition. Wasn't there?

'You know me?' he said and the Scots burr was as clear as it had ever been. Not a hint of change there.

The woman standing beside him laughed. 'My dear Hamish, I dare say lots of people know you. You're a famous man these days, aye on the television!' Her accent was as marked as his, and her voice was pretty, light and soft, and Robin glanced at her and felt a sudden inexplicable moment of gloom. It was ridiculous. Why shouldn't he have a woman with him? His wife no doubt, though she looked a little young for that. He must be – and she did a hasty calculation. He had to be about two years older than she was; or was it just a year? Anyway, around forty-eight or so. And unbidden the thought rose in her mind – more than ten years younger than Sam.

'You've clearly forgotten me!' she said as gaily as she could. 'Well, never mind. Anyway, if you see anything you want – ' She looked directly at the woman. 'Do try it on. I'll be with you as soon as I can – ' She looked over her shoulder to where Buffy was making clear indications of impatience and then glanced at Hamish again. He was staring at her fixedly and she managed a smile and then turned away.

It took Buffy and the monosyllabic Sally almost an hour to decide what they needed for the programme and all the time as Robin made quick sketches or pulled garments from her rails to show them, she watched the Todds covertly. The woman was clearly enchanted with all that she saw, and took garment after garment to hold against herself while she peacocked in the mirror, and he watched her gravely, standing quietly beside her with his hands lightly clasped in front of him as she twittered on.

Lucky woman, Robin found herself thinking, and then was furious with herself. Why on earth should such a ridiculous notion cross her mind?

Buffy was at last satisfied and bore off with her the copies of the drawings she had finally agreed for Sally's costumes, swiftly traced through onto greaseproof paper by Robin, taking with her assurances that the samples would be ready, to Sally's size – which was happily a stock size ten – within a fortnight. Robin looked over her shoulder at the Todds, still happily browsing among the rails, and risked a phone call. She'd have to get the work in hand fast if she was to fulfil her promises. After all, important work came first, she told herself, before gossiping with old friends, and tried to be convinced by her own argument. But she knew the real reason for her eagerness to make her phone

call was a sudden extraordinary unwillingness to face Hamish
Todd again.

She made her call to the workshop which did most of her
making-up, explaining what had happened, and Cynthia, the girl
who cut the patterns and did most of the sewing, was agog.

'Ooh, I love Sally Sampson. She's ever so good as the staff
nurse in it!' she burbled. 'I'll be ever so thrilled to make-up for
her – what does she want?'

'I've got drawings,' Robin said. 'Pretty accurate ones, I hope.
The people in charge – well the woman really – she's tough.
You'd better be sure you can do it. I'd as soon tell them it's not
possible at the start as find we can't cope.'

'We'll cope,' Cynthia said blithely. 'Just you see – I'll pick up
the drawings first thing in the morning on my way in – will that
do? I can have the pattern cut and a toile ready by – oh, the next
day. You could have the dresses – how many do you say? Three –
by the end of the week. How would that do?'

'Magic,' said Robin and had to hang up at last, and she went
back to the shop with a slightly dragging step, hoping they'd be
gone. But he was still there and she took a deep rather shaky
breath and let herself admit the truth. She would have been
heartbroken if he'd vanished. Seeing him again had made her feel
quite – well, she didn't know quite what. Exhilarated. Young.
Hopeful again –

'I'm sorry I couldn't be with you,' she said. 'And at least no
one else came this afternoon. Fortunately it's usually quiet on
Mondays – did you find anything you like?'

'Masses I like – but I'm not sure it likes me,' the woman said
and laughed. 'I'm getting a bit old for this sort of stuff, damn it.
I'd love to wear it though. Such fun – but can you imagine, in
Edinburgh? The skies'd fall in with shock!'

'I don't see why,' Hamish said and his voice was more cheerful
now, more definite. 'Do you, Mrs Landow?'

Robin felt her face crimson with pleasure and tried to pretend
she didn't know it. 'Then you do remember me!'

'Of course I do! I was just so dumbstruck when I first saw you
that I couldna' believe it!'

'Oh!' The woman looked from one to the other sharply. 'Then
you *do* know each other – I mean, it isn't just that you appear on
television?'

'We go back a long way, Moira,' Hamish said gravely. 'Let me see – nineteen forty it would be – '

'Good heavens!' Moira said. 'A quarter of a century, near enough!'

Robin winced. 'Help! You make me feel older than God.'

'Well, let's face it, time goes on,' Hamish said. 'I'd never have thought you'd become the sort of silly woman that would fuss over a few birthdays, Robin.'

'I'm not,' she said. 'I mean, I never used to be. But lately –' she smiled brightly. 'It's dealing with such young people in the shop, you see. It sort of brings it home.'

'I must say I'm surprised to see you in such a business.' Hamish sounded as pedantic as he ever had, and it warmed her a little. It was like being back at the old London, sitting in Casualty over snatched cups of tea or – and then she had a sudden visual memory so intense it was almost as though she were there again; she and Hamish, running from the crump of bombs to get to the shelter, half pushing and half dragging with them an old man who wouldn't be parted from his old pram and its load of his precious belongings – and she had to shake her head to bring herself back to the present.

'But you look pretty young yourself,' Hamish said consideringly and he looked slowly at her clothes – and today she was wearing one of her own dresses in a rich green over white boots –and then at her hair and face. 'Verra fashionable.'

'It's only for business,' she said at once, needing to convince him she wasn't merely frivolous, that there was more to her than met the eye. It was important suddenly that he should approve of her. 'Otherwise I'd look as – well as ordinary as anyone else.'

'You were never ordinary,' he said and smiled and again she was aware of the warmth of memory and found herself thinking – I thought I was in love with this man once. And dared not look at him.

'Well, Moira,' she said then. 'Can I interest you in anything?'

'I think not.' Moira sounded genuinely regretful. 'Here it looks wonderful, but at home – no, there's nowhere I'd be able to wear it. And what would Joe say? He'd have seventy kinds of fit!'

'Joe?' Robin said involuntarily and Moira, who was again looking yearningly at one of the cheekiest dresses on the rail, a confection in cherry red, said absently, 'My husband,' and Robin felt almost dizzy with the rush of feeling that burst over her.

'Oh,' she said and didn't stop to think. 'I thought you were married to Hamish!' And Moira looked up, caught her eyes on Hamish and then looked at Hamish and said slowly, 'Married to Hamish? Oh, no, my dear. Hamish is a widower, and has been these many years, is it not so, Hamish? So he's footloose and fancy-free, as you might say. I certainly am not. I'm just here to keep him company tonight – if that's what he wants me to do, of course – ' And she turned her smiling face with its sharp little eyes and even sharper glances from Hamish to Robin and back again as they stood and looked at each other and said nothing at all.

17

'I think I'm entitled to close early,' Robin said. 'Seeing I had no lunch. And it's almost five anyway – I hope you like big fat sandwiches. Only, well, it's all they do at this place – '

She turned the last key in the lock and tugged on the door to check it before turning back to them. 'Everyone around here eats at Chubbie's. Their coffee's great – '

'Wherever you like, Robin,' Hamish said. 'It's good of you to offer us your hospitality at all.'

'Oh, hardly my hospitality.' She led the way along Foubert's Place towards Carnaby Street and the tangle of alleys and streets beyond. 'I wish I could take you home and give you a proper dinner, but we're right out in Hampstead and you wouldn't have time. But at least this place we're going to is typically London in lots of ways – ' She was chattering absurdly and she knew it, but she couldn't stop herself. The whole thing was getting too ridiculous; not just meeting Hamish again after all these years, but being so excited by him; what else could she do but chatter?

Chubbie's was its usual crowded noisy clattering steamy self, smelling delectably of toast and coffee and cream cakes, and she ordered smoked salmon sandwiches, feeling an obscure need to be extra generous, and settled them at a corner table, and as they ate and drank went on chattering. But not so much that Moira couldn't do her share and Robin managed to pick up a good deal of information about Hamish that she was fascinated to hear, without actually asking Hamish himself, as he sat and ate his sandwiches and listened and said nothing at all.

Hamish, according to Moira, was quite the most remarkable man who had ever breathed. He was the perfect neighbour – which was how Moira and her Joe knew him, since he lived next door in a

153

flat in what Robin understood to be a tall and handsome Edinburgh house; since he was quiet and thoughtful and helped her fetch her parcels up and down which was more than Joe ever managed to do; since he was wonderfully clever, and there wasn't a research biologist anywhere in Edinburgh to touch him and as everyone knew, Edinburgh was the centre of the Universe as far as medical research was concerned; and since he had become famous appearing on radio and television as well as being interviewed at length in the *Scotsman* which was, of course, the crowning accolade.

Hamish sat through all this glowing praise listening with every air of courtesy as though he was hearing a discussion not of himself but of someone entirely different, and Robin realized after a while that in fact he wasn't listening at all. He was watching her, and that made her pink and a little damp with embarrassment. But it wasn't a disagreeable way to feel at all.

'So that's why I'm here,' Moira finished gaily. 'Someone had to hold the poor wee man's hand for this BBC programme he has to do – it's not the same as doing it in Scotland where everyone knows him, so I reckoned he needed some company, and anyway I wanted a chance to do some window-shopping. Not real shopping, you understand, Joe couldna' be doing with that – but just looking about – '

She rattled on and Robin risked a glance at Hamish, trying not to laugh aloud at Moira's description of him as a poor wee man and found he was looking at her with his brows raised in comic dismay, showing he found it as funny as she did, and they both laughed, and Moira beamed at them and seemed delighted to be found witty, whatever it was she'd said.

How it happened Robin couldn't be sure, since she led the way out of the sandwich bar back into the street when she'd paid the bill, and she didn't see; and she wondered afterwards for one wild moment whether it had been her own guardian angel who had made it happen. Or perhaps her guardian devil –

Whatever the cause, Moira let out a wail of dismay and pain as Robin made her way in front of the two of them into the street, and she turned to stare. Moira had stepped sideways to avoid a puddle left by the day's rain, which had at last stopped, but in doing so had caught the heel of her shoe in a broken paving stone and fallen, and was sitting on the pavement with her legs spreadeagled and a look of almost ludicrous pain on her face.

'Oh, no!' Robin cried and knelt beside her as passersby stopped to stare, and Hamish too dropped to his knees on Moira's other side to try to help her stand up.

She managed to get upright, but not without considerable grimacing and Robin checked her ankle carefully.

'I don't think you've broken anything,' she said. 'But you ought to have it seen, just to be on the safe side – '

'Not a bit of it,' Moira said. 'There's no need for any such fuss. I'm always doing this. It's a funny ankle – unstable joint they call it. It hurts when I do it, but it's no more than a nasty stretch of the muscles and tendons, I've been told – I know what to do – ouch.' She had put her weight on her foot tentatively but clearly that wasn't a good idea at all. 'I'll have to bind it and rest it. Oh, what a nuisance it is! Why cannot I be more careful where I put ma feet – you'd think I'd have learned by now. It's the same as I did last Christmas, you'll remember it, Hamish – '

'I remember,' Hamish said. 'Are you sure though? Robin's right, I think. You should have it X-rayed and – '

'I will not!' Moira said. 'I've had more than my fair share of X-rays this past few months as it is what with my chest and that barium meal, I'll have no more when I don't need them. All I have to do with this is rest it tonight and it'll be well enough tomorrow. I've a supportive bandage in my case at the hotel – I never travel without one. So you be seeing me back and I'll settle down and –ah!'

'What is it?' Robin said anxiously. 'Has the pain increased?'

'Och, no, that's no problem. It's the show, Hamish's programme!' She turned her head to stare at him mournfully. 'I came all this way to keep you company and now I go and make such a fool of maself. Now what do we do?'

He laughed, kindly. 'Moira, you make me feel like a daft bairn! I'm well able to take care of myself. I'll take you back to your room at the hotel and I'll do the programme and then I'll be back to make sure you're all right. And if you're not, will you, nill you, I'll have you off to the casualty department of the nearest hospital – '

'There'll be no need for that, Hamish Todd, and don't you even think it,' Moira said, and leaned against him as he put an arm round her and she began to hobble carefully towards the kerb, where Robin had managed to flag down a taxi. 'You take me back to the hotel and then – Och, I know! *You* go with him, Robin!'

Robin gaped at her. 'I?'

'Indeed, you. And why not? You're old friends, and you'll be better able to keep him company than I would, being a Londoner as you are. We'd have been a couple of babes in the wood at the studio, but you'll know all about it and how to handle the people so that they'll treat him right – '

'Moira, I've no more experience in a television studio than a flea – less than you that's for sure, if you've been to other programmes Hamish has done – and you'll be all right, Hamish, won't you? You don't need company?'

'I'd appreciate it,' he said in a low voice. 'I said I could take care of myself, but I've still got a wee problem you see – '

She stood and stared as carefully he put Moira into the taxi, her face red with shame again. She had forgotten completely. He'd been an orderly at the London Hospital when she'd been there because he had been a conscientious objector, and had to do the work as an alternative to going into the army. And later he'd gone on to work in the coal mines, even though he suffered quite dreadfully from claustrophobia. She remembered the night the two of them had been caught in a bomb incident, in the lower corridor at the London Hospital, and had only escaped damage because there had been a casualty department trolley there for them to shelter under; and how Hamish had developed symptoms of claustrophobia as they sat there waiting to be rescued, how he'd shaken and sweated and needed to hold on to her –

'Of course I'll come with you, Hamish,' she said quickly, as he turned from the taxi where Moira was now comfortably ensconced. 'I'd hate to have to go to do a TV programme alone – '

'I'm not shy about admitting it any more, Robin,' he said. 'I was when I was younger – full of pride and therefore of shame, I was. But I've more sense now, I'm not so bad as I was – I can cope well enough in most places – but in these studios they have no windows, do you see. You're locked inside a dark place that has too many lights at its centre. I had a bad attack the first time I did a programme and I just canna cope among strangers in a studio since. If I have a companion I'm well enough – that's why Moira came.'

Moira poked her head out of the taxi. 'So you'll go with him, Robin?'

'Of course I will – what time?'

'They want me at Lime Grove out by Shepherd's Bush at around seven,' Hamish said. 'I'd cry off, and say I just canna be there, but there'll be others in my field I'd not like to offend and you understand they'd be mortally put out if I just didna' – '

'You'll be there and so shall I.' Robin said. 'And I'm so glad you don't make it a secret any more – '

He smiled a little crookedly. 'I don't tell the world you understand. Just my friends.' He reached out and took her hand. 'And you're a very old friend.'

She let her hand stay in his for a little longer than she should have done, and then pulled it away, a little flustered.

'Of course – now, seven o'clock you say? I think I've just got time to get things sorted out there and I could meet you at your hotel – where are you staying?'

'Very near here,' he said. 'Moira likes Oxford Street, you see, so I said we'd book at the Berners' Hotel. It's comfortable enough – '

'It suits me fine,' Moira said. 'Robin, I'm sorry about this, and grateful too. I don't think you'll have a bad time of it. He's great company – ' And she looked at Hamish sharply, as he got into the taxi himself and then at Robin. 'But I don't have to tell you that, old friends as you are. I'm on the third floor of the hotel, so come and say hello when you pick him up, will you?'

'And my room's on the first floor, and I'll meet you in the foyer at – shall we say, half past six? Can you manage that in time? The studio's sending a car for me – '

Robin looked at her watch. Half past five. 'I'll be there,' she promised, and watched the taxi as it pulled away before hurrying to the underground to get home and organize them all there – and to make herself look as good as she could – before rushing back to see Hamish again. It was a busy hour, but she enjoyed it. The day might have started disastrously but it was clearly ending in a crescendo of excitement. So much so that she didn't dare think about it.

Poppy phoned Sam at a quarter to eleven.

'Sam? How are you? Good, good. Sorry to call so late, but could I have a word with Robin? I'll tell you all about it in a moment, but I ought to tell Robin to start with, I think – '

'She's not here,' Sam said.

At the other end of the phone Poppy frowned. There had been a note of flatness in his voice that alerted her and she said quickly, 'Is something wrong?'

'Wrong? Of course not. Not more than usual!'

'And what does that mean?'

'Nothing. Just a bad joke. No, she's just out – '

'Oh, then I suppose – ' She stopped. 'Dammit, where? None of my business, I know, but she usually says if she's going to be out when we talk on the phone and I spoke to her earlier this morning and she said she'd be home tonight.'

'It was all rather unexpected. She met an old friend,' Sam hesitated and then said, 'You know him of course. Hamish Todd.'

'Hamish Todd – ' She was silent and then said slowly, 'Oh, Hamish Todd.'

'I said you'd remember him,' Sam said.

She did, of course. She'd worried about him for quite a while. He'd been tall and bulky and quiet and very attractive in his silent sort of way and Robin had had more than a passing crush on him. Poppy remembered perfectly well how she'd worried about that and how glad she'd been when he went off to be a miner to work out his anti-war conscience underground in the most difficult circumstances he could find. She'd known him to be an admirable person, but had known equally well that he wasn't the man for her beloved Robin. She had breathed a deep sigh of relief when Sam had quietly moved into the space left in Robin's life after Hamish had gone, and made her happy to forget him.

And now he was back. She thought for a moment and then said cautiously. 'So where is she?'

'She went with him to keep him company in a TV studio. He's become rather well known in his field, it seems. Quite famous in Scotland and now it's spreading here. He was on "Probe" tonight, on the BBC. It seems he's made a considerable breakthrough in recognizing mutations in epithelal cells and identifying not only the causative agent but a system that could reverse the effect – '

'What does that mean? In my language?'

'It might be a lead on a treatment for cancer,' Sam said. 'It's important work. I admire what he's done considerably. I watched the programme – he was impressive. Very much so.'

'Oh, then Robin'll be home any moment if she went with him – "Probe" finishes at nine o'clock, doesn't it? Before the News?'

'Yes,' Sam said in a colourless tone.

'But it's getting on for eleven now, I mean – '

'Dear Poppy, I know no more than you do. She agreed to go to the studio to keep him company. That is as far as my information goes. She'll be back in due course, I've no doubt. They're probably whooping it up with drinks or whatever. They do that after TV shows you know. I did one once – '

'I remember.' Poppy smiled, recalling the way ripples of excitement had gone through the entire family when Sam had been asked to take part in a discussion of the role of psycho-analysis in the crime of shoplifting. 'But you came home right afterwards – '

'I preferred to.' Sam's voice was still colourless. 'Robin's clearly having fun.'

'Yes – ' Poppy said and sighed. It was no part of her role to say more, though she ached to do so. She talked too often to her daughter not to be aware that there was something wrong in the Hampstead household, but she knew better than to ask outright what might be going on. She'd find out soon enough if it was important. She roused herself then and said, 'I'd better explain why I called.'

'Not just social then?' Sam sounded amused for a moment. 'Not just checking up on us?'

'Sam, shut up. You know me better than that.' She was genuinely incensed and he recognized that at once.

'I'm sorry, Poppy. Of course I do. Put it down to fatigue. What's up then?' His voice sharpened. 'Oliver's all right? There's no problems at the Bittacy?'

She laughed. 'No, no problems. Not with old Corbett to watch over him. Even your Oliver'd be hard put to it to get into trouble there. No, this is something else – '

She stopped then and took a little breath. 'I may be fretting over nothing. Look, have you a copy of tonight's *Evening News*?'

'Somewhere, I suppose. Helga usually gets it. Why?'

'I've only just seen it – but – look, go and see if you can find it, will you? There's something in it that worries me.'

'I'll look – ' he said absently, put down the phone and went padding off to the kitchen to seek out the evening paper. Helga had gone out, so he couldn't ask her and he peered around vaguely and then found it under the cat's dish, a little spattered with milk, and bore it back into the drawing-room.

'I've got it,' he said down the phone and Poppy gave a sharp little intake of breath.

'Good – now you can see for yourself. The picture on page three – turn to that, will you?'

He did so, though not without difficulty, for the damp milk patches had spread and made the soft paper difficult to handle. But he managed it at last and looked down at a large picture of a woman in very expensive and fashionable clothes waving a hand at the camera and beaming happily.

'I've found it,' he said.

'You see what I mean?'

'I'm not sure. Let me see the caption. Just a moment.' He read it. ' "A new arrival in London that should save our souls, or so she hopes. American TV evangelist, The Lady in White – so called because of the shimmering costume she wears in her show – flies in from New York to discuss the chances of airing her show here. The anonymous star – she refuses to use her own name, since she says that she's here on the planet to glorify God, not herself – says she's praying for a happy outcome. If it keeps such glamour here, perhaps we should be praying too." '

'That's no proof of anything, is it?' he said into the phone and Poppy almost snorted.

'Did you ever hear such ridiculous nonsense! Not wanting to glorify herself, I mean. It's all she ever wanted.'

'You're sure, then?'

'Aren't you?'

He sighed. 'It's so difficult to tell with newspaper pictures. They're so grainy and – anyway mine's got some of the cat's milk on it, and that makes it harder than ever to see.'

'All the same, you knew at once what I was getting at, didn't you?'

'Yes,' he said after a long pause. 'Yes, I knew.'

'Chloe.'

'Possibly.'

'I'm sure of it. Oh, Sam, what will she do?'

'My dear Poppy, I'm not psychic!' Sam said dryly. 'There's nothing she can do that'll upset anything. When the courts awarded Bertie to you for adoption and agreed he should live with us, it was final. She can't take him away if that's what you're afraid of.'

'Of course I'm not afraid of that,' Poppy said a little acerbically. 'I'm well aware of the legal situation. It's the emotional thing that worries me. Suppose she wants to see him? Tries to beguile him? You know what Chloe's like. She could make him so miserable. And Bertie's so vulnerable.'

'Bertie's a lot tougher than you think, Poppy,' Sam said bracingly. 'He's a level-headed happy kid. He'll cope whatever she says.'

'So if she wants to see him, I have to agree?'

There was a longer silence and then Sam said, 'If you're right and that it's Chloe who's arrived here, and she wants to see Bertie, then there's only one person who can answer that question. And that's Bertie himself, isn't it?'

18

Jessie loved summer mornings when it was hot. She had a way of knowing just when the right day had arrived, and would wake early and insist that Barbara and Lally wrap her up and put her in her chair and wheel her into the park, with much manoeuvring and holding up of the traffic across the Bayswater Road at Marble Arch, and then would sit and bask in the sun like an elderly lizard, her face turned up to the sky and her eyes closed as they bumped her awkwardly over the grass to her favourite spot.

Bertie knew where he would find her on this late June morning. The weather had at last agreed to behave as though it were midsummer and he'd awoken to cloudless skies and the sound of birds shouting their fool heads off, as he put it to Sam over breakfast, and there was no doubt in his mind she'd be the best person to talk to this morning.

'D'you mind if I skive off school today, Uncle Sam?' he said abruptly as Sam got up to leave. 'It's all right, you know. They're all heads over elbows with the people doing their O's and A's and Mocks, and people like me they're quite happy to leave to muck about mostly. They wouldn't miss me – '

Sam stopped and looked down at him as he sat a little hunched over the remains of his breakfast. He had always been a good-looking child, with some of his mother's beauty in his small pointed chin with the hint of a cleft in it and the widely set dark blue eyes that tilted at the outer corners. Today he looked even more than usually handsome and that was in part, Sam knew, because of his pallor. He's slept badly, poor kid, Sam thought and wanted to lean over and hug him. But it was getting hard to do that with Bertie these days. Pushing his way through puberty as he was, with his voice taking alarming swoops from time to time and his bony wrists and ankles seeming to sprout out of clothes that had fitted him perfectly well just a few weeks ago, he found direct physical contact with Sam uncomfortable. He still hugged Robin – when she'd had time, Sam thought with sudden irritation – but even that he didn't like to do too often. Well, at least he had Jessie; she might seem an odd confidante for a boy of thirteen but clearly she was right for him; and Sam nodded.

'That's sounds reasonable to me. You're going to see Auntie Jessie, I take it?'

'I didn't think I was that obvious,' Bertie said and looked a little put out. But then he grinned. 'Well, at least no one can say I'm getting into bad company the way they keep on saying about poor old Brett at school. Poor fella. D'you know, he's almost six foot already and keeps on getting all silly about girls. His father gives him a bad time over it.'

'Poor old Brett indeed. He can't help growing up.'

'If we could stop it happening, some of us, we would,' Bertie said with a note of bitterness in his voice that made Sam look at him sharply. But then he looked up and grinned. 'It's all right. I'm not too fed up about it. But I would like to talk to Auntie Jessie. She's so – well, you know.'

'I know,' Sam said and turned to go. 'Well, I'll do you a note for school. Drop it in, will you, before you go up to Marble Arch? And Bertie – ' He stopped at the door, and Bertie looked up enquiringly. 'You really must do what *you* want, you know. Not what anyone else thinks you should. *You* have to choose.'

'I know,' Bertie said. 'That's the trouble. It'd be so much easier just to do what I'm told. I know you're supposed to want to do things for yourself when you get older, but sometimes – ' His voice trailed away.

'I know,' Sam said. 'Sometimes it's awful. But you'll have to get used to it.' But there was a smile in his voice that took the sting out of the words.

Bertie didn't even go to the flat. The sun was so very agreeable this morning, promising to be too powerful by the afternoon, that he was certain Auntie Jessie would already be in the park, and after he dropped his note into the Head's office (where the secretary received it with a sniff, clearly sure she'd been given a forgery since she was convinced that every boy in the school was the deepest dyed of villains who committed every crime there was and several new ones they'd especially invented to upset her) he took a bus to the Lancaster Gate entrance, and wandered in past the great iron tracery to make his way across the grass to the side of the Serpentine.

It was a long walk and one he enjoyed, despite his limp, but even if he didn't he would never admit it to Barbara and Lally. First of all, they made the same difficult journey pushing the heavy wheelchair with Auntie Jessie in it, and carrying the inevitable baggage without which they never stirred out – vacuum flasks and sandwiches and handkerchiefs and medicines and cold drinks for the old lady, just in case; and secondly because they'd worry so if he showed the least sign of fatigue.

He didn't think very often about his handicap. It was a mild one, consisting of little more than one weak leg with a dragging foot and less sensation on the surface than on the other. There was a big scar on his back of course, but he couldn't see that so he didn't worry about it overmuch. The thinness of his weak leg worried him sometimes; would it be difficult later on when he got like poor old Brett and girls were important? Brett seemed to think having good legs and no spots and the right sort of hair was very important when it came to girls, so Bertie supposed he would worry then. But at the moment it was all right.

Taking it all round, he didn't have a lot to worry about at all. He had the fun of having two homes and two sets of people to regard as parents, though he knew they weren't really. But who needed an ordinary mother and father when they had someone as delightful as GranDave and Gramma to spoil them and as sensitive as Uncle Sam to love them and as pretty and funny as Auntie Robin to live with? He had the others too. Penny and Sophie, and all the other aunts and uncles – especially Uncle Josh who was the best fun of all of them, and of course there were Lally and Barbara – so it had never mattered.

But now it did and he didn't like it a bit. It had been Sam who'd told him about her, this natural mother who'd turned up out of the blue, and about whom he had to make a decision. He'd talked afterwards to Auntie Robin, but she'd gone rather vague, since the shop and even more so lately. You talked to her, but she never seemed to be listening properly; she looked pretty of course – prettier than ever, lately, now he came to think of it, but she didn't actually *listen*. Not like Uncle Sam.

But that was all he did. He didn't tell you what to do. He said it was a thing you'd have to think out for yourself, but how could you? You have to know what to think about before you can make decisions, and he just didn't know enough.

'She'll tell me,' he thought then, as at last across the shimmer of the grass he saw the little knot that had to be them. That old-fashioned wheelchair was very distinctive; and he speeded up his walk a little, and wondered what it would be like to paint a picture of them sitting there by the glitter of the water; he liked painting. One of these days, though he hadn't mentioned it to anyone, he might be a famous painter. One of these days.

Auntie Jessie was happy sleeping in her wheelchair, and beside her, leaning against the wheel, Lally was dozing in the sun and Barbara was sitting just looking at her. They'd spread the big green tarpaulin – it was heavy to carry but they always brought it – and there was Barbara's little radio on it, playing softly, and a basket which was the picnic they also usually brought, and Bertie, unseen, stopped to look at the scene, not wanting to break in on it, feeling almost embarrassed to do so.

It was the look on Barbara's face as much as anything that made him feel he had to wait. She stared at Lally so intently, a bit like the way the cats sometimes stared at the birds they were stalking in the garden, but not as hard as that. More like the way Uncle Sam sometimes looked across the room at Auntie Robin when he thought no one else was looking; pleased and sad at the same time, a sort of wanting look –

Lally moved against the wheel of the chair as overhead a kite swooped, dipped and fell and a child a few yards away began to wail his distress, and Jessie woke and said irritably, 'What's all that? What's the matter?' And Barbara turned her head and saw him, all in the same moment, and she scrambled up awkwardly and came thudding across the grass towards him.

'Bertie! Is something wrong? You should be at school. Why are you here? Do Uncle Sam and Auntie Robin know? Is there something the matter?'

'Give the boy a chance!' Lally said and smiled at him. 'Come and sit down, Bertie. I've got some cokes in the bag, because I like them. Would you like one?'

'Oh, yes please, Lally,' he said eagerly and flopped down beside her on the tarpaulin. 'Hello, Auntie Jessie!'

But she'd gone back to sleep, and Bertie looked at Barbara, who had sat down again.

'Uncle Sam said I could take the day off. There isn't a lot happening at school at present except for people doing O's and A's and Mocks.'

'Hmm,' Barbara said. 'Not sure I think that's a good idea. School's school, when all's said and done. You shouldn't play about with it.'

'I'm not playing about with it,' he said with great dignity. 'I have matters in my mind to discuss.'

'Oh,' Barbara looked at him with some dismay. He looked as solemn as he'd sounded and his eyes, though they were wrinkled against the sun, were big and intense in his rather pale face. 'Can you tell us about it?'

'It's why I've come,' he said. 'Uncle Sam thought it was to talk to Auntie Jessie, but it's really to talk to you.'

Barbara glanced at Lally. 'I see,' she said and no more. Bertie had never been a boy you could rush. He had to say what he wanted to in his own time. She could fuss over him as much as she liked on minor matters, and he took it with great good humour; but she knew when to leave him space and time to do his thing his own way. This was clearly one of them.

There was a silence between them as Jessie snored gently in her wheelchair and the children around them laughed and ran and wept and the birds on the Serpentine splashed and squawked as their natures took them, and still they sat unspeaking as Bertie finished his coke and several biscuits which Lally found for him.

'Have you heard about anything?' he said then, looking at Barbara. 'Has anyone told you?'

'Told me what?'

'Well, it's my mother, you see.' He leaned back and burped gently as the coke settled and smiled at her. 'Doesn't it sound funny? I've never really said it before. My mother.'

Barbara had whitened and clutched both hands in front of her, staring at him with her eyes wide and dark.

'What about your mother?' she said, and her voice was husky. 'What's been going on?'

'Nothing yet,' Bertie said. 'It's just that she's here, you see.'

'Here?' Barbara looked round wildly as though she were expecting to see someone pop up out of the ground. 'Where?'

He laughed. 'Silly Barbara! In London. She lived in America, Uncle Sam says, all this time, and now she's come back. She wants to go on telly here.'

Lally lifted her chin. 'I did wonder,' she said softly. 'I did wonder when I read about it.'

Barbara looked at her sharply. 'Wondered what?'

'I saw it in the *Evening News*. This "Woman in White" thing. I threw the paper away before you saw it, actually. I thought, it looks like her and that'll upset our Barbara no end. And I don't like to see you upset. So, I threw it away.'

Barbara was even paler now and staring at Lally. 'You saw a picture of her, of Chloe? And you never said?'

'I wasn't sure. It sort of looked like her. But I wasn't sure and I thought, why worry you?' She looked pleadingly at Barbara. 'I hate it when you're unhappy, Bar. You know I can't bear it.'

Bertie watched them interestedly. They were talking to each other as though he weren't there and he liked it best when adults did that. It was the best way to find out the truth about things. But as they went on, speaking in low voices with Barbara getting more and more agitated and Lally more intense, he felt uncomfortable. It was the way he felt when Uncle Sam and Auntie Robin were talking sometimes, though they weren't so obviously angry in the words they said. But the feeling was the same.

'Anyway, I don't know why it matters so much. It's up to me if I see her or not,' he said loudly, needing to alter the mood, and the two women stopped and turned to him in smooth and identical movements that looked quite funny and he smiled at them, relaxed and content now. It seemed easier to think about it all now he'd told them and they'd shown how important it was by getting so upset with each other.

'How do you mean?' Barbara said.

'Gramma said. I didn't have to see her if I didn't choose to. She wants to see me, though.' He seemed to preen a little. 'She phoned Gramma and said so. She wants me to go and have dinner with her in her hotel. She's staying at Claridge's. Over there.' And he waved vaguely in the direction of Park Lane. 'I could eat whatever I wanted.'

'You can eat whatever you want any time,' Lally said sharply. 'Has anyone ever kept you on short commons?'

He thought about that. 'Well, a bit. I mean, I can't have

167

anything I want, can I? If I go to Claridge's to see her, I could have – oh, I don't know. Oysters?'

'Not in June you couldn't.'

'Why not?'

'Out of season. No R in the month.'

'Oh,' he thought about that. 'Well, frogs' legs, then.'

'Disgusting!'

'For heaven's sake, you two,' Barbara burst out. 'Stop talking nonsense! It's not to do with food, it's his whole life!'

'How can it be my whole life to go and have dinner at Claridge's with my mother?' Bertie said with great reasonableness. 'It's only one dinner.'

'But it wouldn't be – she'd try to make you go with her – she'd take you away to America and make you into one of her horrible choirboys who walk around and collect money and – '

He stared. 'Barbara, what are you talking about?'

Lally got to her feet determinedly. 'Nonsense, Bertie, just nonsense. No one can make you do anything you don't want to do. Listen, Barbara.' She knelt beside her friend and put both arms round her. 'You're working yourself up into a state over nothing. He was adopted by Mrs Poppy, you know that. Mr David and Mrs Poppy. No one can change that. It's for ever. He's safe – '

'She can! She can do anything she wants to. You don't know her! I hate her, I hate her – she'll persuade him – ' Barbara was weeping noisily now, gulping and sobbing and her eyes had swollen already and Bertie scrambled across and put his own handkerchief into her hand. It was grimy and bore a number of ink blots, but she didn't seem to mind and blew her nose lusciously.

'It's all right, Baba,' he said and the use of his infant name for her made her cry even more. 'It's all *right*. I won't go to Claridge's if you don't want me to. I truly won't. Don't cry. It's horrible when you cry.'

Lally's own eyes were wet now and Bertie sat back on his haunches and stared at them with a frown.

'Listen,' he said. 'This is silly. She isn't the devil. Just my real mother! Is she so dreadful that you have to get into this sort of flap?'

'We're all so happy as we are,' Barbara said and put one hot hand on his. 'Us here with Mrs Jessie and you with the Landows and at Mrs Poppy's – why spoil it all, letting her come in and – '

'I only wanted to talk to her,' Bertie was looking stubborn now, his lower lip held in a sort of pout, his upper a thin line. 'It's just wanting to know what sort she is.'

'A bad sort – ' Barbara began and Lally held her hand firmly and spoke loudly. 'Barbara, no! You can't say things like that to the boy. His own flesh and blood – you can't say it – '

Barbara took a deep breath to retort and then stopped and turned and looked at Bertie. Her face was streaked and pouchy but she had stopped crying and he looked back at her with that same mulish look and after a long moment she managed to smile, tremulously, but a smile for all that.

'I'm sorry, Bertie. She's right, of course she's right. It's just that I love you so much and I couldn't bear to lose you – '

He shook his head. 'I can't be lost,' he said. 'I'm not a – a something you carry in your pocket, a half-crown or something. I'm a person – '

She nodded. 'Yes, of course you are. A sensible one too. I'm the silly one. Sorry, Bertie. You do as you think best. Your Uncle Sam was right. It's up to you.'

But she looked at him yearningly for all that, as did Lally in an odd sort of way, and as though he heard her voice, Bertie knew she wanted him to say something that would please Barbara.

He thought for a while and then he nodded very slowly. 'I shall see her,' he said. 'It's because I want to have a look, you see. But not on my own and not at Claridge's.' He flashed a grin then. 'No point if there's no oysters and frogs' legs – well, it's not important. I'll ask Gramma to have a supper at her house, shall I? And I want all the people there who have to be there to help me, Uncle Sam and Auntie Robin and Gramma and GranDave and you and Lally – and maybe Uncle Josh if he can get away from his girlfriend. I don't want her, just Uncle Josh and – well, anyway, that's what I'll ask Gramma to do. Will that be all right, Barbara? Will you be happier then? Then you can see I'm not going anywhere. Just looking at her. I want to have a look, that's truly all.'

And Barbara nodded and sniffed and hiccupped, all at once

and Lally took a deep breath of relief. And Auntie Jessie woke up and said querulously, 'Where's my tea? I want my tea.'

And then they were all laughing.

19

They came out into the dust and petrol fumes of Kensington Gore and stood there blinking in the sun, very aware of the heat radiating up into their faces from the paving stones and the smell of dried, almost burned, grass in the hot breeze from the park across the road, and Robin stretched a little and yawned.

'Marvellous,' she said. 'It doesn't matter how often you hear it, it comes up fresh and new.'

'That's Beethoven for you,' he said and turned back to look at the building behind them. 'I wish I liked the place as much as I liked the music.'

She looked too. It lowered back at her, all red brick and frieze and she laughed. 'The Albert Hall's been part of my life for so long I hardly even see it any more. It's just there, you know? I suppose some people would think it ugly. Actually, I think I rather like it.'

'It's amazing what you can get used to.' Hamish tucked his hand into her elbow and they began to walk. 'Now, what? Tea perhaps? Are you thirsty?'

'Not particularly.'

'Then shall we stretch our legs? After sitting still for so long – '

'Oh, I'm sorry. I just didn't think. It must be hell for you, being so tall, and – I didn't mean to be so thoughtless.'

'You weren't.' He smiled down at her. 'I doubt it was an accident we were at the very end of the row of seats we were in.'

She went a little pink. 'Well, I did ask for them,' she admitted. 'I thought you'd find it easier than – '

'Yes,' he said. 'It helps a lot.' They walked on in silence for a while, and without consulting each other crossed the road at

171

Alexandra Gate to go into the Park. Then he said, 'I'm not as bad as I was, of course.'

'Indeed you're not,' she said warmly. 'You managed marvellously at the studios. I thought the programme was great and no one would have guessed for a moment that you were anything but calm and comfortable.'

'I was calm and comfortable,' he said. 'You were there. That's why.'

He held her arm a little more tightly to guide her past a group of strolling Arabs in full Middle Eastern dress, the men walking in front of the veiled women and the children bouncing along among them like so many puppies, but when they'd passed he didn't release her; he just went on holding her very close. She was very aware of the warmth of him beside her, and knew she ought to extricate herself, but she didn't want to. She revelled in the way he made her feel, thinking of nothing but the sensation of his hand against her inner arm, glad it was high summer and she was wearing a sleeveless dress.

'This is getting difficult, isn't it?' he said suddenly and she turned her head and looked at him.

'Difficult?'

'Oh, Robin, let's not just pretend! I've stayed down here much longer than I'd meant to, or have any cause to. We can't go on just being polite. Or I can't.'

'I think we'd better sit down,' she said a little unsteadily, and pulled away from him and made for one of the benches beside the broad path, and sat down as close to the corner as she could. He hesitated a moment and then came and sat beside her, but not too close.

To their right the water of the Serpentine danced and glittered in the bright afternoon sun, and the parents and children out for a Sunday afternoon stroll shouted and laughed at each other as toy boats essayed out from the side, and sometimes came back and sometimes turned over, and ice-cream vans rang their chimes and from somewhere far away the faint sounds of a military band came to them. She could see the red brick of the Serpentine gallery on the other side of the path and the beds of drooping azaleas and geraniums and petal-shedding roses and tried to concentrate on them. But she couldn't, of course.

'So, here we are sitting down,' Hamish said and she could hear the amusement in his voice. 'Does it make a great deal of difference?'

'It makes a lot,' she said. 'I'm not good at walking and being sensible all at the same time.'

'Being sensible? What would being sensible mean, now?'

'It would mean telling you that it was fun to see you again, that I've enjoyed seeing so much of you these past few weeks, and that it's high time you went back to Edinburgh and disappeared.'

'I know that full well,' he said. 'I've been thinking it myself for some time. There's a limit, after all, to the number of lies you can tell to your colleagues about why you can't come back and get on with your work. Like over the holidays and the extra library research – they'll begin to twig soon that there's something more interesting here in London than the medical libraries.'

'Lying?' she said and her voice was unsteadier then ever. 'And there's me thinking you were a man of conscience.'

'I've the sort of conscience that makes sense,' he said. 'It'll no' let me kill people in wars, but it doesna' make an unseemly fuss over lies that hurt no one. And which make me feel better.'

'Oh,' she said and could say no more.

'I shouldna' have gone away to the mines, should I?' he said then.

'What?'

'If I'd stayed in London all those years ago, it would all have been different. We might have been here in the Park like them – ' And he lifted his chin to indicate a couple of middle-aged people who were walking arm in arm with their heads together, talking. 'An old married couple – '

'There's no guarantee it would have been different,' she said. 'You're taking a lot for granted.'

'If we're like this now, surely we felt it even more when we were younger?' he said. 'I know I did.'

'You never said.'

'I had no right to. What did I have? No prospects, no future – '

'No future?' She laughed then. 'Oh, no of course no future, Professor Todd!'

He laughed too. 'Well, who was to know then? The thing is, now is now. And it's – '

'I wish you wouldn't,' she said urgently, and tried to pull

closer into the side of the bench against the iron arm rest. 'This is silly and dangerous.'

'Dangerous,' he said and sighed. 'I suppose it is for you. For me, of course, it's no such thing. For me it could be – well, it could be everything.'

'Everything – ' It wasn't a question nor was it a statement. She just let the word drift between them, and he nodded.

'I'm alone, Robin. Sarah died ten years ago and there were never to be any children. She wasn't the sort of woman to be interested in children anyway – so there's just me and the work. And now I've seen you again and it all seems so – ' He shrugged. 'I wonder what I've wasted my life on.'

'Wasted your life? Ye Gods!' She almost shouted it. 'How can you say that? You've done incredible work, pushed the research into cancer miles forward – how can you possibly say you've wasted your life?'

'My personal life and my working life are two different things. Public success and financial success aren't worth a lot if you're not as happy as you could be – are they?'

She was silent and he leaned closer and took her hand. 'Are they?'

She thought of the shop and how busy it was, thought of the way her customers thanked her and squealed their delight over what she had to offer them and thought of how it was at home in the evenings, and how all she wanted to do was get to bed and sleep so that she'd be nearer the time to go to the shop again, and couldn't answer him.

'I feel cheated sometimes,' he said abruptly and leaned back and turned to stare across at the flowerbeds and the grass and she mimicked his action and they both sat silently staring ahead.

It was probably at the same moment that they became aware of the fact that they were looking in exactly the same direction. Among the couples lying untidily on the grass, some of them asleep and some kissing in a desultory fashion, there was one pair, she in the skimpiest of shorts and a sun top, and he wearing only a pair of white cotton trousers, his shirt on the grass beside him, who were much more enthusiastic. They were kissing and caressing each other with an energy and a lack of inhibition that even on a hot day in the middle of the Park, and in these much more open-minded days, Robin told herself, was a bit much; and

174

she felt her face begin to redden as the couple rolled together and their hands moved across the expanses of bare flesh, both clearly completely oblivious of the fact that they were being watched by more than one bystander.

It was Hamish who managed to break the spell. 'I wish I were like them,' he said and his voice was harsh and tightly controlled. 'I wish with all the heart I have that I could be as brave as them and as honest as them and as strong as them. I'd take you now and I'd make love to you in just that way, only even more –'

'Hamish, for God's sake, will you be quiet!' she cried and put her hands up to her face to cover the redness, but he wasn't going to let her do that. He turned and took hold of her roughly and pulled her close and began to kiss her with the same sort of abandon as the young people in the grass and she was so startled she could do nothing to stop him. And then she no longer wanted to stop him and responded as eagerly as it was possible for her to do.

It seemed a very long time before they broke apart breathlessly and then he was speaking in her ear, letting words come out between the kisses and soft bites he was giving her, and she listened and nodded and didn't care about anything at all, only the here and the now and that they were together. There wasn't anything else that mattered.

She woke suddenly and lay staring in puzzlement at the rich blue of the square window that was in her line of vision as she lay there on her side; and was puzzled. Someone had moved the window in the night, she told herself muzzily. It should be on the other side, surely? And she turned to peer at her bedside clock, but it wasn't there and she turned to look at Sam's, on his bedside table, and then she remembered in a great rush and sat up suddenly. And beside her he stirred and reached up one hand for her.

She could see better now and stared around, feeling the distaste rising in her. Her clothes were scattered about the floor, her dress, her bag, her sandals, her underwear, and his too, and what had seemed right and natural before, when they had come into this room, was now only messy, even sordid, and she lifted her hand to her mouth and rubbed it. There was a roughness

175

there and she knew she had hurt her lip, so intense had been her kissing, and that made her feel ashamed too.

He had dozed off again and she slid out of the bed and moving as quietly as she could picked up her clothes and looked around for a door that might lead to a bathroom and her heart sank. This was a very small and old hotel. The old wardrobe with his suitcase on the top, the anonymity of the dreary furniture, and the meagreness of the curtains and bedcovers told her that. And there was only one door. She would have to go out to find a bathroom, to wash and dress and make herself look decent, and who she might meet out there was something not to be thought about. So she picked up the dressing-gown he had left lying over an armchair and shrugged into it and collected her things and crept out.

She found the bathroom the hard way, trundling along the anonymous dusty corridor in which she found herself until the smell of damp and cheap soap and talcum powder announced success, and locked herself in, grateful no one had been around, and set to work to make herself Robin again; for as she was, naked under a man's dressing-gown in a strange hotel, the last person she felt herself to be was the respectable wife and mother and shopkeeper she had hitherto thought herself. She was a wanton, a slut – the words tumbled around in her head, getting more and more ugly, more and more insulting, and she tried to shut them out by scrubbing herself dry on the rough towel she found hanging on the back of the door, until her body glowed and her skin actually hurt.

It was odd, she thought when she was dressed and looked in the mirror. I look the same as I did. Don't I? But I'm not the same. I'll never be the same again –

She let herself out of the bathroom and went back down the corridor and stopped outside his room. There was silence, no hint of movement, and she stood uncertainly, trying to think what to do. Just hang his dressing-gown on the door knob? To just go and leave him, not to see him again – could she do that? For the first time since she'd woken she allowed herself to remember, and it was, she had to admit, a good memory. He had been a quick and eager lover but a tender one for all that; that his need for her had been voracious was evident but he had been concerned that she should be as eager as he was, and had deployed considerable skill in making sure of it. Sam had always been all she had ever wanted as far as sex was concerned; a little dull and predictable after a while, but what else should a married woman expect? It would be childish to think that it could be all the time in a marriage bed the way it had been this afternoon in this illicit hotel one.

And this could get the same way, a secret voice began to whisper. It was like this with Sam at the start. Remember? And she made herself remember how it had been with Sam all those years ago and she couldn't. Her body still glowed too much with the memory of Hamish to conjure up anything of Sam. When she thought of this afternoon she remembered with her body. When she thought of Sam she remembered only with her mind. It was quite different.

And this could get the same. Next time, if there is one, could be as exciting and perhaps a dozen or so times after that. But then? Wouldn't you start to think of Sam and the house in Hampstead and the children and the shop –

She stood there staring at the silent door, horrified by her own thoughts. To put her house and shop in front of love, in front of the sort of love that Hamish had shown this afternoon? What sort of materialistic creature was she, for heaven's sake? How could she be so calculating? Surely she should be prepared to throw all her cautions away, should go back into that room and tell Hamish that she'd come with him to Edinburgh and leave everything behind for the sake of his love, that the future would be the two of them and her past would be dead, quite dead –

Somewhere in the depths of the building a clock began to chime, and she still stood there, trying to think, not listening but aware of the sound. A Westminster chime, ringing the quarter, then the half, and then the three quarters, and finally the hour, and she began to count the strikes automatically. One, two, three, four, five, six, seven, eight –

She was so startled by her reaction to the time that she actually took a step back. Eight o'clock? It can't be. I'm supposed to be at Ma's by seven thirty, in Norland Square. They're having a dinner party for Chloe and I have to be there for Bertie –

She had dropped the dressing-gown and was half-way down the stairs before she realized she'd even moved. But she didn't stop. She had her bag hanging over her shoulder and she scrabbled in it for money for the phone, and found no change, and by then she was at the foot of the stairs and across the lobby saw the receptionist's desk and ran for it.

She didn't stop to consider what the woman might think, of what effect her presence might have on Hamish's reputation in the hotel. When they'd come in he'd just led her quietly across to the staircase and up to his room, and there had been no problems, but now as she reached the desk she had a fleeting concern for appearances. Did she look as though she'd spent the past few hours in a strange man's room making desperate love to him, leaving her husband and children forgotten at home? What does such a woman look like? a part of her mind wondered, even as she said breathlessly to the receptionist, 'I have to make an urgent call – no change – sorry – please, I must use your phone – please – '

The woman was startled and looked dubious, but Robin was already reaching across the desk in her urgency and the woman didn't stop her when she picked up the phone and began to dial her mother's number, just standing there staring at her.

'Ma?' as Poppy answered. 'Oh, Ma, I'm so sorry – been held up – on my way – is she there yet?'

'Of course not.' Poppy's voice was crisp and a little curt. 'When did she ever keep decent time? But I thought better of you, Robin – '

'Couldn't help it, Ma – I'll explain when I see you – ' Stock-taking was what she'd said she'd been doing, in order to get away on a Sunday afternoon. How can there be emergencies when you're stock-taking? Oh, God, I'll have to think of something. 'Tell Sam and the children.'

'They've been worried – ' Poppy said and her voice was even crisper. 'But I'll tell them. Be as quick as you can, she'll be sure to be here soon – ' And she hung up and Robin slowly cradled the phone and looked at the woman behind the desk.

'Thank you,' she said and turned to go and then turned back. 'Please would you tell Professor Todd – '

She stopped helplessly and the woman stared at her in the same silent fashion, her eyes round and rather fishlike, and Robin tried again.

'Tell him I was – I had to – Oh, it doesn't matter. It doesn't matter at all – '

And she turned and ran, out into Berners' Street, praying that in the early evening of a fine Sunday heaven would smile on her and send her a taxi.

20

Bertie was very aware of what he was wearing. It had been Barbara who had said he should have something extra nice and Uncle Sam had agreed when she'd phoned him, and he'd had a dreary morning trailing round Selfridge's and Marshall and Snelgrove's and Lord knows where else in consequence. But he had to admit that he liked the way he looked. Barbara had let him choose check trousers instead of the usual dark grey and that felt good, and they were a good grownup sort of fit. To go with them she'd chosen the shirt, which was a dull ordinary old blue thing, but he'd been allowed to choose his tie in bright red and his blazer and he had one with brass buttons which he liked a lot. Much better than his school uniform blazer with its scuffed sleeves and bedraggled pockets which was perfect for school but not for meeting natural mothers in.

He was beginning to feel a little bothered. So far, thinking about this evening had been quite fun. He'd imagined his mother throwing her arms wide at him and crying, 'My Child!' and himself saying nicely but firmly, 'Well, actually, I'd rather not go to America just at present, thanks, though maybe next holidays for a few weeks,' and everyone smiling at him approvingly. Natural Mother included; but now it was here and she had almost arrived it was different. Worrying, in fact.

They were all here. Lally and Barbara, who had actually agreed to get someone else in to keep Auntie Jessie company so that they could both come, and Auntie Lee and Uncle Jeremy and Sophie and Penny and Uncle Sam as well as GranDave and Gramma. Auntie Robin had just arrived, looking very pink and anxious because of some sort of problem at the shop; she'd gone there just to do some stock-taking, but someone walking past the shop had had a heart attack and she'd had to look after him and take him to the Middlesex Hospital and by the time everything was sorted out she'd been late; but she looked nice even though she was apologizing to everyone for not having time to change. Very nice really, all shiny and bright somehow.

Together with himself they made nine people. The only important one who wasn't here was Uncle Josh, who had to be in Birmingham where he was rehearsing some music for one of the shows he was involved with. Otherwise here they all were. It made him feel very strange to have so many people gathering together, and all on account of him.

They weren't making as much noise as they usually did when they were all together, Bertie thought, and that made him uneasy too; and then as suddenly Lee, who was standing by the window, said 'Hush!' and they all stopped and turned to look at her, he knew they were as nervous as he was. And that made him feel really very bad indeed.

'She's here,' Lee breathed, peering down the side of the curtain and Sophie and Penny ran across, though their father tried to pull them back, and then they all gave up and joined in the group staring down into the street. All except Bertie. He'd wait and see her properly the first time, he decided.

Downstairs he could hear the people Gramma had got in from the hotel to do the cooking for tonight. She'd thought Oliver would be one of them but he'd said he had to do night duty at the Bittacy and couldn't manage it (which had quite pleased Bertie, because Oliver wasn't bad – as cousins went – but could be quite mean when he was in the mood) so there were just three of them; and they were making a certain amount of clattering noise down there and some very pleasant smells. It had been nice to look forward to supper when he'd first smelled the roast chicken and the rich salady scent of mayonnaise, but now somehow he'd lost his appetite. Maybe it would come back when they actually sat down.

The doorbell pealed and he felt everyone in the drawing-room stiffen. And then Gramma moved forwards and said comfortably, 'I'll let her in myself. The others are busy in the kitchen,' and went away down the stairs and somehow Bertie managed not to follow her. It was difficult, because what he wanted to do very much indeed was follow her down, go straight into the kitchen and out of the back door before his mother came in at the front.

Uncle Sam seemed to understand. He'd been standing next to Auntie Robin trying to talk to her, but she hadn't much to say, just standing looking as though she'd only just woken up, in a way, and when Bertie looked at him he seemed to know and came over to stand beside him.

'Feeling all right, old man?' he said and put his hand on Bertie's shoulder. It felt good there, and Bertie took a deep breath and even managed to smile.

'I'm fine thanks, Uncle Sam,' he said. And he really was. Well, almost.

There was a sound of voices outside, one of them Gramma's rather low one and the other high and a little breathless and giggly and there was a wash of marvellous scent as the door opened. He closed his eyes to breathe in the scent, which he liked a lot, and then slowly opened them.

The thing that amazed him was how small she was. A little person, shorter than Gramma, who wasn't exactly huge. In fact she wasn't a lot taller than he was himself. Old, of course; he could see that at once. She had a face that was very smooth with make-up, like Johnson's mother when she came to school to meet him or talk to the teachers (which she did a great deal more often than Johnson liked). She used a lot of make-up too, and she had that pale smooth polished sort of look.

But Johnson's mother's colours weren't so good, Bertie decided. This polished person looked golden. Her dress was yellow and over it she had a floaty sort of coat in a darker yellow. Her shoes were the same colour and so were her gloves, but her bag was a big splash of bright orange against her skirt. Her hair was the yellowest of all, he thought, cut into fancy shapes a bit like Auntie Robin's but not quite so hairlike. It could have been painted on her head, it was so smooth and shiny.

She came towards him, talking all the time, looking at everyone in the room as well as him, her eyes seeming to dart about like fish in a bowl.

'It is, isn't it?' she said breathlessly. 'Of course it is. It just has to be. Oh my, but you're so *big* – '

It all happened rather fast. She was almost in front of him with her head poking forward so that she could kiss him. He felt it coming, knew it was inevitable and was determined it shouldn't be, and he pushed his hand forward and said loudly, 'I'm-Bertie-How-do-you-do,' in one loud gobbling breath and grabbed her hand so closely to her front that she had to step back a bit before they could shake properly. But it stopped her kissing him and he thought – one to me.

'Oh, so English, bless his little heart!' she cried. 'So polite – ' and she made the word sound odd, saying each half of it evenly; po-lite, so po-lite and inside his head Bertie practised it. It sounded silly, he decided. Po-lite –

Then everyone began to talk, his mother most of all. He'd have to think of her as Chloe. She didn't look like a mother, that was the thing. Auntie Robin did, even though she'd gone so smart lately, and certainly Gramma did and even Barbara and Lally did though they had no children. The small person in yellow looked like none of them and therefore calling her Chloe was the only thing he could do.

She sounded like the people on the films and that was funny. She talked a lot and he listened to the words mostly rather than to what she was actually saying while they all had drinks (Sam gave him a little sweet sherry with some lemonade in it which pleased Bertie. It wasn't his favourite drink but it was a proper grownup one and he was one of them tonight, no question) and slowly he began to relax.

She was all right, really, wasn't she? He tried to imagine what Brett and Johnson would think of her if they saw her, and some of the older boys at school, and decided that on the whole they'd approve. She wasn't an embarrassment, at least. Odd, certainly, but not unpleasantly peculiar.

Until they all went down to dinner. That was when he changed his mind. The table looked great, all glittering with candles and glass and he could see Gramma was pleased with the people from the hotel and they knew it and were very pleased too. That made everyone feel good, and they took a lot of food on their plates and were eating happily. It was the sort of meal that Bertie most liked; a cool sweet melon to start with and then cold roast chicken and piles of potato salad and other salads and masses of mayonnaise; perfect. Everyone else seemed to like it too, except for Chloe who had hardly anything on her plate and didn't eat what she did have, using her mouth just for talking.

He'd settled to enjoying his supper and paying no attention to the others, but then suddenly she said, 'Colin,' and he felt Gramma beside him go stiff and that alerted him.

'Bertie,' Gramma said quietly. 'Let's be clear on that, Chloe.'

Chloe laughed, a high little sound. 'Oh, I'm sorry. It's so hard for me to remember. It's how I always think of him in my yearnings you know, in the dark nights – well, if I must. Bertie.'

He stored the exchange away in his head to ask his grandmother about at some later date and looked at her warily.

'Yes?'

'So tell me all about yourself.'

'Er – ' he said. 'Er – I go to school.'

'Well, sure, of course you do. And what grade are you?'

'Oh, really, Chloe!' GranDave said suddenly. 'Don't come the acid with us! You were at school here yourself, and you know perfectly well they don't count in grades in England. Bertie's a fourth former. You remember the system as well as I do.'

She looked a little pained. 'For pity's sake, David, I have lived in Russelville, Alabama, for so many years now that I have quite forgotten I ever lived here – '

'Oh, I don't think so, Chloe! You found us well enough tonight!' David said cheerfully and went back to his chicken. 'Anyway, for the record, I haven't forgotten what life was like in Baltimore back in the twenties and earlier, before I came to live in England, and that, Lord help me, was something like thirty-five years ago. I guess I have a better memory than you, hmm?'

'And I guess I have a very busy life in the States,' Chloe retorted. 'So maybe that's why I have no time to think of the old days.'

There was a little silence and then she turned back to Bertie. 'So, do you like school – Col – Bertie?'

'Yes,' Bertie said.

'And do you go to church?'

He stared and shook his head. 'We have prayers at school,' he said after a moment.

Uncle Sam laughed. 'Clearly he thinks that's enough,' he said dryly. 'I'd agree with you, old man. I felt the same in my school days.'

Bertie flashed a glance at him and grinned. Another one to our side, he thought and then was a little puzzled. He hadn't meant to see this as a battle. Just a chance to meet her. Oh, well.

'But he ought to go to church,' Chloe said loudly. 'Everyone should!'

' – Or to synagogue perhaps?' David murmured.

Chloe lifted her chin sharply. 'I suppose. Anyway, I was talking to Bertie. His mother's a Christian so of course he is too.'

'Am I?' Bertie said. 'I don't think so.'

'You see – ' Chloe was shrill suddenly. 'He's had no proper religious education! I'm sure if the Court knew that, Poppy – '

'That it wouldn't make the slightest difference. Not after thirteen years of silence from you,' David said and lifted his brows. 'Do we have to talk this way? Meeting Bertie is one thing. Making him so very uncomfortable is surely another.'

'I only wanted to know how he worships,' Chloe said and wiped her lips on her napkin, leaving a heavy smear of lipstick which made Poppy look disdainful.

'Well, he told you – ' David began and then Bertie cut in.

'I'm not sure about worshipping,' he said clearly. 'I don't think it's a good thing just to worship. It stops you thinking.'

'That's a terrible thing to say!' Chloe cried. 'You just have to look in the Good Book to know that – '

Bertie ignored that. 'I think you have to be – to be thoughtful about everything,' he said. 'I talked to Mr Webber about it at school and he says I'm just a natural animist. Anyway, I think that's what he said. I told him I thought everything has its own special sort of spirit, you know, stones and ants and trees? They all mean something. They wouldn't be here if they didn't. So you have to be respectful to everything. That's better than worshipping, Mr Webber said, and he's right. If you worship one thing it might make you hate another and hurt it. That can't be right.'

There was a little silence and then Sam said softly, 'Attaboy!' and Robin looked up from her plate at which she had been staring blankly and gazed at him in startled awareness.

'That is downright pagan,' Chloe said. 'You can't tell me that's the right way to raise a boy, to be a pagan.' She turned her back on David and looked directly at Poppy. 'Why, if I went to the Courts here and I told them what this poor benighted child here has said in front of us all – we're all witnesses – why, they'd agree it was high time he came to a real good Christian home where he'd get the best sort of education a boy could have – '

'Working for you, Chloe?' David said softly. 'Being one of your angelic choirboys? Oh, I can see it. He's a handsome child and he'd look *divine* in a ruff and a cassock. And of course he limps so you can make a real exhibition of him! Is that what you want? Well, you can't have that. Bertie is Bertie. This is his home, we're his family and there is no way I would ever let you spoil his life for him. None of us would. We love him too much.'

Barbara leapt to her feet, clapping, and Lally pulled on her sleeve to make her sit down. The others sat looking from one to the other in a state of great embarrassment, but with a sort of relish too; Jeremy was bright eyed and excited and Lee too had a watchful calculating air. And then Bertie stood up.

'Thank you for my supper, Gramma. May I leave the table, please?' he said politely.

Poppy looked at him worriedly and held out a hand to him and he took it. 'Darling, if we could have protected you from this, we would have done. But we all talked about it and we thought you're such a sensible person and so – well, you know we love you, don't you? You know you're safe with us? I thought, after we all talked, we all thought, you'd be better knowing the truth of it, once and for all. That your mother wants to take you away to America to be part of her work there – '

They were all very still watching him; even Chloe was staring at him. He'd never felt so important or so lonely in all his life. He looked from one face to another; GranDave, smiling and nodding, talking to him with his eyes, telling him it was all right, everything was all right, no need to worry, they'd sort it out; and Uncle Sam worried and sitting very straight trying to will him to think for himself, and Barbara and Lally both sitting very still with white faces, and the others – and he lifted his chin and looked at Chloe closely for a long time. Looked at her face with its smooth polished surface and the dark blue eyes that were so like his own and the bright yellow hair and he took a deep and slightly shaky breath.

'It has been very interesting to meet you,' he said clearly. 'But I know now you're not my mother. I don't have a mother. I've got something much better. I've got Gramma and GranDave and Uncle Sam and Auntie Robin and Barbara and – and everyone.' He made a vague gesture to take in the table. 'And that's enough for anyone. I'll go to America one day, I dare say. When I'm a famous painter, or maybe I'll be a famous actor. I haven't quite decided yet. But when I do, I'm sure I'll go there. For me, not for you, or anyone else really. Maybe for GranDave – ' He looked at him and grinned. 'He's told me so much about Baltimore I have to go and look at it again for him. But not to see you. So, do you mind if I go now? I really don't want any more supper, and Gramma said I can watch telly in her room before I go to sleep, and there's a programme on I like. Good night. I hope you have a nice stay here.'

And he thought, that's three up to me, and I think that's the winner, looked round at everyone and said, 'Good night,' and went out of the room.

There was a long silence after he'd gone and then Chloe stood up.

'I know what it is,' she said shrilly. 'You all ganged up on me and poisoned his mind against me. Well, you can keep him. He's been ruined, you hear me? Ruined. I wouldn't have a boy like that anywhere near me or mine. He'd pollute the minds of the other boys in the choir with notions like those. You've put the devil into him, all of you, and I hope you burn in hell, every one of you, for the evil creatures you are. I'm going now and I'll never come back again – you're all evil, every one of you. You always have been – '

She slammed the dining-room door and after a moment the front door and they could hear her footsteps outside as she ran along the square until they vanished into the distant rumble of the traffic in Holland Park Avenue, and then there was a sudden burst of chatter from Lee and from Sòphie and Penny who had been sitting enthralled and open mouthed. Barbara was weeping noisily in a mixture of anticlimax and relief and Lally was comforting her, and even Robin was talking to Sam as Poppy and Lee and Jeremy sat with their heads together chattering busily.

David got up quietly and under cover of the chatter, went out of the room and upstairs to Bertie. He liked the same telly programme and anyway he needed time to dry his eyes. The boy could still make him weep, even after thirteen years, he thought. Only tonight it was a different sort of weeping. The right sort.

21

'Please, Robin, I don't think I want to know – ' Chick said but Robin didn't seem to hear her. She just went on talking, sitting with her head down over her coffee and stirring it as though she was trying to bore a hole in the bottom of the cup.

And anyway, Chick thought as desolation filled her, what's the point of stopping her? She's told me now, I know. And I hate her. I hate her –

It was a horrible feeling. She and Robin had been friends for twenty-five years – more than half their lives. How could she hate her? How could she turn her back on her when she was so obviously miserable?

And what about me? she thought, as she too stirred her coffee. What about how I'm feeling? And what about Sam? And as Robin's voice went on she let her mind drift away into a story all of its own, quite out of her control. It was as though she were a spectator at the theatre of her own imagining, and she was enthralled. There was Sam sitting at his desk in his cluttered office at the Clinic, staring miserably into space as he contemplated Robin's cruelty to him, and there was she herself, Chick, coming to stand behind him and touch his shoulder to comfort him, and he turning to her and taking her in his arms and telling her how wrong he'd been not to notice her before and Robin was a thing of the past and the future belonged to them, to Chick and to him and –

'It's as though it was someone else, not me,' Robin said. 'Do you know what I mean, Chick? Chick?'

'Mmm?' Chick roused herself and looked up at Robin. 'Someone else? Yes, I think I know what you mean.' And she refused to watch her private theatre any more, though she knew that somewhere deep inside her mind, behind its curtains, the

188

performance continued to its logical and, to Chick, dreadful yet so desirable conclusion.

'I can't think what possessed me.' Robin sounded fretful now, like an irritable child and that sharpened Chick's tongue.

'You can't escape your own actions by pretending it was all out of your control, you know,' she said. 'He didn't exactly rape you, did he?'

'Chick!' Robin stared at her, horrified. 'Don't say that! I mean, how could you – '

'Oh, I'm sorry! It's just that – well, it won't help to make excuses, Robin. You weren't possessed. It was something you did. Presumably because you wanted to.'

'That's what's so dreadful. Of course I wanted to. I've never felt anything like it in my life. I was – my God, it's shaming to remember – I was desperate for him, I didn't give a damn about anyone or anything. Just getting back to that room and – and – ' Again she bent her head. 'It was like – '

'Spare me the details, please,' Chick said and got up to fetch more coffee, although the pot on the table was still half full.

Robin bit her lip, mortified at her own stupidity. Chick widowed, alone – how could she, her closest friend, be so wicked as to talk about such things to someone who might now be feeling the loss of her own partner more keenly than ever? Chick and Harry had been passionately happy together, as Robin well knew. In the days when they had been young brides who confided in each other there had been times when Robin had marvelled a little at Chick's evident delight in sex. She'd always enjoyed it herself, of course she had, for Sam had been a considerate and caring lover, but it had never been quite as intense as it seemed to have been for Chick. And now, when for the first time in her life sex was a powerful drive, she was telling Chick about it in a way that might make it seem that she was crowing over her, and at the very least would sharpen her sense of loss.

'I'm so sorry,' she said. 'I didn't mean to – well, I'm sorry. But dearest Chick, who can I talk to if not to you? Ma? Can you imagine? Lee – We've never been close, even though we're half-sisters. It's the age gap as much as anything else – that's why I came to you. I need help, so badly.' And she looked appealingly at Chick who was at once all compunction.

'Oh, it's all right, love,' she said and sat beside Robin and took her hand. Who are you, she was asking herself furiously, to think ill of Robin for falling in love with someone else? Haven't you done precisely the same thing as she has? If not in reality, in your mind. And wouldn't you do it in reality if you could? If you'd had the opportunity she'd had, if Sam suddenly noticed you and how you were feeling and showed an atom of interest, wouldn't you be there, ready for anything?

But that's the thing, she thought then as she leaned over and gave her handkerchief to Robin, whose eyes were now brimming. I wouldn't. I couldn't. It's different for me, with my Harry dead; it wouldn't really be wrong, but I still couldn't do what Robin did, because she still has Sam and he has her –

She shook her head then to clear her confused thinking and squeezed Robin's hand.

'Has he gone back to Scotland now?' she asked.

Robin shook her head. 'I can't tell. He keeps phoning as much as he ever did. He doesn't come into the shop any more, which is one comfort. He used to just walk in and want to see me, and it got so bad I had to hide in the back. I told Beckie he was an old flame who was making a nuisance of himself and I wanted to get rid of him and she thought it a huge joke and did all she could to help. She made him so uncomfortable about coming in he stopped. But he phoned and phoned – and still does. So maybe he's calling from the hotel still. Or maybe he's back in Edinburgh. I just don't know. I just hang up – '

'Why don't you talk to him? Find out?'

Robin stared. 'Haven't you been listening? I can't – '

'Why not?'

'I don't trust myself. If I talk to him I might – I can't – '

The devil in Chick sat up and took notice. 'You might what? Go again to his hotel?'

'Anywhere,' Robin said miserably. 'Anywhere at all.'

'Then perhaps you should talk to him,' Chick said calmly, watching her face, and Robin gaped at her, amazed.

'But Sam – the children – '

'Yours wouldn't be the first marriage to end in a divorce court. It's happening all the time these days – it's different now. If people are unhappy, if they don't love each other any more, it seems the best thing to do.'

Robin shook her head. 'I didn't say I didn't love Sam.'

'But you're besotted with Hamish! Are you trying to tell me you're one of these romantic-novel heroines who're in love with two people at the same time?'

'No,' Robin said with all the dignity she could. 'I'm not. I'm not in love with Sam – I just love him. He's been the middle of my life for – oh, for ever. I can't imagine him not being there for always. But I'm *in* love with Hamish and it's the maddest thing that ever – I have to cure it. It's like a disease. An infection. I have to stay in isolation until the bug loses its virulence. Haven't I?'

Chick said nothing but she shrugged slightly and Robin frowned.

'Chick, are you trying to force me to – I mean, I came to you to help me be sensible, and here you are telling me to end my marriage. What about the kids?'

'Will they be any worse off than they are at present?' Chick said. 'You're not exactly the ideal mother right now, are you? Not that it matters too much with Oliver – for good or ill he's an adult now. The girls – well, they'll get their A levels, that's for sure, and they'll be off to University, and that leaves just Bertie and he's just as happy at Poppy and David's as he is with you – it's not as though you were tied with really young children.'

'I don't understand,' Robin said and shook her head in genuine puzzlement. 'What happened to you? You were always the most –I don't know – sensible person. The one who believed in doing the thing that was best for the majority. Not the selfish thing but the wise thing. And here you are encouraging me to go potty – I don't understand.'

Chick shrugged again, keeping her head down so that she didn't have to look at the expression on Robin's face. 'Times change, I suppose. We hear about it all the time. It's not the way it used to be. These days people are more relaxed, more – well, they know they've only got one life and they want to make the best of it. They're not the way we were, terrified virgins till our wedding days – '

'I wasn't terrified!' Robin said. 'As for virgin – dammit, Sam and I came as close as – I mean, long before we were married we – and as for you and Harry – I remember, if you've forgotten! You told me – '

'I know, I know. And I don't mean in virtual fact, but in mind. There's only ever been one man in my life and that was Harry and we knew we were going to be married so it made no difference. But now the young ones – they have all sorts of affairs long before they marry. Eventually, people'll probably stop marrying altogether and they'll just wander from one to the other. It's so easy now, isn't it? No need to worry about having babies before you want to, and with penicillin and all there isn't even any worry over infections or whatever – so maybe we're wrong to be so stuffy. If you've found that you get more out of life with Hamish, maybe you ought to accept the fact and go off with him – '

She stopped, horrified. It wasn't her own voice she was hearing, it couldn't be. This wasn't Chick, being the sort of friend she ought to be. This was Chick being greedy and self-interested and wanting Sam. And it would be so much easier if Sam's wife wasn't around and had no right to complain –

She put up both hands and rubbed her face. 'Don't listen to me,' she said unsteadily. 'I'm talking nonsense. I'm tired and – '

'But perhaps you're right,' Robin said slowly. 'I came to you because I thought you'd do a Jiminy Cricket for me.' And she hummed in a cracked little voice, 'And always let your conscience be your guide – '

'I'm not here to be your conscience or anyone's but my own,' Chick said, and her voice was rougher. 'I've got enough to cope with on my own. Don't load me with your decisions, Robin.'

'Well, I'm not going to, am I? It looks like it's me who says it'd be wrong to see Hamish again and you who are saying go ahead – '

'I'm not saying another word. I've said too much already – '

'But it's – ' Robin sighed. 'It's what I wanted to hear, I suppose. I keep having these daydreams, real ones, like sleep ones, you know what I mean? I don't sort of choose what I'll dream about or make plans the way you do – when you're awake and thinking. I just see it all happening in front of my eyes, as though it's nothing to do with me, I've got no control. It just happens – '

'I know what you mean,' Chick said. 'It happens to me too.' And they sat in silence for a while, thinking their own thoughts.

Chick stirred first. 'I've made a decision of my own,' she said abruptly. 'It might upset Sam, a little.'

Robin lifted her head. 'Upset Sam?'

'I'm leaving the Clinic.

192

'Oh, no! He'll be devastated!'

Chick looked wistful for a moment and then steeled her face. 'Will he? Well, it can't be helped.'

'Why? Is there something?'

'No. It's just that – ' She hesitated. 'It's time I moved on.'

'Moved on where? And why? That's not a good enough reason for –'

'I can't cope with psychiatry any more.' Chick was getting desperate now. Until she said it she hadn't realized what she was planning to do, but she knew now she was right. Whether Robin chose to go off with Hamish or not, she couldn't stay at the Clinic any longer, seeing Sam every day and feeling her attachment to him grow. It's just a transference, she tried to tell herself, drawing on her new knowledge of psychiatry to explain her own reaction. It's just the gratitude and dependence I'm feeling because he helped me through a bad time. Well, I'm through it now, I have to wean myself away.

'Oh,' Robin said, and hesitated. This was hard to argue with. 'Will you do something else instead?'

Chick laughed, though there wasn't much real mirth in it. 'I have to. I'm not that well off, remember. And there's Charlie – he's still only fifteen. He'll need a deal more money spent on him before he's off my hands.'

'Like Penny,' Robin said. 'She's fifteen too, of course – I suppose she still needs looking after – more than the others, anyway.'

'Yes, Robin,' Chick said. 'Yes, I'm afraid she does. It'll be quite a while yet before she's away at University – '

'And you said it'd be all right to go off with Hamish, because the girls were nearly off my hands!' Robin flashed. 'You've changed your mind very quickly! Now it's one of your own you're talking about.'

'Let's not squabble,' Chick said. 'I don't think I could bear that. There's enough changes going on. Don't make it worse by spoiling what we are.'

Robin opened her mouth to speak and then closed it and then tried again. 'I suppose so. I'm sorry. It's just that – oh, Chick, what's happened to us all? It used to be so easy, didn't it? There was you and Harry and Sam and me and the children were little and no trouble except for earaches and sore bottoms, and now,

193

you're on your own and Sam and I feel like strangers and there's Hamish and Oliver – who knows what Oliver'll do next?'

'Did you fall in love with Hamish as a way of forgetting how upset you are about Oliver?' Chick said with a sudden flash of insight and Robin grimaced.

'That'd be a depressing thought. I hope not. But I can't deny I fret over him. He's happy enough at the Bittacy but I still don't trust him. It's horrid not trusting your own child. I feel – '

'I know,' Chick said and again they were silent for a while, drinking coffee and listening to the faint sounds of the house around them; the dripping of a tap, the faint hum of the refrigerator, music from Charlie's faraway radio. Then Robin stirred.

'So, what will you do?'

'I'm not sure. Private nursing maybe. It'll give me more control over the hours I work.'

'Horrid, though! Dreary rich people imagining they've got symptoms.'

'Rich people get ill too. They're not all hypochondriacs.'

Robin sighed. 'I suppose so. But I remember how we used to despise them so at the London, do you remember? We had no time for any but the ward patients.'

'Well, I've been with private patients this past couple of years,' Chick said. 'Sam's Clinic isn't NHS, after all – '

'He runs it as though it were,' Robin said with sudden bitterness. 'Works all the hours there are and gets hardly any reward for it.'

'Except the job itself.'

'I know, I know. The way we used to. But it's different now. We're a family – at least there's the shop – '

Chick set her head on one side. 'Is that part of the way you feel, Robin? A bit of anger about the shop being a major source of income now?'

Robin made a little face. 'Oh, I don't know. I've thought and thought about it. Don't think I haven't. This past few weeks I've thought about nothing else but why I'm being so ridiculous. It stops me from remembering that afternoon – what am I going to do, Chick? I'm obsessed with the wretched man!'

Suddenly she began to laugh and pushed her cup and saucer aside and folded her arms on the table and set her head on them so that she could let the laughter go. Her shoulders shook and after a while she lifted her flushed face and damp eyes to Chick. 'Honestly, it's like being twenty again! All I think of is fashion and a good-looking bloke and – dammit, I'm forty-eight! This is daft. I've started the bloody menopause even, and here I am making a complete cake of myself.'

'It could be the menopause that's doing it,' Chick said. 'I've heard it can do that to people. Me, I'm not noticing any difference yet. Or I don't think so – ' And she stopped and wondered: Sam? Could she be having just a midlife fuss, the sort of thing that the magazines went on about so darkly, the madness that seizes women in the change? Oh, heaven forbid! There has to be a mind of my own in there somewhere – I can't blame only hormones – and she looked at Robin.

'No, you can't blame your hormones. You're still the person you are. What you do is in your own control. You're in charge of your life.'

'I sometimes wonder,' Robin sat up and wiped her face. She was not laughing now. 'Oh Chick, thank God for you. I don't know what I'd do without you to be my friend. I can talk to you about anything, anything at all. It helps hugely.'

'Don't depend on me,' Chick said sharply. 'I'm a person with needs of my own as well, you know. Don't assume I'll always be on your side.'

'You always have been,' Robin got to her feet. 'Why should I expect anything else after so long? Thank you, Chick. I do love you – I do hope I've not hurt you in any way, talking this way to you tonight. I didn't mean to – I wouldn't do anything to hurt you – '

'Nor I you,' Chick said and wanted to cross her fingers. Because who knew what was possible? If Robin chose to leave Sam, what mightn't her best friend be capable of? It didn't bear thinking about.

Robin yawned. 'I'd better go. It's a busy day tomorrow – the TV people are coming back for more of my stuff. It's a whole new world, and it's paying me handsomely. But they ask a lot of time and attention, so – good night, Chick.'

'Let me know what you decide to do,' Chick said as lightly as she could. 'I'll be here – '

'I will. Right now I'm sure I – sure that I'm not sure.' She managed a laugh. 'Daft, ain't it? I must go – '

Chick took her to the door and went out with her to take a deep breath of the sunny smells of her garden roses and stocks and a hint of nicotiana, making the air rich and soft.

Robin stopped with her hand on the garden gate. 'Have you told Sam yet you're leaving?'

Chick shook her head. 'I'll do it soon,' she said. 'When the time is right. Soon.'

'Well, be kind to him.' Robin said. 'He's going to be very upset.'

'Yes,' Chick said. 'I'll be kind.' And she watched her walk over to her car and heard the engine start and the clutch let in. 'But will I be kind to myself?' she said into the dark sky and went in and closed the door.

22

Poppy had spent the whole morning on it, and she was no further forward, and at twelve o'clock she folded all the papers back into their folder and went across to Richard's office.

He frowned as she came in without stopping after her perfunctory knock. He was sitting with a tall rather heavy man of about fifty who rose courteously to his feet as she came in.

'I'm rather tied up at the moment,' Richard said pointedly as she walked in but Poppy lifted her chin and carried on. Normally she would have left if she'd interrupted a meeting. Although she regarded the business as very much her own, she would never poach on Richard Melhuish's ground; he was Chairman of the Board and as such was entitled to respect. But this morning she was too bothered by the contents of her folder to remember the niceties.

'I won't keep you long,' she said a little grimly and came to the side of his desk. Richard, recognizing defeat, got to his feet and smiled.

'Let me present to you Mr Arthur Dickenson of Dickenson Brothers,' he said with a meaning tone in his voice. 'We've been discussing a few future plans – '

'Indeed we have,' Arthur Dickenson said, shaking hands with her. He seemed an agreeable man and under normal circumstances she would have been happy to stop and speak to him. But these weren't normal circumstances.

'Richard,' she began, after nodding quickly to Dickenson. 'I'm sorry to interrupt you, but I really need a fast answer on this matter of the shares. I've been through this folder several times and there are factors that just don't add up. I'd appreciate a rapid response, please.' She turned to Arthur Dickenson. 'I'm sorry to have charged in like this, but this is one of those things that – '

'Please!' He held up one hand. 'Please, no apologies. I know how it is to run a difficult business. And we were finished I think, Richard? Yes, I'm delighted in fact to have had this chance to meet you. So sorry you were always too busy to join us at the other meetings.'

She had been on her way back to the door, but now she stopped and returned.

'I'm sorry?'

'The last three times I was here – I'd hoped to meet you then. You are after all legendary in this business we're in. But I fully understand how it is when you're under pressure. Anyway, Richard and I have reached a happy outcome. I'm sure we'll sort very well together.' And he turned and shook hands with Richard, who came round his desk to lead him to the door.

Poppy stood in the middle of the big office with her head down, thinking hard. Dickenson. Three meetings? And now, a completed arrangement? What arrangement?

Richard came back in at last, closed the door behind him and returned to his desk, whistling softly between his teeth, but she wasn't deceived. He was thoroughly rattled.

'And what was that all about?'

'A rather nice piece of business. I wanted to surprise you and I flatter myself I've managed it.' He smiled beatifically at her, but she was too angry to respond in kind.

'I'm not sure I like surprises,' she snapped. 'What was he doing here? Is he who I think he is – one of the Dickensons from south of the water – '

'The very one. Time we got another toehold in that area,' Richard said and tilted his head at her in a beguiling fashion. 'Don't you think?'

'What have you done?' She was very blunt. 'Let's get this one clear first and then I'll get on to the next point. And be straight with me, Richard. I'm not in the mood for any – '

'Any what?' he said softly, because she'd stopped short.

She took a deep breath. 'Anything less than the direct unvarnished facts.' She had been going to say 'truth' but thought better of it. There was no need to alienate him completely.

'I wish you'd sit down, Poppy,' he said fretfully. 'You make me tired, standing there looking like a Boadicea. What on earth's upsetting you? Has your Oliver been up to mischief again?'

She reddened. 'This has nothing to do with Oliver! And he has hardly been up to mischief, as you put it. Any number of our staff get a bit sloppy about punctuality and have to have their knuckles rapped. It was no more than that – ' As if she didn't have enough to put up without being put on the defensive over Oliver! Wretched boy, she thought, and then was even angrier with Richard for making her feel that flash of anger against her own grandson. 'Will you get on with it, please?'

He sighed a little theatrically. 'Of course. Dickenson's retiring. Old man, that is – Arthur here wants to spend a little time amid the fleshpots. And when I heard that I thought – there's some goodwill there, and some useful equipment. They've got three of the biggest and best marquees in the business. So, I started to negotiate. And I'm happy to tell you I've made a very good deal. A share option – three of ours for two of theirs, and that makes a nice bonus for Arthur and saves us a great deal of fuss with their senior people messing us about. I assured him we'll keep on his staff, though of course after three months I'll be able to see some of them on their way – we don't want to be top heavy with employees, do we? That was a big mistake always, I thought – too many full-timers, not enough freelancers – and with no union to meddle with us, it'll go well. So there you are. A nice lollipop for you, Poppy. In one stroke I've increased the size of the firm by a third!'

Now she had to sit down, for her knees had lost all their control. 'You did what?' she gasped. 'You did *what*?'

He almost smirked. 'I knew you'd be pleased.'

'Like hell I am!' she shouted and he stared back at her over his folded hands with his brows lifted in what was meant to be a pained expression, but she knew that he was lying, that in every action and word he was as devious as a man could be, and she almost spluttered her fury.

'How dare you go ahead with a deal like this and not consult me and the Board?'

'I have every right to, Poppy,' he said. 'I'm Chairman of the Board and you're Executive Managing Director. You chose that role not long after I joined the company, you know that. And I didn't act totally alone, of course I didn't! I have Gillian's full consent and agreement and she is, after all, an equal partner – '

'Partner, yes. But not the sole owner.'

'Any more than you are,' he said smoothly. 'When you made Gillian a partner, then brought me in. Like it or not that's how it is. She and I, we're very close,' and he smiled again, and she could have hit his smirking face.

'Is this deal signed?'

'Tomorrow.'

'Well, it won't be,' she said firmly. 'I'll put a stop to it at once and – '

'Why?' He sounded very silky. 'Now, why should you throw away so lucrative a deal? Out of pique, because I acted on the say-so of the Board and didn't consult you? Hardly good business. And anyway, let me remind you I do have Board consent.'

'At what meeting was this agreed? I have no memory of it – '

'I'm afraid you weren't available. This offer came up and I couldn't waste time. I called a meeting late that evening – now, let me see – ' He leaned forward and flicked open his desk diary. 'Ah, here it is! You were at the Festival Hall event and I did applaud your being there. It's the way we got our reputation after all – when you choose "Food by Poppy", you're very likely to get Poppy herself supervising. What could be a better advertisement? But it did mean you weren't available for a meeting – I had some of the Board here, however. A quorum, you know!' And he reached for a ledger and pushed it over to her, and she looked down at the page he indicated. It bore the signatures of four of the Board members, as well as his own and Gillian's and each of the signatories were those of the members she regarded as his creatures. She didn't want to think her Board was split, but there was no doubt that while she had her own allies, so did Richard. And he'd used his to excellent purpose.

'That explains the share confusions,' she said slowly.

'Confusions?' He lifted his brows at her.

'You know perfectly well what I mean. The file came through to me, and I started to check it – normally I'd have let it go through, but this time I looked for some reason and the figures didn't add up. Now, I can see why – '

'Here's all the documentation, Poppy.' Richard leaned over once more and handed her yet another file. 'It explains it all. If you check the share holdings against these new figures and check out what it's really cost us to take over Dickensons you'll be impressed, I know you will – I've plenty of time. Take a good look.'

Silence settled on the big office as she sat there, her head down and her pencil flickering over the columns of figures as she checked it all. Bookkeeping had been her first skill in this business, and she could still read a balance sheet without any difficulty and could spot any errors or evasions in a matter of seconds.

There were none. It was as he had said, an excellent deal. The company they'd merged with had very useful real property in the shape of glass, china, silver and marquees, not to speak of a small fleet of fitted delivery vans, and the figures Richard had achieved had been shrewd to the point of parsimony. 'Food by Poppy' was the gainer in every respect; and she lifted her head slowly and stared at him.

'Why didn't you tell me? Why leave it for me to find out and misconstrue? Why the secrecy, damn it? I'd have done all I could to help, if you'd told me – '

'I didn't need any help, Poppy.' He smiled. 'And as for the secrecy – I was just trying to please David.'

'David?' She was amazed. 'My David? What had he got to do with – '

'At the last party we were at – remember? He was talking to me. Told me he was worried about you. Thought you were overworking, wanted you to take life a little easier – ' He coughed delicately. 'Seemed to think that as the – er – years were passing you expected too much of yourself. As he put it, "We aren't chickens any more." '

She went scarlet. 'Are you trying to suggest I'm past it?' she cried wrathfully. 'Because if you – '

'No, no!' he said soothingly. 'I simply tried to please your David! I thought, give you a fait accompli, you'll be delighted, he'll be happy that you hadn't been worried over it all – and there were some worrying days over the deal, I do assure you – and everything in the garden would be lovely. What more could you ask for?'

She shook her head, nonplussed. 'I don't know,' she said at length. 'A little honesty, perhaps – '

'I am not dishonest, Poppy,' he said very softly. 'It would pain me greatly to think you might be suggesting otherwise – '

She shook her head irritably. 'Oh, for heaven's sake – I don't mean to suggest – I suppose I should have said "openness". Yes, that's what I meant. More openness. Less secrecy.'

'I told you, I was only trying to please David.' He sighed and got to his feet and came round the desk to crouch beside her and take both her hands in his. He was a big man and she couldn't pull away without threatening his balance. 'My dear, I hate putting the wrong foot in it with you. I try so hard to be all you want. I accept it, when you put your scapegrace grandson in the Bittacy – no, not another word! He's doing excellently well, of course he is, in spite of his poor time-keeping – and then I try to make the running of this place smooth and easy for you, and all I get is suspicion. You want to be careful, Poppy. You don't want people saying you're getting cantankerous with the passage of time!' And he laughed charmingly and patted her hand.

She was defeated and she knew it. He'd done it again; made her feel she was stupid and paranoid. But how could she be otherwise? He was too smooth altogether – and somewhere at the back of her mind the thought germinated, grew and shaped itself and became concrete. He'll have to go. Somehow I have to get rid of him before he gets rid of me –

But there was no more she could say now. He was right; the deal he'd struck was faultless and she remembered the conversation he'd had with David that night. She'd laughed and paid no attention. It was just David doing his usual protective thing. But Richard had used it shamelessly and her anger seeped more deeply into her and lay inside her belly in a hard little knot.

He got to his feet with a little grimace as his knees protested and went back to his desk. 'So, we're friends again? Splendid! And now so that you don't think I'm keeping things from you, let me talk to you about the September Tide Ball – '

She blinked. The sudden change of subject bewildered her. 'The what?'

'In aid of the Support the Elderly Fund,' he said. 'I do all I can for them, since it seems to me to be – what do they call it these days? Enlightened self-interest, that's it. Enlightened self-interest.' He managed a musical little laugh. 'Who knows when I mightn't need their efforts on my own behalf? Anyway, I'm on the committee for the big fund-raiser of the year. We're doing the food, of course, and it's a nice contract. The charity will still raise all its money, never fear,' he added quickly as a faint look of doubt crossed her face. 'If someone else did it they'd charge even more and be half as good, so we may as well have the business. The whole evening raises the best part of twenty thousand, what with the tombola and the advertising brochure and so forth. Now, I've taken a table. It's the least I can do. Out of my own pocket, mind you – not the company funds!'

'We can spend some money on charity,' Poppy said. 'We have an allocation – '

'Then keep it for other needy groups. This one is my affair. I've taken a table, as I say, and that means twelve people. Now, I want you all to be my guests – all of you.' He beamed at her. 'Let me see, you and David, that's two. Robin and Sam, another two, Lee and Jeremy and your Josh – that's seven – and I have to say, if I didn't include your Josh my Caro would never speak to me again! These young things, too delightful – now, where was I? Ah, yes, the other two places. Gillian wants a cousin of hers and his wife, but have I left out any of your people? Oliver perhaps and – '

She shook her head swiftly. 'No, not the young ones. There are too many – and there's the problem of the very youngest – there could be jealousies. Better none of that generation and be done with it – ' She stopped and frowned. She'd been trapped somehow into letting him assume his invitation had been accepted and it would be hard to refuse now. And she badly wanted to.

'I should perhaps be supervising if it's such a big booking – ' she said then, hopefully. It would be as good a get-out as any.

He lifted both hands. 'I won't hear of you working that night, my dear! What sort of firm would we be if we couldn't find one of our staff to take charge and to do so splendidly? Mary Wheable can do it. She'll enjoy it – poor creature, so dreadfully plain that it'll be a treat for her to be at the Dorchester for such an event!' And he laughed again.

Poppy was feeling worse and worse. There seemed no way out of this; she wanted to protest about the way he spoke of Mary Wheable, whose only problem was a pockmarked skin left from girlhood acne, but who had an otherwise pretty face and a lovable personality to go with it, but she knew that wouldn't help. Instead she opened her mouth to argue that her family couldn't be expected to accept just like that, when he interrupted.

'Don't tell me they won't come, dear Poppy,' Richard said, and smiled widely. 'I'm sure they will if you put on a three-line whip!' He laughed merrily. 'Anway, I have your David on my side. I told him about this yesterday, and I suspect he's very keen. I'm sure the family will come to please you – so let's say it's agreed, hmm? September twenty-fifth – last Saturday in the month. Half past seven in the private suite for a champagne reception and then dinner and dancing till dawn. It'll be splendid. And you'll all be there!'

'I see no point in going,' Sam said. 'It's not as though we enjoy each other's company all that much, is it?'

Robin took a deep breath. She wouldn't be riled, she wouldn't, she wouldn't. 'That's up to you, Sam. But I'd like to go. I have a new dress and anyway Ma says it helps her if we all turn out. Pa's fussing – he's got it firmly in his head that somehow he needs a night out like this. I think really he wants to dress up in evening clothes. He doesn't often get the chance – '

'But you agree we're not going for ourselves, Robin? That you don't particularly care whether you're with me or not?'

'I agree nothing of the sort,' Robin said. 'And really, Sam, you're being very silly. Such stuff you talk! I dare say I've been a bit busy lately and that's meant I've had little time for talk – but to read any more than that into it – that's silly.'

Sam sighed softly. 'I see, Robin. Very well. I suppose I'm silly. And you do want to go?'

'Yes.'

'Then I suppose we must.'

'Lovely,' said Lee. 'I adore a dressing-up event. Such fun – and maybe a chance to pick up some useful business.'

Jeremy laughed lazily. 'Do you ever think of anything else?'

'Not a lot,' she said cheerfully. 'Except you.'

'Does that mean if I say I hate big balls of this sort, and don't want to go, you'd stay home with me – '

'Oh, no! If you wouldn't I still would. I dare say someone'd dance with me – '

He sighed in a theatrical fashion. 'Then I suppose I'd better go.'

'As if there was ever any doubt of it,' she said, and began to tickle him.

Once again it was long after they should have done so that they got up, but, as Lee said, where was the point of being in love if you didn't behave that way when the fancy took you?

'Oh, help,' Josh said. 'I hate those sorts of events. Of course I'm not going.'

'Oh, Josh, please!' Caro wailed. 'I want to so much! It's one of the best there is, you know. Very glitzy – disco music as well as a band, and masses of food and drink. And anyway, Gillian and Daddy'll be devastated if you don't come.'

'You mean you will and you'll make their lives such a misery over it that they won't know what to do with themselves.'

'Something like that!' she said sunnily. 'Do say you will, Josh. I do so love dancing – you know that.'

'And I hate it and can't, and you know *that*!'

'But it won't matter. I'll find someone else to dance with. I just want you for the dinner and so forth – '

He sighed. 'Because a girl's best accessory is a man on her arm?'

She laughed again and tucked her hand into his elbow. 'Something like that.'

'But I – '

'No buts. You're coming. I've made up my mind to it.'

'Oh well,' Josh said. 'In that case there's nothing more to be said, is there?'

'I'm going to gatecrash,' Oliver said gleefully. 'In full bib and tucker – '

'You wouldn't dare!' Suzy looked appalled. 'How can you?'

'Very easily. I'll just turn up, walk in, and be there. It's not that difficult. Come with me and try it.'

She shrank back. 'Oh, no!'

'I will alone then.'

'You can't.'

'Try to stop me – '

'Oh, damn you!' she burst out at length. 'You really put me on the spot.'

'How?'

'If you do this, I'll have to do it too – '

'Have to? What nonsense – though I'd love you to be with me.'

'I promised Mummy I'd look after you, so of course I'll have to do it too – to look after you.'

He roared with real laughter. 'I've heard some special pleading in my time, but you take the biscuit.'

She risked a smile. 'It's not special pleading. It *is* my conscience about you. So I'll do it too – as long as you promise to pick me up when we're chucked out.'

'Bet you a quid we aren't.'

'A quid?' She was doubtful. 'That's a lot of money – '

'Then you expect to lose?'

'No! They will chuck you out – '

'Well, let's go and see shall we? And – ' He hugged her. 'Quid or not, it'll be great fun.'

23

Robin made a considerabie effort with her appearance, not so much because she cared what effect she would have on the people at the ball, as to give herself something to occupy her mind. While she was climbing into first the soft skin-coloured body stocking and then the cream crocheted long dress with its silk backing that she had chosen to wear ('You're older than you should be for it,' Beckie had said judiciously. 'But you're thin enough, so it's all right.') and then had spent half an hour painstakingly doing her make-up and her hair, she couldn't think of anything else. So she was in a tolerably relaxed mood when she came downstairs to join Sam who had been dressed and ready even before she began, and who was sitting over a drink in the living-room waiting for her.

'Good God,' Sam said without stopping to think. 'You look incredible.'

She felt it like a slow trickle of warmth moving from her chest into the rest of her, and she smiled at him in the old comfortable way and did a small pirouette. 'Thank you kindly, sir,' she said.

Sam, who had been startled not so much by his approval as by a degree of shock, for had he been asked to put his reaction into words, he would have had to say he thought her dress, elegant though it was, more suitable for seventeen-year-old Sophie; but he was quick-witted enough to build on her reaction, and came over to her, one hand held out.

'It is a pleasure and a privilege to escort you tonight, Mrs Landow,' he said gravely.

She went a little pink. 'Er – thank you, Professor Landow.' It was the old silly routine they had always used, in the days before she had retreated into her misery over Hamish, and for a moment she wished heartily that she had never clapped eyes on Hamish, that he would vanish into the past where he belonged and never bother her thoughts again. It would be so comfortable, so peaceful, so altogether right to be as they had been used to, she and Sam. And she seized on that feeling and determined to hold on to it.

'Have fun,' Oliver said lazily from the depths of the armchair on the other side of the fireplace, and Robin looked at him with her face a little creased.

'I wish you'd been invited too, darling – '

'Oh, I wouldn't fret over me!' Oliver said. 'I have plans of my own.'

'Are we allowed to know what they are?' Sam asked, a little sardonically.

'Oh, a night out is all, much like yourselves.' He smiled sweetly. 'I promise you you'll find out. How's that? Just let me think about what I'm going to do and make my arrangements – '

Sam nodded resignedly and turned to Robin. 'I suppose that's something. Ready, Robin?'

'As ready as I'll ever be. I hope this turns out to be – all right.'

He looked surprised. 'Is there any reason why it shouldn't?'

She shrugged. 'Ma's not entirely happy over it, I gather. It was all Richard Melhuish's idea. He's paid for the table and Ma feels – well, she's not comfortable.'

'Oh!' They were outside now and climbing into the car. 'I thought we were guests of "Food by Poppy".'

'So did I till Ma told me this morning. Well, never mind. A party's a party.'

'Yes,' he said and touched her hand briefly as he put the car into gear. 'So let's enjoy it.'

'Yes,' she said, and turned to smile at him. 'Yes. Let's try hard to enjoy it.'

And Sam grinned at her, and set off for Park Lane feeling better than he had for weeks.

'It's supposed to be pleasure, this evening,' David said into Poppy's ear as they moved with all the other guests slowly up the corridor that led to the room where the private reception before the ball was being held. 'Try to look as though you think so, even if you don't.'

'I still think it's all wrong the way he's done it,' she murmured.

'I'd rather have paid for myself – and the rest of the family come to that.'

'Not at these prices,' David said. 'Believe me. Settle for it, darling. Forget your prickles and have fun. Look, there're Lee and Jeremy. They look – well – very up to the minute!'

'Don't they just?' Poppy said and giggled, for Jeremy was resplendent in a crimson velvet jacket and flowing cravat in matching satin, and Lee had chosen the simplest of mini-skirted evening dresses so glittering with psychedelic diamanté that it made people blink. 'I'm glad I went into food as a career. At least I don't have to compete all the time – look at that woman over there! She can't be that much younger than me and she's wearing the same sort of dress Lee is – '

'Tonight,' David said contentedly. 'Is going to be fun. I do so adore watching people make cakes of themselves. People-watching – there's no sport like it. Hello Melhuish! And Gillian – good to see you both – '

'Looks as though your cousin and her husband aren't going to make it then,' Richard said over the table to Gillian, who reddened.

'I told you – their daughter's baby's due any moment. They did say if anything happened – '

'They could have phoned,' Richard growled. 'Then we could have found someone else who'd have liked to join us.' He glared at the empty places left at the table, each adorned with an uneaten first course of smoked-salmon cornets filled with cream cheese. 'I'll get the waiter to clear the places. Looks so miserable like that – as though someone had a couple of teeth out.'

'I'll manage an extra starter,' David said cheerfully. 'Food's great, as usual – ' and he reached for one of the plates and began to tuck in. The others laughed and Josh leaned forward and took the other one.

'Who am I to let my father make a greedy exhibition of himself without doing something to cover up for him? I'll be greedy too – but it's for his sake, of course.'

Caro giggled. 'Oh, do watch out, darling. People are staring!'

'Don't care,' Josh said, his mouth full. 'This is too good to waste – who's staring?'

'That chap at the next table,' Caro said and jerked her head. 'He's been staring over ever since we sat down.'

'Looking at you, Caro!' Richard said and laughed fatly. 'You'll
have to look to your laurels, Josh. She'll be snatched from under
your nose!'

Caro, who was wearing a blue silk dress that was as near to
being topless as it was possible to get without being just a skirt,
wriggled her shoulders with pleasure.

'Oh, Daddy, do shut up – it's Josh he's staring at, not me. I
told you. He thinks he's greedy and so do I!'

Josh had lifted his head and looked at the next table and then
had looked away, apparently uninterested. 'Well, let him think
it,' he said. 'I need a lot of dinner tonight. Had no lunch.' And he
finished the salmon just as the waiter arrived to bring the next
course.

There was a bit of fussing as Richard, being very self-
important, instructed him to remove the unused place settings
and ordered more bread and then more wine, and then the rest of
the table fell into general conversation, with Caro in earnest
chatter with her father, who was on her other side, leaving Josh
free for a moment to look about him. Which he did carefully but
apparently casually, looking at the adjoining table for a brief
moment and then away. But he had seen what he was looking for,
and a faint flush appeared on his cheeks.

The dinner wound on to its end, punctuated by speeches,
the selling of raffle tickets and auctions of donated goodies in
the usual charity ball fashion, and from time to time people at
the table wandered off to the tombola which had been set up at
the far side of the ballroom, to bring back their winnings, if any,
and commiserate with or compliment themselves over them, and
after Poppy had won a rather handsome set of costly bath soaps
and talcs and assorted oils and toilet waters, Caro clapped her
hands and demanded that Josh go and win something for her.

'I'll stay here,' she said. 'And pray hard that you get something
wonderful. Whenever I try a tombola all I ever get is blank
tickets, so I'm obviously a Jonah. See what you can get for me,
Josh!'

Josh got to his feet obediently and reached into his pocket.
'How much are the tickets?' he asked Poppy and she grimaced.

'A pound each! But it's a good cause – and they seem to have
some nice prizes. Go and do your stuff, darling! We'll all pray for
you!'

He laughed and then made his way through the crowds of people who were table-hopping to talk to their friends, or bound as he was for the tombola, relaxed and comfortable, and Caro looked after him fondly and smiled; and Richard murmured in her ear, 'It's time you two made up your minds.'

'Mmm?' She looked sideways at him and then smiled. 'None of your business, Daddy!'

'Anything which affects my little girl's my business.' Richard said, with his voice down so that the others could not hear him. 'And I think it's high time he proposed. You know how to make him do that, surely? I thought every little girl was born knowing that.'

'Oh, Daddy,' she said and giggled again. 'Do shut up.' But she watched Josh till he disappeared among the crowd and then sighed and turned to look at the floor as the music for dancing started, taking over from the piano which had accompanied their dining.

'Come on, Caro,' Jeremy said good naturedly. 'I know you love dancing, and Lee here wants to table-hop and see who she can pick up for the agency. We'll go and struggle our way round the floor, what say you?'

'Great!' Lee was on her feet at once. 'I never waste an opportunity. Keep him happy for me, Caro, there's a lamb!' and Caro and Jeremy went to dance as she went off happily to prowl round the room, and Poppy and David got up to dance too, not so much because David wanted to, as because Poppy pinched his leg under the table to tell him she had no intention of staying at the table with Richard alone, since Robin and Sam had spotted friends at another table and gone off to talk to them; and Richard sat with his elbows amid the debris, watching the dancers, and especially Caro, as Gillian sat discontentedly beside him, wanting to dance but knowing Richard hated it, and having more sense than to suggest it to him.

The evening wore on, and after a while, as none of his guests reappeared, Richard got restless and got to his feet. 'You'll be all right if I go and find old Dickenson?' he said. 'It'll be politic. Won't be long.' And he departed in a cloud of cigar smoke leaving Gillian alone.

It was half an hour later that the table began to reassemble, Jeremy and Caro scarlet with their exertions on the dance floor where they had been rocking and rolling with great verve, and the others looking ready to relax too. They were all getting a little weary now, for it was well past eleven and the place was hot and noisy and not a little stuffy with tobacco smoke.

Caro stopped short as she came up to the table, a small frown between her brows. 'Where's Josh? Didn't he win anything?'

'Doesn't look like it,' Jeremy said and collapsed into his chair. 'Maybe he's still queueing up to see what he can get for you.'

'Hmm,' she said and looked across the ballroom. 'Maybe I'll go and see if I can find him – have you seen him, Daddy?' as her father came back.

'Mmm? Josh? No – has he wandered off? Better go and round him up. Time soon for the cabaret – they say it's a good one – ' He sat down. 'I want us all here for that – '

'Did you see him, Gillian?' Caro asked and Gillian, who had managed somehow to doze off as she had sat at the table alone but would have died rather than admit it, shook her head.

'Sorry,' she said and added mendaciously, 'I wasn't here all the time.'

'Blow him,' Caro said crossly and went off in the direction of the tombola. She felt aggrieved. It was all right for her to leave Josh to dance, because he wouldn't dance, but there was no reason for him to wander off, was there? She wanted to find him and tell him so, and also to do something about what her father had said. Quite what she didn't know; but she had a hazy notion that her female intuition, whatever that was, would help her, if she could just get him alone; and she was bright eyed and hopeful as she found her way to the tombola.

She had learned to regard Josh as very much her property. He was funny and nice and wonderfully attentive and a complete gentleman and that was rare these days, as she well knew. He never pounced on her the way so many men did, making a pest of themselves and ruining her make-up. He'd never done more than hug her or kiss her cheek affectionately and she loved that. It gave her a frisson of delight when he did it because it was so sweet and old fashioned and his face was so smooth and felt so nice.

But now she was ready for more and she wasn't ashamed to admit it to herself. She had to face the facts, she told herself as her eyes raked the crowds; Josh was, for all his elegance and his sophistication and his brilliance at his work, a basically shy person. He had to be encouraged and she, no question, was the girl to do that encouraging. Hadn't her father said so? And wasn't he one of those people who was always right?

He'd come up behind Josh as he'd stood in the small queue that had formed for the tombola and murmured in his ear, 'I thought you'd never get away from them.'

'Eh?' Josh stiffened and then very deliberately relaxed his shoulders and turned away to stare ahead at the tombola shelves and their heaps of vapidly staring teddy bears and bottles of far-from-premier-cru wine and out-of-date books and records in garish sleeves. 'I don't know what you mean.'

'Of course you do.' The whisper was sharper. 'I saw you looking at me.'

'Once,' Josh muttered. 'And then only because someone pointed out that you were staring at me. Please don't.'

'Why shouldn't I? You don't answer my letters, you don't ring me, you're never in when I phone. What else do you expect me to do when I manage to come across you like this?'

'Not now, for pity's sake! Not here!'

'Where else then? You disappear out of my life like – like I'm some sort of tart, and expect me not to notice? We see each other regularly for months on end and then suddenly, nothing – ' His voice was rather louder now, and the person standing in front of Josh looked over his shoulder and Josh caught his breath and turned and went, leaving the queue to shuffle up closer, and plunged away through the crowd.

The other followed him and caught up with him as he reached the corridor that led to the cloakrooms and managed to get ahead of him and head him into the hall. Josh was cornered and had to stop and look at him.

He stood there with his mane of thick blond hair flopping into his eyes in the familiar way, and Josh felt the old lurch. He was a sweet person, Greg; he'd been fun to be with, calm and undemanding. Josh knew he'd treated him less than kindly, as a sort of bandage to comfort himself after Adrian, and that was something to be ashamed of; and the awareness made him relax his guard now. He looked around quickly at the other people wandering along the corridor and said softly, 'Listen, Greg, not here. There has to be somewhere we can talk privately. For both our sakes.'

Greg stepped back and also looked round and then nodded. 'Care for a drink, old boy?' he said loudly as a couple of large men talking earnestly, apparently about laundry charges, went past and Josh let his lips quirk and nodded.

'Good idea,' he said equally loudly and followed as Greg led the way.

'There're a couple of private rooms along here,' Greg said. 'I've worked here sometimes and – yes, there you are.' And he made his way across the corridor towards a pair of doors.

'Can I help you, sir?' It was one of the waiters, who was passing with an empty tray, and Greg said swiftly, 'Is anyone using these rooms?'

'Those, sir? No, they were wanted earlier, for the champagne reception, you know, but there's no one in there now – '

'Excellent,' Greg said with great aplomb. 'Then we can use this one for a short business discussion. If anyone tries to interrupt us, send them on their way, will you?' And he smiled at the man who nodded, showing not a hint of surprise, and Greg opened the door and led the way in. And after a moment's pause, Josh followed him, and closed the door behind him.

24

Caro wandered disconsolately round the tombola area again. There weren't so many people here now, for the shelves were sadly depleted, with only a few of the less interesting prizes being left, and she could see clearly that Josh wasn't there.

She went back to the edge of the dance floor, though prudently out of sight of her own table (no need to irritate her father at this stage), wondering if by any remote chance someone had invited him onto the floor, but she knew that was a nonsense, and left after a while, now thoroughly bothered.

It wasn't like Josh, polite attentive Josh, to treat a person so. One of the delights of going about with him, one of the reasons she so often called him and persuaded him somehow to take her out, was his respect for her. To disappear in the middle of a ball was anything but respectful, and anger began to mount in her. She didn't often get angry, but when people treated her without the concern she believed herself entitled to, she could become spectacularly aroused. And she was on the way to that now.

She went to the cloakroom, as much to tidy her face and catch her breath as to visit the lavatory, and looked at herself judiciously in the glass. Pretty, undoubtedly; a good figure, no one could argue with that. Lively and fun, well, every one of her girlfriends said so. And well off; with a father like hers, how could she be otherwise? Take it all round, she was much too worthwhile a girl, she told herself with mounting wrath, to be treated as Mr Josh Deveen was treating her this evening.

She came out into the corridor and stood hesitantly looking around. From the ballroom she could hear the music, bouncing and fun; they were playing Latin American now and she loved that, and she did a little rumba step to comfort herself and then

215

slipped into a samba rhythm. She might as well dance with herself if there was no one else to dance with, she told herself with considerable self-pity and made another little twirl.

That was when she saw the waiter, leaning against the wall with his arms folded, grinning at her, and she made a little face to cover her fluster and said sharply, 'I've mislaid my partner. Have you seen him wandering around?'

'Hard to say, miss,' the waiter said. 'Not knowing what he looks like, can't say.'

'Tall,' Caro said. 'Dark curly hair. Nice face.'

The waiter thought about that. 'There's two gentlemen talking business in there,' he volunteered. 'One of them's very striking. Fair he is, like Marilyn Monroe, a real blonde. Not got the figure mind you.' He laughed, caught her eye and straightened his face. 'And the other fella – well, can't say as I really noticed that much. Dark I think, might've been curly – '

'Then I shall look for myself,' Caro said, and marched down the corridor towards the two doors he'd indicated.

'Oh, no, miss. They said not to disturb them! Business it was, they said – '

'Not at a ball,' Caro said firmly. 'I won't have my partner talking business at a ball. And if he isn't mine he's someone else's and so's the other chap, and they ought to know better.'

The waiter shrugged and prudently took up his tray and vanished. He'd been hanging around hoping to get a tip out of the two men when they reappeared; this young madam had put paid to that, he told himself crossly, and went off to see if the pickings were better elsewhere. And Caro put her hand on the first door knob, turned it and pushed the door open, in one firm gesture.

It was a big room, a little cluttered with the remains of the champagne reception; a long table covered with a white cloth and a few unused glasses and dishes of peanuts on it and several rows of empty bottles. There were overflowing ashtrays and a tangle of small gilt chairs, but Caro hardly noticed any of them. She could see only the two men in the middle of the room.

The smaller of them was blond and rather slender and he was holding the other man very closely and resting his head on his shirt front. He was weeping, small soft gulping sounds, and his companion was stroking his hair gently and murmuring soothingly into his ear. It was the most intimate scene she could remember seeing, and she stood there her mouth drying, staring at the man who had been stroking his companion's head.

'Oh my God,' she said. 'Oh my God!' and turned and ran.

Richard was getting bored. Perhaps, he thought, not so much bored as a bit bosky. Once the evening was well on its way and he was over the irritation of the defaulting cousins (a daughter expecting a baby? What sort of excuse was that?) he'd been happy enough; but then Caro had vanished, looking for her Josh, and then to crown it all, that young villain Oliver had turned up at their table with his cousin, as cool as you please, to greet his parents and to kiss his assorted relatives and to tell Richard smoothly that they were guests of someone else at the ball and thought they'd drop over to say hello.

Sam and Robin had looked amazed, and then pleased to see them and had accepted their arrival happily, though Sam, to do the man credit, Richard thought, had looked somewhat doubtful. But Richard knew a gatecrasher when he saw one, and had talked a long time to the young wretch to find out who he was with. After all, didn't he, Richard, know everyone who was worth knowing at this ball? If young Landow really had been a guest then it should have been easy to find out who to. But the boy had stared him coolly in the face and said he was a close friend of the bandleader, who had invited him along with his crowd, and Richard, certain though he had been that the boy was lying, had been unable to shake his story. Which had left him too angry to do anything but drink more than he should have done. Which was why he was now feeling what he called bored and bosky.

Where was Caro? He looked around for her and there was no sign of her. Damn it, he hadn't seen her since they'd finished eating and that was ages ago; and as the room darkened to a great crash of drums and trumpets to announce the start of the cabaret, he lumbered to his feet and set off to find her. That Josh was his guest and he needed teaching his manners, he told himself with some truculence. To leave Caro and then not come back was not the sort of behaviour he expected from a future son-in-law, and so he'd tell him.

He pushed his way past the tables and the chattering crowd, and emerged at the lavatory corridor, prudently decided to stop off, and re-emerged buttoning himself just as a door up the half-lit corridor slammed shut and someone came running along past the cloakroom at a rate of knots, almost cannoning into him.

'Hey! Just a minute – ' he cried, and reached out and now he could see it was Caro and at once all sense of muzziness from the drink vanished and he was as sharp and alert as he ever was.

Her face was white and awash with tears. Her mouth was open and drawn down into the sort of grimace he hadn't seen on it since she had been a small child who had fallen over and genuinely hurt herself, and the sobs that were coming from her were piteous. He seized her and half dragged her, half led her, up the corridor and out to the deserted but better-lit lobby, to sit her down on one of the settees there and look at her closely.

Everyone connected with the ball had gone to watch the cabaret, and they could hear distant laughter as the comedian who had been hired launched himself into his routine. The sound made her tears seem even more pathetic.

'What on earth's the matter?' He peered at her and his voice thickened. 'Has that bastard upset you? If anyone lays a finger on my little girl I'll have his balls off – what did he do?'

She shook her head, speechless, and then clung to him, burying her head in his shirt and then, as though stung, pulled herself away and set her hands one to each side of her face and stared at him miserably.

'He was doing that,' she whispered and began to sob again. 'Oh, God, he was doing that.'

'Who was doing what?' The effects of the wine he'd drunk began to come back, but not the muzziness. He felt flat and stale yet at the same time as though he were on the edge of a cliff and about to fall off. He had to concentrate, had to speak clearly. 'Where've you been all this time?'

She managed to take a deep shuddering breath and he waited, knowing she'd speak now and after a moment she managed huskily, 'I was looking for Josh.'

'And you found him.' It wasn't a question.

'Yes, I found him.' She gave another convulsive sob. 'He wasn't on his own.'

His face cleared. Bad as this was, it wasn't what he'd most feared, and he made a face and growled, 'The young bastard! I'll have his balls twice over if he's been two-timing you with some floosie or other – no daughter of mine gets treated that way – '

'It's not like that,' she managed and began to weep again helplessly.

'Dolly, do stop!' He was getting angry now. 'I thought he'd tried it on or something, made you go too far. At least it isn't that – so he's been having it off with some other girl? Better to find out now than later. We'll be rid of the lot of them soon, sweetie, just you see. I'll show them, these bloody Deveens. He'll go down with the rest of them – '

She sniffed lusciously and looked at him with some puzzlement, and he shook his head. 'Never mind all that. Just you tell me where he is and I'll give him what for – and then I'll take you home and you can forget all about him. There's plenty more where he came from, and better value – '

Again she shook her head, almost petulantly now. 'He wasn't with a girl,' she said. 'Do stop and listen, Daddy.'

There was a little silence and it was filled with a louder than usual roar of laughter as the comedian said something even ruder than usual. 'Listen to what?' he said then, and moved closer and put his arm around her.

She was sitting curled up smaller now, and she slid into the security of his grasp gratefully, keeping her head down so that she didn't have to look at him.

'It'd have been easier if it had been some girl. You know where you are with a girl. I could soon have got rid of her and showed him what I felt like – but how can I – how can anyone – I mean. I don't understand – '

He was silent again, his eyes bright and shining with an oddly excited look. 'So, it's like that is it? Well, well – these theatre people. Listen, can you tell me what they were doing? Or do you want to write it down?'

She looked at him then, her face crumpled. 'Write it down? Whatever for?'

'I thought you might be embarrassed.'

'Embarrassed?' She thought about that and then shook her head. 'I'm furious,' she said. 'I feel like I've been slapped. I'm miserable. I'm – ' And again she began to weep. 'But why should I be embarrassed?'

He waited as long as he could, which was only a matter of moments and then shook her a little. 'Tell me what they were doing. Who was it, to start with?'

She reached for his breast pocket and pulled out his handkerchief and blew her nose loudly. 'It was that chap, the one at the next table. The one I said was staring at him – I was right! Oh, God, I was right – ' And her eyes brimmed again.

'I know the one you mean,' he said. 'The fair one. I saw the one – '

She nodded. 'They were in the champagne room – you know, where we were before dinner. There was no one there but them, and I just walked in and he was – he was – '

'Take it easy, girlie,' Richard said and hugged her again, but he was hurrying her, needing to know every detail he could, and she felt the pressure and tried to pull away from him. But he wouldn't let her. 'What were they doing, for God's sake?'

She took a deep breath again. 'He was crying.'

'Who was? Josh?'

'The other one.' She gulped and then sat up straight. 'Just like I nearly did on you. Being hugged and crying on his shirt front all romantic and Josh was stroking his hair and murmuring at him, I mean, you could see it – it was like lovers – '

'It's hard to explain, sweetie,' Richard said carefully and she shook her head at him, furiously.

'Oh, Daddy, do stop! I'm not stupid, you know. I know all about queers!'

He went a dull brick red. 'You shouldn't know about such things!'

'Why do you think I was so upset, for God's sake?'

'Well, to find out that he – well, I don't know. I mean, they might have been doing something different. Not just hugging, I mean – '

'Well they were. And I'm so upset because – because – ' She made a face. 'I feel such a bloody fool.'

'No need to swear.'

'Yes there is! Every need!'

He let that pass. 'Is that the only reason? Because if it is – '

She shook her head, the tears welling up once more. 'Oh, of course not! I really liked him. I wanted to – you thought so too. You said he ought to propose and – ' And she was gone again, the tears cascading down her face and leaving her eyes puffy and reddened.

'I'll murder him,' he said and reached for her and held her

close, rocking her slightly. 'I'll see to it that he doesn't do this to some other man's daughter. He needn't think he can make a fool of my girl and get away with it.'

She lifted her head. 'What are you going to do?'

'Report him, of course! I don't need to make my hands dirty touching him. This dirty thing he's doing and people like him – they can be stopped. I just inform the police, that's all.'

'They'll send him to prison,' she said.

'I'll say they will.' He nodded in high satisfaction. 'But not till there's been a trial in open court and every bloody newspaper for miles around splashes him all over their pages. He'll never work again in a decent business! Just you wait and see – '

She thought about that for a while and seemed to find some comfort in it and slowly the tears dried up for good and all, and her puffy eyes seemed to settle down. They sat there for a while longer, holding on to each other as beyond in the ballroom the singer who had been warbling a shrill ballad gave way to what was clearly a conjuror or something of that sort, for there were just a series of 'oohs' and 'aahs' and bursts of applause. And then he stirred and pushed her away and leaned back in his place, digging in his pocket for a cigar.

'Come to think of it, sweetie, it might be better at this stage not to say anything,' he said slowly.

She turned and looked at him, almost sleepily. The waves of emotion after the excitement of the evening, and the wine she'd drunk, had left her half exhausted.

'What?'

'I was just thinking – there are more ways than two to skin a cat.'

'Don't talk stupid riddles, Daddy,' she said fretfully and he laughed and patted her hand.

'Trust your old Daddy. This is no riddle. Look, I told you, it's time we dealt with all the Deveens. I want them out. You understand me? I want to run things my own way. Well, I could, if I had a majority shareholding.'

'I don't know what you're talking about,' she said and wriggled irritably in her seat.

But he went on almost dreamily, as much to himself as to her. 'That Josh of hers – he owns a chunk of shares. They all do. I want as many as I can get – and this could be a way of swinging the pendulum, know what I mean? Or do I mean the see-saw?' He laughed, a happy little chuckle. 'Anyway, it could make all the difference. I'll see this Josh of yours, put it on the line for him. He sells me the shares – don't want to cheat him, he can have the market price – but he has to sell 'em. Then I own the majority, with Gillian's, and there's an end of it. Madam Poppy's on her way to the knackers. She gets only money out of the business – and once she's pushed out of the day-to-day running she'll lose heart and want to sell out anyway. Oh, yes, indeed. It's all mine. It's going to turn out beautifully, sweetheart. Just leave it to your old father. Listen, you've had a nasty shock. An upset. You need a rest, a chance to get over it, hmm? How about – oh, I don't know. A few days in Paris, shopping? Gillian can take you.'

She lifted her chin and looked at him, her eyes wide. 'Could I?'

He patted her hand again as a roar of applause and loud music signalled the end of the cabaret.

'Of course. Do I ever promise and not deliver? You go to Paris, get over your hurt heart – and it won't take long, pretty girl like you – and I'll deal with your young man. Queers!' He almost spat. 'They make me sick.'

Caro said nothing. She just sat and looked into the distance with her eyes glazed and tried to think about Paris and Josh and how she felt. It was very difficult because really all she wanted to do right now was go to bed and sleep.

25

Caro sat curled on the sofa in the corner of the drawing-room, the Sunday papers spread around her and a pot of coffee on the floor beside her. She was beginning to enjoy her role of Wronged Woman, for her father's fussing (echoed by Gillian who always did what Richard wanted her to do) was very agreeable.

But she wasn't entirely comforted. She had started out being rather proud to be going out with Josh. He was older than most of the men she knew, and a good deal more interesting and attentive, which made the girls that she knew agreeably jealous. All that had been well worth the effort of having to phone him and beguile him into dates, since he just didn't ask her if she didn't make a move first. She'd regarded him more as a catch than as a person she actually cared for, to start with. But over the weeks she had found him more and more attractive and was, she told herself now, deep in self-pity, thoroughly in love. And though she might have exaggerated the degree of her attachment, there was little doubt that she had been hurt to discover that Josh, as her father put it so bluntly, was definitely not the sort of chap any sensible girl would touch with a barge pole even if she got the chance which was highly unlikely seeing he didn't know if he was Arthur or Martha.

Maybe, she told herself now, she'd misunderstood what she'd seen. Maybe Josh was just being nice to the young man, whoever he was, who was weeping for some ridiculous reason – why would a man cry, after all? – and she'd just jumped to a silly conclusion. But she knew she couldn't pretend that. The scene she had interrupted had been crackling with emotion and sexuality. That had been the shocking part of it, for they hadn't actually been doing anything much. It had been the pain and the yearning the young man had been showing, and the controlled distress that Josh had been filled with that had hit her so hard.

Now she gazed out at the golden late September sky and grieved for her pain. It had all been so much fun when Josh was around, and now it was all so dreary. Even the promise of a trip to Paris, which her father had reiterated, didn't make her feel any better.

Behind her the phone rang and she sat up and grabbed it immediately, just as her father came thudding in with a hand outstretched from the other room, where he'd been sitting over some papers at the table.

'No,' she hissed at him, furiously, her hand over the mouthpiece. 'I *will* talk to him if it is him. Go away!' For he had insisted on answering a couple of earlier calls that morning to keep Josh away from her, in case he had the gall to phone, he said. But she'd been thinking since then and had decided not to let him interfere with any further calls, which had been why she had set the phone with its long flex so conveniently on the table behind her head.

She took her hand away from the mouthpiece and said in a husky voice, 'Stanmore seventeen eleven.'

'Caro,' he said and she caught her breath and turned to look furiously at her father, who was still standing there, and grimaced him to go away; but he shook his head and went and sat heavily in the armchair by the fireplace and stared truculently at her.

She hunched her shoulders and turned away from him, trying to talk quietly.

'Hello,' she said.

'Hello.' There was a long silence and then he sighed softly and said, 'You were very upset last night.'

'Yes.'

'I wish you hadn't rushed off.'

'What did you expect me to do?'

'I wanted to talk to you.'

'You could have come to find me.'

'I did. Once I felt – as soon as I could. But you were sitting with your father and I realized – I thought there'd be an argument.'

'There would have been,' she said with emphasis and managed not to look at her father, who still sat glowering at her.

'Yes – I imagined – look, I owe you a good deal of explanation. Not an apology, mind you – '

She had begun to melt, but now she stiffened again. 'Oh?'

He sighed again. 'I have nothing to apologize for, Caro. I've never said anything to you or done anything to make you think I was anything other than a friend. You'll agree with that?'

She thought for a while. 'I suppose so.'

'It's important you agree, Caro. I like you. You're a fun girl, pleasant to be with – amusing, pretty – one day a man somewhere is going to be very lucky to have you as his wife. But it won't be me.'

'I realize that now,' she said.

'And you know perfectly well that there was never any suggestion that it would?'

'I'd thought so.' She began to gain some courage.

'You had no right. But look, we can't talk like this. May I come and see you?'

'No!' she said quickly.

There was a little silence. 'Is that because you don't want to see me, or because there's someone there with you?'

'Yes,' she said desperately, and he laughed a little.

'I'm sorry. It has to be yes – no question, is that it?'

'Yes.'

'Right. There there's someone with you. Your father?'

'Yes.'

'Hmm. Is he – is there going to be a problem with him?'

'Yes.'

'I see. He wants to horsewhip me? Or something equally original?'

'Yes.'

Richard could bear it no longer. 'Stop bleating yes at him!' he roared.

'I will if you go away and let me talk in peace!' she cried furiously, not covering the mouthpiece this time and in her ear Josh said, 'Oh hell! Family fights.'

'Yes,' she said into the phone and then glared again at her father who had reached out his hand. 'No – I'm not talking to you!'

'You give me that phone,' Richard said and she held on to it with both hands and shook her head vehemently.

'If you don't leave me alone to talk in peace I shall go out and find a phone box,' she said breathlessly. 'It's my private life, not yours.'

225

'You made it mine last night,' he growled and then stopped and stared at her. And suddenly to her amazement, smiled.

'All right, all right. What does it matter after all? It just adds to the case. Okay, Caro. You talk to your nancy boy. Much good it may do you. Or him – ' And he went into the adjoining dining-room and with some ostentation pulled the pair of sliding dividing doors shut.

She took a deep breath. 'He's gone,' she said into the phone.

'I'm sorry he's, well – it's understandable, I suppose. I dare say if you were my daughter I'd – well, never mind. Look Caro, are you all right? I wouldn't have hurt your feelings for the world.'

'No? But you did.'

'I – ' He stopped and then said carefully, 'I'm not going to discuss this. No apologies, no explanations even. Only to say I'm sorry you were upset and I hope we can still be friends.'

She gaped at the window, amazed. 'Do you mean still go out and all that?'

'I don't see why not. Nothing's different. I'm still the same person – '

'But you're a queer!'

There was a little silence and then he said in a level voice, 'Yes.'

'So why take me out? Is it to hide it from people? You know, pretend you're normal?'

'I would deny I was in any way abnormal,' he said with sudden strength. 'Different perhaps than some, but neither better nor worse. Just different.'

'It's not normal to – you know what I mean.'

'Not to want a girl?'

'If you want to put it that way.'

'But I do want friends. I thought we were. I hoped we were.'

She sat in silence, trying to understand, and then sighed. 'I'm not the sort,' she said eventually. 'I mean, there are tomboys and that, like to go around with sporty chaps, just as – well – like sisters and brothers and so on. But me, I like a man who *is* a man. I couldn't go out with you knowing you'd rather be with a fella – ' She swallowed. 'It's all wrong. Peculiar.'

'Oh, I wish I could make you understand! It's not peculiar. It's just the way I am. Like the colour of my eyes.'

'Well, I'm not like that. I have to have a boyfriend who's likely to – I mean, I don't want to waste my time.' She swallowed again. 'I'm not exactly a teenager, you know.'

'I see. Simple friendship is wasting your time?'

'I want to be married!' she wailed. 'I want to have babies!'

'I'm sure you do. And I'm certain you will. But why can't you have friends as well? Oh, Caro, let's stop all this. I'd hoped you'd understand, but there it is. You don't, so – let's just say goodbye, shall we? I meant you no harm and I still don't. I'm sorry you were upset last night but so was Greg and – '

She couldn't help it. 'What was the matter with him? Why was he in such a state?'

Again there was a long silence. Then he said painfully, 'I'd just had to tell him it was – that there was no future for him with me. We'd seen a bit of each other recently, and I'd thought that it would work, that I was ready for a new – but it didn't and I wasn't. So I tried to tell him it was over and he – well, seeing me last night started it all up again for him. I had to make it clear and he – he was upset.'

'Like me,' she said and suddenly laughed, a hard little sound. 'My, but didn't you have a field day yesterday? Two people all of a flutter over you!'

'If you think that gave me pleasure then you've learned nothing about me in all this time,' he snapped and she bit her lip.

'Sorry. I suppose – it's just that – well, there it is. No need to go on. Listen.' She hesitated. 'My father – '

'Your father? What about him?'

'He's – he's pretty annoyed. I didn't mean to cry to him but he sort of was there and – well, he's a bit peeved. He gets nasty when he's like that.'

'Nasty?'

'Tries to get his own back.'

'But I've done nothing to him.'

'He thinks you have to me.'

'Oh hell,' he muttered and there was another of his long silences. Then he said, 'What's he going to do?'

'I don't know. I'll – I'm not sure. Just – I'll tell him not to, whatever it is. I just hope he'll listen.'

'You're a very nice person, Caro. I do wish we could go on being friends.' His voice was warm and she felt the little frisson

227

of pleasure he had always been able to create in her crawl across her shoulders. 'I get the feeling you do understand about me, and don't mind – '

'I mind like hell!' she said, trying to sound perky, terribly sophisticated and yet understanding. 'There was I thinking I'd met the man of my dreams at last and it turns out I've been dreaming the wrong dream. Tell me, do you fancy Paul McCartney as much as I do? It could be cosy if we both had a thing for the same fella!'

'Not funny,' he said after a moment. 'Sorry. Not funny.'

'Well, you can't win 'em all,' she said as flippantly as she could and then it was her turn to be silent for a while. 'Josh.' She stopped.

'Yes?'

'I will try to understand. It's not easy.'

'Thank you,' he said. 'I can't ask for more. And Caro, do remember that even though you don't feel we can go on as we did –out and about and so forth – I'll always regard you as a friend. If you ever want anything or – well, you know where I am – '

'Thanks,' she said a little bleakly. 'Goodbye, Josh.'

'Goodbye, Caro.' And the phone clicked in her ear and then reverted to the buzz of the dialling tone and slowly she replaced it.

He came in so promptly that it was obvious he'd been listening at the door. 'So? What did the creep try to pull over your eyes this time? Fairy dust?'

'Oh, shut up, Daddy,' she said absently, still staring at the phone.

'You're daft, you know that? The bastard's a toe rag, treats you like a – '

'He didn't,' she said levelly and now she looked at him. 'He's a very decent person. It was my own fault. I jumped to conclusions.'

'Your own fault? How can it be, when you're the one he cheated? Lets you think he was a normal bloke and then he goes off and – '

'He is normal. Only different,' she said, and swung her feet to the ground. 'I'm bored sitting here. I'm going over to see Jenny. I'll have to start putting myself about a bit and she knows everyone and goes to all the parties – Listen, Daddy,' she stopped with her hand on the door in the hall. 'Leave him alone, will you?'

'What? Let him get away with it?'

'He's done nothing wrong,' she said stubbornly. 'He's just what he is. It's like the colour of his eyes. He can't help it. Leave him alone. The things you said last night – don't do it.'

'Don't do what?' He opened his eyes wide.

'You know perfectly well what I mean,' she said angrily. 'The things you said last night.'

'And what did I say last night?'

'About reporting him to the police. *I* wouldn't say anything against him and you might as well know it. So how'd you prove anything?'

'I said last night I'd changed my mind,' he said. 'Remember?'

She shook her head. 'I'm not stupid. You just had a better idea, you thought. You were going on about shares.'

He shrugged. 'Well, if you don't care he made a monkey out of you – '

'He didn't, so I don't,' she said. 'Just forget it ever happened. I'm going to.'

He stood there listening as she went out and thudded up to the stairs to her room and then went back to the dining-room and the table full of scattered papers. He'd been working out just how his position would be once he'd forced Josh Deveen to sell his shares at the risk of being reported to the police for being homosexual. No matter what idiots like that fella Wolfenden might say, this was a decent country, and characters like Deveen would never be allowed to get away with their filthy ways. All he needed was time to sort it out and the chance to talk to the man and it'd be a fait accompli. Either way, he'd get his come-uppance.

The letter arrived on Josh's doormat three days later. It was brief – exceedingly so – and to the point and until he'd read it to the end right as far as the signature, he didn't understand it. But then he read it again, and it made the most clear and ugly sense, and he sat and stared at it in cold disbelief.

Dear Mr Deveen,
    This letter is an official request to purchase from you your voting shares in the company 'Food by Poppy Ltd'. of

229

which you own six (6) per cent. The price offered is that which will obtain on the market at the time of exchange of contract.

I am sure that when you consider all possible outcomes of refusing this reasonable request you will agree that it is to your benefit to make this sale to me as soon as possible. I will arrange for my brokers to be in contact with you within the next three days to finalize the deal.

Yours etc.

[signed] *Richard Melhuish*

26

'It's such an odd thing for him to want to do,' Poppy said fretfully and peered again into her mirror to see whether she needed more foundation, decided she needed less and began to scrub it off again. 'I'd much rather have eaten here where we can be comfortable, and I love cooking for him on the few chances I get – why do you suppose he was so dead set on this?'

David, who as usual had been ready for ten minutes and was now waiting patiently for Poppy to finish her make-up, sighed. 'I've told you. I don't know any more than you do. You were the one he spoke to on the phone, not me.'

She leaned back and looked judiciously at her now rather rosy face and then set to work with the powder. 'He just said there were things he wanted to talk to us about. Both of us. And when I said fine, come to supper, he said no, it'd be easier if we went out. Do you suppose he wants money?'

David laughed. 'I doubt it. Has he ever? And he has his inheritance, remember – '

'Yes – ' she sighed and set to work with lipstick, talking through her stretched mouth with some difficulty. 'And he's never been shy about talking about money. And he was definitely bothered about whatever this is.'

'Sex, then,' David said lightly and got to his feet. 'It has to be one of the big three, doesn't it? And I've never known him talk about politics – '

Poppy said nothing, concentrating on neatening the edge of her lipstick, careful not to catch his eye in the mirror. There were some things she and David just didn't talk about and one of them was Josh's private life. But maybe, she thought, tonight will be

different? And wondered hopefully about Caro Melhuish. Just
for a moment.

'Will I do?'

'As ever. Green looks great on you.'

'Mmm.' She twisted and turned a little in front of the mirror.
'It always has.' She stopped then and looked at him with a rather
comical expression of dismay on her face. 'It's about time I
stopped being so dreadfully vain, surely? At my age, to be
fussing over what I look like! I should be ashamed.'

'The time to worry is when you stop caring,' he said firmly and
took her elbow. 'I have no intention of going around with an old
crone with a shiny red nose and thick white whiskers sprouting
out of her chin. Keep up the camouflage, kid – '

She laughed and they went down into the square to find a taxi
to take them into town, apparently contentedly enough, but she
was worried; Josh had sounded remote and chilly on the phone
and had been so adamant abut this evening's arrangements, and
all that had built itself into a sense of premonition that made her
very twitchy indeed. It had been a dreadful couple of days
waiting for this moment; now at last it was here, a part of her
wanted to run back into the house, to jump into bed and hide
under the bedclothes for the rest of her life, which was of course
nonsensical, and she scolded herself silently as the taxi rattled up
Bayswater Road towards Oxford Street and the tangle of Soho
streets where they were to meet Josh.

'I've heard a lot about this place,' David said, as the taxi
arrived. 'The gossip columns have been on and on about it. Very
trendy, it seems.'

'And the rest,' the taxi driver said. 'Got more front than
Brighton, this place has. Very full of itself, it is – that'll be seven
and six, guv'nor – ' And David, muttering a little about the
exorbitant cost of taxis these days, paid up and then turned to
lead Poppy into the restaurant.

'Trattoria – ' David said, peering up at the neon lit fascia. 'Not
like any of the ones I saw in Italy.'

'I've heard of this place too,' Poppy said, all her professional
curiosity aroused. 'They're really doing very well – maybe I can
pick up a few ideas – '

There were plenty to be picked up. The restaurant was light
and bright and glittering with excitement. She couldn't be quite

sure what it was that mattered most: the pale bright tiles with a few rush mats on them here and there that made up the floor, the high-backed rush chairs with their almost ferociously rural air, the tables clad in the brightest of pottery on blindingly white cloths, the sounds of tinkling Italian music or the almost overwhelming smell of garlic and basil and oregano; and then decided that it was in fact the customers.

The place was solid with people, because it was now nine o'clock. Josh had wanted a late meeting even though his parents usually ate their dinner at seven or so; but he seemed to have forgotten that and Poppy hadn't reminded him. Now they stood close together feeling rather conspicuous in a place that was so overwhelmingly young. Unbelievably pretty girls in the scantiest of mini skirts and the palest of make-ups, with luscious heavily painted eyes staring out like small coals from pallid faces, and equally beautiful young men with legs in such tight trousers that they looked like deep-water fishing birds, were stalking through the hubbub, crying joyously in greeting to their friends and yelping excitedly at the things that were said to them, and Poppy caught David's eye and giggled softly. And he, hearing her thoughts about the incongruity of their presence in this modern kaleidoscope of colour and noise, laughed back.

The head waiter – or so Poppy assumed him to be, though he was dressed very casually in an open-necked full-sleeved pink shirt over tight black trousers, an outfit she would never have permitted in her own establishment – looked at them with a very supercilious air as they approached him and Poppy saw there were several people sitting about in the small bar section at the front of the restaurant, who were clearly waiting for tables. But David showed no unease at all and said firmly, 'Josh Deveen. He has a table – '

The scornful air vanished at once and the head waiter thrust out his hand. 'You must be Poppa of Josh – such a pleasure – ' He broke into excited Italian which Poppy was convinced was staged especially for their benefit, and then shook her hand with unusual vigour, and still talking at the top of his voice led them into the restaurant to a table at the far side, where Josh was already sitting.

He greeted them warmly, getting to his feet and fussing them into their chairs, with the head waiter and one of his acolytes hovering and fussing too, and that gave Poppy time to take a good look at him. And her heart sank. He was pale and clearly hadn't slept well lately for there were violet smudges under his eyes and he was visibly thinner. This was not a good news event.

'Let's not say a thing till we've ordered,' he said firmly. 'Now, let me show you this menu, Ma. You'll love the stracciatella – the best chicken soup anywhere. And then I'd recommend a little of their tagliolini pesto – it's the best in the world – and a ragout of kidneys and – '

'Darling, no!' Poppy protested. 'I've never managed more than two courses in the evening and that's pushing it a bit – I'll have something simple – please, nothing special.'

'You can't come here and not have something special,' he said. 'The soup then, and the ragout with a little gnocchi to round it off. We can talk about pudding later – you won't be able to resist the zabaglione – '

There was a good deal of animated chatter between David and the waiter, with David showing how knowledgeable he was about Italian food by ordering squid in its own ink – which slightly startled Poppy, for all her culinary expertise – and Josh selecting food which was clearly small in quantity. He's very unhappy, she thought, as the waiter made a note of his request for the stracciatella and a very small piece of sea bass to follow. The sooner he tells us whatever it is the better.

But he clearly had no intention of saying anything yet. He poured wine for them, a crisp and a very pleasant Soave, and urged grissini on them and chattered about the people around them, pointing out the more famous ones Poppy might have missed.

'That's Joey Constant, the rock and roll bass player – absolutely marvellous, he is. Oh, and look, there's the girl from that Sunday night variety show, with an MP, no less – she's riding high! And that's Peter Geria, the dancer – he's had a huge hit at the Garden – see, Ma?'

Obediently Poppy looked, watching the people he'd pointed out in spite of herself; they were all so very exotic, it seemed to her. The men seemed to be as carefully and fashionably dressed as the girls, and more than one of them seemed to her to be wearing a certain amount of make-up. There were one or two rather over-emphatic tans, she thought, as well as more than one who had clearly adorned his hair with a streak of bottled silver. That they looked exciting and wonderful she couldn't deny, but still they were a little overwhelming, and she looked at Josh, in his usual comfortable open-necked shirt with a scarf knotted in it, and his old but much loved tweed jacket, and thought he looked rather dull in comparison with them. Sometimes, in family settings, his casual style of dress had made him seem as exotic as these parakeets here. And she sighed and was a little amused at herself; clearly comparison was all.

The inconsequent chatter went on all through the meal; and then as they reached the pudding stage – which David greeted with delight and Poppy not at all – Josh said abruptly, 'These people I pointed out to you – what do you think of them?'

'What?' Poppy was bemused.

'The dancer over there. And that actor – and the rock and roller – ' He indicated them again with his chin. 'What do you think of them?'

'Think of them? Well, nothing, really. I mean, I don't know them. I'm sure they're delightful people to their friends and families, of course, but – '

'I don't mean that!' He sounded irritable. 'I mean, make a judgement. What sort of people do you think they are?'

She stared at him, deeply bewildered. 'Darling, how can I know what sort of people they are? What sort of judgement could anyone make on just looking at them? They're people, that's all. Interesting, I suppose – ' She looked again at the bright fashionable clothes and the extreme hairstyles and faces. 'A touch exotic even. But no more than that – '

'What about their love lives?' Josh said abruptly and again Poppy frowned and opened her mouth to speak. But David leaned forward and set a hand on her arm and stopped her.

'If you mean, have we realized that all these men you've indicated are homosexual, Josh, then the answer is I have, but Poppy hasn't. I suspect she doesn't notice things like that. A lot of women don't, you know.'

Poppy was sitting very still. Josh tilted his head a little stiffly and said, 'Is that true, Ma?'

She swallowed, for her mouth had suddenly dried. 'Yes,' she said after a while. 'I – sex isn't something I think about much –

235

not at my age – ' and she tried to smile; but all she managed was an ugly rictus.

'You know I don't mean that. You surely must know what I do mean. And what I've brought you here to tell you.'

'Yes.' She took a deep breath. 'Yes, I know. I suppose I always have. Well, at least I have for some time. Tried to pretend it wasn't so – Caro – ' She let her voice trail away.

'It's because of Caro I have to talk about all this to you,' he said. 'It's been hell this past few days – ' And he bent his head and Poppy leaned forward and took his hand, for he was clearly weeping. David reached into his pocket and shoved a handkerchief under the table into Josh's hand, and he took it gratefully and blew his nose.

'I've been dreading this evening,' he said simply.

'I wasn't exactly looking forward to it,' David said. 'I suspected it would be something like this – '

'Like what?' Poppy said, still trying to hold the situation at bay.

David shook his head firmly. 'Don't make it harder than it has to be, Poppy. So our Josh is homosexual. What's the word these days, Josh? In my days in the army, it was queer – '

'It still is,' Josh said. 'Or gay. Or camp – '

'Camp – ' Poppy echoed and then stopped. What was the use of talking, after all? She'd heard the word camp too. Lee sometimes used it when she she was talking about her actors, or about a particular style of play, and even without trying Poppy could remember some of the jokes the men would make long ago when she'd been an army nurse and they'd treated her like one of themselves and not thought to censor their conversation when she was around.

She had always known, of course. A part of her hadn't wanted to know. She'd tried to pretend to herself it wasn't true. She'd always wanted to see her Josh settled with a loving wife and babies of his own, like Robin and now Lee, though she had no babies yet, but it wasn't just a hunger for grandchildren that drove her. She slid her hand across the table and took David's and was suddenly burning with gratitude for him. Without him always there, totally reliable, totally hers as she was his, life would be unbearable. And she wanted no less a comfort for her children.

David seemed as usual to know what she was thinking,

because he said, 'There's no reason why you shouldn't be a perfectly happy and successful person, Josh, whether you're gay or not. I hope you can find a partner – '

'I did, once – '

David touched his hand again. 'Adrian?' Josh nodded, unable to speak. 'I did wonder – ' David said.

Poppy had caught her breath by now. 'It's all right,' she said, and she too took one of Josh's hands. 'I suppose – well, I'll get used to it. And there's nothing any different really. You're still what you've always been, my Josh, and I love you to pieces – '

He looked at her directly then and said in a sort of burst of pain, 'Oh, Christ, I wish I'd told you years ago!'

'So do I,' Poppy said. 'If being silent's made you miserable.'

'It's got me right into the crap,' he said savagely and she recoiled a little from the anger in him.

'How do you mean?'

'If you'd known you wouldn't have pushed Caro at me, and she'd not have developed a – a sort of crush and her bloody father wouldn't – oh, what's the use of playing the might-have-beens? I'm sorry – I just wish I'd told you sooner. It's my fault I didn't. I didn't have to go along with you – '

'You're not making complete sense,' Poppy said carefully, though she felt she had a pretty clear picture of what had happened. 'Are you saying that Caro – '

'She thought I meant more than I did. I took her out because –oh, because she asked me, mostly. And to please you, I suppose. Silly, isn't it? It's not as though it'd even have gone anywhere, my taking a girl out, but there you are. I thought I'd please you.'

'Oh, no, Josh,' David said quietly. 'Oh no, I can't have that.'

'What?' Josh stared at him.

'You feel bad about Caro. I can see that. But I can't have you shifting the blame to us – to Poppy and me. That fact that we didn't know for sure that you were gay – though I have to say I've thought so for some time – doesn't mean that you were forced to cater to our supposed ignorance by misleading someone. A girl. You can't say you took her out to please us, because it just won't wash.'

Josh took a deep breath as Poppy threw a furious grimace at David, and then he nodded. 'That's fair, I suppose. In fact, I know it is. Sorry, Pa. It was just – it's been so lousy this past week or so. I've got myself in a right tangle. And I just don't know what to do next.'

David stiffened. 'There's more then?'

'Yes.'

'Then you'd better come out with it. Has there been – are the law involved?'

'Not yet,' he said grimly and took a deep breath. 'But unless I do what Melhuish wants, it will be.'

Afterwards Poppy was always to remember that fifteen minutes as almost the worst she'd experienced, as Josh explained to them both about what Melhuish had said after the ball. Around her the bright sparkling restaurant with its bright sparkling people glittered and grinned at her, and across the table her beloved son poured out a chapter of misery that hurt her as much as if he had rubbed her softest skin with wire wool. All around her were other men, like her son, who experienced a need that someone somewhere had decreed was illegal. They seemed happy enough, able to run their lives safely and securely, even in the public eye, like that very famous ballet dancer and the rock singer; why should it not have been so for her Josh? Because it clearly wasn't.

'So there it is,' Josh ended at last, and his voice was a little husky now. 'He extended the deadline by three days and then another three, but that's the end of it, I'm sure. If I don't sell him my six per cent in "Food by Poppy" by tomorrow night he'll shop me. I know they've got no evidence, but they've got their ways, these police. They hate us and they'll do anything to make trouble – no, don't look like that. Our police may be wonderful if you're a conservative, conformist, white, well-behaved, heterosexual person who pays large sums in taxes. But try being a gay not-so-conservative sort of person like me and see what happens to you – I just don't know what to do, Ma. I know he wants the shares to harm you in some way and that's why I had to tell you about all this. I wouldn't have exposed you to any of this for the world, unless I had to. Do believe that. It was to make it easier to tell you that I insisted on coming here. It's always so much easier to talk about very private matters in public, I find. Less likely to have great emotional storms when you've got an audience. Do believe me, I wouldn't hurt you two for the world!'

238

'Of course we believe you,' David said in his usual matter-of-fact way. 'Why shouldn't we? The thing we have to do now is decide how to cope – '

'Do you think I haven't thought myself to shreds? I've tried everything – even thought of just disappearing – but then he'd make it hell for you, no doubt. I'd have been suicidal if I didn't have more cowardice in me than courage, believe me – No, Ma, it's all right. That was a sick sort of joke. I'm sorry.' And he clutched her hand, for her knuckles had whitened with her sudden rush of fear.

'The only thing to do with a blackmailer is to refuse to give in to him,' David said. 'We should call his bluff – '

'How?' Josh said bitterly. 'If I do that he'll scupper me. And that means not just me but all of you. Imagine the fuss – you're a vulnerable person, Ma. The papers are interested in you and your business – no, I can't go to the police and complain I'm being blackmailed. I wouldn't trust 'em to treat me right anyway. They're as hateful to people like me as any of them – '

'But you can't sell to him!' David said. 'It'd be – '

'It'd take Ma's business away from her,' Josh said. 'I know. I've worked it out too. It's what he wants, of course – '

'Is Caro in agreement with him?'

He shook his head vigorously. 'Absolutely not. I've talked to her. She swears she'll never speak to him again because of what he's trying to do to me. That's made him even worse, of course. Oh, hell and damnation! What am I to do!'

'It's fairly easy I think,' Poppy said calmly. 'I'll buy your shares. Then he won't have any reason to blackmail you, will he? You won't have what he wants. I'll buy them tomorrow, Josh. End of problem.'

There was a silence between them into which the chatter and the noise of the other people flowed like a river and then Josh took a long unsteady breath. 'It won't work.'

'Why shouldn't it? Tell him tomorrow that we know what he's been doing, tell him we made you sell your shares to us and tell him to do his worst and much good may it do him. There's no evidence, you say – '

'None at all. Not that'd stand up in a court of law, that is.'

'Then that's that. I'll arrange it all tomorrow. And tonight,

239

darling, you can sleep.' She touched his hand again briefly. 'And do relax, sweetheart. It's all only sex after all – '

27

'He's taken it too quietly, that's the thing,' Poppy said. 'I keep expecting something awful to happen and it just doesn't. It's like waiting for the thunder before a storm starts.'

'Maybe it's the other way about,' Robin said. 'Maybe he's lying low, expecting you to do something awful to him.'

David shook his head. 'No. Not Melhuish. I'm realizing now just how clever that man is. I have to agree with Poppy. He's taken it much too quietly.'

Sam leaned over and poured more whisky into David's glass, and lifted his brows in query at Poppy, who shook her head. 'I think,' he said, as he put the decanter back, 'that the only thing we can do is wait and see.'

'I wish we could persuade Josh to charge him with blackmail,' Robin said. 'Surely the man's committed a crime? Josh has done nothing wrong –'

'But dammit, he has,' Sam said with some force. 'I don't think so in human terms, and neither do any of us, but the law is the law and though I'm convinced it's a stupid law and they'll have to change it sooner or later, men like Josh suffer all sorts of injustices – and Josh was right when he said the police don't like people like him. The chances are they'll side with Melhuish if it ever comes to the crunch.'

'It mustn't,' Poppy said. 'I've told Josh – and he said it won't. That there's no way he'll do anything in the least risky – oh, if only I could persuade Gillian to take her proxy away from him! It's the only way we can ever get rid of the man.'

'I can't see that happening,' Robin said sombrely. 'Can you? She seems so cowed by him –'

'I tried to talk to her,' Poppy said and got to her feet. 'But she

241

went off like a scared rabbit and then the next thing I heard was that she'd gone away for a holiday somewhere. Melhuish is making sure I can't get at her – all we can do now is wait for the next Board meeting. I've an idea about what I might be able to do – but it's no use talking about it because I can't be sure it'll work. And anyway, I'm much too tired right now. Take me home, David.'

Robin pushed her coffee cup away and got to her feet too. 'Stay the night – ' she said. 'The spare room's ready and – '

'No thanks,' David said and kissed her. 'I love you dearly, Robin, but I love my own bed better. Come on, Poppy. And thanks for dinner, you two. It's helped Poppy a lot to be able to talk about it all. She wasn't coping at all well having only me as her safety valve.' He looked after her, for she'd gone out to the hall to visit the lavatory before the long drive home. 'I'm so glad Josh told you so that we could start talking as well. It does help.'

Sam smiled a little crookedly. 'It usually does help to talk. It's the main remedy in my medical bag, talk.'

'Then use it – ' David said softly as Robin too went out into the hall, to help her mother into her coat. 'Here at home – '

Sam opened his mouth to speak and then closed it again as the two women came back. 'Come on, David,' Poppy said. 'I really will stay the night unless we go right now. I'm so tired I can hardly think.'

'Great,' David said cheerfully. 'You only find problems when you think. Instead, you can doze in the car going home. Good night, you two. And try not to fret too much. I dare say we'll weather this storm as we've weathered most of them over the years – and thanks for the strudel, Robin. It was splendid. Not as good as Auntie Jessie's used to be, but splendid.'

There was a flurry of goodbyes at the door, and they came out onto the porch for last hugs. Then Sam and Robin went down the path to see the older pair into their car.

'That's odd,' Sam murmured. 'That car's been parked there all evening – and I saw it this morning when I left.'

'Mmm?' Robin glanced at the shabby old Ford across the road. 'I think it must be a commercial traveller's or some such. There was a chap sleeping in the driver's seat when I came home. Good night, Ma. Take care – I'll phone you – '

When Sam and Robin came back to the house and closed the

front door behind them, Sam stood for a while in the hall. Robin had gone back into the dining-room to clear the table, not wanting to leave too much to Helga in the morning and after a moment he followed her and began to help.

They worked in silence, fetching and carrying beween dining-room and kitchen and then, when the dishes were stacked in the kitchen to Robin's satisfaction and she tried to leave the room, he stopped in the doorway so that she couldn't get past.

'Robin,' he said, and she looked up and then away, swiftly. She hardly ever did look at him directly these days; he'd noticed that and it had hurt. But he had decided he would bear the hurt in silence no longer.

'Your father said something important tonight,' he said and Robin nodded.

'He usually does. He's right about the way to deal with all this. As long as Josh is sensible there should be no more – '

'I didn't mean about Josh,' Sam said steadily. 'I mean about us.'

She stiffened. 'He didn't talk about us.'

'He did at one point. Reminded me of the value of talk. We haven't been talking.'

'Oh, really, Sam!' she said as lightly as she could. 'At this time of night?'

'The time of day is hardly relevant. It's just that – we've been dodging it. For weeks. Months even. There's something wrong between us and I can't bear it any longer. I need to know. In words – just what's happening. How are we?'

She stood with her head bent, staring down at the tiles on the kitchen floor. Helga keeps them amazingly clean, she thought. Each of the joins between the tiles was carefully scrubbed. She's really marvellous. I must tell her how much I appreciate her. She deserves that –

'It's too easy to stay silent, Robin,' he said, not moving from the doorway, so that she couldn't escape. 'It's time to talk.'

She remained standing there, still staring down at the tiles. There was a small crack in the corner of one of them. They'd been hard to install, she remembered; that crack must have happened because the floor was uneven, and the tiler had been in a hurry –

'Whatever it is you have to say, it'll be better than this silence,' he went on. 'Oh, I know we talk commonplaces, but we don't talk honestly. Not about what really matters. I'm very lonely, Robin. I don't think I can cope much longer. Not unless you tell me what's wrong.'

Keep looking at the tiles, she told herself, keep looking – but it didn't help. The words came out of her mouth and she listened with a sort of amazement. It was as though someone else were speaking, not herself.

'Hamish Todd. He stayed in London a good while after that TV programme he came to do. He's gone back once or twice but he kept coming back. We had an affair.' Be quiet, her inner voice shrieked. Be quiet, don't be such a fool, be quiet –

'I slept with him,' she said and then she did look up at last, directly at Sam. 'I slept with him.'

There was a long silence and she went on looking at him, trying to read his expression, but it was smooth, looking no more than thoughtful. His eyes were dark, though, and she thought there was a glitter there. Tears? Anger? It could be either.

The silence went on, broken only as the old wood of the house settled round them into its night-time creaks, and somewhere out beyond in the streets there was the rumble of traffic. Then he said carefully, 'You *had* an affair with him. Does that mean it's past? Over?'

'Yes,' she said, almost surprised. She hadn't thought about the possible reaction from him since she hadn't expected herself to tell him so baldly, but if she had, it certainly wouldn't have been this. 'Yes. Well past. As soon as I – it happened once. Only once.'

He took a deep breath and closed his eyes, and she was even startled for he just stood there with them tightly closed and said nothing.

'Sam? Did you hear what I said? I slept with Hamish Todd, dammit. I – '

He opened his eyes and looked at her and then slowly a smile began to stretch his lips and it grew and took in his eyes and then he was gazing at her as happily as if she'd given him some piece of news that he'd been longing to hear; and she stared back, totally nonplussed.

'Past,' he said simply. 'Past. You came back to me. Only once. You came back to me.'

She shook her head, letting her bewilderment show. 'I don't understand you – I thought you'd be – ' She shrugged. 'I don't know. Not like this.'

He moved towards her, his hands out as though he were about to put his arms round her and then awkwardly pulled them back and put them firmly in his pockets. 'You thought I'd scream and shout? Be jealous? Of course not.'

'Why not?' she said bluntly. 'If it had been me – if you'd come and told me – '

'Why not? Because I'm me and you're you. Because all that matters to me is the present and the future. What terrified me was the possibility that you were involved with him now. That you had plans to stay with him in the future. That would have been hell' He smiled again, even more widely if that were possible. 'But it was only once. And you came right back to me – '

'Of course I did,' she said and now sounded irritable. 'As if I'd do anything else.'

'You could have done. You could have decided not to bother with me any more. Couldn't you?'

'I suppose so – ' She bent her head again. 'I'm so ashamed. I hate myself. I'm so disgusted – '

Now he did come out of the doorway and took his hands out of his pockets and set them on her shoulders. 'That helps no one. Guilt – it's the most corrosive thing there is – '

'Thus spake the psychiatrist,' she said with a sardonic note in her voice. 'My God, but you really are – it's like you're living your own life through a textbook, as though you were your own doctor treating yourself for your problems.'

'It'd be a poor show if I learned nothing from my working life to help me cope with my own more important life,' he said. 'And the most important thing I've learned is that you can't lock up the people you love. They have to be free if they're ever to be as loving to you as you want them to be – '

'You sound so bloody *good*!' she burst out. 'You make it impossible to – oh, Goddammit, any other husband'd have screamed and even hit me or something. But you – you go all philosophical on me and – '

'You want me to hit you?' His face creased. 'I don't really think I could manage that.'

She almost laughed. 'God almighty, Sam, of course not! It's

just that you – you're so – I never would have imagined you could be like this over something that's made me feel so dreadful. I'm eaten with guilt, I'm so ashamed I could die and all you do is – '

'All I do is be glad you're here,' he said and put his arms around her and held her close. She remained stiff for just a moment and then gave in, and let him hold her, and took a deep breath of relief. For the first time for months she felt safe. It wasn't very exciting, it wasn't at all passionate, there was no fire in it, but it was the best feeling she could imagine having.

Oliver had been waiting for them to come to bed, getting more and more irritable. For God's sake, the grandparents had been gone ages! What were they talking about down there for so long? But at last the stairs creaked and he heard their soft murmurings and he rolled over again and pulled the blanket over his ears. At last!

He heard his door latch click in its usual way, and made a convulsive and very visible turn in bed, and at once the door closed again and he lay there and listened as their own bedroom door closed and then there was the sound of water running in their bathroom and he could sit up and push the bedclothes back. It was shaming at his age to have to go in for such ploys. Didn't he have a job? Wasn't he earning his own money now? To have to skulk around at home like this so that his mother could go through her ridiculous ritual of making sure he was in his room and in bed was something no man of his age should have to put up with. The sooner I can earn a bit more, rent a place of my own, the better, he thought as he slipped into his shoes and smoothed the few creases that had appeared in his shirt and trousers as he lay under the blankets. Then I'll be able to lead my own life in my own way. And about time too.

Suzy was waiting in the usual place at the corner, and she slid out of the dark shadows as he came round it and hissed at him, 'I was just about to go home again. Where've you been?'

'I couldn't help it. There's some sort of fuss going on at home. The grandparents came and stayed for dinner, and then the olds didn't go up till all hours. Anyway, so what? We'll be there in plenty of time.'

'We'd better be,' she said. 'Or this'll be the last time I'll come.'

'Suit yourself.' He was flippant. 'You don't have to tag along, you know. I'll be perfectly happy on my own. Come on. There's a cab – ' And he ran and she had to run too or stay behind.

It was odd, she would think sometimes, how things had turned out. It had all started to please her mother, to help Oliver settle back into London, but now it was part of her life too, and so was he. Sometimes it depressed her to admit that she enjoyed his company as much as she did; at other times it exhilarated her. The important thing was that at least he was behaving better than he'd been used to. Tonight's escapade was an unusual one, rather than the run-of-the-mill sort of thing they'd been for him before. She could claim some success in making him behave better, she would tell herself sometimes, full of optimism; and then he'd say or do something that would show her that nothing had really changed; that Oliver was still as selfish and careless as he'd ever been. Maybe he just wasn't able to be anything else.

'That's odd,' Oliver said suddenly. 'There's that car – '

'What?'

'There's been a car parked outside our house the past few days – usually a chap in it fast asleep. I see him in the mornings when I leave, and again when I get home.' He peered through the taxi's back window. 'Now he's driving along behind us! Oh, well – another night bird, I suppose.'

'Is it someone you know?' She was alarmed. 'Could they tell my mother about this?'

He scoffed at that. 'What a load of codswallop you do talk sometimes, Suzy. As if anyone was interested in following you! You've been reading too many thrillers. Listen – about this place we're going to,' And he shuffled along the seat to sit closer to her, with his arm thrown negligently over her shoulders in a way that still made her shiver inside with excitement. 'It's nothing all that special, you know.'

'Then why are we going there?' She forgot the car behind them. It was hard to think of anything else when he sat as close to her as this.

'I just fancied it. It's popular with musicians and sometimes you get a really big-name guy playing a set or two. Good jazz, you know?'

'I like jazz.' Suzy brightened. Now they were safely on their way it didn't seem so wicked. She'd been feeling bad about deceiving her mother about what she was doing, especially as Chick always trusted her and never dreamed of checking up on her. Let's face it, Suzy thought then, she's never really had to till now. If she knew I was going to a jazz club at midnight, on a school day, she'd go up the wall – but she won't know, and I can manage, after all. I've only got a revision day tomorrow.

'And there may be some other interesting activities too,' he said with elaborate casualness. 'So fasten your seat belt. It's going to be a bumpy night!' And he bent his head and started to kiss her, after which she didn't really care much at all about anything.

28

It was six o'clock when the phone dragged her out of the deepest possible sleep and she found herself sitting bolt upright, staring at it. The room was bright, for they had not drawn the curtains when they'd climbed into bed and she sat for a moment trying to work out the day and the time and the reason for the ringing, and then, as Sam stirred beside her and reached his hand for the phone, collapsed back on her pillows.

A patient, she thought and tried to push herself back into delicious sleep, but she couldn't. She was vaguely aware of Sam beside her muttering into the phone and thought muzzily – did we? Did I imagine it or did we? They'd fallen asleep, she held close in his arms after weeping her sense of guilt and confusion and above all of relief all over his chest and then there had been the time in the night when – Or had there? Had it just been an intensely erotic dream or had it really happened? Had Sam really reached for her and –

'What?' Sam was suddenly sitting upright beside her and she opened her eyes and squinted up at him. 'What did you say?'

He listened and then said crisply, 'I'm on my way. Ye Gods, I had no idea – wait till I get there, will you? It'll take me – oh, an hour or so I'm afraid. I have to dress and we're out in Hampstead –yes – by all means tell him. And the other one, you say is – oh. You've spoken to the family. All right, all right – I'm on my way –'

He dropped the phone and almost fell out of bed in his hurry, and made for the bathroom and she stared after him and then called, 'What is it? An emergency at the Clinic?'

'You'd better come in while I shave, so I can explain,' he called. 'It's – come in, for heaven's sake – '

The lavatory flushed and then the taps began to run and she

249

dragged on her dressing-gown, very aware of her nakedness – and since she'd worn a nightdress to go to bed last night, clearly it hadn't been a dream she'd had – and followed him into the bathroom.

'Listen,' he said through the shaving soap he was plastering on his face. 'Try not to get too agitated but listen. It seems that Oliver went out last night – '

'Went out? But I saw him! He was in bed when we came up and that was almost midnight. He turned over in bed and – '

'And must have got up and sneaked out when we were in bed.' His voice was muffled as he tilted his chin to use his razor. 'That was the police station at Vine Street. They say they've got them both there – '

'Both?' She could have slapped him. 'Both who? And why?'

'Oliver and Suzy – they were caught up in some sort of police action, it seems. They can go if someone signs for them – police bail is it? They may have to come up in court – I won't know more till I get there – '

'I'm coming too – ' She ran for the bedroom, to pull clothes out of her wardrobe. 'Tell me the rest in the car – '

She didn't stop to wash and was ready to go as soon as he was, waiting only to leave a note for Helga and the girls and Bertie, who was with them this month, to say they'd had to go out for a while and would be back soon; and clambered into the car as he started the engine and hurled it out of the drive.

'Right!' she said. 'Now, what's he done?'

'I don't know. The woman on the phone was very cagey – '

'Woman?'

'Policewoman, she said. I suppose because they're children. Under twenty-one, anyway.'

'Suzy – ' Robin said and bit her lip. 'I never thought of Suzy as being – as being – '

'Like Oliver?' Sam said grimly. 'A right villainous scapegrace who's about to get his come-uppance? No, neither did I.'

'What are you going to do?' She was on the defensive at once and he knew it and wasn't going to be put off by that.

'It's no use, Robin. You've been too easy on him altogether. He's going to find out life isn't all roses. He's going back to school. That'll teach him to behave himself, to be somewhere he'll get some real discipline and where he can't charm birds out of trees the way he charms you. I love him too well to allow anything else, so don't argue. This young man's overstepped the mark this time. Whatever he's done as far as the police are concerned, what makes me angry is that he sneaked out of the house last night. It's that I intend to deal with and it's no use arguing with me –'

She didn't.

Chick was already there when they arrived, looking tousled and drawn in a pair of battered old trousers and a cotton shirt and she turned a face of such anguish to Robin as they came hurrying round the corner after parking the car that Robin could have wept.

'They told me you were on your way, so I decided to wait for you,' Chick said huskily. It was clear she'd been weeping. 'I have to know what's been going on before I – before we talk. I thought of all of them, my Suzy would be all right – ' Her eyes filled with tears again. 'Oh, God, if only Harry were here!'

Robin slid her arm into hers. 'Darling, I'm sure it'll be okay. And whatever it is, it's obviously Oliver's fault, and I'm dreadfully sorry and – '

'Let's not jump to any conclusions,' Sam said and led the way into the police station. 'Facts first. Come on – '

The policewoman was friendly and cheerful and smiled when Chick said a little breathlessly, 'What have they done?'

'Nothing very much, Mrs Amberley,' she said. 'Been where they shouldn't have been, lied about their ages, of course, but not much worse than that. But they've had a nasty fright and I think it'll have done them good.'

'What happened?' Sam was very crisp.

'We got a tip that there were a lot of drugs changing hands in a jazz club. And that there was some indecency going on – no, don't worry. It didn't affect your children. They were there to hear the jazz, that's all. He's a lovely young man, I thought, very sensible and reliable and was terribly upset to discover that he'd taken his little girlfriend to such a place. But there it is – the good get caught up with the bad, don't they, when things go wrong? Anyway, we got the tip, our people went in and arrested some men for – ' She glanced at the two women and dropped her voice a little, speaking directly at Sam, 'Indecency, sir, you know the sort of thing – in the lavatories at the back. And then there was this chap we've been wanting to get, with some of the grass in his pocket, and we got him. But when we brought in the others to check up and found out yours were under age – well, the little girl only looks seventeen, doesn't she? Well, we couldn't just let them go without notifying you, their parents. Sorry to have startled you, but we wanted to call you when it was a bit nearer getting-up time.' She laughed cheerfully. 'But we couldn't leave it too late, or the day people would be here and they might make it a bit hotter for them. And as I say, he's a nice sensible boy, and I wanted to do the best I could for them both. Now, if you'll just come this way – '

Sam glanced at Robin and lifted one brow and Robin bit her lips as they followed the policewoman's broad-hipped swaying gait along the corridor, which smelled of Jeyes fluid, floor polish and faintly of sick and old plimsolls, and she made a little face back, knowing how right he was; for as clearly as if he'd said it she'd known what he meant. Oliver had once again worked the miracle, turning on his famous sweetness to persuade someone that whatever anyone else did, he was an innocent abroad.

They were sitting hunched up over a formica-topped table in a canteen with cups of cocoa in front of them and a plate of thickly buttered toast between them. Oliver was eating cheerfully, but Suzy, looking pinched and wan, was just holding her cup between her hands and saying nothing, staring miserably at Oliver.

When Chick came in she jumped to her feet and hurled herself across the room to the imminent danger of several chairs and tables. 'Oh, Ma!' she wailed. 'Oh, Ma, I'm so sorry!'

'It's all right,' Chick said and held her close, and as Suzy wept bitterly on her front said very clearly, staring at Oliver, 'It's my fault. I made a point of asking you to spend time with Oliver, to help him settle in London. I should have known better – '

The policewoman, who had gone over to Oliver and was standing with one hand on his shoulder in a friendly yet protective way frowned for a moment and looked at her and then Sam said quietly, 'Are you ready, Oliver?'

Oliver jumped to his feet and swallowed hard, and wiped the back of his hand across his buttery mouth and Robin saw for the first time ever what it was that clearly Sam had known for some time. He was looking at them both with wide frank eyes, an expression of total innocence mixed with rueful embarrassment on his face and looking altogether delightful. The edges of her mind began to melt a little as they usually did when faced with one of Oliver's escapades; the way they always had ever since his childhood, but she looked again at Sam and saw the pain on his face and knew it couldn't go on this way. And she took a deep breath and forced the warmth to dissolve and vanish and said firmly, 'Oliver! You will apologize at once for the trouble you have caused this police officer and her colleagues.'

He gaped at her, startled by her sternness, and for the first time a hint of his familiar sulky expression trembled on his mouth and then he nodded with a quick understanding and turned to the policewoman and said with an air of confiding boyishness, 'Oh, I'm so sorry, Eliza – Constable Parrish! I wouldn't have been anywhere near that place if I'd known what sort of place it was, truly. It was like I said – that wonderful music – it's great that you like jazz too. You sort of understand – ' He threw a glance at his parents and then turned his wide-eyed gaze back to the policewoman's face. 'It's so difficult when people don't understand – '

She pressed his hand and smiled warmly. 'Well, any time you need to know if a club's all right, you just pop in here and have a word with me,' she said. 'I know 'em all – the bad as well as the good – and I'll see you right.'

'Oh, I will,' he said fervently. 'I will,' and turned back to Chick.

'I'm so sorry, Auntie Chick, to have dragged Suzy into this. She didn't mean to be disobedient – it was all my fault – '

Sam, sickened, said with a snap in his voice, 'That's enough, Oliver. We'll deal with all this outside. Is there any paperwork, Miss Parrish? Papers to sign or anything?'

'Not a thing,' the policewoman said heartily. 'We'll make no fuss over a natural enough mistake. Young people'll be young people, and this pair have had a nasty fright, like I said. Goodbye Oliver – ' and she smiled at him. 'Remember I'm here if you ever need any advice.'

'Oh, I will,' he said with another of his wide earnest smiles, and they left with Sam leading the way.

'We'll go by train, thanks,' Chick said, when they were on the pavement again and Sam offered them a lift home. 'We need time to talk, Suzy and I. And – Sam – ' She took a deep breath and then glanced at Robin.

'This may seem an odd time to do it, but I have to – I mean sometimes events overtake you. I can't stay at the Clinic any longer, that's the thing. I need a different sort of job. If you can manage with Mary and Jenny – they're very good, both of them –until you get a replacement for me, that'd suit me very well – '

'I see,' Sam said after a long moment and then nodded gravely. 'I see. It's as bad as that?'

'I think so,' she said after a long pause. 'It's been a long time we've known each other, but I think the time has come for a little –space, you know what I mean? I'm thinking of selling the house and moving on. Hal's already away and Charlie quite likes the idea, I think, of a little time with his other family – '

'Other family?' Robin said and stared at her. The street was beginning to get busy now, with early workers scurrying along in the morning sunlight and because Chick was standing with her back to the sun, she seemed to be haloed. It was almost like looking at the Chick she had known all those years ago when they'd been girls together at the London Hospital; the lines and slight heaviness of the face that were an inevitable part of the passing years were not so visible, and that added to the illusion. 'Other family? Aren't we your family?'

'Of course you are and you always will be. But it's time for me – for all of us – to try a new tack. We'll be going to Canada for a long visit as soon as school breaks up. And then, after that – who knows? So, goodbye, for the present anyway. Come on, Suzy.'

The three of them stood and watched the two figures go to the corner of the street and then as they turned it and vanished Oliver said disgustedly, 'Well honestly! What a fuss to make just because – '

'Just because you took her daughter out to a place that was raided by the police? Just because you encouraged her to be as deceitful and lying as you are yourself?' Sam was blazing with anger. 'Don't you dare to criticize Chick! She's seven times the parent I've ever been! We've allowed you to get away with murder, Oliver. Well, the road ends here, my young friend. Back to school you go, and we'll have no more of the sort of life you saw fit to choose for yourself – '

'Oh, for God's sake!' Oliver said and threw his glance upwards in exasperation. 'Where's the harm, for pity's sake? So we were at a jazz club! So what? I'm not a baby any more – I told you –I've got my own life to live and I'm going to live it. Is it my fault someone shopped us?'

'I still don't understand what happened, not fully,' Robin said, needing to defuse the situation, frightened of where Sam's anger was leading him. 'Why should they bring you two here instead of just sending you home?'

'It was Suzy's fault.' He was sulky now, and fell into step as Sam began to lead the way to the car which was parked round the corner. 'She put on those unisex clothes, so that's why!'

'What've her clothes got to do with – ' Robin began, more bewildered than ever, and Oliver made an odd little snorting sound of disgust.

'They thought in the bad light that she was a bloke. Thought we were gay or something – it was gay people they were after – not just the dope. Anyway, the copper shoved us both into his bloody van and there you are. Once we'd got to the police station and they found out she was a girl they stopped pestering us – someone had seen us go in apparently and told the police.' He shook his head then. 'It was odd. They called me Mr Deveen at first. How did they know that was one of our names in the family?'

Sam stopped suddenly, just as they reached the car, and turned to stare at him. 'What did you say?'

'I said, they called me Deveen. Once I showed 'em the things I had with my name on, they said it was all right – and then they laughed when they saw Suzy and that she was a girl. Said it was all a mistake – and the policewoman was all over me. You heard what she said about me. For heaven's sake, there's no need to over-react to all this. I mean, I did no harm, did I? Just went to a jazz club.'

'You cheated and lied,' Sam said. 'You pretended to be asleep when your mother looked in and then sneaked off. I've had enough of that sort of thing. You go back to school.'

'And if I won't?' He stood there with the morning breeze lifting his hair slightly so that he looked younger than ever and Robin looked at him and wanted to weep. But Sam was right. He had to be right. She couldn't stop what was going to happen, however much she wanted to.

'Then you must manage on your own,' Sam said levelly. 'You

can no longer live in our house. You will have to keep yourself on your earnings. Somewhere else.'

Oliver whitened. 'But I don't earn enough to pay rent and so forth!'

'Then you'll have to be a resident worker full time at the hotel, won't you?' Sam said, implacable.

'But they'd drive me mad there! I stay there when I have to but the way they check up on you all the time and make so many stupid rules and – '

'Precisely,' Sam said. 'So the choice is yours. Either you do it my way, or you do it yours. I have the final trump card, you see – money – and though I hate to play it you leave me no option.'

'Oh, hell!' Oliver said loudly. 'Oh, bloody hell!'

'I agree,' Sam said, and unlocked the car. 'It is. For us in particular, though I doubt you'd see it that way. Are you coming back to sleep or are you going to work? I imagine it's where you should be by this time?'

Oliver looked at his watch and made a face. 'Well, I can take the day off, I suppose – '

'If you do that you might be fired. And then what'll you do?'

Oliver looked at him for a long time and then turned his gaze on to Robin. 'Ma – '

'No, Oliver,' she said softly. 'No. This time it won't work. He's right. I should have agreed with him years ago. He was right then and he is now. The choice is yours.'

There was a little silence and then Oliver said ungraciously, 'Then I'm going to work.'

'Splendid!' Sam said heartily. 'At your age the loss of a night's sleep is no great handicap.'

'If I have a dreadful accident because I'm so exhausted it'll be all your fault!' Oliver snapped.

'Oh, I doubt you will!' Sam was in the car now and Robin had joined him. 'I really doubt that. You're used to late nights, after all! What would you have done if you hadn't been caught tonight? Gone home in time just to change and then go to work? You'd have had no sleep – '

'That'd have been different.' Oliver made a face, seeing the trap too late. 'I mean, I've had a most unpleasant shock. It isn't every night you get arrested for something you didn't do – That's what's made me exhausted.'

'I'm sure,' Sam said courteously. 'Go to work, Oliver. And when you come home tonight, let me know your decision. Either back to school or out to earn your own keep. Good morning!' And he let in the clutch and moved the car along the street and away, leaving Oliver's figure standing on the kerb and dwindling in the rear view mirror as they gathered speed.

29

'And you managed to raise enough cash?' Josh said. 'Surely it must have been a hell of a lot.'

'It was,' Poppy said with considerable feeling. 'The only way I could make it sound convincing was to pay a good deal more than the market price. But it's worth it – '

Josh got to his feet and began to prowl the room. 'It can't be.' His voice was no louder than it normally was, but there was a violence in it that made it seem to reverberate in the big office and Poppy got to her feet and went over to him.

'It is,' she said and led him back to his seat against the wall, beside David, who sat and watched, alert but quiet. 'It's not just to protect you, and never think it. I'm not making any major sacrifice here. Dammit all, I have to be hugely grateful to you. If I hadn't found out from the way he tried to use you just how dangerous he was, I might have gone on blissfully unaware of the risk I was under. He'd have pulled the whole damned business out from under me and I'd have been none the wiser. So, don't go thinking you're some sort of – of jinx. Anything but.'

He smiled a little twistedly. 'That sounds good, Ma, but can I believe it?'

'You can believe it,' David said. 'I'm part of this too, remember. I helped raise the money. With Jessie's support.' He looked sombre for a moment. 'She's not entirely well – got a nasty cold – but she's as sharp as she ever was and wanted very much to be part of this when I explained it all. So she's delighted to be on board, and so am I. For heaven's sake, Josh, we'll make it back in no time! Now your mother's got what she wants. Take it from me, all will be sweetness and light chez nous, and all because of you! Howzat, then?'

Josh shook his head and managed to laugh. 'I'll try to believe you. You certainly make it sound like happy ever after – '

'We're not out of trouble yet.' Poppy went back to her desk and sat down again. 'He's an aggressive devil and vindictive too, I suspect. He may try to make trouble for you just because he's been clobbered – well, we'll have to find out.'

'Does he know yet?' Josh asked.

Poppy lifted her hands in a gesture of uncertainty. 'I wish I knew. I told Gillian not to say anything at this stage – told her it'd be better to let me – and she agreed. Thought it'd save her some trouble, I suspect. Poor thing!' And she sighed. 'She doesn't deserve all this.'

'I'm not so sure,' David said. 'She married him.'

'You make that sound as though she'd committed a crime,' Poppy said. 'Any woman can make a mistake.'

'She certainly did,' David said feelingly. 'When I think of it – '

The intercom on Poppy's desk buzzed and Poppy made a hushing sound at David and flicked the switch. 'He's coming in now,' her secretary said rapidly, just as the door opened, and Poppy leaned back in her chair and looked enquiringly up at Richard Melhuish.

'Good morning, Richard.' Her voice was so neutral she might have been telling him the time. 'Thank you for coming to see me.'

'I find it a touch irritating that I should be sent for like an office boy,' he said, walking directly to her desk. She could not believe it at first; she'd arranged Josh and David's chairs against the wall alongside the door, not wanting their presence to be too obvious when he first came in, in case he turned and went straight out again. She wanted very much to deal with this matter in her own office, where she felt secure and in control. It was her territory and she needed to be in it; and she'd been afraid he would steal that advantage from her if he saw she had supporters. But he was so angry and walked in so fast that he didn't see them at all, and just stood with his fists clenched on her desk, leaning on them, so that he could bend over and push his face closer to hers. 'If you wanted to talk to me, what was so difficult about coming into my office to see me?'

'I might have been unwell,' she said as mildly as she could, forcing herself to sit very straight and not to recoil from his closeness. 'Had you considered that?'

He looked at her uncertainly for a fraction of a moment and then shook his head firmly. 'You'd have said so.'

'You're quite right. I would. Wouldn't you be more comfortable if you sat down?' She indicated the chair alongside him and after a moment he threw himself into it. He still hadn't seen David and Josh and she wondered just how long it would be before he became aware of them. She couldn't imagine herself ever being in a room with other people and not knowing they were there, but then that was Richard all over, a part of her mind told her. So self-confident, he has no time for awareness of others.

'So what is it?' He sounded very belligerent and she lifted her brows at him, feeling more in control of the situation by the moment. His anger gave her strength and she smiled gently at him.

'Now, Richard, why should you be so aggressive? Are you trying to hide a guilty conscience?'

'A guilty – what are you talking about? I suppose I am a bit annoyed – I don't expect to be made – to be made to come trotting to your call like an office boy – '

'You've already made that point.' She smiled again.

He looked at her and then quite deliberately relaxed his shoulders and tried a smile of his own. It was far less emollient than it usually was, but at least he tried, and she applauded him for that by smiling even more widely herself.

'So perhaps you'll explain what it is you made me come for?' He looked at his watch. 'I can spare ten minutes, no more. I have someone coming in to see me then – '

'Something for the benefit of "Food by Poppy"? Or – '

'What else? Of course.'

' – Or for your personal benefit?'

He seemed to stiffen and looked at her warily. 'What do you mean?'

'I thought perhaps you were counting your chickens. Or shall I say your shares? Interviewing replacement managing directors, perhaps.' Her smile was now positively beatific, it was so wide.

There was a long silence as he stared at her and then it was his turn to smile sweetly. 'I think you'd better explain,' he said softly.

'No,' she said. 'Oh, no, Richard. I think the explanations have to come from you. I need to know just why you set a private detective on to my family. What was it you were trying to do, I wonder?'

Behind him David moved in his chair and Richard, who had been sitting very still, shifted his head slightly, but didn't look round. 'So, we're not alone,' he said.

She laughed. 'Of course not! I wondered how long it would take you to realize that. Would I take a foolish chance like that?'

'If you're going to have a witness to this discussion then I think I must too.' He moved as though he were going to get to his feet. 'My solicitor perhaps – '

'That's up to you,' she said with a fine judicious air. 'If you want him to know the sort of tricks you've been up to. I suspect there have been laws bent here, if not totally broken. Blackmail *is* a crime, is it not?'

'If you're accusing me of blackmail – and what's all this about detectives?' He began to bluster and then looked sharply over his shoulder, no longer able to ignore the other people in the room. And at the sight of Josh his face went stiff. 'What the hell are you doing here?'

Josh stood up. 'Looking after my mother,' he said quietly. 'I thought she might need some protection. We both did.' And he looked briefly at David.

Richard turned back to Poppy. 'So, he's gone crying to his Mummy to tell, has he? Now you know what you've got in your precious family, do you? A pansy? One of the fancy nancy boys who – '

David had moved so fast that Poppy was hardly aware he had until he was standing over Melhuish with one hand on his shoulder, pulling him round. His face was blazing with rage. 'We'll have no more of that, Melhuish. Not another word, you hear me? If you do I'll – '

'You'll what?' Melhuish said and managed a snort of laughter. 'Hit me, old man? I can just see it!'

'Is that all you can think of, violence?' Now it was Josh who was standing beside him, on his other side, and Poppy reacted strongly.

'Sit down, both of you. We'll talk about this like civilized people, to the best of our ability. I want no nonsense about hitting people. That's stupid – now, Richard, let's get it clear.

261

You set a private detective on to us in order to get evidence to prove Josh was breaking the law, is that it? You wanted to get some sort of evidence you could use to force him to sell his shares to you so that you'd get control of my company.'

'It isn't your company,' he said. 'It's half mine.

'Partly Gillian's,' she said. 'Only partly. And certainly not yours. Most of the shares are in my family's hands – '

'And once I get Josh's shares, the majority will be with me.' Melhuish stretched his legs in front of him and pushed his hands into his trouser pockets, ignoring David and Josh who had returned unwillingly to their chairs, where they both sat on the very edge, alert and ready to jump up again at any moment. Poppy could feel the tension in them and had to concentrate hard to prevent it transferring to her. She needed to be as cool as she ever had been; that was all that mattered right now. To keep her temper. Then she could be sure to win properly, without Melhuish making trouble for Josh. The business she was sure now was safe – not that Melhuish knew that yet. But there was still Josh –

'But you aren't going to get Josh's shares,' she said quietly. 'He isn't going to give in to your unpleasant blackmail.'

Melhuish raised his eyebrows. 'I wasn't particularly concerned about them. For all I know you are the sort of people who tolerate these characters who prey on boys – '

David got half-way to his feet and Poppy threw him a glance of such ferocity that he sank back. She turned back to Melhuish. 'That is an outrageous accusation,' she said softly.

'Is it? He preyed on my daughter, didn't he, even though he prefers boys?'

It was more than Josh could bear. He was on his feet and shouting. 'I did not! I never at any point was more than her friend. I wanted to please my mother by being friendly to her, to start with, but learned to like her for herself. That's all I ever did, and she knows it. I can't believe that she'd say anything different.'

Melhuish didn't look at him, only half turning his head to spit the words out. 'Oh, you've managed to pull the wool over her eyes too, I know that. Stupid bitch won't say a word against you – but that doesn't mean you've had the same effect on me. I'll get you punished if it's the last thing I do – you're a disgusting

object, a worm, not fit to be on this earth, you and your kind –
perverted, revolting – '

'That sort of talk is singularly pointless,' Poppy said with great
incisiveness, though inside her belly was shaking with a painful
mixture of rage and fear and disgust and a desperate urge to go
running across the room to cradle Josh's stricken face between
her hands and soothe him. But she sat tight. 'I have just two
things to tell you. That I know – we all know – of the way you
tried to get Josh into trouble. You sent a detective to follow him
everywhere, only the man you hired was too stupid to know what
he was doing. He watched my daughter's home rather than my
son's. I know from Robin and Sam that he's been hanging
around their house for some time – and from Oliver that he
followed him and his girlfriend to a jazz club. He let himself be
confused by the fact that like so many young people now she was
wearing the same sort of clothes as Oliver. Jeans and a shirt – and
both have the same length hair. So he told the police Josh Deveen
was in a jazz club where there were other homosexuals, and that
he'd taken a young boy there – he couldn't even see that Oliver
was little more than a boy himself. I don't know how much you
paid your detective to sneak around watching people in the dark,
but take it from me, Richard, you wasted your money.'

Melhuish was sitting staring at her, his face impassive and
when she stopped he still sat silent. But then he shook his head
slowly.

'All right.' His voice was suddenly husky. 'All right. So this
time he's got away with it, your precious pervert. But there'll be
other times. His sort always get caught eventually – and I'll see to
it that he gets no peace at all. In the pubs and the clubs where
bed-bugs hang about and the public lavatories and the parks and
Hampstead Heath and – '

Josh was standing up again, white and stricken. 'It isn't like
that! It doesn't have to be like that. It's because of people like you
and your sort that harmless people like me are driven to such
places! We're no different from you. Just ordinary people who –
why do you hate us so?'

'Because you're hateful,' Melhuish said loudly. 'Because
you're vermin. Because you're degenerates who – '

'The gentleman doth protest too much, methinks,' David said
softly and shook his head. 'Is that it, Melhuish? Have you found

263

that somewhere inside yourself you have some of the same feelings my Josh has? Only you've buried them so deeply you've made them into ugly festering things instead of the honest loving feelings they are in Josh? His partner died and he's grieved as sorely as any man ever grieved for a partner. As perhaps you grieved for your first wife, before Gillian – though we can't know that. But your hatred and your anger now do make me a shade suspicious, Melhuish. Look at yourself, my friend. Look deeply into yourself.'

Melhuish was heading for the door now. 'I've had enough of this!' he roared. 'I'll get them on to you, you see if I don't. I'll see that every policeman in London knows about you and what you do – '

'It'll get you nowhere,' Josh said wearily. 'I live the life of a recluse from now on, believe me. No friends of either sex. It won't be worth it. I had hoped Caro was a friend, but even she I won't see – though she wants to continue to be part of my life. But we'll forget it – and so can you. Because you'll never get any evidence at all. Never – '

'Oh, I'll get it. If I have to spend every penny I have on detectives and – '

'Ah, pennies.' Poppy said in a quiet voice and stood up as well. 'That's the second thing I have to deal with. Richard, I have to tell you that you no longer have any employment in this company and therefore no more salary. Your post as Chairman of course is no longer suitable for you as a non-shareholder and that means no more dividends either – '

'What are you talking about?' he roared. 'I'm still holding enough of this company to be powerful here and never you think otherwise. I can – '

She shook her head, with every display of regret. 'Oh, no, Richard. Not any more. I bought Gillian's shares, you see. All of them – '

The man became very silent. Outside they could hear the clatter of the typewriter as Poppy's secretary went on with the mundane matters of the day, and the distant sound of the vans in the yard where the drivers were loading them ready to deliver the day's orders. Poppy was very aware suddenly of the whole weight of the establishment around her. It was as though her disembodied self was wandering from room to room, watching the accounts department getting the prices out and the invoices ready, watching the cooks down in the great kitchens packing the big trays ready for the day's events, watching the clerks counting the china and the glass and the silver in the high store rooms and she thought –it's mine. It's still mine. All of it. And felt a great weight of tiredness fill her. It was too much. Time she took life a little more easily, surely, rather than overloading herself with work –

'You can't have done,' Richard said hoarsely. 'She'd never – '

'Oh, I lied to her,' Poppy said cheerfully, her weariness vanishing as suddenly as it had come. She was in full control again and ready to fight on for as long as she had to. It would be exhilarating to be in complete control again, wonderful, and now she was. 'I told her you were ill, you see. That you'd insisted it be kept a secret from her to stop her worrying, but that the doctors had told me after your last attack of fainting here at the office – which of course she knew nothing about – that unless you stopped work you'd be at real risk of a heart attack. So she sold me all the shares. She loves you a lot, you see. Wants to keep you alive rather than own any part of the business. She was really happy when we'd finished the deal. She's full of plans to take you away on a long rest cure. Enjoy it, Richard. You might as well.'

He went. There was nothing else he could do. He slammed the door behind him so hard that it banged against the frame and swung back open again and they could see Poppy's secretary in the outer office staring after him, her face agog with amazement and excitement. And then Poppy, moving very carefully, sat down. Her legs were shaking so much she could no longer stand up.

'Oh my God,' she said. 'Oh my God!' And burst into tears.

30

'I told you she would,' Lally said with great satisfaction. 'Take more than a bout of bronchitis to do any damage to my old dear. She'll be with us years yet.'

'I said the same!' Barbara protested. 'I never said anything different.'

'Oh, yes you did.' Lally was very firm. 'You were thoroughly miserable, sure everything was going to be awful – you can't tell me. I know you – you were planning the funeral.'

'I was not,' Barbara said and Bertie threw up both hands and covered his ears.

'Shut up, shut up, shut up,' he chanted. 'I shan't stop saying shut up till you stop arguing, so shut up, shut up, shut up – '

'And that's enough from you, young man,' Barbara said, pulling his hands from his ears. 'Now, are you ready to get dressed?'

'I haven't finished my apple!' Bertie said and Barbara snorted and took it from him.

'You'll get more than enough to eat at the party. Now, you know exactly what you have to do?'

'Of course I do.' He was scornful. 'As if I'd forget.'

'Go through it again,' Lally said and reached over to reclaim his apple and give it back to him while Barbara returned to his shirt and her iron.

'But I've told you three times – '

'Tell me again.'

He sighed theatrically. 'Such a fuss! All right. All right. I go to Gramma's office. I tell her GranDave sent me because one of his friends has turned up from Baltimore and he had to meet him at the Savoy, and please will Gramma come in the taxi with me to

266

collect him on the way home, because he's a bit tired and doesn't want to spend all evening with the friend who'll try to make him stay at the hotel with him for ages, and if Gramma turns up she'll be able to rescue him. Then we go in the taxi and I tell Gramma when we get there that GranDave and his friend are in the bit of the hotel that's at the back and I take her there and I open the door – and I *do* know which one – it's the room called Pinafore, and it's all dark in there and I say, I wonder if it's this way and reach in and switch on the light and there you all are shouting, "Surprise, Surprise". I told you I knew what to do.'

'That's all right then,' Lally said. 'Would you like another apple?'

'Leave him be,' Barbara said at once. 'He has to get dressed and he'll get lots to eat later – here's your shirt.'

'No thank you, Lally,' Bertie said and sighed and got down from the table. 'I'll be as quick as I can,' and he took the shirt and went off to the bathroom.

'I do hope nothing goes wrong,' Barbara said fretfully, and began to bustle about the kitchen to make sure that everything was tidy. 'Let's see now, Mrs Jessie's cocoa tray's ready for when we get back, and yours, and the washing's almost dry – shall I take it down or leave it up there till tomorrow?' She squinted up at the drying rail above her head and pursed her lips. 'A little longer won't hurt it, and did you boil the dishcloth when you'd finished washing up?'

'Stop fussing!' Lally said and went over to the other side of the kitchen to hug her. 'You're like a cat on wire wool, for heaven's sake.'

Barbara turned and hugged her back. 'Oh, I know. I'm sorry. You're right, you know. I was frightened for Mrs Jessie. I thought she was going to die. She was so blue and she sounded so awful with her breathing – '

'Well, she didn't die,' Lally said. 'She's over it. There'll be another time of course and one of them will be the end and that'll be that. But there's not much you can expect that's different, is there? She's going to be ninety-nine – it's a remarkable age! She can't last for ever.'

'I wish she would,' Barbara said. 'I wish everything would.'

'Stop the clock? What for? There's a lot of bad things people have to go through as well, you know. Suppose you'd been able

267

to stop the clock that time Chloe was trying to get hold of Bertie – wouldn't that have been awful? This way we know it's in the past – she'll never bother him again.'

'Who can say?' Barbara sounded sombre. 'Who can possibly say? Here's poor darling Josh so unhappy and we thought he'd be all right – '

Lally's face clouded. 'Yes, I know. But things will change for him again, you see if they don't. It'll get better – '

'How?' Barbara sounded belligerent suddenly. 'How can they get better? Everyone hates people like him. Like us, really.'

'No,' Lally sat down again. 'Not everybody. They'll change things – they'll have to – '

'I hope so. It's awful being illegal. Just because we're well – you know what I mean.'

'I'm not sure we are illegal,' Lally said. 'I never heard we were. I know lots of other people like us, just friends living together – '

'It's not legal for Josh. So why should it be for us?'

'I don't know,' Lally shook her head. 'Anyway, there's no sense in dwelling on it. Just as there's no sense in trying to stop the clock. It'll get better, you'll see if it doesn't.'

'And Mrs Jessie'll die.'

'Yes,' Lally said. 'One day she will. But not as long as I can stop it happening. And after that, we'll just have each other to look after. And that's something to be grateful for, isn't it? That we've got each other?'

'Yes,' Barbara said and reached up and kissed her cheek. 'Yes. We're luckier than Josh. We've got each other – '

Lally brightened then. 'We could look after him, couldn't we? Then he'd be all right too.'

'Yes,' Barbara said after a moment and then with more assurance. 'Yes. We could. And you can tell him that when he gets here. It'll cheer him up. Listen, we'd better check Mrs Jessie's all ready to go, and see Bertie on his way. We'll just have time to change ourselves then – oh, Lally, it is exciting, isn't it? She ought to be so thrilled!'

'You're absolutely sure?' Sam said and squinted at her anxiously. 'I thought you enjoyed it so much.'

'I did, for a while,' Robin said and manoeuvred the car carefully into the fast traffic of the Finchley Road, pushing her way into the centre lane. 'But the moment's passed. And it's a hell of an offer – '

'There's more to life than money,' Sam said, and stared out at the passing crowds and the busy restaurants, and part of him wondered if people in Swiss Cottage ever did anything other than eat, there were so many. 'You have to enjoy what you're doing.'

'I'll enjoy being at King's Road,' Robin said. 'After we get back. And Lee'll be there too, of course. I haven't seen much of her since she got married so it'll be nice to get some time together.'

'As long as you're not selling the shop because of me,' he said. 'I love you and I trust you, Robin. You don't have to prove anything.'

'Trust me?' She grimaced as a black cab cut across her into the space in front. 'I don't know why you should.'

'Because I love you. And because you – well because. So you can keep the shop going as long as you like and no arguments from me.'

'I'm bored with it,' Robin said. 'How much excitement can you generate over two sleeves, two pockets and a placket anyway? It'll be more fun to deal with "Food by Poppy". Ma's always wanted me to join her, so I shall.'

'Well, if you're sure – '

'I'm sure.'

'Then that's all right. Isn't it?'

'It is,' she said and looked sideways at him. 'Thank you, Sam.'

'What for?' He squinted at her again.

'Just thanks. That's all.'

'Oh,' he said. 'Well, that's all right then, isn't it?'

'I can't think why he sent a taxi,' Poppy said crossly. 'So unnecessary. I could have gone by tube.'

'He said it was because it would be fun for you,' Bertie said, improvising. 'A treat.'

'A treat!' she snorted. 'You mean he thinks I'm too old to go on the tube any more. Well, he'll soon find out how wrong he is.'

'Well, he didn't actually *say* that,' Bertie said hurriedly. 'I sort of guessed it.'

'So! You're as bad as he is,' Poppy said and looked down at her grandson and then reached over and touched his cheek. 'You think I'm too old to go on the tube as well, do you?'

'I just like being in taxis,' he said and pointed out of the window. 'Look at that, Gramma! Doesn't that look fab?' The taxi was held up in a knot of traffic opposite Peter Jones in Sloane Square where several Daleks from 'Dr Who' were being chased about the pavement by men dressed as space travellers and passing children stopped to stare and laugh. 'I'll be one of those one day.'

'A Dalek?' Poppy said, distracted, and laughed. 'If you go on eating as much as you do you'll be shaped like one.'

'No, a spaceman. I'll walk on the moon and I'll walk on Mars and – well, not Mars. It's too cold there. Or is it hot? But there'll be other planets we can go to, when they get hyperdrive and I'll be able to go – '

'You've been reading too much fantasy, Bertie,' Poppy said and Bertie turned to her immediately.

'Not fantasy! Just looking forward! That's all I'm doing – making real plans. I mean, Gramma, when you were my age if someone had told you you could sit in your house and watch people singing and dancing hundreds and thousands of miles away you'd have said they were daft, wouldn't you? But you do watch television now, don't you? Well, this is the same – '

She looked down at his eager face and the way his hair flopped in his eyes and thought for a moment and then said, 'Yes, Bertie,' as the taxi at last extricated itself from the jam it was in and took off again towards Eaton Square, and she reached forward to push the hair out of his eyes. 'You're absolutely right. I suppose I am getting rather old after all. It's not every day a person has a seventieth birthday, is it?' She leaned back in her corner and stared out of the window and said as much to herself as to Bertie, 'Not that anyone seems to have remembered.'

Bertie looked at her with his eyebrows up. 'Oh, Gramma, is it your birthday today? I knew it was around now, but – '

'It is,' she said a little grimly. 'January the twenty-second has always been my birthday so I don't see why it shouldn't be this year.'

'Oh, well,' he said comfortably. 'I'll get your present tomorrow. Sorry I got the date wrong.'

'That's all right,' she said and smiled at him. 'It's not so important once you get old, anyway. Now, who did you say GranDave had to meet here?' for the taxi was drawing up outside the Savoy.

'He didn't say the name.' Bertie was scrambling out so he didn't have to look at her. It was getting harder to tell lies, he found, somewhat to his surprise, or at least to tell them without the fact that he was doing so showing on his face. 'But I know where they are. Come on – ' And he led her into the hotel.

'It worked beautifully,' Lee said with great satisfaction and hugged Jeremy's arm. 'Did you ever see anything like the look on her face? Wonderful.'

'I thought she looked as though she was going to be sick,' Jeremy said. 'But so do I if I get a shock. Have you ever noticed?'

'Now and again,' Lee said and pinched him hard. 'Was that shocking enough?'

'It will be when I get to you,' he said as she dodged away and he followed her, and Robin, who was sitting on the other side of the same table, shook her head a little wistfully and watched them. It must be fun to be so silly and light-headed with your own husband, she thought, and then stole a glance at Sam.

He was staring across the room at David, so she could study him for a moment without him realizing, and she thought – I do love him. He's not the most exciting husband in the world, not romantic and silly, like Jeremy, or whatever it was that Hamish was, but he's safe and good and I feel right with him; and then he turned his head and looked at her and suddenly she felt a lift in her belly of sheer excitement, the sort of sexual excitement she had known with Hamish, and she felt her face flame. And he seemed to know what was happening, because he murmured 'Mmm! Like that, is it? Later, my love. Keep your fires banked up for me,' and leaned over and kissed her.

'It's funny how things turn out,' she said after a moment, trying to cover her confusion in silly words. 'Who'd have thought we'd all be here like this for Ma's seventieth? All the family – '

'Almost all,' he said sombrely and she glanced at him.

'I know,' she said. 'I'm sorry about that too. But the time had to come. People have to break away sometimes to find themselves – and that was what was necessary.'

'Yes,' he said. 'But I still miss her – and her children. They were good news.'

'She'll be back,' Robin said. 'She said as much in her last letter from Toronto. And she's sending a telegram to Ma for tonight –

what, darling?' as Penny came running up to her. 'Is there something wrong?'

'Yes – it's Oliver! I've asked him to talk to me and he said he wouldn't be caught dead wasting his time with me – Tell him to stop being so hateful – '

'We'll do nothing of the sort,' Sam said briskly. 'You'll have to find someone else to talk to. Oliver has every right to choose his own company.'

'Oh, blow it,' Penny said. 'And blow Oliver. He always gets away with everything.'

'Not quite everything,' Robin murmured and watched Penny flounce away to complain to her sister about her brother's shortcomings.

'He's all right,' Sam said with great satisfaction. 'I wish I hadn't had to wave the financial stick, but never mind. It worked. He'll do all right at this school, you know. It's so difficult to get away with rule-breaking there that he just doesn't bother to try any more. And he's working! It's really amazing. I keep wondering when the bubble'll burst.'

'Don't be unfair!' she said at once. 'He's trying hard, you said so yourself and – '

'Yes, I know,' he said. 'I'm not criticizing. It was our fault in the first place, I suspect. Sent him to the wrong school.'

'It was no one's fault. It's just the way things are when children grow up. Difficult.'

'You noticed.'

'Wait till it's the girls,' she said darkly. 'Penny, I think, is going to be hell on wheels.'

'I'll worry about that when it happens. Hush – David's on his feet.'

There was a little sporadic applause and slowly the big room fell silent. The tables were a wreck of the elegant creations they'd been when they'd all come in, as bottles of champagne had been emptied and food had vanished and streamers had been thrown. Now the diners sat replete and contented, ready for David, and he looked round at them all and took a deep breath.

'I'm bad at speeches,' he said and Lee clapped loudly and there was a general laugh. 'But I have to make one today. My Poppy, your Poppy, our Poppy, has hit the big one. Seventy. Doesn't seem possible, does it? Just look at her.' He turned and looked at her and the rest of them broke into applause and Barbara called out, 'I wish I looked as old as you, Mrs Poppy!' and Lally nudged her furiously. Barbara had undoubtedly had more champagne than she was comfortable with.

'So I just want to wish her a happy birthday. To tell her how much we all love her, and how much we want to be here to celebrate her next twenty or thirty birthdays. And if she's anything at all like our dear Jessie, that's just what we'll all do!' And he threw a glance towards Jessie, who was snoozing gently in her wheelchair between Lally and Barbara, and she woke up for a moment, beamed round at them all and promptly went back to sleep. 'So all of you, glasses up – the toast is Poppy.'

They drank the toast, calling her name, they clapped and called, 'Speech, speech,' and then at last when she stood up they sat down and fell silent and expectant.

She looked round at them all, trying to control the tears she knew were very near the surface. There was Jessie, who had woken again and this time had stayed awake, peering up at her with her tired old eyes with their milky rims and now almost vanished eyelashes, and she thought about her mother, Mildred, and the long years when they'd been so distant with each other, and then the happier ones when they'd become closer. She looked at Bertie and remembered Bobby, his grandfather, and also Chloe, his mother, and the painful times they had all shared. She looked at Robin and remembered most of all the years when there had been just the two of them, before David had come back into her life, and then at Josh, and for him the memories came thick and fast and now the tears were very close.

But she managed to speak all the same.

'You're wretches, all of you,' she said. 'To surprise me like this and to give me so many delicious presents. I'm spoiled rotten, I really am. And the best present of all – Lee and Jeremy's baby on the way.' Beside her David said loudly, 'And about time too,' and Jeremy blushed crimson and Lee laughed and everyone looked at them and smiled, and Poppy caught her breath and went on. 'It's a wonderful party and I'm having a wonderful time. It's the best time I can ever remember. And I remember a lot – '

She stopped and stared down at the table then, thinking, and then went on. 'It's so odd, isn't it? I was born into a London that was lit by gas and travelled by horses and full of fog and now London's lit by spotlights and full of fast cars and crammed with skyscrapers and there are spacemen wandering about – ' She caught Bertie's eye, who grinned widely at her. 'And here I am still going strong. So much has changed in the world while I've been here – so very much – '

Again she looked round at them all, her children and her grandchildren and saw in her mind's eye the people who weren't there but who had filled her life and they jostled for space in her private vision. Her father Lizah, and Bernie, Jessie's scapegrace son, and Mabel, the girl she had met the day she went to a Suffragette meeting as an active worker for the cause, and who had brought her this whole room full of people who were her family, when she had introduced her to her brother Bobby – and at last she stopped trying to control the tears. They trickled down her cheeks and she wiped them away with the backs of her hands and sniffed lusciously and said, 'Thank you, all of you. I do love you, you know.' And sat down.